BOOKS *by Kay Boyle*

Generation

Without Farewell

We are the generation without farewell. We may live no farewell, we must not, for on the stray paths trodden by our feet our wandering hearts find endless farewells. . . . We have many encounters, encounters without duration and without farewell, like the stars. They approach, stand for light-seconds beside one another, move away again: without trace, without ties, without farewell.

WOLFGANG BORCHERT

Generation

Without Farewell

BY Kay Boyle

 1960

Alfred A. Knopf / New York

L. C. Catalog card number: 59-11822

© Kay Boyle, 1959

THIS IS A BORZOI BOOK,
PUBLISHED BY ALFRED A. KNOPF, INC.

FIRST EDITION

For Siegfried

The year is 1948
The place is the American Zone of Germany

The principal characters are:

Jaeger

A German newspaperman, aged twenty-seven, who returned to Germany in late 1946, after spending over two years as a prisoner of war in Colorado.

Colonel Roberts

An American colonel in the Occupation Forces in West Germany. Now in his late forties, he is commander of the army post of Fahrbach, Hesse.

Catherine Roberts

The Colonel's wife, a native of Philadelphia, who is ten years younger than her husband.

Millicent Roberts

The only child of Colonel and Mrs. Roberts. She has just completed her freshman year at college, and has come to spend the summer with her parents in Fahrbach. She is eighteen years old.

Seth Honerkamp

An American civilian serving as director of the America House in Fahrbach. He is twenty-five, his college education having been interrupted by his enlistment in the air forces during the war, and by his present employment with the War Department in Occupied Germany.

Lucius Stephany

A lieutenant under Colonel Roberts' command. He is the same age as Jaeger.

Mike Dardenella

> *The American manager of the local U.S. Army Post Exchange. He is of Italian extraction, and in his late thirties.*

Christoph Horn

> *A German groom at the riding-stables, twenty-one years old.*

Herr Knau, *a German forester, and his family.*

Generation

Without Farewell

———————

1

The things
that went through his mind were thought in English as he
walked up the lane that mounted between gardens, and
tidy little orchards, and neatly spaced vegetable rows. At
this level, the place had a bourgeois look to it, but, higher,
there were finer houses, and a great dark saddle of needle
trees was flung across the summit of the hill. The houses
he passed were stucco, with flat modern roofs, and their
façades, paunched with balconies and bristling with boxed
geraniums, were turned toward the summery valley that lay
below. But the stucco walls were cracked and scarred, as
if by the sorrow of their lot, and the paint on the closed
doors and the lowered venetian blinds was peeling away.
But they were still as smug as *Bürgermeisters*, these houses
of his countrymen, in spite of what had taken place. The
roofing that had kept them from rain and snow had been
patched with strips of tar paper, made in Ohio, probably,
he thought, and filched from the back door of an army
supply depot. They had been built in a period of hysteri-
cally made national promises, when a *Volkswagen* was
God's final commitment to every man who did his duty in
Hitler's *Reich*, and their architects had exposed them with
fanaticism to the sun, as if the cure for all the ailments of
man's flesh and spirit lay in its healing rays. The look of
them had been altered only through neglect, so they had

3

not taken on the stature of monumental tragedy as the ruined cities had. They were as alien to him, these close-mouthed dwelling-places, as the entire country was. No matter how long he lived, he knew he would speak of the honeysuckle he passed, and the fruit trees on the other side of the stone walls, in a language used perhaps like a hand to shield his face and heart, but which he had come to believe was more explicit than his own. "Lindy, did you smell that honeysuckle vine last night?" he liked to sing to himself through his teeth; or: "Mah Lindy Lou, did you hear that mockingbird last night?" It filled him with sentiment, the American lingo, for it spoke as simply and eloquently to him now as when he had heard it in the jukeboxes of Colorado, not roaring out marching songs, not the "*Badenweiler*" or "The Entry of the Gladiators" or "The Old Comrades," but singing of mares eating oats, and of the lights coming on again in a world of death that men were sick and tired of. "Oh, Lawd, I'd lay right down and die if I could be as sweet as that to you!" he sang in a voice that he liked to think was as tender and deep as the voice of a cello. Since he was done forever with the vainglory and the black possession of the Nibelungs of his youth, he wanted speech to be as simple as that. He wanted to say "hi" to whatever grim, defeated faces leaned over spade or hoe in the German gardens that he passed. To free himself of the old, accursed heritage of class, he wanted to face himself every morning in the cracked mirror in his furnished room sustained by a casual, pseudo-American identity.

Yet here he was on this June afternoon climbing up from the valley to the American Colonel's house to give lessons for the money there was in it, knowing he could teach the Colonel's wife nothing but the past tense of the German tongue. For the language served him now merely for speech with the phantasmic men and women of his memory—with

4

Goethe, and Schiller, and Büchner, and his own dead people, and a girl he had slept with in the grass by the Rhine ten years before; or else for the journalism he wrote for a living and that any schoolboy might set down. "Mares eat oats, and does eat oats, and little lambs eat ivy," was the vocabulary that touched his heart and made him grin. He wanted to take a ferocious pleasure in the taste of the air, in the smell of the leaves, in the white drop of honey that hung on the delicate pistil of the flower that he picked from the vine. He had had enough of history.

As he walked, he sang out loud about love to no woman in particular, not even this time to the waitress in the Nevada diner who had been the substance of woman for three years to him, although he had seen her for only twenty minutes one hot summer afternoon. Because of the currency of passion in her flesh, she had lingered like heat, like poppy petals, like desert sand, her damp soft fingers touching the letters on the sleeve of his general-issue shirt once she had put the slice of pork in gravy and the French fries down. "Police Officer—or maybe Police or Petty Warrant—or maybe Police on Wings?" she had tried working the P.O.W. out. Her dress was pink, and the white collar of it was starched, and her throat as white as the collar as she stood beside his chair. "Say, it's the first time I ever seen that insignia and I could've sworn I knew them all," she said. Inside her dress, her breasts stood separate, hard, and young. "This one you couldn't have known," he said, trying to put some humor into it. "We don't get out very much. That's my guard over there with the roast-beef sandwich. I'm on payroll duty with him, interpreting. It stands for prisoner of war," he said.

As he walked, he broke off another delicate, sweet-stemmed flower from the honeysuckle vine, and put it between his teeth. He would have gone straight up the Colonel's driveway then, and turned off the gravel to the handsome flagstones of the path, and found the door, had not a military car, an Opel Kapitän, with its metal polished high, blared out in warning behind him; and he stepped aside. The car mounted the incline of the drive smoothly and fast, and came to a halt in the sun where the rock garden began, and he saw the two G.I.s who rode in front, and the officer who rode behind, with a woman seated on either side. The corporal got quickly down from his place beside the driver to open the door that caught on its shining surface the rich, bright miscellany of flower and shrub and sky, and the young man with the honeysuckle flower in his mouth saw the women's slender ankles as they stepped out, and their skirts lifting lightly in the summer air.

One was younger than the other, but about them both there was cast such a magic area of life and beauty that he could not take his eyes from them, nor could the commanding officer of the post, who had got down with them from the car. For it was Colonel Roberts who now sought to hold himself erect, as if sensing that his uniform lost its authority when they were near. His belly was sucked in beneath his ribs, and his figure might have looked almost boyish had it not been for the great weight of his shoulders in the olive drab. They were wide and thick, and every now and then he jerked them back in irritation as if they were an unwieldy burden he could not set down. His square, greying head was turned toward the women with an intensity that excluded time and place and man, his uniform nothing but a sad, unlovely shade that one turned quickly from for the delicate coloring of the women's arms and throats and the smooth silk of the leaves beyond. And the young man who had stopped short in uncertainty in the drive thought: *I must have mistaken the day, or anyway the hour, or maybe misinterpreted his urgency when he asked me last week to come.*

He's too much the male at any time to want anything but subordinates around. Had he himself been a short man, the German would have turned then and gone down the hill, but he had learned a long time back that a tall man is never quick enough, never nimble enough in thought or act, to evade anything with ease.

"Quite a place, isn't it?" Colonel Roberts was saying to the younger woman, who was little more than a girl. He ran his finger inside the collar of his shirt, speaking almost savagely to her because she had turned and was looking down into the valley where the river lay. *Look at the house ahead of you!* he might have been roaring at her. *Don't give a second thought to Germany!*

"Oh, yes, it's very nice. I like it," the girl said, speaking quickly, and she let the valley and the river go. She put her bare arms behind her, and clasped her hands at the back of her blue skirt, and stood, a slender, bare-legged figure looking up in quiet obedience at the house above them, with its white prow riding a surf of vine and apple and plum leaves. It seemed to float upon a tide of sun, so light and airy it was, and then, from behind it, the land descended in sudden menace on the Colonel's quarters, for there a forest of ancient needle trees cast its deep shadow on the entire rear. "I'll always go in and out by the front terrace. I think I'd be afraid to go around the other side," the girl said shyly.

"There's no door on the terrace. Just long windows!" cried the Colonel in strange irritation with her. He might have been shouting out: *Will I have to put signs up so that you'll know window from door, officer from enlisted man, Kraut from American?*

"You can climb over the terrace railing and not go toward the back at all," said the other woman, and in her voice there was the disturbing sound of an America the young man did not know. "That's Wotan's and Donar's territory in back. I've been reading about them at night when I'm here alone."

And then Colonel Roberts turned in his impatience and saw the young man standing below them in the drive, and he called out:

"Hi, Jaeger! Come on up! I'd forgotten it was for today."

"Hello," said Jaeger quietly, and he took the honeysuckle flower from his mouth.

"We're twenty-four hours behind schedule," the Colonel said, his flushed face struck hotly by the sun as he watched the corporal and the *Hausmeister*, who had come down the garden path, take the suitcases out of the car. "My daughter should have got here yesterday, and then we'd have settled down. But she stopped overnight in Paris; that's the way women are. This is Mrs. Roberts," he said, and he jerked his shoulders fiercely again as if to fling the weight of them down on the path. The older woman smiled, and Jaeger saw that her mouth was not painted, and that her teeth were straight and white. "After making out all right for four months here, she's decided she wants to learn the language. She'll tell you why. For God's sake, Matterhorn, nobody's asking you to take all three!" he said to the *Hausmeister*, who stooped, wizened as a monkey in his starched white coat, his hands clawing at the fine leather handles of the bags. "This is my daughter, Milly, Herr Jaeger. Herr Jaeger spent three years in America recently—a guest of the War Department," the Colonel said, and he gave a laugh.

They were almost identically boned, the younger and the older woman, and they watched Jaeger with the tact and delicacy with which deer speculate on a stranger's presence in their lives. Whatever had happened to them on earth so far, in the forests or fields, in sunlight or shade, they had not been hurt, and it was clear they had not begun to calculate on how to defend themselves if danger came. *Like poets*, thought Jaeger, for it was poets he loved better than other men; they had that look of purity in their eyes which all men are given at birth and which they exchange, year by year, for one of bitterness, or avarice, or vanity. They wore plain linen dresses, the mother's grey, the daughter's peacock blue, with nothing that tinkled or glittered on them, no buckles, no jewels, no sequins, no ornaments, and Jaegar stood in almost unbearable homage before their beauty and their elegance. The mother was slightly taller than the girl, and her hair was auburn, wavy and dark and incredibly alive with health as it rippled back from a point on her square brow. It was the hair that betrayed without a glance being given, a word being said, the hot fire of love to which the outcast, the defeated, the lost, to which children and men could come to warm themselves in comfort for a while. The silky threads of her hair escaped the pins and the copper net of light cast by the sun, and wound like honeysuckle tendrils in her white neck and at her carefully made ears. The girl beside her was muted and remote, her shyness turning shy those who looked at her and tried to speak, and so delicate that the bones of her wrists and ankles seemed ready to break in two. When she moved her head, the darker plumes of her hair brushed softly across her shoulders, and Jaeger asked himself how she ever found speech and presence if her mother was not there.

The Colonel began to speak with authority of the disposition of the rooms in the requisitioned house, as if it had been his own decision, and not that of a German *Burger*, that had placed the largest rooms and the widest windows on the valley side, so that they faced a great medieval *Schloss* upon the opposite hill. They could see it as they walked up the path, standing across the valley, high above the University buildings and the slate roofs of the town, its ram-

9

parts flung far and wide, and its breast and bulwarks and heart made of the coldest stone.

"The only thing wrong about this house is that the kitchen's downstairs," said the Colonel's wife, turning her head to say it to Jaeger as well as to her daughter, who walked by her side. "You know, a kitchen in the cellar, so that the lives of the lower classes would stay where they belonged. So we have to have three servants, which may seem like a lot, but there're always guests, there's always entertaining to be done. The lonely of every country are always ready to come and dine, bringing their loneliness with them like an extra guest," she said, and there was no hint of the South in her voice, thought Jaeger, as in the voices of many army wives, and no twang of the jukebox to be heard.

"Three servants and a dumb-waiter!" the Colonel said, and he looked ahead at his wife and daughter and gave a loud, uneasy laugh. "We've even got nightingales in the dumb-waiter's ropes! You'll hear them warbling, Milly, every time a meal's pulled up!"

"Perhaps your houseman should oil the pulleys," said Jaeger, speaking quietly, respectfully. For a moment, it occurred to him that he might be able to fool them into thinking him a practical man.

"But nightingales don't want oil!" the Colonel's wife said softly, and she walked on in her grey dress before them, her shoulders as tender, her waist almost as narrow, as the girl's. "Haven't you read about nightingales pressing their hearts against the thorns of a rosebush, and singing and singing until they die?"

"Herr Jaeger has certainly not read anything as romantic as that!" cried Colonel Roberts. "The only thing the Germans read are their *Fragebogens*, just to see if they've slipped up and told a straight story anywhere!"

"But he could have read it when he was a boy in school!"

said his wife, and they might have been arguing about something quite different from this, about the very quality of life, thought Jaeger. Their voices, their wills, were two rapiers crossed there in the sunlight, and, for all the lightness and delicacy of the women's, hers was as strong as the man's, and would not give.

"The Germans weren't in the habit of telling their students fancy tales. You can say that much for their education," the Colonel said, and he jerked his shoulders back. "They probably gave him Bismarck instead. They like to think of themselves as realists, and I'm inclined to think they're right!"

"Richard Wagner and a couple of others told their countrymen some pretty tall stories," Jaeger said, his voice not loud, but so American that the Colonel seemed to jump inside his skin.

"Oh, the deep, dark mire of German myths!" said the Colonel's wife, and she gave a young and happy laugh. "I've been studying lithographs of heaven and hell, and reading the poets in translation, in the hope that the secrets of the dark forests of Germany will be revealed to me."

"Certainly nothing as clear and simple as a nightingale giving its blood to a white rosebush so as to turn the roses red," said Jaeger, pleased with these things she said. Around them now lay the well-tended, tilted grounds, with spruce and lilac, apple tree and pear, growing out of their separate islands of fresh loam. "I read Oscar Wilde in Colorado. For the first time in my life, I had time to read, and books weren't banned the way it was when I went to school. I discovered Heine and Thomas Mann. We weren't allowed to read them in Germany."

"You as a prisoner of war, and us as prisoners of the occupation," said the Colonel's wife, speaking scarcely aloud as she climbed the path. "I'm reading the *Portable Plato* and the *Portable Faulkner* from the PX. I start reading the moment I get up in the morning, and I read straight through every meal, not looking up because I can't bear to see what happens to people when they win."

"Look, Jaeger," the Colonel said, speaking sharply, "you come up to the house and get this lesson business settled— the hours, the pay. You won't have to hang around," he said, his veined blue eye glancing at the watch on his wrist, the snap of his voice making the presence of the national barrier clear. "We'll just settle what day of the week Mrs. Roberts—"

"Milly, while you were gone, I had another child," said his wife, saying it without warning as if to stave off the threat of him shouting aloud: *The way out is down the hill and through the gate, Herr Jaeger! You'd better get moving fast!*

"A brother or a sister?" the girl asked in a low voice, and she and her mother took each other's hands.

"Another daughter. I named her Persephone," said the Colonel's wife, and she halted in the last few steps of sun. Just this side of the advancing shadow of the needle trees was a shallow, sunken pool, and in the center of it knelt the terra-cotta figure of a maiden, life-sized, long-haired, and naked, set on an ivy-covered pedestal. "She must always have been a stranger here, so with you so far away, I took her for my own," the mother said, and Jaeger felt then that if he had the courage to walk up the sloping land and look at her, he might see tears upon her face.

But the Colonel began speaking coldly, savagely.

"You will be told by any number of people, by American civilians and by Germans, Milly," he said, the contempt in his voice making the two categories one, "that the marks on her rear end were made by the bullets of enlisted men who were stationed here in 1946. You'll be told that when the men had drunk a little on Saturday nights, they used that part of her for a target. Believe it if you want, Herr Jaeger. But I can tell you it isn't true."

"I'm sure she'd be the first to admit that it's the climate, or else snails," said the Colonel's wife. They had halted before the sight of the statue's sloping, terra-cotta shoulders, and the side of her bowed, grieving head, but Jaeger looked at the living women, seeing now in the beginning of the shadow that they had mermaids' sea-green eyes, and that their lashes were wet. "The fog comes up from the valley as thick as smoke all winter, scarring everything that stands in its way, even the flesh of Persephone," the mother said.

"Who told you about the fog? You've never been here in winter," said Colonel Roberts, flinging his shoulders from right to left.

"The German brewer," said his wife.

"But he's dead!" the Colonel cried in greater irritation.

"Not always. When you're out hunting at night, he comes to life," she said. Before they walked on past the statue kneeling so humbly in the ivy leaves, she turned and looked at the two men, and her eyes met Jaeger's, and it was as unequivocal as if she had spoken his name. He felt the blood mount in his face, for he was certain she saw him pale-haired, uncomfortably tall, bony-shouldered, lean, as part of the local landscape, as Teutonic as the great, cold *Schloss* across the valley, standing immutable against the tender sky. Even a Leica camera could not have caught in its sensitive lens the double exposure of what he was: a man in a shabby ersatz-wool suit and a cast-off American army shirt and a pair of American tan shoes that were not new, and that he had never known when they were new, and two vocabularies. Everything he had was secondhand—the suit, the shoes, the second vocabulary even, and he could not tell her that Bing Crosby had begun singing sweeter than any operatic Siegfried to him as long as four years ago. And then she turned,

13

and she and the girl went on up the path past the statue with its stone flesh pocked by G.I. bullets, and water running through the broken fingers of its terra-cotta hands.

Inside the entrance hall, a mirror hung the length and height of the wall, the glass, held fast in a frame of gilded, wooden grapes and tumultuous cherubim, coming suddenly alive with the reflections of the two women and the men. The *Hausmeister* and the corporal set the bags down on the polished parquet floor, and the Colonel gave his orders to them.

"Bring the car up at eight fifteen tomorrow morning," he said to the one in uniform, and to the other: "Matterhorn, take the bags upstairs. The large one first, and then come down and get the other two." When the young man in khaki had jerked his arm up in salute and gone out the door again, the Colonel indicated the coat rack with a thrust of his chin. Placed on the shelf above the brass hooks was a brown felt hat with a snap brim, and, beside it, an officer's garrison cap, and the *Hausmeister* made an attempt to pronounce the names of the callers who had come. He spoke in a high, obsequious treble, his gaze fixed on the rosy folds of skin that hung, as thick as plush, at the Colonel's throat below his lifted chin. When he had said the names, he let his lids fall in mock humility, and he sucked his leathery lips closed over his empty gums, and he waited there before them in his tight, white butler's jacket, abject, and servile, and sly. "Lieutenant Stephany and Mr. Honerkamp? Is that what you're trying to say? Now, get going with the bags, Matterhorn," the Colonel said, and the *Hausmeister*, wincing from the lumbago that warped his spine, stooped to lift the bags again, a film of artifice drawn over the shrewd almonds of his eyes. It was then, as his small skull bowed before them, that Jaeger saw he was an old man, a very old man, and that the sparse strands of hair drawn wetly across his ivory scalp had been dyed to the shade of dark mahogany. *So that he could pass for fifty instead of seventy, and get the job*, thought Jaeger, and the *Hausmeister* made his way, stiff-jointed, on bowed legs, up the highly polished stairs. "Let's get this business of the lessons settled, Cat," the Colonel said, and his manicured fingers touched his belt, "and then we can let Herr Jaeger go."

"I don't think I can give him the picture of what I want in five minutes," the Colonel's wife said softly. In the shadows of the hall, she turned her calm, balanced face, with its square brow, its wide-set mermaid's eyes, its wide, warm mouth, to her daughter, saying: "Milly, whatever post we were on, it's never been like this before. I never felt I had to explain anything, not even my heart. I took for granted that people knew."

"Knew what?" said the Colonel, and he jerked his shoulders impatiently.

"Oh, simply knew!" she said, and Jaeger watched her reflection in the mirror move toward the girl's reflection, and watched their hands touch in the glass. Then they turned toward him in the shadows, like mermaids turning in the clear depth of a wave. "This house belonged to a brewer," the mother said. "He made a Bluebeard chamber out of the library on the second floor. There are forty-five heads of his victims hanging on the walls."

"Oh, come!" cried the Colonel. He pulled in fury at his shirt cuffs as he glanced up at the hats that waited for recognition on the shelf, but his pride in her incomprehensibility was as hot as passion in his eye.

"Yes, he was a hunter," said his wife. "I found some of his belts in the attic, big enough to gird an elephant. But he never hunted anything his size. He went after animals without paunches, or trunks, or fangs, or claws, and once he had shot them, he cut off their heads as if they were helpless

Marie-Antoinettes. You can see them, dozens of little roe-bucks with their brows still furrowed in death on the upstairs walls. They tell me he died at the end of the war, the brewer, but he couldn't have died. He's living here still, both he and his wife. We can't do anything to make them go." And now the picture of it seemed uproariously funny to Jaeger, and he found he was laughing, and he could not stop. "He probably wore a Bavarian outfit all winter, the kind with stag-heads in the lapels," the Colonel's wife was saying, "but now that it's warm, he's put on his *Lederhosen*. Oh, I've been reading books about the traditional things that Germans do! His wife wears shoes with elastic set in the sides, and a black straw hat with a periscope fixed upright on the front of it." The girl beside her looked at the Colonel, and then at Jaeger, with her shy, darkly fringed, green eyes, and she too was laughing without making any sound. "She's come back not out of love of country, or for her people," said the mother, "but because of this furniture that was hers. She has to come back and touch the old chests of drawers, and the wardrobes, and the tables, to see what harm we've done to them. And what if I asked her what harm her people have done to the living? That might be the biggest joke of all," she said, but nobody was laughing any more. "Sometimes I can hear her in the attic, probably turning the portraits of the ancestors around so that the light will strike the medals on their breasts again."

"Your mother—" the Colonel started to say, and he flung one arm out as if to embrace the girl, wanting to end it quickly now. But the story of the brewer and his wife had to be told, for it was this sweet-scented woman's version of Germany.

"He's there, holding on to every window so that you have to fight to push them open or get them closed," said the Colonel's wife. "And he drinks beer quietly every night, case after case of it. At first I thought it was Matterhorn, but I know now that he makes use of Matterhorn to put the caps back on the bottles again so that you think the cases are still full. It's only when you want to serve beer to people who drop in that you find there isn't any left." She was laughing again, her lip drawn back from her white teeth, her straight nose a little wrinkled up, her long, tilted eyes half closed. "Sometimes when I'm here alone at night, Milly, I can hear the brewer breathing behind me as I go upstairs to bed, and I want to scream, but how could I explain the scream to Matterhorn and the others when they came running from the lower regions? How could I say, 'He can't bear it because it's the Colonel's turn to be out in the woods with death in his heart!' Oh, it's terribly funny, terribly funny, Milly! It's absolutely insane! It's not the loss of honor and prestige or the war that broke the brewer's heart, but the fact that somebody else has the right to the roebucks, and the pheasant, and the deer." The three of them stood there laughing so foolishly that the Colonel seemed on the point of shouting them down. His shoulders tossed, and his veined eyes blazed with blue fire, but before he could get the words out of his mouth, his wife said the one thing that could find an echo in his heart. "I'm told they have three sons prisoners of war in Russia still. Perhaps that's what they've come back looking for. Two hundred and fifty thousand dead at Stalingrad, and a hundred and twenty thousand frozen and starving and wounded taken prisoner there. Isn't that how it was, Herr Jaeger?" She had tried to say these words in German, as they had perhaps been said to her, but the numbers came haltingly. "And by now, this June, not more than three or four thousand have come back," she said, finishing it in English. "You see now how badly I need lessons, Herr Jaeger," she said, and then her voice ceased. It was as if the deep waters of the mirror had flowed like a river over them, and, except for the Colonel's labored breathing, there was a sudden quiet in the hall.

"For God's sake, let's go in and have a drink!" the Colonel cried out. In his impatience with the three of them, he included Jaeger in the abrupt gesture he made.

He stepped forward and pulled open the left half of the heavy double door, and, at once, a shaft of luminous sun-dust bisected the hall. Like an outraged shepherd, he herded them through this falling, shimmering beam. In the wide, elegantly furnished room that lay beyond, there was a climate that was not Germany's. A meridional light came through the long windows that stood open on the terrace, turning the flowers on the cretonne covers of the sofas and armchairs to the richness of tropic vegetation, and giving the polished, blond wood floor a higher sheen. But there, across the valley, was the castle on the other hill, watching in iron censure lest the disruption of foreign men and women carry things beyond the bounds of the long endurance of history.

"Hi, Mrs. Roberts! Hi, Colonel!" cried a totally American voice as the civilian in the room jumped to his feet and moved quickly forward through the sun. And *Never*, thought Jaeger, watching him, *never could I cross a room with that absolute certainty others would be pleased to see me come.* He would have liked to have on his own back the white shirt the young man wore, but he knew, almost without envy, that this, and the casual, college-boy, flannel suit, and the shoes with their thick, crêpe soles, belonged to men who had not lost a war. It would have been with hearty young men like this that the girl had walked the streets of the college town from which she had just come (the name forgotten, although the Colonel had told it to him a week ago with pride), or walked the campus with while they talked to her of poetry and philosophy, or merely of ice-cream sodas and banana splits, and it brought alive to him again the bitter knowledge that his own life could never have this continuity. "I'm Seth Honerkamp," the young man said in a forthright voice, and he held his hand out to the girl.

"Oh, Seth, it was nice of you to come!" said the Colonel's wife, for the girl said nothing. And Jaeger found himself waiting with anxiety, as the young men on the campus must have waited, for her to speak. It made all one's weaknesses stand out, all one's uncertainties even less certain, he thought, when they were received into the utter silence of her eyes. It might be she had never spoken, never yet listened, never heard the clamor of life all around her, he thought, except when she turned her head to whatever it was that she and her mother saw and heard with absolute clarity from the moment they touched each other's hands. "The committee of welcome for Milly," the mother murmured, including the young man in uniform who was standing, too. She moved, a faint smile on her lips, quickly, efficiently, in the room, absorbed with the ash trays as she set them out, and the newspapers she folded and put out of the way. The girl stood still.

"This is my daughter, Millicent," said the Colonel, and he brought her forward with his arm around her, seeking to focus even the direction of her gaze so that it would not slip between his fingers and rest on something that he could not see.

At first glance, Honerkamp seemed short in stature, but he was not. It was perhaps because the flesh of boyhood had lingered in a defensive armor on his shoulders, and chest, and limbs. Even his belly might go to fat in a little while, thought Jaeger as he looked down on him from his own gaunt height. He had a small-featured, rather worried face, this Honerkamp, with the plumpness of the cheeks and chin giving a perhaps wholly false impression of joviality. *Oh,*

19

she must have known them by the dozen on the campus!
Jaeger thought, as he too had known them in America, with
the stubbornness of boyhood in their minds as well as in
their flesh, so certain of what they had heard in the lecture
hall, and so baffled by what no one had told them yet, or
what could not be told, that they would stop in the middle
of exposition or argument, and the blood would rise hot in
their necks as they drew their hands in perplexity back and
forth across their crew-cut skulls. Honerkamp was given a
look of added innocence by the brown curly head of hair.

"This is Millicent," said the Colonel, holding her there
in choleric pride for them to see, and the young man in uniform gave a half-bow.

Lieutenant Stephany was of another tradition from
Honerkamp, one that might have been acceptable to
Hollywood, and he stood there, dark and debonair, aware
of the pleasure that a first sight of him afforded anyone he
met. He wore his battle jacket and his combat boots as if
they were fancy-dress or trappings put on for a musical comedy, and his soft, nearly black eyes were filled with blandish-
ment, his red-lipped mouth weakened by apology for what
he knew he was. Behind these two young men who faced
the Colonel and the girl, the backdrop of afternoon shone
in the open windows: first, the terrace railing, and then the
deep surf of green leaves fluctuating on the boughs, and,
across the valley, the chimera of the medieval castle drifting,
derelict, above the bluish slates and shingles of the town.

"I wouldn't have let her out of my sight, not even to go to
college. She looks young enough to play with dolls," said
Honerkamp, and he might have been speaking of someone
who had walked out of the room. "I'd have gone to college
with her, disguised as her twin."

"You'd have had to take some weight off first," said Lieutenant Stephany, his teeth showing white in his red, irresolute mouth.

"Well, we're going to make up for it now. We've got all summer ahead," said the Colonel, and he ran his finger inside his collar and laughed at nothing except for pleasure that she was here at last.

"Only maybe she doesn't know how to hold a gun, or ride a horse," said Honerkamp, the humor not quite humor now as he looked the Colonel in the eye. "Maybe she learned nothing at college except how to read a book, or listen to music, and maybe she's been using her mind. With all due respect, wouldn't that change the plans you've been making for her, sir?" he said.

"I can't say that it would, Honerkamp," said the Colonel, and the color in his jowls seemed brighter, and there was a dryness in his voice, that might snap at any instant, that had not been there before. "Stephany will help me out, I hope. He'll take Milly over to the stables. If she feels like it, next week when we go out, he'll show her how to stalk a boar."

"And when she wants to read a book, she can go to the America House and borrow one from Honerkamp," said Lieutenant Stephany.

"Oh, heavens, no one has introduced Herr Jaeger!" the mother cried out softly, her delicately tinted face turned toward him in concern, asking courtesy in place of the things the three of them had said. "Herr Jaeger has just joined the paper here. Colonel Roberts has the greatest respect for his abilities." *This is Herr Jaeger's country, and we are his guests, and this house could very well be his family's house. That is how strange the situation is,* she might have said to the rest of them if she had had the time. But her interest was always a moment or two ahead of the thing that was taking place, and Jaeger watched her as she turned, her head raised, her throat smooth and long, action suspended an instant as if she was harking for statements of passionate conviction to be said. "As President of the German-American Club, I've simply got to learn the language. You can see that, can't you?" she said to everyone in the room. "Herr Jaeger is going to help me." And then she led him to a chair by the window, so that the matter of whether the two men should or should not shake his hand was set aside.

In one corner of the sitting-room, there was a tiled, sunken basin, and the lieutenant crossed to it, and placed one foot on its blue and white porcelain rim just above the highly polished floor. Goldfish or brook trout had perhaps swum captive in it in the brewer's time, but now it was only figures from Aesop's fables, rendered in blue on the opaque white tiles, that gave it life.

"You mentioned boar, sir," said Lieutenant Stephany, and the Colonel's wife waited until his voice was done before she asked what they would like to drink.

"Champagne!" cried the Colonel. "Milly likes champagne!"

"There's quite a situation shaping up out in the Ober-Pastau area," said Lieutenant Stephany, playing the earnest and reliable subordinate now. "They say there's a pig, a very large pig, that comes right down in the village at night. Boar usually hold off until the weather's cold—say, twenty below—before they start looking for food in the village streets. They're shyer than deer, you know. But this one comes stampeding in, and on three different nights, he's charged the peasants in the dark." Jaeger drew the cigarette smoke in deeply, gratefully, as he watched the girl, seeing that she alone, seated among the crimson roses and the dark emerald leaves of the cretonne-covered chairs, was exempted from speech as a child is exempt while adults speak aloud. When the Colonel's wife went out the door, Jaeger thought for a moment that the girl would rise and follow, crying the name of mother, as a child, or bird, or bleating lamb would, in the hall. A bronze, stylized fish gaped from the wall, and Stephany lifted one hand and turned the decorative little wheel placed just below it, and water gushed from the distorted mouth and into the tiled basin built in the floor. "I'd be pleased if you'd undertake a mission with me sometime over the weekend, sir," he said, and he turned the wheel so that water poured from the fish's mouth, and turned it again so that the water ceased to flow. "The forester called me last night. He said there are unidentified Americans coming up after game in a jeep at night. They drive through the village without stopping at the forester's house to pick him up, but go straight out the corduroy road."

"Why doesn't he get the license number?" said the Colonel, and the look of rank, and discipline, and reprimand for whatever interfered with the way he wanted things to be, now glazed his eye.

"They tie potato sacking around the license plates. That's how they take care of that," said Stephany. He strolled back across the room, and sat down on one corner of the heavy table, and crossed his arms in the battle jacket, and his sleeves rode a little short so that an identity bracelet on one wrist, and a handsome Swiss wristwatch on the other, could be seen. There he sat, swinging one leg, playing the role of casual, reckless young officer for the Colonel and the girl. And after a while, thought Jaeger, when nothing very much had come of it—as nothing comes of the mock-heroic roles that movie actors play—Lieutenant Stephany would give it all up, and the rush of energy and charm would perish, and he might turn to the civilians, either the German or the American, for fraternity. But now he was working hard. "This forester, this stalwart character named Knau," the lieutenant said, "he followed them as far as he could,

23

but he couldn't keep up. He was on a bicycle, and he lost them, but he could see the reflection of their headlights every now and then, a long way off, above the trees, and he could hear the shooting for an hour after that."

"How does he know they hit anything if he didn't get anywhere near them?" the Colonel asked, his voice already raised in argument.

"Because he found dead game in the underbrush, and he followed the crippled game in daylight, sir," said Lieutenant Stephany. "Last week, Knau found a dead roebuck, its thighbone shattered by bullets that never came from a rifle or a shotgun. He found it by the smell. Yesterday, he followed a trail of blood, and found a doe gasping its last at the end of it. The jeep had been out the night before."

"All this, Stephany," Honerkamp said with the sound of malice in it, "would indicate that you speak and understand German as well as you do your native tongue."

"Well, no," said the young man, swinging his leg. "We have our contacts, our interpreters."

"I do not intend to be interpreted any further," said the Colonel's wife. She had come through the door, her hair freshly combed, her heels high now, and the room was filled with subtle promises again. "One can't possibly know how much has been left out," she said, and she held the door open for the *Hausmeister* to come in on his warped legs, bearing a tray of fluted glasses and a metal bucket in which swung a champagne bottle's gilt-wrapped neck and head.

"Those deer-jackers aren't army men," said the Colonel, and he flung his shoulders back. "I'd lay my money on that."

"But civilians don't know how to handle guns!" said Honerkamp, and he gave a little yelp of laughter, and ran his fingers through his curly hair.

"Neither do these men in the jeep," said Stephany.

"That's just one more advantage the military has over the civilian set-up," said the Colonel, and he smiled in grim satisfaction at Honerkamp. "We can court-martial our offenders, while you civilians are so fouled up in Occupation Statutes and legal precedents that your crooks and your murderers slip out the back door before anyone can call their names!"

"The military advantage," mused Honerkamp, leaning forward from the soft depths of his chair. "That's interesting, you know. But the boar that terrorizes the villagers, and the jeep that moves through the forest slaughtering game, they could be delusions. The Occupation could have brought about some kind of astigmatism in the Germans. They may see menace and see Americans where there aren't any at all. You couldn't put thin air in the guardhouse, could you, sir? And how are you going to court-martial a myth?" he said.

"If the men in that jeep are thin air, then they're thin air with tommy-guns at their disposal, and with access to standard ammunition," said Stephany.

"What do you think of the military tradition, Herr Jaeger?" Honerkamp asked then, and the small, intent mask of his face appeared to go smaller, more worried still, within the nearly circular frame of boyish curls, and swollen cheek and jowl.

"It got me to America," said Jaeger in a low voice. "I can't complain."

"As a P.O.W.," the Colonel said in explanation as he took the champagne bottle from the ice.

"Damn it. I'm sorry about that," said Honerkamp. "I didn't know."

"I'm not," said Jaeger, his voice scarcely heard. "It meant the end of the war for me."

And now Honerkamp turned to the girl, as if to pursue it

to the end, however bitter it might be. *Speak now!* his earnest, brown eyes exhorted her, the long, proficient fingers of
his young hands clasped in entreaty between his heavy knees;
but his flannel trousers had ridden up as he moved forward
in his chair, and a piece of bare leg could be seen above each
crumpled sock, so that his dignity (although he did not know
it) was impaired. *Speak now so that I may know on which
side you belong! The child of an army man, reared in it,
have you given flesh, marrow, and conviction to it, or are
your mind and will still free? Speak now!* his silence pressed
her urgently, but she was looking toward the terrace and
the *Schloss* across the valley, looking with young, translucent
eyes at this monument to age that stood against the sky.

"You know the village I mean, sir?" Lieutenant Stephany was asking deferentially, taking up the conversation
with the Colonel where it had been before the civilians interrupted it.

"We'll go out on Saturday night," said the Colonel briskly.
He stood, a fine figure of a soldier, except for the weight of
the shoulders that he could not cast aside, carefully working
the cork of the champagne bottle free with the flat of his
right thumb. "It may be lively, tracking them down."

"Which?" said Honerkamp ironically as he stood up.
"The civilians or the boar?"

"And you'll come along with us, Milly!" the Colonel said,
his voice already drunk from the promise of the champagne
or the hunt. "You'll drive out with us, eh, Milly, and the
whole thing will start making sense to you!" he cried so
loudly that no other voice, and no other argument or propo-
sition, could be heard.

Then the cork of the champagne bottle hit the ceiling,
and the laughter of the mother sounded in pure delight.

"That should startle the brewer in his grave!" she cried out
softly, and she watched the fine gold liquid run from the

bottle, that smoked with the cold, into the long stems of the glasses, and stand trembling there. "It's always as wonderful as fireworks," she said, and the others were silent, waiting for the girl to speak.

They saw her green eyes return slowly from the castle to the confines of the sitting-room, and saw her examine their faces in uncertainty, and the four men—even Jaeger now—were abruptly aware of the almost unbearable eagerness with which they waited for the words that she would say. As the *Hausmeister*, dwarfed and gnome-wizened, began to move among them, bearing the glasses of golden fluid to each one, they knew that when she spoke it would be to accept them or discard them, for she was required now to make her choice between civilian and military man.

"Mother told me about the horses," she said, and her voice, like the older woman's, came from an America that Jaeger had not known. "She said there would be Lipizzaners in the horse show on Saturday night. I think I would like to see them more than—" *More than chasing poachers through the forest, more than hunting, and killing, more than waiting in the dark streets of a village for an illusionary boar,* she did not say aloud. Instead, she finished haltingly, in a voice so low that they could scarcely hear: "More than anything else, I would like to see the horses from the Adriatic Sea."

And now that she had specified her choice between the contests offered, Honerkamp looked at Stephany, who sat swinging his leg from the edge of the table still. But he had ceased for the moment to play the role of the debonair young officer exhibiting to the two women in the room the length of his thigh and the softness of his mouth. His identity had seemed to fade, as an inadequately developed photograph will fade, and there was no way of determining now what kind of man he was.

"This is great," said Honerkamp, and his face expanded as he smiled. He squatted suddenly down before the girl, his legs spread wide in his grey flannels, his weight borne lightly on the balls of his feet. "This is wonderful. May I take you there?" he said.

22

Catherine Roberts
wet her lips with the champagne, and then she put her
glass down, and she said she could never learn any language
if it meant sitting down with pencil and notebook and a
grammar. The German lessons must be a part of the things
she had done alone before, or of what Jaeger had done
alone. They would simply do the things together now,
speaking German as they did them, and to Jaeger this
added a sudden peril and wonder to the undertaking, as if
it were not pupil and teacher who would meet in the
appointed places, but as if he fixed a rendezvous with his
own longing to be an honored, articulate man. It was like
this that lovers relinquished their nights of solitude to each
other, he thought, and then he stopped short at the
realization of the implications, seeing himself no longer
crippled and gagged and handcuffed by loneliness, no longer
a prisoner of war released on parole to his own alien
countrymen. The Colonel's wife said that the lessons were
not to be given in time pulled up by the roots from the
rock garden below the house, or out of the hours of horse-
back-riding across the hills, or from the reading of the
histories and guidebooks of Germany, which she had been
doing every day. The horses could be a beginning, Jaeger
said, forgetting to drink the champagne at all. He had
Christoph Horn, the riding-master, to interview for the
paper on the Lipizzaner horses before the Saturday-night
show, and Catherine Roberts could meet him at the stables
the next day.

So before four o'clock on Thursday afternoon, he was
out of the newspaper office and up in the riding-stables
behind the *Schloss*. Christoph Horn gave him a horse to

saddle for himself, a big, bony-shouldered gelding with a greenish tinge to its hide—liver-colored, they called it—and a look of mildew at its fetlocks and its nose. He stood in the fragrant stall and tightened the girth straps under the horse's belly, and the thought of riding with Catherine Roberts through the dark woods and the open fields that had once been the hunting-grounds of the noble owners of the *Schloss* almost made him laugh aloud. For now the fine, noble owners were dispossessed, and they lived in a gardener's lodge beyond the strawberry beds, and ran the riding-school for a living; and the *Schloss* itself was an Officers' Club, and not even the German *Graf* might step inside it, so that Jaeger and the Colonel's wife were allied on the winning, democratic side. But this horse he could have done without, for it seemed a monster to him, with a jaw and cheekbone that looked like a violoncello in the shadows of the place. It had put its ears flat back, and they lay like a pair of discarded kid gloves on the point of its skull, the fingertips twitching slightly whenever Jaeger moved toward its head. Over the tooth-gnawed, hoof-scarred wood of the box's side, Jaeger could see the boy named Christoph in the adjoining stall, moving with such quiet aplomb, such certainty, as he saddled the bay mare that Catherine Roberts was to ride.

"They call your horse 'Snafu,' the Americans," said Christoph Horn, the accent soft, Bavarian, speaking to Jaeger in their native tongue. "When you're up on him, just leave it to him. Set his head to the woods, and he'll find the trails. He's got a mouth like iron," he said.

"And what do I do when I want to come back?" asked Jaeger. He looked across the worn, pine planks at the slender, slightly stooping riding-master whose photograph they had printed in the paper twice, once wearing a jockey's striped silk shirt and cap after winning the steeplechase at Niederstadt, and once in a hunting-jacket of outmoded cut as he rode a Lipizzaner up from Austria, perhaps merely as publicity for the stables, or publicity for the breed with Arabian and Spanish, or with Danish and Italian, blood carried in its veins. Jaeger watched him slip the bridle over the little bay mare's head, and he saw that the riding-master's sharp, sad face was marked by a boyish weariness, an almost feminine and ailing fatigue, and Jaeger thought: *He is grieving now as the entire country grieves, but perhaps his grief has some kind of sense to it, something better than the mere fact of the defeat.* He would have liked to put the questions to him, but the quality of Christoph's presence was like a weary finger laid for silence on the mouth. "What do I do, for instance, when I want to stop?" asked Jaeger, his low voice gone a little humorous now.

"Oh, he'll bring you back if you let him have his head," said Christoph. He seemed exhausted by the effort of being what he was. His cheeks were hollow, and his nostrils pinched as if by hunger, but it could be only the memory of hunger, Jaeger thought, for at this late date the actual pain of it could scarcely be gnawing at his guts, flat though his belly was. He wore a grey cap pushed off his brow, and the visor of it stood straight up from the dark hair that fell loosely above his temples, and hung, long as an artist's, behind his ears. "He's been ridden hard by every G.I. who was ever stationed in Fahrbach. Sometimes by two of them at the same time." He pulled the small mare's coarse forelock free of the brow band, and he said: "If you'll take him out into the courtyard, I'll be along." But Jaeger stood without moving, avoiding Snafu's rolling, white-rimmed eye. "That's *Wehrmacht* branding on his croup," said Christoph, and he undid the stall rope, and turned the mare. His hand on the leather of the bridle was long, and the fingers big-jointed and square-tipped, but it was his face and his accent

gave him a sort of aristocratic weariness, a distinction,
something else that Jaeger could not put a name to yet,
that set him aside from the race of big-thighed men.

"So that means he could have seen Paris or Stalingrad,"
said Jaeger. He watched the afternoon light from the ivy-
hung windows on the other side touch Christoph's face as
he stepped into the cobbled corridor that ran the length of
the stalls, but it did not matter now if Christoph went on
with it, for Jaeger was listening for the sound of a car outside, and for a woman's voice to speak the language that he
liked to hear. "One moment. Is Mrs. Roberts a very good
rider?" he asked, clearing his throat.

"She rides better than most of them," said Christoph,
and he led the little mare out onto the cobbles, under the
ceiling of dark-stained, ancient beams that were as clean
of cobwebs as a ballroom floor. "She's bringing her
daughter for her first jump lesson today."

The irons of the mare's shoes rang through the shadowy,
sweet-smelling place, and through the alternating bars of
dark and sun, and the horses in the twenty or more well-
kept stalls shook their manes, or neighed musically in greeting, or merely turned their heads to watch her pass. Only
Snafu stood motionless, one big hoof cocked and ears quite
flat, his eye on Jaeger, and Jaeger knew the moment had
come to act. He must step forward, unsnap the stall rope,
and follow where Christoph led.

"Oh, Snafu, Snafu," Jaeger murmured. He remembered
riding on Sunday afternoons before the war in the *Wäldche*,
the *Stadtwald* of Niederstadt, and that if the hoofs of one
horse began to pound the turf in a canter, the others would
be flung into panic, reason would reel in their heads, and
they would go thundering down the bridle path with foam
whitening their mouths. That was the secret of mastery

32

over them, he decided now: not to let them get the scent of action on the wind, or hear the stark hysteria of the others. But when he put out his hand toward the stall rope, the horse flung the violoncello of its long, strong jaw up out of his reach. "Snafu, oh, Snafu, did you smell that honeysuckle vine last night?" Jaeger asked him gently, and the horse rang the bit aloud in his mouth and turned his head to look back across his bony shoulder at the man. Then he drew his soft, loose, mildewed lip up, and bared his yellow teeth. There he stood on the golden straw of his bedding, he who had perhaps walked the Champs-Elysées one spring in triumph, or come through the far, deep snows of Russia one winter in defeat, sneering his evil, manlike sneer at Jaeger, who looked uncertainly at him over the *Wehrmacht* markings scarred in his hide. It was perhaps because the stables were cool that the horse did not want to leave his dark, moist cave of April or March to brave the heat, the wasps, and the netting of flies and gnats that would be cast about him in the June woods. Or, just five minutes before, it may have been, he had come to the decision that he had had enough for the rest of his life of carrying men around. *Oh, Snafu, don't defy me! Take me as brother*, said Jaeger in silence. *I am branded, too. I have Afrika Korps and German stamped indelibly on my hide.*

Christoph Horn returned down the cobbled corridor, and he did not seem to look at Jaeger, but he came in his old, scuffed riding-boots into the stall where Jaeger stood. He moved lightly, wearily, past the other man, his shoulders stooped in the grey shirt striped with darker grey, his waist narrow in the grey whipcord riding-breeches; and Jaeger felt a sudden resentment that it should be a German who must help him out. Had the sharp, sorrowing, patrician face been that of an American, Jaeger would have looked with goodwill on it; but it was German, and it belonged to a past that he repudiated, and to a future he did not want to share.

"They haven't come yet," said Christoph, and he moved without concern between the horse and Jaeger. "Mrs. Roberts doesn't keep anyone waiting, not even the horses, so it must be the daughter."

"No, the daughter isn't like that," Jaeger said almost sharply, feeling that he knew them well, and Christoph abruptly raised his head. "I mean, the daughter would take her mother's decisions," Jaeger said.

"Do you know her?" said Christoph, and for the first time they looked straight into each other's faces.

"I met her yesterday," said Jaeger. "She had just come."

"The Colonel brought Mrs. Roberts and his daughter up last evening," Christoph said, and then the two men dropped their eyes, as if they had looked too deeply into each other's lives and hopes for the moment. Christoph shouldered Snafu a little to one side.

"Here, let me take him out," said Jaeger. He felt the blood rise in his face because this delicately made youth, this hollow-cheeked child with his big-knuckled hands, had the courage that should have been his own. "I'll take Snafu, as long as I'm to ride him," he said, but Christoph had undone the stall rope, paying no heed to the big beast's leer or his rolling eye.

"I know them well. I've spent my life with them," Christoph said, and he turned the horse in the wide stall. "He must have been very good in the retreat, Snafu," he said. "He stretches like rubber. He isn't a gentleman, but I've never seen a horse clear a ditch the way he does."

"Does he give any warning before he does it?" Jaeger asked, but Christoph did not smile. He had led Snafu out into the cobbled alleyway, and now the iron of his great shoes rang on the stones. "Did you spend the war years with them, too?" said Jaeger, following after; but he was asking: *What kind of German were you then, and what side are you on now?*

They did not look at each other as they moved from the fragrance of the stalls out into the open courtyard (shaped like the imprint of a horseshoe) which the ivy-covered mews enclosed. In the center was a fountain (living and vulnerable as the fontanel of a horse's foot) where horses, century after century, had lowered their heads, and stretched their necks, and filled their throats deeply from the water trembling in the ancient stone. The dark ivy leaves were pruned in meticulous squares around the stable doorways and the small, barred windows of the stalls. In the tiled, sloping roofs were the lidded eyes of dormer windows that had looked down for generations on the unchanging ritual of men and horses, the unchanging roles, the eternal ceremony of their leave-takings and their returns. Above the roofs could be seen the crests of great, ancient trees, the plumes of their boughs shimmering against the marble clouds that seemed now to be halted in the sky. Underfoot were short grasses, sharply green, and unmature daisy heads, woven like embroidery in and out through the cobblestones.

"I was thirteen when the war began. I went to work with a veterinary outside Munich," Christoph said. As the two men crossed the court, there were only peaceful sounds on the air: the slow clopping of Snafu's hoofs as he followed on the rein, and the moaning of pigeons under the stables' eaves, and the water falling without haste into the basin in the sun. "We had luck. The veterinary stables were hit three times, but we got more than half the horses out. The authorities left me alone. Horses had value, and we were breeding horses, so I stayed."

So it was from the aristocrats who rode, thought Jaeger, from the men with faces slashed with old fencing-scars, and monocles screwed in the sockets of their eyes, bringing their thoroughbreds to the veterinary in time of war and in time of peace, that Christoph had acquired his special air. All through the war, as a child, as a youth, he must have rubbed shoulders with these others, and now their tempered arrogance, and their elegance, had become a part of his blood and bone. Even here, where he was hired by the *Graf* and *Gräfin* to be an underling, he was the worn and grieving prince and he could not be a servitor. And now, at the thought of paid instructor, of hired tutor, a blow struck suddenly at Jaeger's heart. *Where are Catherine Roberts and her daughter?* he asked himself. *Is it possible that they simply will not come?*

"How long have you known Mrs. Roberts?" he asked abruptly.

"Three or four months. She rides several times a week," Christoph said.

And what did you think of her the first time you saw her and talked to her, and the times after that? Jaeger wanted to ask, but he could not say it. Instead, he began telling himself that the Colonel's wife was obviously a very social kind of person, used to a life of daily subterfuge and tact, and one in whom no confidence could be placed. The subtle committing of herself to man, and woman, and child, and beast, must be so casual a thing to her that it wounded those whom it touched far more than it restored their faith. *Oh, the army posts in her career that she must have illuminated with another quality,* he thought; *the hope she must have given for a little while to the ordinary and the dull, and then taken it away!* Across the court stood the bay mare, as tremulous and impatient as a stamping, living heart, waiting where Christoph had tied her in the shade.

"Could I have a look at the Lipizzaners?" Jaeger said, getting down to business now to quiet his own pain.

It was such a pretty, old-world scene that he and Christoph moved through, as charmingly tinted as an English print, with no sign of evil discernible unless you glanced at the entrance from the corner of your eye. Then you saw the two stone towers that guarded the court, set there like grim sentinels to warn the trespasser that this was Teutonic territory. Between the towers, a medieval iron gate stood wide, and over the gate hung a stone arch that held a hall where knights, perhaps, in other days looked through the mullioned windows down into the courtyard on one side and, on the other, out across the hills, and the valley, and far along the winding road below. As Christoph tied Snafu at a little distance from the mare, Jaeger glanced quickly toward the arch, but there was no sign or sound of a car approaching up the hill.

"The Lipizzaners are stabled across the court," said Christoph, and then he began to speak of Mr. Mike Dardenella as he led Jaeger toward the stalls on the left curve of the shoe. Dardenella was manager of the Army Post Exchange in Fahrbach, Christoph said, but this was not the thing that mattered. What concerned him was that Dardenella was a man who wanted to own Lipizzaners, and he had bought two of them, a mare and a stallion, in the past year. It was a passion with him, Christoph said, and he chose them with the greatest solicitude, wanting only the purest and whitest, those with strong, heavy shoulders and small heads, and, above all, those marked with the single "L" on the left lower jaw which denoted the Lipizzan of Italian strain. "He'll go right off, traveling anywhere, and take an expert with him, when he hears of a Lipizzaner that's up for sale." Now they had come to a closed oak door, wide enough for a team of horses to drive through, and Jaeger waited while this slender, hollow-cheeked boy, this stoop-shouldered jockey, with the beak of his grey cap standing straight up from his brow, turned the heavy iron ring in his two hands. Christoph seemed to him now like a younger brother, nearly ten years younger, it might be, and handsomer, more gifted, more adequately equipped to accept existence, and he was filled with a gentle envy for all that Christoph was. It was the horses that had saved him through war and Occupation; they had been his schooling, and endowed him with a contemporary speech. The oak door swung out, and Christoph led the way in, and the fluid sun poured in with them, running across the stone of the floor to the boarding of the stalls, and stopping there against the line of shade. Jaeger followed him to the first wide, padlocked pen, the lower half of which was wood painted emerald green, and the upper half enclosed in fencing wire transformed by sunlight to a golden cage. On a wafer of plywood fixed to the shoulder-high half-door, the name *Siglavy Marina* was printed in black, and the stallion himself lay on the straw. His head was free, and even like this, at rest, with his legs bent under, he had a cold and terrible power. "Siglavy from his paternal line, and Marina from his dam," said Christoph. "Sigmar to us in the stable here. He's a true Piber, with not only the 'L' branded under his jaw, but the 'P' on his left hind quarter." Jaeger looked through the wiring at the horse, and it seemed to him that the animal had as good as lifted a monocle to survey these others without blood and without tradition who had come through the door. "Sigmar's the property of the riding-school. I rode him up from Steiermark. You published the picture," Christoph said. As the Lipizzaner turned his ram-nosed, Arabian head, it could be seen that his left eye was filmed to a milky blue. "It's called a fish-eye, but he's not blind. But still Mr. Mike Dardenella wouldn't have him because of that one flaw. He gave it to the *Graf* to settle the board of the other one he has here."

"And what will Mr. Dardenella do with his Lipizzaners in the end?" asked Jaeger.

"Well, he comes from Brooklyn, so one day, when he goes back, he'll take them to Brooklyn with him." Christoph spoke a little wearily, and Brooklyn might have been the gardens of Schönbrunn stretching away. "He wants to have a stud farm there."

"It would make a good story for the paper," Jaeger said. "The Germans would like it very much: the Brooklyn American buying horses with the breeding of four centuries in their blood."

"As if he were buying a pedigree," said Christoph in sad, gentle disdain. And then he looked sharply at Jaeger, perhaps having caught a little late the sound of irony. "You've been out of Germany, haven't you?" he said.

"I was taken prisoner at the Kasserine Pass," said Jaeger, and Christoph swung abruptly on the worn heels of his riding-boots toward the stable door.

"I thought I heard a car coming up," he said, and the two men listened. But there was nothing, and again the hope of the women coming died.

Yes, a man's life must have continuity, if nothing else, thought Jaeger; *some kind of unbroken lineage of act, of association, some kind of unbroken line of friendship, love. That's where mine has raveled out. This child in his crazy Wehrmacht cap held on to horses, and I held on to nothing.* He remembered Dante Alighieri having written out of his exile: "Truly I have been a ship without sail and without rudder, wafted to divers havens and inlets and shores. . . ." *Ah, how Germanically I dramatize myself!* he thought in impatience. *How like a German I see myself in my slick*

39

brown suit, and these secondhand shoes that walked with another man's gait before they walked with mine! And on these shoes, he followed Christoph into the next compartment of the stables, and Christoph closed the door before a message could run like quick-silver from stallion to mare. In her golden-bedded stall, the plump, white-Lipizzan mare, deep-breasted and muscular of leg, turned restlessly. She could move as she liked in the miniature corral, and at times she stopped to look at the two men, shaking her drooping white velvet ears, and tossing her forelock out of her dark-lashed eyes.

"You can write about them that Lipizzaners have always been good for riding, and driving, and hunting, if you're satisfied to ask only that of them," Christoph said, and he leaned on the half-door of the stall and drew two fingers across the white satin muzzle of the mare; "but that has nothing to do with what they are. They are well-mannered and courteous, each one different from the other. Sigmar, I tell you, has a sense of his own destiny. Mr. Mike Dardenella's stallion plays jokes, but jokes in good taste, with riders he doesn't know. This mare, she is not interested in material gain. She won't take a sugar unless you smooth her nose. Put in that they're noblemen, the Lipizzan stallions," Christoph said wearily, and then he ceased speaking, for they heard a car drive into the courtyard, and they waited as if turned to stone.

"That must be—" Jaeger began, and they started walking toward the door. And now the Lipizzaners were nothing, not the snowy-breasted mare who turned in her pen, or Sigmar, with his monocle lifted. The breed of them could go galloping back on their strong, white legs and their ebony hoofs to another century, for all that either man now cared. They could go back to the studs of Granada and Seville, to the stretches of limestone wilderness on the

Adriatic, for a car had come through the medieval gateway, under the arch between the two grim, dour towers, and had stopped beside the fountain, a long, green car, all polished planes and chromium. "If she's going to be late like this for every lesson!" Jaeger said half aloud, thinking there would be hardly twenty minutes left out of every hour he was to spend with her.

But from the front seat of the car there stepped a short man in a pearl-grey sharkskin suit. On the side of his head, he wore a grey straw Stetson with a flowered, pastel-tinted band around the crown, and there was something flashy, theatrical about him, as he stood there in the sun. He could very well have been an opera singer, or producer, or impresario, and Jaeger turned in despair from the sight of the dapper little fellow, seeing the thing now as it really was. The promise was not to be kept, that promise made by nothing more than the sound of Catherine Roberts' voice in a room, the promise that there would be something else to life, something to which he had not given a name. It had been made merely in the way that she walked out of one room and into the next, so lightly, so easily, and he had accepted it in heavy, German solemnity.

"Hi, Christoph, it looks as good as Florida today!" said the short, well-larded little man as he crossed the cobblestones on grey suede shoes that fitted as neatly as gloves. "What sun, what a sky, what a balmy breeze, for a country as terrible as Germany! Just when you think you've had all you can take of the darned country, along comes Christmas, or *Fasching*, or a couple of days like this, and you think maybe you won't go home after all! *Ich heisse Dardenella, mein Herr*," he said to Jaeger, and he took his grey straw hat from his smooth, black, pomaded hair, and held his right hand out. "*Ich bin Americanische Pferdophile*," he said, his mouth stretched wide with pleasure in his olive face.

The cushion of his thumb was soft, and his fingers warm and eager, and a heavy, silver-linked bracelet slipped forward on his wrist as he shook Jaeger's hand.

"Don't trouble to speak German, Mr. Dardenella. We all speak English here," said Christoph in his weary, eternal disdain, his English so natural that Jaeger looked at him in wonder an instant as he spoke. "Herr Jaeger is a newspaperman. He's come up for a story on the Lipizzaners. He wants to write them up before the show."

"I have a Lipizzaner stallion from the Italian branch, and a mare who's pure Yugoslav Lipizzan, but she defected from the party and got across," the little man said to Jaeger. He stood with his straw Stetson in his hand, looking eagerly from one to the other of them, a smile flickering on his mouth. "When I go home, I'm going to set up a stud out on Long Island," he said, and he stood there like the humblest of opera tenors waiting, not certain until the clapping of hands would come to reassure him that he had understood the part and sung it well. "Archduke Charles of Styria, Carinthia, Carniola, and Istria founded a stud with nine stallions and twenty-four brood mares of the old Spanish Andalusian strain at Lipizza, near the head of the Adriatic Sea. So, compared to him, I'm starting out on a shoestring," he said, smiling still, but watching Jaeger with troubled eyes. "Archduke Charles bred them for artistic riding. That was in 1580, and, I tell you, they're still artists today. They come from Arab, and Danish, and Spanish, and Italian stock, and one book I read says that 'Caesar's snow-white steeds which Hispania did him send' were pretty sure to have been Lipizzaners. That's something, isn't it?" And *Oh, the doomed, outlandish Germans,* thought Jaeger as he listened; *the Germans always so gratified by what they are, so isolated in their destiny! But give a man two drops of American blood in his veins and he'll keep widening the circumference, push-*

ing the horizon farther, ever farther, beyond what he was intended to be. Here was Dardenella with his American-Latin blood pushing the horizon beyond Brooklyn and out over the water to places that were strange to him, flinging it beyond Trieste and Polesina and the Adriatic, and as far as Denmark to the north. "In the seventeenth century, the grandest kind of diplomats were still being sent from the Duchy of Carniola to Spain to buy Lipizzan horses from the studs in Granada and Seville, and a hundred years later they were buying Italian horses to breed with them," Dardenella said with such pleasure, as if he were speaking of his own family tree.

"Herr Jaeger can get all that out of books," said Christoph. Now that the last echo of the little tenor's aria had died, there remained the chill and silence of the disapproving opera house. *You sang it absolutely flat,* was what Christoph had said.

"Well, take a look at the horse I've drawn," Jaeger said in his low, shy voice. He watched the olive-skinned little man turn in the sunlight and place his hat on his smooth, black hair again, and look, still smiling, at Snafu.

"He's a real hood," said Dardenella, and he laughed happily, settling his hat on the side of his head with his golden, silky hand. "They oughtn't to make horses as big as that. I wouldn't ride him if they paid me to. He hasn't any looks," he said, and then he began saying to Christoph the thing he had driven up here to get off his mind. "I'm going to ride Neapoli on Saturday night. I'm going to show him myself," he said, his smile turned painful now. "If I'm a horse-owner, then I ought to be able to put my own horse through his acts. I ought to be able to manage him myself. That makes sense, doesn't it?" he asked. Against the swarthiness of his face, his teeth were polished clean and white, and Jaeger could see gold inlays in the molars of his

43

lower jaw. "I'm going to show Neapoli on Saturday night. That's what I've decided," he said, dividing his grin between the two of them. "That makes sense, doesn't it, Herr Jaeger?" he asked, turning to him for help since Christoph would give him none.

"No," said Christoph. "It wouldn't do. He'd trick you and fool you before the judges just as I've seen him doing it when you're riding him here in the rink."

"Tricked me?" Dardenella spread his hands.

"In the 'Passage,' I've seen him give a quick swing of the back," said Christoph, "so you'll think he's thrusting off from the ground with his hind legs, but he isn't. Sometimes I think I've heard him laughing when he does it, and sometimes he looks at me and winks an eye."

"You're crazy, Christoph," said Dardenella, trying to smile.

"No," Christoph said. "With the Lipizzaners, you accept the tradition or else you let the whole thing go." He stood with his narrow thumbs hooked in the belt of his riding-breeches, looking steadily off through the medieval arch with his old, exhausted eyes. "A king, a maharajah, he can own the horse, but that doesn't mean there is a language he can speak to him."

"Well, we Americans come along, and we change traditions," said Dardenella, the smile held in desperation on his mouth. "So I've decided I'll show Neapolitano Virgilia myself on Saturday night. It's Thursday now, so that gives me two more nights to practice the 'Pirouette' and the 'Passage.'"

"Two more nights isn't enough," said Christoph, his voice cold and spent. "You should have begun to practice in the sixteenth century, and perhaps even that wouldn't have been enough time. I've had seven years at it, and I'm still not proud."

"But I bought him! I own him!" cried Dardenella, setting his patterned necktie straight. He stood laughing at the absurdity of all Christoph had said, but the wound was gaping wide. And then the second car drove in. This time there could be no mistake. It was a station wagon of deep pine green and varnished wood, and it moved slowly under the arch where mounted knights had passed in other centuries, three or four abreast. Two women rode in it, one at the wheel, the other seated beside her, and the auburn-haired woman who drove put her arm through the open window and waved her hand. "It's Mrs. Roberts, Colonel Roberts' wife," said Dardenella in an altered voice, and he took his hat from his head, and held it in homage upon his heart, as if it was royalty that now drove past.

So the promise was kept, and Jaeger felt the cordon of isolation loosening, and the easy generosity of America embracing him again. They were here: Catherine Roberts in a riding-habit the color of sand, and her hair tied back, low on her neck, by a black bow, and the copper threads of it curling at her ears. They had had a flat tire in the country lane, she said, a nail from a horseshoe driven straight through the casing and the tube, and they had sat by the roadside and waited while a farmer, a peasant, had changed the wheel. Jaeger stood listening to the sound of her voice, and Milly got out of the car, and looked straight at Christoph, and laughed. Her breeches were grey, and her white shirt was open at the neck, and her fine black boots fitted tightly around her slender calves.

"Our riding-breaches are just alike!" she said, and the color ran across her cheekbones, and she turned her head away.

"Yours are new, and your boots are new," said Christoph. He had taken the *Wehrmacht* cap from his head, and he stood with his thumbs hooked in the leather of his belt again, his eyes on her in sober rebuke for what she was. If she had turned then to step back into the car, thought Jaeger, this hollow-cheeked boy would have spoken no word and made no move to keep her there.

Catherine Roberts looked down now at Dardenella, and Jaeger saw the gold of the inlays gleam in his mouth.

"I can't thank you enough for the books you've put on sale at the PX," she said. "*The Portable Plato!* Imagine it, Herr Jaeger! And William Faulkner, and Nietzsche. It's going to do a lot for us all. I started *War and Peace* last night, and this time I'm going to get through it. I'm ashamed when I think how many times I started it before."

"That's MacArthur's book, isn't it? It ought to interest Colonel Roberts," Dardenella said, the smile warm, and grateful, and comforted. "I always like making good things accessible." It had been written up in a Hamburg paper two weeks before, the choice of books in the PXs in Germany, and there had been a cartoon, Jaeger remembered, of a G.I. with a package of bubble gum in his hand, and *The Portable James Joyce* under his arm. How uproariously funny the Germans had found it, he knew, for he had been shown it twice at the office, and once by a waiter in the *Ratskeller*, and a copy had even been pinned in derision on the America House door. "Maybe you noticed the kind of perfumes we have on sale. All first-class brands. We've got Schiaparelli already on the counter, and Chanel ought to be in by July," Dardenella was saying, and Catherine Roberts smiled down on him as though he was her child. Milly and Christoph had walked off together to the stables, and Mrs. Roberts pushed up the sleeves of her linen riding-jacket in the heat so that her slender white forearms were bared.

"I see my horse tied up over there. Would you excuse Herr Jaeger and me if we went quickly?" she said. "I'm supposed to learn German before the next meeting of the German-American Club, and I haven't begun—"

"Oh, please go!" said Dardenella. He bowed a little, and stepped back, but his eyes were on her, asking one thing of her before she would leave him with no voice to woo him, no hand to succor him, standing there in the sunlight quite alone. "If I could take just one more minute of your valuable time, Mrs. Roberts, if I could ask you just one question," he said. "You've seen me riding here, you've seen me handling my own horse, Neapoli. Would you say I was outclassed by the horses? Would you say that, Mrs. Roberts?" he asked.

"Outclassed by the horses?" repeated Catherine Roberts in true wonder. "I'm not sure I know exactly what you mean. Or, rather, I wouldn't know at all what you mean if I hadn't been an army officer's wife for so many years, and if I hadn't been four months in Germany. You know, I'm so tired of class distinctions and army rank that I simply can't answer your question," she said quite gently. "I'd prefer you to ask me how many Lipizzan horses can stand on the head of a pin. In time, I might be able to answer that, for I'm changing from one week to the next. When I've read *The Portable Emerson* and *The Portable Greek Reader* and *The Portable Rabelais*, I'll certainly be able to answer anything. Outclassed by the horses? By those beasts with hearts as hard as their hoofs, just because you can't make them do their tricks the way Christoph can? If you can't do the 'Pas de Deux' and the 'Capriole'—is that what it's called?—I'm sure you can 'Zamba' with them!" And Dardenella held his grey straw fedora to his heart, and laughed, with the gold in his mouth glinting in the sun.

"Well, I could perhaps do that, but I'm not so sure!" he said, and he kept on laughing, but there was something else in the sound of it as he drew his breath in at the end.

47

"As for horses, any horses, you don't know what I think of them, Mr. Dardenella," Catherine Roberts said. "If only they'd turn on man, like lions, think how magnificent they'd be! They have no pride—they race for man, and break their necks taking his hurdles, and they step to his music like waltzing bears! They contribute to man's sense of power, and that is wrong. Dog-training schools, and places like that, where the poor beast responds to one firmly spoken word, what sovereignty it gives to man!"

The sound of this was still in their minds as they went across the courtyard toward the horses, and Jaeger could not say afterward how he had managed to mount Snafu. But now Catherine Roberts and he rode side by side out under the medieval arch with nothing between them as barrier except the honeysuckle-sweetened air. They were quite alone, riding the gleaming beasts out into the cobbled lane, their thighs holding the strong, fluid bodies of their mounts in absolute embrace, moving toward the woods that lay beyond.

"I hope we won't have bad luck like this every time we meet," Jaeger began saying. His left hand, in an old leather glove, lay on the hump of the English saddle, with the reins laced through the broken fingers of the glove. The reach of Snafu's walk was longer than the mare's, so that he held him in as he looked down at the side of Catherine Roberts' face. "If the time is to be cut so short, we won't make much progress in our German," he said. "I had started planning a sort of program out. If we can get the genders straight in the first lesson, that will be a lot. Then we can get on to the verbs. But if every lesson starts so late, that will hold us up. German needs a great deal of time, perhaps more time than any other language," he said, speaking rapidly, his voice low. "There are so many complications and

48

contradictions in it, and words that differ in meaning and origin although they are spelled exactly the same—and words that have no precise syntactical relation to the other words in a sentence."

"Oh, dear," said Catherine Roberts. She sat erect and beautiful on the little mare, looking straight ahead.

"It isn't to make the language seem difficult that I say these things," said Jaeger quickly. They had gone through the gate in the outer wall now, and when the horses took the forest trail, the dappled shade of the trees closed around them in tender secrecy. "I've tried to work it all out systematically so that you can learn the language in a certain number of lessons, over a given period of time. But if the length of the lessons is to be cut short, as it was today, then we won't get very far." As he looked down at her, the side of her face, the softly tied hair, the white throat, the slender, sloping shoulder in the linen of the riding-habit, she seemed to him to be a woman in her twenties. "If you think you could manage to be on time, Mrs. Roberts, then we could get on to the regular and the irregular verbs very quickly," he said.

Catherine Roberts leaned forward and straightened the coarse, dark locks of the little mare's mane, and then she turned her head and looked up at Jaeger with her mermaid's eyes.

"I don't really want to learn any grammar," she said. "I really don't. I would just like to be able to talk on two or three subjects, and understand the things that are being said. We could pick out the subjects before each meeting of the German-American Club, and then you and I could have rehearsals during half a dozen lessons before the meeting so that I would know."

"Yes," said Jaeger, helplessly, as the horses walked abreast.

"Of course, any way that you would like it to be. Only we'd have to get out of the present tense every now and then, and into the past or the subjunctive, and that takes a certain amount of study and time. So if we both made a point of never being late for the lessons, we'd get on a great deal faster, and you'd find you were learning more. Also, I felt very nervous about you. I didn't know what had happened to you," he said. He had forgotten his fear of Snafu, and the evil bony shoulders, and the bit that could seize upon its own will and power in the horse's iron mouth. "I had decided you were a person with certain characteristics, certain qualities, and then, today, I found myself thinking about you in another way, and I'm still not quite certain how you feel about the lessons, or if you really intend to take the lessons—"

Catherine Roberts sat quite erect on the mare, and yet without effort, her limbs and body soft and yielding in spite of the straightness of her back rising from the leather seat. The forest lay heavy and fern-like all around them, it was a dark cloak that they would shed in a moment, for the open fields were becoming visible, pale green and shimmering through the branches, like water lying just ahead.

"I shall try to be on time for the lessons," she said in humility.

"From now on, we should speak no English at all," said Jaeger.

"Oh, let us begin that in the next lesson," said Catherine Roberts quickly. "There are so many things I want to say to you first, before we really begin. Here is the whole chaotic drama on the stage, the whole of Germany, and the curtain has risen, and what am I to do?"

"Well, you must get out of the audience. You should somehow start taking part," said Jaeger, and the sound of these words that he could speak so easily to another seemed to echo in mockery through the trees. *Ohne mich, ohne mich, this country and these people, perhaps even life itself ohne mich,* came the echo of it after his own voice had died away.

Catherine Roberts leaned forward to touch the mare's dark mane with a quiet hand.

"I cannot do it without you," she said.

He did not know if it was the sudden tumult in his blood, or else the light from the open field ahead, which startled the horses now, but they sprang to life as if a lash had been brought down across their hides. Perhaps the little mare leaped first, or else it was the fire ignited in Snafu's eye that caused the mare to spin in panic, and now there was no stopping them. Jaeger felt the furious surge of the horse's will like a torrent passing between his thighs, and he saw the black bow in Catherine Roberts' hair undone and the ribbon streaming, pennant-like, as she went past. And then the passage of air and landscape ceased, and the big horse was no longer there. As Jaeger tried to get up from the ground, he could see the little mare's dusty hoofs, her delicate fetlocks, her burnished legs, and the reins looped through Catherine Roberts' arm. She was leaning above him, the silk of her brow, of her hair, of her partly opened mouth, as close to him as if she would embrace him, but she did not, except for the embrace of her fingers on his wrist.

"If it's concussion, then we must keep the blood moving," she said as he struggled ignominiously to rise. "If the blood keeps moving through the veins, then you can manage to outwit the mind. I learned that from a medical handbook during the war. You simply don't allow the mind to know."

"But my skull knows," said Jaeger, and he rubbed his head and tried to laugh.

"Your head isn't bleeding. Whatever happened, happened inside. I think you should walk, if you can. Would you like a cigarette?" she said.

He was up now, the cigarette trembling on his lip, and they began to walk together, moving over the dry earth of summer, over the stones and the thick-stalked weeds and the grasses, with the little mare following on the rein behind. The forest, dappled with light, was close around them, and he lost the thread of memory in it for a moment, and found it again, but he could not find the words of apology to say. The circumstance that seemed the strangest to him was that Catherine Roberts walked, for now only Germans walked on the soil of Germany; all others rode. And in his bewilderment, he thought of the irony that the people of a country who had sent the millions of one race wandering across the continent should now become wanderers themselves.

"You see, if you had stayed with Americans, you would not be walking. You would be riding comfortably," said Jaeger. It was like the prologue to some kind of symbolic play; the fern-like woods in which they wandered perhaps known as the Forest of Consciousness, and they setting out on a mystical journey that had as destination something more significant, more permanent, than mere earthly love. It was all heavy and German, weighted with indefinable meaning, murky, Wagnerian almost, so far from the smell of honeysuckle and little lambs eating ivy that Jaeger laughed suddenly at the awful burden it laid upon their hearts.

"Don't laugh. It isn't necessary, Herr Jaeger," Catherine Roberts said quietly. "When you strike your head hard, as your head struck, then you must try to keep the picture of your life quite clear. You must not forget your name, or what kind of work you do, or where you live, because that is what concussion tries to take away."

"But there's nothing wrong with me! I've simply lost my horse," said Jaeger, and his blood was hot with shame as they walked together back toward the *Schloss,* and the little mare followed, her bit ringing musically on the summer air.

III

Seth Honerkamp's office in the America House had monk's-cloth draperies hung clean and new at the windows, and a square of glossy, grey carpeting laid at an angle on the parquet floor. The walls of this pale-complexioned house had not a crack in them, and it was strange to see German walls bearing no scar of the shattering and the annihilation that had taken place. For everything that was fresh and bright and new in Germany now was American—even the language—and all that was broken and grotesque and too heavy to cart off to the junkpile belonged to Germany. The four walls of the office were the color of mist, and on their opacity bloomed etchings of the old world that had managed to remain intact outside: one of the centuries-old market place of Fahrbach, and another of its tilted, cobbled main street, and a third of the heavy, medieval portal that guarded the entrance from the valley into the slate-roofed town. They must have been made years before, these etchings, thought Jaeger, for the sign that had stood for more than a decade at the portal saying: *"Juden unerwüncht"* was missing; or else the artist had thought of the cold eye of posterity and made the picture as though the words had never been posted there. Honerkamp himself sat in the swivel chair at the official desk, his papers in extravagant disarray before him, and above his head hung further illustrations out of the past of Germany: a reproduction of the brooding Fahrbach *Schloss*, and a portrait of Martin Luther, neither castle nor man relinquishing an instant of their rigor to the college boy who sat below with his young hand scratching at his hair.

"Well, hi, Herr Jaeger!" Honerkamp cried out, and he jumped to his feet with a rush of energy that made the blonde secretary who had shown Jaeger in smile in ceaseless wonder at the race of them. "Gosh, I'm glad to see you!" he cried out in pleasure, and Martin Luther on the wall seemed ready to snap out a word or two of warning to the young.

"My newspaper wanted a piece about books for the Sunday edition," said Jaeger quietly, and why the sound of apology had come into his voice he did not know.

"Sit down, sit down!" cried Honerkamp. He pulled forward a stiff-armed, oak chair for Jaeger, and then flung himself down on his own swinging, jerking, swiveled, executive's throne. He stretched out his heavy legs, and threw one ankle over the other, and the crumpled khaki socks he wore twisted and writhed on his unquiet flesh. "Books, if you like; all right, books, but other things, too, a lot of other things," he said, the words coming quickly as he swung the chair from one side to the other in brief quarter-circles, his brown, nervous eyes taking the measure of this, and then that, of history itself, perhaps, and then hastening on. Jaeger watched the secretary, German, white-skinned, and too broad in the beam, pick up a pile of signed letters from the desk and go. And then, upright behind the door she closed, he saw the skeleton. "That's my scaffolding for the ideal German man," Honerkamp said, his eyes on it, too. "The plaque at his feet doesn't say 'Homo sapiens.' It's Sophocles' words: 'Shall the individual bow before the power of the state?' They found him in the cellar when we cleaned the place out, and I had the medics string him together and set him up for me here. I've got a theory about him that I'd like to thrash out with you." He sat up abruptly, and drew his legs in, the mask of worry on his schoolboy face again. "He was found in a sort of hideout, under the rubble of the one wing that was hit, so either he was in the cellar when the bombs came down, or else he descended with the upper story when it fell. I have two objections to the second possibility: during the war, a young man would not have been sitting in a house anywhere in Germany. Not unless he was wounded, or ill, or home on leave. Otherwise, he would have been off being blown to pieces at the front somewhere. And the medics tell me he must have been young, probably in his late twenties, because only one of his wisdom teeth was through the jaw. The second objection is that none of his bones was broken, and his skull wasn't split, so it isn't likely that he fell."

"Perhaps the cellar was used as an air-raid shelter," Jaeger said, and he watched the sunlight touching the plaster-white bones.

"Then there would have been others disinterred with him," said Honerkamp, speaking fast. "And there's something else: he seems to have had a supply of food with him. There were labels from packages of sugar and cocoa, and there were empty tins all around. For me, he was a man in hiding there—a man alone, a Jew, or a resistance fighter."

"Maybe simply a poet," Jaeger said, his voice muted and shy.

"I haven't got the flesh on him yet, or the brains fitted back into his skull. I thought you'd be able to help me out. You know them well," Honerkamp said, and the skeleton grinned at them from the far corner of the room, its secret contained in its unsigned bones. "Working with old Schumacher on the *Presse*, I know you've got to be good politically, Jaeger, with a past as pure as the driven snow. I've been thinking about you since we met at Colonel Roberts' house," Honerkamp said, and then he ceased speaking abruptly, perhaps because these words had brought the two women to life in the room. "I was going to get you aside at the horse show tomorrow night, but if you can resurrect the ideal German for me on short notice, well, do it now."

"Perhaps he had gone through the Russian campaign," said Jaeger, his voice still low, "and he had had enough. Perhaps he had heard Borchert's old man in the streetcar saying that there were too many dead in the air, so many dead that their voices kept the whole of Germany from sleeping at night."

"No, my man didn't make a sad and grieving decision," said Honerkamp. "He did it with spirit, because his will was free."

"Perhaps he knew what the smoke rising from ovens outside the town meant," Jaeger said. "Perhaps he knew that at a time when others didn't want to know. It took me a long time to find out. I was in Africa, engaged in a very gentlemanly war, a sort of sporting event, with established rules and penalties, where people sometimes even got hurt. I wasn't anywhere near the charnel house of the Russian front, or the extermination centers. In America, I developed the mentality peculiar to collaborators, so how can I say who or what the ideal German is? Schiller, Goethe, Rilke, Nietzsche, Brecht? For years now, I've tried to be as unlike as possible the popular conception of a German, maybe through weakness, or lack of national pride, or moral timidity. I was a receptionist in the American Press Club in Niederstadt when I first came back, and I thought I held a position of more importance than, say, the Minister President of Hesse, because I was young, and because I was on speaking terms with American newspaperwomen and men, while the Minister President was German and old, and therefore of the nationality and the generation that had cheated and misused that skeleton and me."

"My God, you speak our language well!" Honerkamp

cried out, and he took the cover from a faïence box among the papers on his desk, and pushed it eagerly toward Jaeger. "Have a cigarette. And I don't mean merely English, Jaeger. I mean the language of our hopes and fears."

"Maybe Heine covered it all a hundred years ago," said Jaeger. "A lonely man dying on his mattress in a Paris garret, saying that the Germans had started too late in trying to improve their nationality." The lighted cigarette was in his hand, and he smiled shyly, in quiet pleasure, feeling a kind of balm laid on his heart;—*one man*, he thought, *who does not wish to wound another, who honors the other's identity. I have had enough of my uncertainties being kicked in the teeth with every breath I take on German soil.* "Heine said by the time the Germans had perfected it, nationalism would have ceased to be, and they would have to discard it without getting the satisfaction or profit out of it that the French and British always have."

"Then tell me what you are now, you and what's left of our brother, the skeleton," said Honerkamp, leaning across the desk so eagerly, in such concern.

"Deserters from the national cause. A long time ago, when I first came back—almost two years ago—I was held up in Niederstadt one night by four young American paratroopers," Jaeger said, muting his voice and his presence so that they would not impinge upon this circumstance that he described. "They were drunk, and they robbed me, but I didn't mind. I felt superior to them, not as a German but as a member of a group of no specific nationality that might be dismissed as merely kind and decent men. That's where I want to think we both belong, the skeleton and me, but it doesn't give me a country or give him a resting-place. Perhaps it means that the history of this territory where we were born is going on without taking account of either him or me."

"I don't think that's it," said Honerkamp. He jumped up and shook himself, and ran his fingers through his hair. "Let's take a walk together through my democratic commonwealth, the republic of decent men I've set up in this house, and maybe you'll find some fellow human beings—"

So off they went through the halls and the libraries, up the flights of the curved center stairway, with its polished treads and its white-spoked banisters, across landings that were cleared for action like the stripped decks of a ship, past the marble plaque hanging in the main artery on which was engraved the date, January 1948, and the words: "The America House is a gift from the American people to the people of Germany." And the voyage that this handsomely renovated vessel was undertaking, Jaeger knew, was the hazardous passage from total censorship to the uproar of free speech. "America House" was lettered on every volume that served as life-preserver to the newly saved, and lettered as well on the freshly painted benches that were the lifeboats ready to bear all survivors, no matter how difficult the crossing, from bleak and terrible silence to the clamor of another shore. It seemed to Jaeger then that Honerkamp had had the picturesque etchings hung on his office walls and the skeleton placed in the corner of the same room to keep before him the duality of this country which fate had given him to save. And here was the science room, said Honerkamp, lowering his voice because of the students reading there, and here was the domed hall of philosophy. The men and women who sat at the tables with bowed heads seemed dwarfed by the cargo of books that had closed in on them, and they did not look up, but went on reading, reading, and making their notes as desperately as if it was they who charted the great ship's course.

"It was a banker's home before the Occupation," Honerkamp said, his voice and his exuberance quieted. "You can see it in the high ceilings and what's left of the fancy chandeliers. It was requisitioned by our army, of course, like all good things, and it was still pretty bomb-shot when I got here seven months ago, but it functioned as the Officers' Club. Two rooms up the street were considered good enough for me as the head of the Information Center, and the books for the edification of the German people were left in packing-boxes, or piled on the stairs of the place they gave me, while the brass had a pool-and-poker sanctuary here. So I began fighting the American army," Honerkamp said, running his hand through the curls on his head, and talking faster, faster; "I fought the army from the top brass down to Colonel Roberts," he said, and, as he led Jaeger across the hall, the sound of the Colonel's name hung on the air between them. It gave life to Millicent Roberts again, for the Colonel's blood moved in her veins, and it summoned Catherine Roberts out of the accessible regions of her open heart and hands. "And in the end, I won. I won," said Honerkamp, the mask of his face gone small and grim in its frame of flesh. "I turned the officers' bar and what I call 'The Reader's Digest Basilica' into an exhibition hall, and in time I'll get good pictures to show. I'm planning on American painters, and any German painters who aren't lying in their graves, with their canvases not so much blown to hell as simply never painted; and French ones, too, and we've got poetry readings under way: Whitman, and Poe, and Cummings, and Hart Crane. I'll even do Rimbaud and Baudelaire, if they let me live, and certainly Yeats and Joyce and Colum," he added nervously. "You know, the Germans could do with a drop or two of Irish blood, but not too much. I'm on the side of the Germans, Jaeger, I want to make that clear. Even if the books disappear from the library shelves at a rate that makes the blood run cold, even if chapters are ripped out and carried home when the entire volume couldn't be buttoned underneath the overcoat, still I like the grim determined German better than any other European. I like his industry. And he can be the greatest genius that comes when he's Jew and German simultaneously." It was the door of the poetry room they had halted before, and a line from Heine was written in German script, and in English below it, across the newly painted dove-grey wood. "Freedom is a new religion, the religion of our age," the legend went; and Jaeger thought of Büchner's words: "Freedom has become a whore," believing only in humor that the Americans had sent her stalking on high heels across the devastation left by war. And off went Honerkamp in still another direction, saying that they had had to put employees (guards, if you preferred) at the desks placed at the entrance and the exit of the atomic-research room to keep watch over these volumes which the Germans seemed to covet even more than poetry. "I have had to ask their own countrymen to police them, and to look through their brief-cases when they leave," Honerkamp said; and this was true as well of the periodicals-and-statistics alcove, where photographs of lynchings in the South could be examined, the look on the faces of the lynchers, and the impact of the boot kicking in a fallen Negro's teeth, familiar to anyone who had survived Belsen or Auschwitz or any of the other centers of death, he said. "Here, in those files, is the evidence that we are free men," he was saying in a low voice, halted before them, "that we are aware of what is taking place, that we write of it, talk out loud about it, fight to alter it, and do not hold our heads quite so high because we know it has happened and is happening still. Now, the music," he said, moving on again. "That's where I've really got ahead." The music room was empty, and Honerkamp closed the door behind them and leaned against it for an instant, his hands clasped at his back, his head lifted as if he faced a shaft of clear, untarnished light. "I keep this place open three evenings a week so that Germans who work all day can come in and sit down, and hold their heads in their hands the way men do, or have a right to do, in the top galleries of every opera house in the world—at least, in the countries where the opera houses are standing still. Here they can cry their tears, if that's what they want to do, and if they're crying for the Fatherland, that's their concern, not mine," he said. "But, gosh, when I know they're saying to themselves: 'The Amis are giving us this, along with their bombings, and their *Fragebogens*, and their black-marketeering, they're giving us this,' I swear it does something to me, Jaeger. It makes me feel I've worked my passage back at least part of the way." He stood leaning against the closed door of the music room, taking his soul apart for Jaeger as if all that mattered was that Jaeger should know. "I was a pilot, a bomber pilot, during the war," he said, "and maybe it offered some kind of redemption to me, the idea of this crazy, high-minded thing I was going to do. Once I'd blasted the hell out of them, I swore I was going to see they got their music back again, every damned note of it, and a lot of other music they didn't know. Literature, sure, and art, and political reorientation, yes, all right, but first I was going to hand their music back. Look," he said, straightening up and walking toward Jaeger, ready, it might be, to fling one arm across his shoulders, and make a tour of the record cases with Jaeger as eagerly as if he was one of his own countrymen. But, instead, he gestured with one wide-open hand to the busts of Wagner and Beethoven that stood in a shaft of sunlight above their heads. "We're set down here in the Occupation with these gentlemen and others, and the slate's wiped clean, for the Occupier, too, and we're given another chance," he said. "We're so exempted from the past that we can do everything as if we'd never done it before, thinking, acting, talking, arguing. We're all of us allowed to start over again, even to making love as if we'd never made love before." He had halted beneath the two heads now, and Wagner and Beethoven looked down without sympathy for any living man from the smooth protuberances of their empty eyes. "When you're allowed to be born again, you're going to speak out, and you're going to listen for clear answers in return, and you aren't going to shackle the free-wheeling will," Honerkamp said, and he looked up at the two German heads. "I used to roar *Tannhäuser* aloud while I was at the controls and the bombs were going away," he said, "and then, flying home, it was lighter stuff, maybe *Così fan tutte*, and all the time I kept making the promises about giving the Germans their music back as soon as it was through. I'm going to get busts of every composer who drew breath deep enough to carry him from one century to the next, and on to the centuries after that, and I'm going to put them up there with the two I have. I want to meet Carl Orff and have a contemporary sculptor do him. I'm advertising for Brahms and Mendelssohn, and I'll get Gershwin and Menotti if I have to model them out of clay myself, and there're maybe half a dozen others. But I'm shaky on the French. I don't trust Halévy or Bizet or Saint-Saëns in first-rate company." He stood there in his unpressed, brown suit under the two chipped plaster busts, beside the racks of record albums, running his fingers through his hair. "It may be that I'm afraid of the French," he said. "I'm puritan, un-Latin. Whenever I see a French girl walking along the street, I'm a violated man."

He moved forward quickly and took an album from the neat, alphabetically labeled cases, and placed a record from it on the record-player, and he watched it begin to turn. Immediately, the dark voice filled the sealed, record-lined room, humming lazily across the green-upholstered armchairs, passing in low, vibrant thunder from wall to wall, and Jaeger stopped breathing for an instant, scarcely believing the words he heard. "Lindy, did you hear that mockingbird last night?" asked the rich, lazy voice, and Jaeger was smiling as it twined like honeysuckle, hot and sweet, around the busts of the two dead, indifferent musicians on the shelf.

"Why did you choose that one? Of all the records here, why that one?" Jaeger said, the sound of the Negro singer's voice far louder than his own.

"Because I want everybody who walks in here to know that the suspect can be as great artists as any other men," said Honerkamp. "I'm proud of Robeson. I'm proud that we've got a singer like that in America." He began to walk in the room, turning back and forth in his baggy suit, on his crepe-soled shoes. "And there's another reason, too. All my life I've been molded and educated for sentiment. I've been groomed for it by the movies, the magazines, the radio. You must have been subjected to it, too, when you were there. It's air to the nostrils, honey to the tongue. Life in America is one big campaign for love," he said, while the voice sang powerfully and tenderly: "Oh, Lawd, I'd lay right down and die!" "And I've always fallen for it. But this time it seems even better than the other times, because I'm starting over, right back at the beginning again." He ceased walking, then, and his eyes held on to Jaeger's face in concern. For a moment he hesitated, sensing, perhaps, that national boundaries were drawn somewhere between winner and loser, between the Occupier and the Occupied, but the unbaring of his heart had gone too far now for him to recognize that shadowy frontier. The voice sang: "Did you hear that mockingbird last night?"; and Honerkamp could not stop. "I'm in love with a girl I've seen once in my life," he said, speaking quickly, nervously. "I don't know what chance I have with her, or what chance any civilian has with any army officer's daughter."

Jaeger might have said then: "We'll see them tomorrow night at the horse show" or "I'm giving a German lesson tomorrow night to Mrs. Roberts," adding that this time the lesson would be a serious effort, unlike the first one, when not a word of German had been said. He and Catherine Roberts had arranged to meet by the entrance to the court-yard of the *Schloss*, under the medieval arch, and from there they would walk down through the rose gardens to the rid-ing-rink, talking German all the way. "Tomorrow night," he might have offered in comfort to Honerkamp, "I, having been subjected to the same campaign, am living for to-morrow night." But before he could speak, the music-room door opened, the record came to an end, and the broad-beamed, blonde secretary said that Colonel Roberts had been trying to reach Herr Jaeger on the telephone. The Colonel's office had trailed him from the newspaper to the America House, and, once upstairs, Jaeger stood by Honer-kamp's desk, and the twang of the Colonel's voice came through the black arm of the telephone that he cradled to his ear.

"Saturday night, that's tomorrow night," said the Colonel, "we'll be taking a run up to Ober-Pastau to do some hunt-ing, Lieutenant Stephany and me. You're to come along with us, Jaeger. There's some cock-and-bull story going around about deer-jackers slaughtering the game, and we need your German to help track it down. We'll pick you up at the newspaper at five," he said. Then it ended abruptly, the twang of the voice wiped out, without a good-by, as the Colonel put the receiver back in place.

Jaeger stood silent and motionless a moment, looking into the black cup of the mouthpiece, and then the soft staccato of the secretary's typewriter aroused him, and slowly, with great care, he put the beetle-shelled instrument down. So Saturday night had been returned to the impetus of men, he thought, and he felt the world of tender, soft-lipped women die.

It died so utterly that by the next day, as he and the Colonel and Lieutenant Stephany drove through the Hessian hills, he could scarcely recall the scent and the delicacy of Mrs. Roberts and her daughter, or the way their limbs moved in their blowing skirts, or the look of purity, like that in the eyes of poets, that was in their eyes. The Colonel was at the wheel of the long, emerald-colored station wagon, and on either side of the road was farming-country, and strong, tan cows grazed knee-deep in clover, and streams passed without haste under timber bridges, and wound in and out of orchards, their waters at times nearly halted by thick beds of forget-me-nots and flags in bloom. Now and again, they passed an agglomeration of houses, the pure white walls ribbed with cross-bars and beams, and the peasant windows closed against the sight of June. The panes were small, so that for centuries no one had been able to look into the peasants' lives, and geraniums flowered in mock cheer and phony welcome on the cold stone sills. For brief moments, the bold fronts of these houses would break the flowing of the countryside, and then it would pour on again, liquid and lovely: fields shimmering with white flower heads, and dark, still areas of woodland, with the canopies of umbrella pines keeping the light of afternoon from penetrating to the needle-strewn, black, moldering forest floor.

"Jaeger, your work's cut out for you," said the Colonel. It was clear he was pleased with the look of the afternoon and the night before them, and no flush of drink or choler showed on the back of his neck or the side of his firm, bluish jowl. "We've been using the shoemaker of the village as interpreter, but he didn't have any English verbs. He'd hand you a batch of nouns and adjectives, and you'd have to fill in what he left out," he said, his voice genial, amused. He seemed a younger man than when the women were present, for the standards were his own now, and the humor whatever he wanted it to be. Now that he was off alone with men whom he outranked in experience, as well as in rigidity of will, he drew his breath with greater ease. "I'm not sure there's anything going on at all," he said, and Jaeger looked back from the countryside to the Colonel's big shoulders stooped above the wheel, seeing the heavy ears fitted close against the hard, square, greying skull. "It could be some sort of Occupation hysteria, like the stories of our men waylaying German women. But you'll be able to get the straight stuff out of Knau."

The two Americans were roughly dressed for the woods, but Jaeger wore the suit of ersatz wool and the secondhand shoes, having no other things to wear. (*When we left America*, he thought as he sat, detached, in silence, watching the fleeing countryside, *we were allowed to keep one khaki uniform, each piece of which was to be clearly, prominently, and indelibly marked POW. POW the shirt, and the sweater, and the blouse, the pants, POW in white oil paint, faked by some by means of toothpaste, so that they could wash it off when they got back to Germany, but the supervising colonel always knew. Perhaps men are given rank because of that ability to discover the worst in other men. It didn't come into my calculations to try to fake it as long as POW was stenciled indelibly enough on my own past and on my present, and conditioned my future by making me two men. Back in Germany, we could sell them, the cloth being better than anything the country had, and with the money from mine I could buy this outfit schwarz, believing that once I had it on, and German underwear grating my skin, I'd be a German again.*) Lieutenant Stephany had turned from his place beside the Colonel to offer Jaeger a cigarette, and even his slender hand, with the black hair in silk threads drawn through the pores on the saddle of it, seemed questioning and tentative, even the fingers holding the lighter to Jaeger's cigarette preparing the way for what he wished to ask.

Jaeger averted his eyes from Lieutenant Stephany's face and drew the first smoke slowly in. And he thought: *With every drop of his blood, he's afraid of something. Perhaps because he hasn't the male assurance to give women what they want before they'll die beneath his hands. He's not quite the gentleman, and he hasn't a Don Juan's virility in spite of the romantic eyes and hair. He's afraid, mortally afraid.* The lieutenant cleared his throat, and Jaeger watched the fine beads of rash on the white skin draw tight across his Adam's apple and slide up and down as he snapped the lighter closed.

"What outfit were you with during the war, Herr Jaeger?" he asked, his arm crooked on the back of the seat, his fingers turning the lighter around and around.

"The *Afrika Korps*," Jaeger said, not liking this warrior-to-warrior talk that sought to establish them as comrades-in-arms beyond the verdict of capitulation and victory. Although he spoke softly, he could hear his own accent as it must sound in the two Americans' ears.

"Ah, the Desert Fox!" said the Colonel genially. At once, the freshness of the country around them seemed to perish, and the heat of the desert of his memory parched Jaeger's mouth.

"There was some pretty close fighting down there," said Stephany. "I suppose you had your share of it."

"I was wounded before the English took me prisoner," said Jaeger, and he would not give them the satisfaction of any more.

68

"Well, let's have a drink on that," said the Colonel, and Stephany turned back in his seat and took a flask from the glove compartment of the car. When he had unscrewed the three little metal goblets from the cap, the three men drank in silence, the cause, or the nation, or the event, they drank to, not specified.

As they rode into the village street, white geese, with plumage as shadowless as clouds, stood in the straw and cattle urine of the gutter, their tongues hissing venom, their scaled feet the color of pumpkin rind. Before the peasant houses lay cobbled courts, each holding identical plow, and oxen cart, and brimming drinking-trough, but the filth or cleanliness of the courtyard, or of the cart and plow, bore witness to the varying natures of the men who lived within. The coarse, clean lace of the curtains at the windows moved as the peasants, ambushed behind red and coral geraniums, watched the American car go past.

"You probably know the regulations," the Colonel was saying as he drove, and now the delicate odor of whisky hung between them on the air. "Each member of a hunting party is allowed a roebuck, if he can get him, and a dozen pheasant, and six hare." A three-legged Maltese cat began to cross before the car, and changed its mind, and turned and fled, its belly brushing the cobbles in its flight, its gold eyes wide. "You pick up the forester of the area, and give him a gun, and three rounds of ammunition. He's the one class of German national authorized to carry a gun, and then only in the company of Americans," the Colonel said. There was a sudden commotion on the cobbles before them as three orange hens flew, squawking, high into the air.

It was a beautiful time of day as they set out for the forest, with the air washed blue by the approach of evening, and the lumber road, as red as Colorado clay, winding out from the village through fields of lucerne and rye. They had picked up the forester, Knau, at the door of his house, with its reeking dungpile like a monument to the fecund power of the beast set at the courtyard gate, and now that Knau rode in the emerald jewelbox of the car with them, the smell of pig, and ox, and fowl mingled with their whisky breath. Knau was a man still under fifty, stocky and dark, and between the black felt rim of his hat and the rusty black of the jacket he wore, the pores of his neck were studded with nailheads of dirt. He sat beside Jaeger, shouting his words out to the Colonel and Stephany as if addressing the deaf and mute.

"What's he saying now?" asked the Colonel as they rocked slowly out the lumber road, the fields on either side so brilliantly lit with rye that the eyes were startled by the sight.

"He says the jeep doesn't come every night, but only two or three times in the week," said Jaeger. "They have sacking tied over the license plates, and they drive fast. They ran down two geese in the village last week, and didn't stop. He says it's pretty sure to come on Saturdays, and always after dark."

"So it might come tonight," the Colonel said.

"They have a searchlight fixed on the front!" Knau shouted out in German; "and when they get out there, they turn the light into the trees! It blinds every animal hiding in the brush, and once they're blinded, then they mow them down! Ack-ack-ack!" he said, and he made the spraying motion of the illicit guns they carried, looking from Jaeger to Stephany for understanding, and then at the nape of the Colonel's neck, and back to Jaeger's face again, his black eyes blinking fast. "They'll hit doe, or roebuck, or fawn, or even woman and child!" Knau shouted out, and he spoke of the game that stumbled off, wounded, and died alone in the woods, or else refused to die. He had found them, the dead, by the stink on the air after a week, and found the living by the panic of their attempts to rise and flee, dragging their shattered limbs behind them or stumbling forward on their knees, still proud, still asking nothing of man; he gave them the picture of it, and Jaeger could see their breasts stained dark by the slow tide of their ebbing power. "I'm a forester, but I haven't the final bullet to put through their hearts! I haven't a gun to finish them off!" Knau said.

"What's on his mind now?" Colonel Roberts asked, driving ever more slowly as the way through the fields became more rough.

"He seems to be complaining about not having a gun, sir," Stephany said to the Colonel, one arm hooked casually over the back of the seat.

"This whining around for the return of hunting privileges, I tell you they're making a national issue out of it!" the Colonel said. "The deer are eating their crops, and the boar are stampeding in their wheat, so we're to put guns in their hands so they can clear the country of them! I swear I wouldn't risk walking through the woods after dark alone with any one of them if he was behind me carrying a gun!"

And then Knau began telling the story of the blood that flowed in the stream one early morning when he had gone out looking for boar tracks in the marsh. He was crossing the footbridge over the stream, just this side of the forest, when he saw blood staining the water as it ran between the stones. Knau spoke in their own tongue to Jaeger, pronouncing the German words straight into his face, and yet Jaeger knew that Knau had not accepted him as countryman, and could perhaps never accept him because the Americans had brought him here. (*Not even this suit can make a German of me,* he thought, ersatz and German though it was; remembering that in the bottom of his duffle bag, he, like the others, had brought his uncleaned, worn *Afrika Korps* uniform back from America, the sands of North Africa in the seams of it still; and he asked the close air of the car if only by putting on that soiled, faded tunic again would he be recognized as German by the Germans; and the thought of it chilled him as if the blue-dark of the evening was already closing in.)

"What's he saying now?" asked the Colonel in impatience.

"He's telling about finding blood in the stream one morning," said Jaeger.

The forester went on saying that he had followed the current back upstream, walking along the bank beside it, and five or six yards inside the forest he had found the doe's head, hacked from the body and lying under the water, with its eyes wide open, like living eyes. And then the hopelessness of making any one of them understand seemed to come over Knau, and he cried out: "*Verstehen Sie? Verstehen Sie?*"

"Yes," said Jaeger. "Go on. I understand."

"This time they'd killed a doe at the mating time, and so they cut her head off! That's how they get around the law! Knau cried. "They must have slit her wide open before they roped her onto the jeep, if they were stopped by the M.P.s there'd be nothing to show that it wasn't a buck! The whole belly was there in the water, too, and the foxes were watching in the grass, waiting for me to go."

"He seems to have a lot on his mind," said Colonel Roberts wearily. He had brought the car to a halt at the edge of the forest, and here they would leave it, and go on on foot. "Anything based on fact?"

"He says the hunters who come in the jeep will kill anything, in season and out, for the money that's in it," said

Jaeger, and he told the story of the doe. "He says city butchers will pay any price for black-market meat."

"He's pretty certain they're civilians, sir," Lieutenant Stephany added. "He says it's clear in the way they mishandle their guns."

"No," said Jaeger. "He didn't say that. Perhaps the Hessian accent put you off—"

"Let's have one drink around before we start," interrupted the Colonel, stepping down on the short, green grass. "Every damned *Kraut* you run into wants to reorganize the world. That's the trouble with them," he said, and, having spoken in haste, he could not bring himself to look at Jaeger. He could not say: "You speak English like the rest of us, so that lets you out." He lowered his head, and fumbled with the safety catch of his gun, and Stephany turned and took the flask from the glove compartment again. He handed the two little silver goblets to them, keeping the third one for himself, and poured them full. "Have another, Jaeger," the Colonel said when they had drunk, but still he did not look at him. Instead, he jerked his chin toward the forester. "What about Knau?" he said.

"Coming up, sir," said Lieutenant Stephany. He wiped the rim of the cup with the inside of his thumb, and handed it to the forester, and filled it to the brim; and within himself Jaeger grinned widely and painfully, his mind's eye fixed on the sight of two *Krauts* at the edge of the forest, drinking uneasily together like sentenced men.

Then they left the car by the side of the lumber road, and set off two by two, keeping downwind. Stephany and Knau were to cover the marshy area to the north, entering the dark, mysterious forestland from there, and the Colonel and Jaeger would go directly into the section lying to the south. Only Jaeger was without a gun. *Ohne mich*, he thought; *the hunting going on without me, like the horse*

show at the Schloss tonight, and the aborted German les-
sons, and the sound of Mrs. Roberts' voice; like the whole,
defeated, groveling country, ohne mich! The whisky moved
gently in his veins, muffling and muting protest, and he
looked at the forest lying, dark and sickle-shaped, before
them, and waited while the Colonel indicated with a movement of his arm the territory that he had chosen for his own.
He had seen two young roebucks lock horns in a clearing
there one moonlit night at the end of May, he said in a low
voice, and he wanted to get a shot at them. So he and Jaeger took that way, and Knau and Stephany the other, agree-
ing to meet in two hours at the station wagon parked by the
lumber road.

The Colonel went lightly and soundlessly, for all his
weight, knowing the shimmering, summery terrain well; and
Jaeger followed, aware of the heat now, and that the air was
laced with the smell of fox and honeycomb, and difficult to
breathe. He had not noticed the *Hochsitz* above their heads
until the Colonel stepped off the deer trail, and halted, and
shifted his gun, and began to climb. When the Colonel's
combat boots were lost in the green boughs, Jaeger set his
own feet in the wooden rungs that wound like a snake
around the trunk, and he, too, mounted to the man-made
lookout in the tree. There, the two of them sat on the rough
planks, their backs against the railing, carefully drawing their
legs out of each other's way. And from here, as if looking
through a porthole opened on a cool, wide, evening sea,
they could glimpse through the boughs a portion of the
open, airy marshland. But close below them lay the suffocation of the woods, steaming with gnats and thin young
wasps, and the underbrush dappled still with the last sun.
Once a great golden bee, droning with sound, zigzagged in
fury across their becalmed raft on the unrippling tide of
leaves, and instantly was gone. Everything waited and

harked now for the beasts of the deep woods to come; everything listened and watched, and the light falling through the trees quivered with the heat, and Jaeger's nerves were taut as wire. After a little, he felt the Colonel's eyes fixed on him, and he looked quickly up, and he saw that the other man's lips were shaping words, but emitting scarcely any sound.

"What if it was something else we were out after tonight, Jaeger?" the Colonel's lips were saying, and the blue eyes fixed Jaeger with a strangely icy light. "What if it wasn't the deer this time?" he said, and even the barely audible sound of his voice outraged the deep, unbreathing hush. The gun was on the planks beside him, and his hand was on it, and it seemed to Jaeger that in a moment he might slowly, dreamily, in retarded motion, lift the gun from under the terrible weight of heat, and place it against his shoulder, and take aim. His forefinger would hook around the trigger of it, and, like a sleepwalker groping for direction, he would seek to focus the long, dark barrel across the drowsy air. But the Colonel's eyes were not the eyes of a dreamer; they looked straight at Jaeger, furiously awake and blue. "Come, Jaeger," his lips were whispering, "let's establish what we are. You have your past and your people, and I have mine, but somewhere those two histories must run parallel, because we're men, and because we were once engaged in the same war." He said the words softly across the *Hochsitz*, and yet it seemed to Jaeger that he was ready to shout them out and break the tenseness of the listening, waiting woods like glass. "Save your hides!" he might roar at any moment to the roebucks and hare. "I'm out after something different tonight, something whose belly you can't slit without facing the verdict of twelve men!" But he went on whispering: "You were a soldier, too, Jaeger, and that gives us at least one set of rules in common, no matter what side we happened to be on. Perhaps if we talk enough we'll find that we have more. That's what I want to know. I think you'll agree with me that soldiers know what direction they're moving in, either backward or forward, either retreating or advancing, if you like it better that way. But they don't slide sideways off the line of march." His hand did not lift the gun yet, but turned, restive, on the burnished wood. "The good ones don't," he whispered, "and that's the kind I like to have around."

"Haven't we all had enough, after two wars?" said Jaeger softly across the stillness, his eyes fixed on the gun.

"I'm not talking about war," the Colonel whispered in impatience. "I'm talking about conduct. I'm talking about deportment. What was your father? How did he bring you up?" he said; and now Jaeger's father, who had been a soldier in both World Wars, was resurrected from the frozen soil of his death in Stalingrad five years before.

"I was brought up to take rank seriously," said Jaeger while the Colonel watched his face. "My father was an *Offiziersstellvertreter* in the First World War," he said, deliberately drawing the syllables out, but the Colonel had no time for humor now. Jaeger did not add that his father had not advanced because the military had suspected him of socialistic tendencies, and that it was probable his own men had killed him, shot him in the back, when he placed the honor of the army above human life and refused to surrender his platoon.

"Well?" said the Colonel with the blue fire burning in his eye. "Go on. Keep talking, but not loud."

"There's not much to say about him," Jaeger answered in hesitation. He wanted to take his handkerchief out, and mop the drops of sweat from his brow, but he was as uneasy as if he stood at attention before a court-martial tribunal, his muscles bound rigid by protocol, and he could not stir.

"So you had no respect for him because he was nothing but a sergeant. Is that it?" the Colonel whispered across the breathless air.

"I had no respect for him because he used to strike us, my brother and me," said Jaeger. "That's what mattered, not his low military rank. He beat us, and all our teachers beat us. Every German of his generation beat whoever was weaker than himself, I suppose—every German, that is, except the Jews."

"So the Jews seem better to you than other Germans, do they?" said the Colonel. His face had begun to flush now in the heat. "Where did you get ideas like that?" he said.

"I would say from my mother," said Jaeger in a low voice, not wanting to speak of this woman who had lain a long time quiet in his heart. The Colonel's hand was on the gun, and a strange light gleamed in his eye.

"Go on," he whispered. "Go on." His face was red, and his breath came, labored, through his nose. "I'm interested in finding out about you," he said. Lying between them on the boards, like one of those figures of queens who have died too young and who lie in replica in stone on the covers of their tombs, Jaeger saw the vision of that thin, small woman he had loved. "Go on," the Colonel said.

"My mother stood between my father and us, between us and the whole of Germany, taking the blows. But she couldn't go to war for us," he said.

"So that put you on the side of women, all women, I suppose?" said the Colonel, and there was a wiliness now in his hushed voice. "I suppose that made you feel women understood you better than men did?"

"On the side of women?" Jaeger repeated.

Everything was absolutely still as the Colonel raised the gun from the planks, and fitted it to his shoulder, and it seemed to Jaeger then that he was fighting for something more vital than comprehension as he faced the Colonel, that he might even be asking the Colonel for the gift of life.

"Yes, on the side of women. That's what I mean," the Colonel whispered, taking aim. "Some men have a kind of weakness in them that rots them down to the core." His eye was fixed to the metal sight on the long, smooth barrel of the gun, and he covered first Jaeger's face, then moved to his throat where the pulse beat swiftly, and then to the bull's-eye of the heart. "They can't take discipline, so they look around for sympathy, female sympathy," the Colonel said, the gun still moving slowly, unerringly, seeking its resting-place. "Tell me, have you a woman of your own, a mistress?" the Colonel asked in a voice so gentle that Jaeger sensed rather than heard the words.

"No," said Jaeger, and, facing the judge on the court-martial bench, he felt his mouth suddenly parched dry.

"And you'd like to have a woman, the right kind of woman, not just any cheap little *Fräulein*, wouldn't you?" the Colonel whispered. At the same instant that Jaeger felt the air go past his cheekbone and ear, the woods were shattered with the sound. "You can look now. I got him," the Colonel said, speaking out loud. "It went in just under his ribs, and got him in the heart." Jaeger turned as he sat, and looked down through the railing, his blood still trembling, his breath coming uncertainly. There it lay on the deer trail below, a small, dead beast in a golden coat, so glossy, so rich in color in the fading light that it seemed to be breathing still. Its neck was stretched long, russet and bright, and its head was laid wearily down, with a clover leaf pressed on its mouth. Jaeger turned away from the sight of it, and looked at the Colonel, who was feeling for a cigarette in the pocket of his shirt. But the Colonel's hands were shaking, and they would not do the things he wanted them to. "I've been watching him for five minutes or more. You didn't even know it, Jaeger," the Colonel said, and he gave a laugh, but his teeth were knocking in his jaws. "You need some training. You'll have to come out more often on maneuvers with us. You haven't got forest-trained eyes or ears yet, Jaeger," he said, trying to hold the lighter steady in his agitated hand.

How much time passed then before the other thing came to life could not be said; it was as long, or as short, as a dream, and the quality as undefinable, that interval in which the Colonel sat smoking in order to quiet the uproar of his blood. Jaeger waited with his head averted, his eyes on the little dead buck below or else scanning the distance through the porthole in the trees. And then, far in the open area of the marshland, he saw the grasses part in a wire-thin furrow, as if a silver thread were being drawn through the fabric of the fields, raveling quickly and steadily to the threshold of the woods. There it ceased, and Jaeger watched for the slithering snake of movement to come through the brush, but nothing moved in the forest, and no whisper was heard. For a long moment this interval, too, endured: the Colonel smoked, the roebuck lay dead, and then the living thing that had parted the tall marsh grasses emerged on the deer trail below: a fox, with golden-tufted ears and heavy tail carried just clear of the ground, moving silently, alert to a thousand warnings on the air. Its tiny feet were shod in smooth, black kid, and it stepped with caution; but the smell of the freshly killed was richer than the smell of living man in its nostrils, and it moved irresistibly toward the dead. It was perhaps the scent of tobacco that suddenly halted the fox's advance. It paused and raised its narrow-muzzled head, and its eyes, dark, calculating, incredibly bright, looked up at the *Hochsitz* and the two men sitting there. Its muzzle was sharp and suave and neatly finished, a hard, tapering bone in the triangle of its lifted, softly feathered face. For an instant it looked into Jaeger's eyes, and they faced each other's alien identities, fox and man, or criminal eying the self-appointed guardian of some moral code, and then the fox turned, the movement as swift and weightless as the closing of a fan, and was gone in the undergrowth again. But the smell remained, more fluid than the odor of skunk cabbage, but as inescapable on the air.

"There's the stink of a fox around," said the Colonel, turning his head abruptly. "They come out like maggots when you've drawn blood."

And Jaeger knew suddenly that he, too, was fox, and that they moved surreptitiously together, part of a network of sensibility and sound that the Colonel could not feel or hear. The Colonel was solid as a boar, it seemed to him now, and the coarse, grey bristles that sprang on the other man's neck were somewhat like the hide of a boar, and the neck was as thick and the eye as fixed in shallow belligerence.

"Would you like me to go down and get the roebuck back to the car?" Jaeger asked in a low voice, but the Colonel had clattered loudly to his feet on the *Hochsitz* boards.

He wanted to leave at once now; he could scarcely get down the ladder fast enough. He broke the silence into pieces ruthlessly, for he wanted to get home. It was as if he knew that elsewhere love or lust was stirring in passion in men's and women's hearts in the summer dark, and he not there to witness it and shout it down. "My wife and my daughter are up at the *Schloss*, talking with all kinds of men," he might have been saying. "They're up there talking to grooms, and riders, and PX managers, and God-knows-what!" Now, at this instant, he must return to Fahrbach, and find his women, and take them home. Although it was scarcely nine, and the light not gone, and the country merely washed with blue, still he must go. "I've had my reckoning with you, Jaeger," he might have been saying as they carried the dead buck between them back along the trail. "I've given you warning, and you know where matters stand." The Colonel held the buck by its forefeet, Jaeger by its hind, while its head, with the sprays of antlers on it, as beautiful as a young girl's head, dragged sorrowfully through the leaves. "But you aren't the only one, not by a long shot, Jaeger," the Colonel might have been saying as they laid the little beast on the floor of the station wagon, behind the seats. Stephany and Knau could get back to Ober-Pastau on foot, the Colonel said as he started the motor, and he made a sign for Jaeger to sit beside him now. "The Germans asking for a return of their guns and their hunting privileges! What do you think of it, Jaeger?" he asked, and he swung the station wagon swiftly around as the first deep wave of evening washed across the land. "Pour me a drink, will you? You know where the flask is," he said, and he drank twice from the metal cup, driving with one hand, and exhaled the strong, sweet smell of whisky in an "ah" of satisfaction on the air. "It's become a kind of symbol for them, that hunting-gun and the right to track things down. But all the time they're asking for something else. Do you get what I'm trying to say? They're asking to be given arms, an army, a shooting equality with us. But we're on to them, Jaeger," he said a little craftily. He switched the headlights on, and the light that sprang ahead channeled the red ruts of the lumber road and turned to April green the strip of grass that zigzagged down the center, and the car went fast. "In spite of Knau and the rest of the whining lot of them," the Colonel said, "the hunting-laws will stand."

They had come to the village, with its livestock now silenced and effaced by night, and the lamps in the houses masked for sleep, and the Colonel drove faster, faster, with his thoughts of the Germans, and all men, knotting and un-knotting in irritation in his head. The headlights illumi-nated the dungheaps and the oxen carts in the courtyards, painted the boxed geraniums brighter than reality, the houses whiter than bone; faster, faster, he drove up the cob-bled street toward the conflagration of the flesh that might be consuming his wife and daughter and the strangers with them now.

"I don't trust that upstart, Honerkamp," he said. "I don't like the look of any of them, the German baron up there at the *Schloss*, or the riding-master, Horn, or the crook who's buying the white horses so that he'll get himself some kind of pedigree. I can trust Stephany because he's under orders, my orders, military orders. He knows what to expect if his conduct isn't what I, or the U.S. army, will take. And now that I've put things straight between us, Jaeger, perhaps you'll abide by the standards, too. That's what's meant by manhood and vigor; just that. Not how many women you can satisfy a month, or how many times a night you do it, but the ability to say things out and make them stick. That's why some men are officers, and others lick their boots," he said, and his hand reached out and took the flask, and he drank the little that remained in it straight from the metal mouth.

"How will Lieutenant Stephany get back to Fahrbach to-night? That's thirty kilometers," Jaeger said.

"Back to Fahrbach?" repeated the Colonel, bringing his mind in irritation to the lieutenant when he wanted to think of getting his women home. "I'll send a car back from the motor pool to pick him up. Just let me say this about deci-sion: it's knowing your own mind that makes the difference between officers and enlisted men. Your officer sees the situation from the *Hochsitz*, or wherever, and he knows, for that day anyway, which heart he may have to put the bullet through."

And then, down the narrow street between the diagonally ribbed houses, they saw the other headlights coming toward them fast. The Colonel did not slacken pace, and in the moment when the two cars passed, their sides almost grazed, and they saw that the other was a jeep, and that there was sackcloth tied across the license plates.

"There it is," said Jaeger, scarcely aloud. "We can turn in the next courtyard and follow it."

"I'm not chasing any jeep tonight. Not tonight," said the Colonel through his teeth. He drove straight on through the village, past the drinking-troughs and the plowshares. *My women, God damn it, my women!* his heart may have been crying out. "Stephany and Knau can take care of the high-jackers tonight," he said. "That's what subordinates are for."

IV

Jaeger had been
sent by the newspaper to cover the second monthly get-to-
gether of Occupier and Occupied, and he walked up the
hill not knowing if either the Colonel or Mrs. Roberts
wanted to see him there. For a quarter of a mile, American
cars lined both sides of the roadway, while humbler German
vehicles, having deposited their cargo, crept down the hill
again to wait below in the unpeopled dusk. Six nights before, the Colonel and Jaeger had carried the roebuck in and
hung it high in the cellar, and then the Colonel had said
good-night, without the ritual of a drink, and had not held
out his hand at the door. And now Jaeger came through
the early evening wearing the same brown suit, the hunting-
suit, the riding-suit, the only suit, the suit that was like his
own skin to him, and that would become his own skin if
salaries didn't go up or the currency reform come fast. He
smoothed the double-breasted front of it, thinking he might
one day be buried in it, or, given a little warning of approaching death, that he might get the uniform out of the bottom
of the duffel bag, and, even with food stains on it still,
stretch out in his coffin in fine Teutonic dignity. Except
the boots were gone, so boots would have to be borrowed or
bartered for that final march. *Perhaps for a pack or two of
cigarettes*, he thought, *and then I'd sleep a long sleep with
the military, on equal footing at last with the brass of every
nationality*.

In the Colonel's house, there were aging Germans with
naked heads, wearing tails that had gone rusty a decade before, and there were smart young Americans with pomaded
hair, in white linen dinner-jackets or in midnight-blue tux-

edos with satin cummerbunds. There were grim, big-boned women with iron-grey braids pinned up in crowns upon their heads, and women who sought to be girls forever, with shining locks hanging to their shoulders, and cigarettes jerking as nervously as the laughter in their mouths. Here was the new, expensive cloth of American officers' uniforms, and, within hand's reach, the ancient wine-colored silk, the wisteria and mustard velveteen, of German evening-dresses, the cut and style forgotten since the interval of peace after an older war, the gloss of sitting wearing the broad seats thin. Here were the American bayonets of women's voices, and the deep funereal German thunder of men's, for this was the German-American Club of Fahrbach, composed of the fat and the lean, the young and the middle-aging and the nearly old, admitting both winners and losers, with the losers better larded than the others, as if this much at least had been granted them in the humiliation of defeat. On the terrace above the valley, the musicians played for those who had taken one another's hands to dance and for those who mourned their dead still, for those on eager alien high heels and those on the same worn soles that had paced back and forth, back and forth, month after month, as the news of wholesale annihilation had darkened the air. Jaeger heard the music weeping its tears for the dreamers who leaned on the balustrade above the valley, and for the others who stood by the buffet tables in the entrance hall, eating the hot *Wurst* laid on slabs of bread, and raising the cold clay steins of beer. *I'm hungry too*, he thought, and he looked at the sausage, and pickles, and cheese, set out; but Honerkamp, in black tie and dinner-jacket, spoke his name and drew him to one side of the hall.

"I started to put this vest on tonight, and what do I find but that it wouldn't button across me any more," Honerkamp said. The music of violin and zither and accordion came through the windows and entwined the men's and women's heads with tender leaves of memory, the love and the longing of its score erring in grief through the three big rooms that opened on the threshold of the night. "So I split the seam right up the back, and then pinned the two separate pieces to my shirt, which means I can't lift my arms very high," Honerkamp said, and he stood there laughing and running his fingers through his hair. "That's what *Kraut* and beer and an administrator's desk have done for me," he said.

Six nights before, the horse show had taken place, and the Lipizzaners had danced, and Jaeger had sat in the *Hochsitz* with Colonel Roberts instead of being there. Since then, no word of the German lessons had been sent to him; no voice had called; and now his eyes sought through the people for the color of one woman's hair and the white square of her brow.

"I must find Mrs. Roberts and say good-evening," he said in a low voice to Honerkamp, but he did not know if he should speak to her in apology or blame.

"Good old protocol," said Honerkamp, and his eyes were seeking too, with no time for the faces that he saw. "I danced one dance with Millicent, and now she's disappeared," he said. Through the long open windows, the troubling music touched their hearts and drew them gently to where it played. Here, at both ends of the terrace, hung paper lanterns, pleated and tinted to the likeness of great, soft-breasted pigeons with glowing eyes; but the length of the front wall was unencumbered, and the deep valley below lay filled with dusk. On the opposite hill, the town mounted, roof by roof, street by cobbled street, through the early evening to the castle that stood against the fading golden summit of the sky. "So they dragged you all over the countryside last Saturday night," Honerkamp was saying as they walked.

"I've been thrashing it out with Stephany ever since. You were taken out to find out from the peasants not who the men are, but who the men aren't who ride that jeep. The Colonel isn't going to have them army men."

"But we saw the jeep. It was a military jeep," said Jaeger. Here the air smelled sweetly of the vines and flowers and grasses that flourished in the gardens just below, smelled of honeysuckle even. "It passed us on the road."

"Justice," said Honerkamp with bitterness, walking lightly, hastily, with the mask of worry shifting on his face, "is, to the military among us, for the eggheads or the birds."

The *Hausmeister* moved among the guests in his starched jacket, bearing a tray of squat, wide-mouthed glasses, half filled with liquid redder than a fox's brush, the cherries, the ice, the liquid, in the glasses swinging with his unsteady gait. When he rocked near on his warped legs, Honerkamp reached out and absently picked up a glass, and with thumb and forefinger fished the cherry out.

"Hi, Matterhorn," he said as he chewed, but his eyes were seeking something else.

"Hi, Mr. Hönig," the *Hausmeister* said. An infinitesimal gleam of hope appeared in the opaque almond of each eye. "You good man, Mr. Hönig," he said.

"Oh, Matterhorn, you're my friend!" said Honerkamp, and then he took the little man's arm. "Look," he said, lowering his voice. "Where's Miss Roberts got to? Where did Miss Roberts go?"

So back they went now through the musical and fragrant night, following Matterhorn past the fat and the thin, the shabby, the smart, past the victors and the vanquished, entering the brilliance of the house again, moving into the hallway where the Germans in rusty tails raised their stone steins and devoured the rolls of pig. Nearby, the German wives and unwed daughters lingered still, shapeless and timid in their faded silks and their strapped, brocaded slippers, holding fast to folded Venetian fans (always Venetian, Jaeger thought, brought back to them as souvenirs before the war and preserved in tissue paper as perishable as the dreams of Italian palaces reflected on the dark glass of motionless canals), fearful that someone might ask their opinion of the coming monetary reform or the Occupation Statute. For it was only the husbands, the fathers, the dead sons and brothers, who knew the answer to any question, even if it was only as to whether there were stars in the night sky.

Matterhorn's tray was empty now, and, without pausing, he slid it onto the dumb-waiter, and, twisted and warped, he led them down the flight of cement stairs to the vast, illuminated regions of kitchen and laundry, wine cellar and storage room, that opened below. In the kitchen, spacious enough to serve a restaurant's clientele, the girl sat on the table, bare-armed, bare-legged, in a pale, soft, summery dress, with a highball glass held in her hand. On one side of her stood Mike Dardenella in an oyster-white linen dinner-jacket, well groomed, Italian-eyed, theatrical, perhaps just having finished speaking, and just having set his glass down, empty, with a smile still on his mouth. On the other side stood a small-boned man whose head was fixed directly to his shoulders, wearing a tuxedo too large for him, and a marmot's uneasy grin.

"So now it's really turned into a party," the girl said, but she did not lift her mermaid eyes from the depths in which they contemplated wing-footed mollusks and Conchifera and sea anenome. She seemed a modest, withdrawn schoolgirl sitting there, her voice soft as the murmuring of a dove.

"Hi ho, a conspiracy!" Honerkamp called out, and the mask of worry dropped from his face now that he saw Lieutenant Stephany was not standing by her side. The four men shook hands and repeated one another's names aloud:

Honerkamp, Dardenella, Jaeger, Overstreet. *Overstreet, the marmot,* Jaeger thought. He saw the long, incisor teeth, and the skin patterned dark with freckles that mounted from the jawline, and crossed the cheeks and the flat short nose and the forehead, and moved in under the pepper-and-salt cap of the new man's hair. "That's one of the things I learned in high school," Honerkamp said; "it takes three to make a conspiracy, a complot, or a cabal."

"I learned it different in school," said Dardenella, and he smiled in pleasure at them all. "I learned three was a crowd."

There were two white polished stoves and a row of out-sized sinks, making a puny thing of the American refrigerator that stood by the pantry's double doors, and despite the three years now in which people of another country had lived under this roof, the mammoth saucepans on the wall were for the preparing of such quantities of food as no American family would ever eat. In a moment, thought Jaeger, the brewer with the girth of an elephant and stagheads in his jacket lapels might tower at the door. Matterhorn brought the bottle of Scotch out on a tray, and the soda water, and the glasses, and ice, and Honerkamp served drinks around.

"Not for me," said the man called Overstreet, the incisors long on his lower lip, the voice as flat as the middle-western plains that Jaeger had crossed, and he raised one freckled hand. "I'm a strictly Coca-Cola man."

"Then we'll let old Matterhorn in on the complot instead," said Honerkamp, and the *Hausmeister's* leathery fingers, dark as the talons of a Raptores or Accipiter, closed in trembling need upon the glass.

"You good man, Mr. Hönig," Matterhorn said. His lips were wet, and he looked at the American with shrewd, obsequious eyes. "Why you have no uniform? You good enough for uniform."

"The best men, my friend," said Honerkamp, speaking his own fluent, inaccurate German now; "the very best are the men like Herr Jaeger, and Herr Dardenella, and Herr Overstreet, the kind who have laid aside just that because it stands between them and what they cherish as the beating hearts of all humanity. We civilians, we're the true emissaries of democracy, and we say to hell with the hierarchy of army men. Our role is to loosen the soil at the roots of things that have not been permitted light or space or air. I tell you, we bear gifts of imponderable value, Matterhorn," he said, and he took a quick swallow of his drink as he stood looking in rapt, earnest, schoolboy frenzy straight at the girl. "We've entered into a proletarian cabal on German soil and don't think there aren't any Germans in it with us."

"*Ja, ja,*" the *Hausmeister* murmured, wisely, wisely, shaking his wizened head.

"There's a man who stands in my office, a skeleton," Honerkamp said, going on with it in English now. "He was perhaps a Jew, but he could just as well have been a *Wehrmacht* soldier home on leave, one of those Germans in the Occupation of Paris who used to slip away to the cemetery in Montmartre to kneel in homage at Heinrich Heine's grave. Let him be that, or a Jehovah's Witness, or Quaker, who was hiding in the cellar when the bombs happened to fall. Or let him be merely one German who was ashamed, just one."

"*Ja, ja,*" the *Hausmeister* said.

"If you came to the America House and met him, Millicent, you'd be in the democratic complot with me and Jaeger and all the rest of us," said Honerkamp, and, standing there drinking quickly, nervously, before her, revealed in all the bleak urgency of love, he watched her for a word, a sign. "You could help us put the brains in his skull and the words in his mouth," he said, but she did not lift her head or speak.

Overstreet had walked to the icebox, and as he turned and

looked back at Honerkamp, grinning his long-toothed, marmot grin, it seemed to Jaeger that any tuxedo would have been the wrong size for him because it was the wrong thing for him to wear.

"You seem to have conspiracy on your mind tonight, Seth," Overstreet said, the voice nasal, pitched a little high. "Isn't it all aboveboard and played straight, the program we're administrating here?"

"He's intelligent. That's why they put him in Intelligence," said Dardenella, and he winked his opera singer's eye at Jaeger. And, suddenly, the girl spoke.

"I'd like another highball, please," she said.

Matterhorn swayed on the horseshoe of his warped legs, taking his drink in one long draught, and then set down his glass.

"My sister's Inge, she like one G.I.," he said. He sought to stand steady by the table, pouring the Scotch into the girl's glass, spilling the soda, fumbling the ice cubes from the tilted tray. "If they get married, that way they make me American civilian, too. *Ja, ja,*" he said.

"Sure, the program's fine, but then the grafters and highjackers come along to break your heart, Mr. Overstreet," Honerkamp said. He had little or no use for his drink, and he put it aside to forage for food in the cannisters and the bread- and cake-boxes on the kitchen sideboard. Finding nothing there, he reached to open the cupboard doors above his head, and Jaeger could see the split vest under his dinner-jacket seize him by the armpits and stop him short. "You'll always get the poachers on the domains of other men," Honerkamp said, and he pulled his vest down into place. "You get the guys who gum up responsible procedure. You get them not only in an Occupation, but in literature, and in music, and every art. You're faced in the end with Plato's three classifications of men, the lovers of wisdom, the lovers

91

of honor, and the lovers of gain," he said, and Overstreet's hand paused where it was on the refrigerator door. "Say I'm the first, and Jaeger the second, and you the third, for the sake of argument," Honerkamp said, his voice squeezed small in the fury of his search from shelf to shelf. Then, abruptly appeased, he came back to the table with an open box of Triscuits in his hand.

"Where do I belong?" asked Dardenella, ready to laugh out loud.

"Gain, Mike, nothing but gain," said the man called Overstreet. He had taken the bottle of Coca-Cola from the refrigerator now, and removed its cap, his eyes on Honerkamp as he lifted the bottle to his mouth.

"The lovers of honor are rare," Honerkamp said, and, chewing, he held the box of Triscuits out to the girl. But she looked deeper and deeper into the fathomless power of her glass and slowly shook her head. "Sometimes it scares me, how few there are," Honerkamp said. His fingers broke a Triscuit into bits, and he fed the pieces rapidly, nervously, into his mouth. "Sometimes it scares me pink," he said, his small mouth chewing fast.

"I thought I detected a faint rosy tinge, Seth," Overstreet said through the portcullis of his teeth.

"You did a fine piece on the Lipizzaners, Herr Jaeger," Dardenella said, bringing the Germans in the room into the conversation now to bolster his pride. "I bought fifty copies of the *Presse* to send back home. It looked pretty good, that paragraph about the Duke of Newcastle and the way he trained the horses, and me owning their descendants now. I didn't mind your linking my name with his, Herr Jaeger! I don't mind at all!"

"Maybe it's the horse that trains the man to ride," said Jaeger, his voice shy and low. "Christoph Horn says the

Lipizzaner's dance is nothing but the natural movements of the way he plays when he is free. Maybe the Lipizzaners have that gift—"

And then Colonel Roberts was suddenly there, crossing the room quickly, with a separate reprimand for each of them in his blue, blazing eye. Non-fraternization scarcely laid in the grave, he might have been shouting, and here were German nationals making free with what he owned. *Hausmeister, at attention! Daughter, sit up straight and be a child again! Honerkamp, I'd like to get a uniform on you! Dardenella and Overstreet, you're out of order! Jaeger, who the hell asked you to come?*

"Where would your Lipizzan horse be today if ex-Cavalryman General George S. Patton hadn't stopped his tank advance across Austria when he saw a white horse doing its tricks?" the Colonel said, his eyes on first one and then the other of them, gauging the disciplinary measure each deserved. He tossed his shoulders from right to left, and the men stood motionless before him, except for Matterhorn, who sought to rise from the corner where he sat, and could not rise. "Overstreet, if you know your modern military history, you can tell us what happened," the Colonel said, and Overstreet put his empty Coke bottle on top of the refrigerator, and his bared incisors hung long on his lip.

"I guess I've forgotten that footnote to history, sir," he said.

"Footnote to history, Christ!" said Colonel Roberts. "Did you ever hear of a general in any army in any country in any century you can name detailing a tank column to bring a breed of horses back where they belonged? That's happened only once, and I was there when it happened, so you can say I've had my part in making history. General Patton sent a column into Czechoslovakia to bring the Lipizzaners back to Austria, two hundred mares and a bunch of foals! But who gives the army credit for it?"

Honerkamp passed the open box of Triscuits respectfully to him, but Colonel Roberts shook his head.

"Yes, I know the story," Jaeger said, pleased that, for once, he could bear the Colonel out. "I read about it in the States. I read that General Patton said America must save the old European culture, or as much as it could, so he got the horses out."

And now the girl's laughter gasped soft and foolish in the kitchen.

"Oh, that's funny, that's terribly funny!" she whispered through her laughter, and she rocked back and forth on the table in her pale, summery dress. The empty highball glass was in her fingers, and her head was lowered so that they saw only her shining crown of hair.

"Come now, Milly, they're waiting on us upstairs," the Colonel said, the gentleness in his voice sequestering her. But his eyes blazed darkly when he looked at Jaeger's face. *If you turn my women against me, you with your old European culture, I swear I'll break you, Jaeger,* said his hard flushed jowl. *I'll have you kicked off the paper in two minutes. I'll fix you for the duration of the Occupation if you don't do things my way.* "Come, Milly," he said, and he took the glass from her fingers. "Here, Matterhorn; straighten up down here, and then get upstairs where you belong."

At the sound of his name, the *Hausmeister* tried to cross the room to where they stood, holding to the row of sinks and the two white stoves as he came. Dardenella pulled out a chromium-tubed chair, as bandy-legged as Matterhorn himself, and helped him to sit down.

"He's tired, little Matterhorn," said Dardenella. The

94

Hausmeister's arms lay as if discarded on the table, and his head dropped on them. His dark hands, prehensile as a monkey's, lay helplessly on the bright white tabletop. They had been defeated a long time back, thought Jaeger, and he kept his eyes fixed on these hands so as not to look at the Colonel and the girl who stood now in submission by her father's side. They had been defeated a long time before the country was, and not by war, but perhaps by the furiously limited campaign of one man's conflict with his undetermined self. "He's worn out by something, all right," said Dardenella, speaking as gently as a mother, while his manicured fingers smoothed the dyed strands that lay across the old man's skull.

And now, in the momentary silence in the room, the strains of music drifted from the terrace above, and Honerkamp raised his head.

"What did I say about that, nothing more than *that*, wiping out in the end the sound of the bombers going over?" he said. "I tell you, I've driven to Paris a dozen times this spring, driving all night because the music I wanted was going through my head and I couldn't lie down and sleep until I'd got to the record stores. And once I had the albums I wanted, I didn't even stop for lunch, but drove straight back to Germany again, either because I love these people who think in oratorios or canticles, or because I'm scared of what the French are capable of doing to me," he said, and then, as if the music had recalled to him why he was here, he went quickly out of the kitchen and up the stairs.

"Tell me, Mr. Dardenella," said Colonel Roberts briskly when he was gone. "Last Saturday night you missed the horse show. I can't understand it."

Dardenella's hand ceased moving on the dry hemp of the *Hausmeister's* hair.

95

"Missed it? I wouldn't miss that! I had to be there," said Dardenella. "Horn was showing my horses. What would I be doing, staying away?"

"That's what I'm interested in knowing," said the Colonel. "Think back. I want your alibi."

"Well, no, sir, I didn't go up there, after all," Dardenella said, and a look of pain came slowly on his face. "That *Graf* up there, and the *Gräfin*, they make the rules, and Christoph Horn writes the tickets out. What they tell you is that there has to be some kind of understanding between the Lipizzan horse and the man, so I couldn't show Neapoli myself. He doesn't understand me culturally. That's what they say. Horn says there's got to be one rider to a horse, but I say he's nuts. I'm not taking any German national home with me when I go. They tell you there has to be some kind of loyalty. Maybe Horn's talking about the sixteenth century. I wouldn't know."

"He's talking about *now*," the girl whispered, not lifting her head.

Jaeger closed his eyes as he took a long swallow of his drink, not wanting to see the centuries that lay between man and man, not wanting to know there could be no mingling of American and German in this room, this house, despite the proximity of their flesh and the deceptive mingling of their voices coming down the open stairs.

"And you haven't got that kind of loyalty. Is that it, Dardenella?" the Colonel went on with it.

"We're investigating him now, sir," Overstreet said, and he stood there pulling at his cuffs and shaking with laughter at his own wit, but the Colonel paid no heed.

"So when you found they weren't going to let you show that horse, you took a ride out in the country in your jeep," the Colonel reconstructed it. "You thought that communion with nature might do the trick."

"Well, I took a ride, sir, that's correct. I drove down to Niederstadt," said Dardenella. "I took in a few night-clubs to get a change of scenery. But not in a jeep. I don't have a jeep," he said. "I was just damned sore."

"But your friend here has a jeep," said the Colonel. His jowls were brick-colored as he turned his head to look at Overstreet.

"He's not my friend. We have a nodding acquaintance, Colonel," Overstreet said.

"Oh, he's lived too long in Alaska to know about thoroughbreds and the finer things of life," said Dardenella with a wink of his eloquent Italian eye. "He won't look at a horse. He's a trapper by trade. He's after smaller game."

"I was out on business, government business, on Saturday night, sir," Overstreet said, the upper lip sheathing the long teeth in sudden gravity. "That's as much as I'm able to say." He pulled at the too-long shirt cuffs in the tuxedo's hanging sleeves, the pattern of freckles standing dark on his brow. "Sometimes even the boys in the office don't know where I am," he said. "That's part of the calculated risk we run."

"So you're a trapper, are you?" the Colonel said, paying no attention to the rest of it. "What about having a try at the wild pig who's terrorizing the men and women of Ober-Pastau? That's the way the story goes. Give us guns and we'll get him, the peasants tell you. But I want to know the German I hand a gun to. I want to know him well." He had had more than enough of it, and the pulse beat in impatience in his jaw. "Come, Milly," he said. His arm in the uniform sleeve went under the girl's bare, slender arm. "Let's clear the kitchen. Let's go!" he shouted at the lot of them, and he led them up the stairs.

There, in the press of people in the hall, each man was on his own again, and Jaeger saw Catherine Roberts coming toward him, and his heart went strangely muted in his breast.

"I was waiting for you. I was going to have someone call the paper to find out why you hadn't come," she said. She spoke in a low voice, and she did not look into his eyes. "I don't know how to seat them," she murmured; and she had no age, no flesh, it seemed to Jaeger, no commitment to any man, for she was not even woman. She was air to breathe, and of such unexpected purity that he could scarcely bear it in his lungs. "I don't know who takes precedence, the *Herr Oberbürgermeister* or the *Rektor* of the University," she said, and if this was intended as humor, he could not laugh. He could only turn when she turned and follow the dark, copper fire of her hair through the maze of people out of the hall and into the reception rooms where German maids sought to place the gilt-legged chairs in rows. "Speak to them, reassure them, show them to seats," Catherine Roberts whispered to him. She paused and looked through the archways down the vista of pale rugs, glass chandeliers, cretonne-covered sofas, looking across the chairs and the people for the waters of humanity to part and order to be made.

But even as the assemblage found seats, German was drawn to German, American to American, by something as fixed, as inevitable, as polarity. Honerkamp was seeking to intersperse them, an American here, a German there, but after an awkward word or two had been exchanged, they would rise to merge again with those whose national history they shared. Jaeger herded droves of his own countrymen into the ranks of the Americans, but before his back was turned, they had shifted from the chairs where he had sat them down, and moved, singly or in couples, apologetically, back against the tide. In the end, the Germans sat in a body in the middle room, with the *Herr Oberbürgermeister* and the *Rektor Magnificus*, as dissimilar as owl and crow but wholly German, sitting side by side in the front row. Behind them, Americans were in possession of the south room, their glasses in their hands, their cigarettes on their lips. The north room, too, was the territory of the Occupier, but here the chairs were turned so that those seated on them faced the middle room and a barrage of German eyes. And down the strip of neutral ground between them strode Colonel Roberts, and took the seat on the *Rektor's* right which the *Herr Direktor* of the *Krankenhaus* vacated for him with a nervous bow. On the Colonel's right sat the army Chaplain of the post, a man of forty or somewhat more, cherubic and clean and bland, with pleasantly waved hair. The boyish Chaplain jumped like a rabbit in his seat when the Colonel struck the palms of his hands together and roared his orders out.

"Let's get going now!" Colonel Roberts shouted, and throughout the rooms the voices halted. The Colonel swung around in his chair, and his blazing glance shot fire and brimstone over the German company and the Americans closing on their flank.

It was the obligation of his wife, the President of the German-American Club, to stand up under the archway between the middle and the north reception rooms, and turn her back on none as she told those on her right hand and those on her left why they were gathered here. The people of their two countries had come together in this club to establish a friendship that functioned, she said, and perhaps they should begin with a language that they all could share.

"I have begun to take German lessons," she said, with hesitation and shyness in her voice now, but she did not look at Jaeger, who stood in the north room, alone among the Americans, a cigarette in his hand, leaning against the wall. "I shall soon be able to say all these things in German to you," she said, but now she must say in English to them that this functioning friendship required concerted action from them all. Some members had spoken of outdoor excursions as a way of bringing the two nationalities together, she said, excursions with a definite purpose in them, such as the identifying of mushrooms, or of wild birds in the early morning, or the study of astronomy at night under the stars. Some had suggested a course in German and American literature, with discussions in both languages, she said, while others had thought that musical instruments could give them a reason for being together, either in chamber-music groups or in an orchestra. Although she spoke with the greatest simplicity, there was confusion on the faces of many of the Germans, and they looked tentatively about them. The *Herr Direktor* of the *Krankenhaus* glanced at the *Rektor Magnificus*, and the *Herr Oberbürgermeister* looked at the Colonel. The words that seemed to whisper through the rooms in query were "functioning friendship," for the explanation for this was not in any book that they had read. "We hope that our new members here tonight will have other ideas and suggestions to make," said Catherine Roberts, her voice grave. "After the speakers of the evening have addressed us, it is our hope that you will turn this gathering into an open forum, a town meeting in which everyone takes part."

By now it was clear that an interpreter was needed to make her words as well as the situation comprehensible. Jaeger had listened as he smoked, held by the vision of Catherine Roberts contained and armored in her aura of purity, but what her words meant he did not know, for he was not certain, even, that he knew what she had said. When he sought, at a later moment, to recall the color of her dress, he could not, for she appeared to drift on a soft wash of light, like Botticelli's Venus on the wave. But now that the voices whispering for clarification could no longer be denied, he saw her waver, saw her green eyes seek her husband's eyes, and the Colonel, tossing in his seat, called Jaeger's name aloud.

"Hey, get up there and do some enucleating!" he shouted, and at once the moment was eased by American laughter. But Jaeger saw his own hand trembling as he threw his cigarette away.

He stepped nearer to her, and as she spoke again of functioning friendship, going back to the beginning and pronouncing the words with care, each time he waited until she paused, and then he repeated the words in German to the assembled people. And now his flesh went hot with shame at the intimacy of this act which they performed in public together, for she would give him the words from her own mind and mouth, turning to look at him as she did so, and he would savor them for an instant, and then transform them to another sound upon his tongue. It was unbearable to him that they should be standing here on public view, exposing, before the words were quite pronounced, their understanding of each other's speech. At moments, he felt the thoughts swoon in his head, for it was as if they stood up here before the Chaplain, and the *Oberbürgermeister*, and the *Rektor*, and the countless witnesses, and exchanged vows that no man had the power to undo, and that they themselves were never to betray.

The *Rektor* of the University was the next to speak, standing with shoulders as narrow and sloping as a bird's, his long nose beaked and sorrowing. His hands were clasped out of sight under his rusty black tails, and he began to speak in German, saying that education was a highroad that all free men must share. American and German alike, he was saying, must walk together on this highroad as men had followed it in olden times out of the darkness of the barbaric ages; and then the Colonel's voice rang sharply out.

"Speak English, Rector!" he shouted, and the members of the German-American Club sat frozen on their chairs.

"My English," said the *Rektor Magnificus* in a halting voice, "is poor. I have not spoken in many years."

"Speak it anyway," said Colonel Roberts, his shoulders casting the weight of his impatience from one side to the other.

So the *Rektor* began to speak again, but this time in another tongue, groping for words, lost in the labyrinth of structure, the beginning of each sentence nearly forgotten once he neared its end. His arms hung limply by his sides, and his eyes were glazed like those of a man who has been stricken. His beak and brow were as narrow as an ailing bird's. He was saying, or he sought to say, that the German was emerging now, like barbaric man, from the long silence of modern German history, and the time had come for new legends of Beowulf to be sung. But his voice faltered as he spoke, and in a moment the blue underlid of the bird's eye might rise to shutter from the others the mark of the blow the Colonel had dealt. He spoke of Goethe's "Metamorphosis of Plants," but whether any American seated there, or any German, except Jaeger, recognized the syllables or followed the tortuous way he took, could not be known.

"I would, but could I, inexperience in this language, to strive, to tell about the classification, the three types of changing—*die Verwandlung*—metamorphosis," said the *Rektor* in a voice of indescribable pain. "I would speak of that classification Goethe exploded, expanded, into three —namely, progressive, we will say, and the backward, reversed, movement of progress—"

"Retrogressive," said the *Herr Oberbürgermeister* deferentially. His accent was Oxford and assured, for who else in the room was entitled to put this word or any other into the *Rektor's* mouth?

"Progressive, retrogressive," the *Rektor* repeated, continuing to turn his "p's" into "b's"; "and the third, namely, arbitrary. I would compare the three types of this changing proved by Goethe to the progression, the developmenting, of the German man like the universal plant. In ultimacy, this makes the mind turn to follow, if common men could dare, to the *Urpflanze* of Goethe. That is to say, that German genius proved in science a fantasy, a hallucination of poetry, that all plants—and in allegory might be charged all men—arrive from the *Urpflanze*—"

"Could you make that a little clearer, Rector?" Colonel Roberts called out.

"*Die Urpflanze*," said the *Rektor* bleakly, and he did not turn his head.

"*Urpflanze!*" the *Herr Oberbürgermeister* cried out in a distressed whisper, his eyes as yellow as an owl's and his ears as feathered. "*Ach, Gott,* I cannot find the English equivalent—"

"I think it is called the primitive plant, the prototype of all plants, that Goethe sought," said Jaeger, leaning in uneasiness against the framework of the arch.

"The way men sought the Holy Grail?" Catherine Roberts asked from her seat beside the *Herr Direktor* of the *Krankenhaus.*

"*Ach,* no, it was not religious. It was biological," said the *Herr Oberbürgermeister,* and he leaned forward to catch the Chaplain's eye in confirmation. "Or would you say the mystic experience of Goethe's findings was more spiritual than scientific at its source?"

"Well, that could very well be," said the Chaplain, nodding pleasantly, as he, too, leaned forward in his chair.

"All right," said Colonel Roberts. "Now we know where we are. Let's get on with it, Rector," he said.

The *Rektor Magnificus* spoke for twenty-three minutes

by Jaeger's watch, and when he was done and turned to take his seat again, he seemed to move unsteadily. For this was perhaps the evening he had thought of through the years, the night when, if he survived, he would speak in an official capacity to men who recognized his worth, and the light of their understanding would illuminate the darkness of all that he and others like him had endured. Had he not dreamed of tracing for them in his own tongue the metamorphosis of the German through Goethe's theory of the metamophosis of the plant, not in exoneration of any German crimes, but to establish that the highly organized individual in all countries, all centuries, is the same, advancing a few evolutionary stages, and leaving behind his fellow man? Had he not wished to stand humbly among his peers and say that all men proceed, some slowly, some more rapidly, from an identical root? But now he had been stripped even of his modesty, deprived even of the arms of his learning and language, which were the only arms he had ever wished to bear. As he took his seat, his beak and his brow seemed to have gone narrower, and his eyes to merge as one cold, tearless eye above his nose.

It was after ten when the speeches and the intervals of discussion were done with, with only Honerkamp and the *Herr Oberbürgermeister* seeking to bring animation and logic to the scene. And then the guests saw with relief that the buffet tables were being spread anew in the hallway, and the zither and two violins again took up their complaint in the auditorium of the wide, soft night. The Americans began at once to drink, and the Germans to devour *Wurst*, as if no talk of functioning friendship had ever interrupted these activities. And there were those among his countrymen here, thought Jaeger, moving through them, who had certainly been invited only because they had the proper jackets to wear. It would have been highly impractical, he reflected sardonically, and the burdened dumb-waiter cried and groaned aloud in the hall, to plan a club whose members had not been able to save jacket and tails or watered silk from the holocaust, no matter what courage or defiance marked their pasts. Matterhorn stumbled from room to room, setting the gilt-legged chairs against the wall, while the maids passed among the guests, bearing trays of Rhine wine in long-stemmed glasses, elaborately cut and colored emerald, and topaz, and blue. *There is no reason for me to stay*, thought Jaeger, and he put his notebook and pencil in his pocket as if putting away all hope for what the evening might have been; and then Catherine Roberts stood close beside him, her face turned from him, but her hair like a dark fire burning near his heart.

"If you would just go up to the second-floor library," she was saying without seeming to speak, "I will come as quickly as I can."

Upstairs, before the dark, heavy, double doors, Jaeger knew this must be the entrance to the Bluebeard's chamber that she had spoken of in the garden the first day. He turned the gun-metal knob, and the door swung out with the deliberation of a drawbridge descending, and he walked into the inner mystery and gloom, and the drawbridge closed behind him again. A lighted lamp with an opaque, bottle-green shade stood on the library table in the obscurity, and out of the semi-darkness of the walls around sprang a white forest of roebuck skulls and stony horns, a petrified forest, it seemed, of bleached, desert residue as brittle as eggshell and intricately branched. Facing him was a massive fireplace over which hung forty or more of these perishable cheekbones and brows, with their trim little sets of rugged horns; and high above them was a heavy cornice of six deerheads, each mounted on a shield of wood, each head raised on the glossy, reddish, curved throat in separate fear of what had stirred in the forest on that last flight. The heavy sprays of the antlers were rooted like iron in the fur-clad bone. This room must have served the brewer as retreat, thought Jaeger, for here no flavor of cabbage boiling hour after hour could permeate, and no sound of women's voices could affront, speaking of lesser things than man's concern. Nor could the voices of children who had grown now, or were dead, or who were held prisoner in another country, be heard from the terrace, or from the orchard, or from Wotan's and Thor's dark woodlands behind the house where they once had played.

Below the roebuck skulls were shelves of books, dense as underbrush, but the worn, uncertain gilt of their titles gleamed here and there like the wary eyes of wild things in the dark. Other books stood upright between sober, iron bookends in the shape of hunting-dogs, and Jaeger took one volume from among the others, one entitled in English *Natural History*, and, as he waited, he turned the pages in the lamplight, not wanting to look at the army of almost human skulls upon the walls. "The Harvest Mouse," ran the headings; "The Hamster," "The Water Vole," "The Lemming," "The Agouti," and there were illustrations of them; "The Common Dormouse," "The Jelerang," "The Common Marmot," and he stopped at the engraving on this page. For here, with each hair faithfully rendered, was the flattened head, the short arms on which coat sleeves seemed to hang too long, the protruding teeth, the small chin, of the man called Overstreet. The description ran: "*Arctomys Marmota* is a creature given to subterranean habits of life, digging large and rather complicated burrows. It is very common in all the mountainous districts of northern Europe where it associates in small societies. The hoary marmot, or whistler, is found from Alaska to the high mountains of Idaho. The body is heavily and clumsily made, the head is large and flat, and the incisor teeth are extremely large and project beyond the lips." *Alaska*, thought Jaeger, and out of the past came the echo of Dardenella's voice, saying: "He's lived too long in Alaska to know about thoroughbreds or the finer things of life."

He put the book back in its place, and he turned and looked at the heavy, double doors, over which three tusked boarheads hung. The evil snouts of the wild pigs might have been filled with breath still, for wet spittle seemed to bead the stiff, black leather of their lips, and the tilted, orange eyes were made of something more living than glass. And then one side of the heavy door below the boarheads opened, and Catherine Roberts came in.

"Herr Jaeger," she said, speaking softly. "It's Milly." Her eyes were lowered as if she could not bear the sight of the roebucks' naked white brows, and the concave frontal bones, so young, so friable. "I thought you wouldn't mind coming with me. If you could walk down to the end of the lane, I'll pick you up there. I think I can get the car through the others now that people have begun to go."

𝑉
—

The warmth and fragrance of the night was close on either side in the narrow lane as they drove, and honeysuckle vines brushed soft as water against the side of the car. Catherine Roberts had perhaps waited a long time to speak of this, and now her voice touched Jaeger in every nerve, its tenderness breaking at times as if wounded past all healing, and then recovering its passionate urgency. *How will you recognize her if you come across her tonight unless I give you the dimensions of her terror or the sound of her wild, panting breath? For you and I are the posse, the bloodhounds setting out on her trail,* she might have been saying to him. *You've read in the papers sometimes about a child who is lost in the mountains, or who was last seen wandering by the sea, and the night comes down, and still no trace, no footsteps at the edge of the canyon or the water, still no answering cry. And, God, what do you do then, which way do you turn, how do you keep your reason from reeling in your head?* And yet it may have been that she did not say these words, or even speak of the loss of a child, but of losing a possession like identity that can escape through your fingers if you are not able to give it a name. *When children wander off in the dark alone, it isn't after flower, or bird, or firefly, or anything the eye can see or the hand can touch,* she might have been saying, but Jaeger was not certain that these were the words she used.

"I saw fireflies for the first time in America," he said when her voice ceased for a moment. "We don't have them over here."

"But I wasn't speaking of fireflies," Catherine Roberts said in soft impatience with him.

"Still, I was thinking of them. I don't know why they came to my mind. Perhaps because of the dark and the smell of honeysuckle," Jaeger said.

"But maybe I was thinking of them too! Maybe that explains it," Catherine Roberts said. "I truly don't know what I'm thinking. Perhaps of will-o'-the-wisps. I've drunk too much white wine, and that is why the heart speaks clearly, but not the mind, and I am so pleased by the taste of cold white German wine, dry like tonight, so touched, Herr Jaeger, so terribly moved by the doors of the heart, the ducts of pity, that it opens. But I should have the courage to pour every long-necked bottle down the hillside, and let it drench the stones of the lane and the roots of cabbage. I should do anything at all with liquor except let Milly drink it. Whenever she lifts a glass, I should strike it from her hand. And I—I should not drink when Milly is near." The air that had been warm on their faces changed suddenly, and they seemed for a moment to be passing through the moist rock of a tunnel, but it was the bridge over the quiet, unhastening river that they crossed. And then they moved through the tepid night again as the car mounted the hill. "You may think this has happened so many times before that I know exactly what to do, but I don't know anything at all, Herr Jaeger," Catherine Roberts was saying, her voice low. "When children wander off in the dark alone, it's because the question is hammering louder and louder in their blood, and they can't bear it any longer. They gallop in fright like colts, the way Milly has gone, direction or distance meaning nothing, and if they don't find the answer as they run, then they stop long enough to pick the poisoned flower in the underbrush and they eat its petals and heart, or they plunge under the surface of the water, with the songs of the wild birds that have lured them roaring in their ears as they go down. I've had too much wine," she whispered. "Does it seem to you sometimes that all of us in Germany are living in limbo? Nothing has been decided about any of us yet, not even the duration of our sojourn, so perhaps it is more like purgatory. But Milly has never gone off like this before. She has never fled from us. She has borne us in uncomplaining docility. Ah, but I can understand her running out of the mausoleum of that house where you saw the heart of a man cut out of his breast while he still lived—or lived in limbo, anyway—and offered to the guests with the plates of hot *Wurst* and the beer. I should make a sea of all the beer in Hesse and drown the brewer who haunts that house, and hold his wife under with both hands so that she'll stop dreaming and dreaming of the sons who are prisoners of war in Russia still! Two of them, or three, or four, perhaps a whole regiment of them, who cares? I should send her body floating, bloated and horrible, as a warning to other mothers down the mainstream of German identity. It is they, that man and woman, who have driven Milly out! Oh, stop me, Herr Jaeger! Stop me from saying all these things I do not want to say! What has happened to us here in this country? I crying out things to you so mad that they should go down in silence to the grave with me, and you, a young man, with life quite simple, quite attainable, before you, having nothing better to do with your nights and days than throw them away like this!"

Jaeger trembled with pain and love for her as he rode beside her on the cushioned seat of this car that had borne him, and the Colonel, and Stephany, out into the hunting-country, that had rocked so ponderously out over the corduroy road. Now it soared lightly toward the *Schloss* that brooded in darkness above them, and he asked the other, rushing dark at the windows how she had borne the years of marriage with the red-jowled, arrogant man in uniform, how she had slept in his bed at night and yet carried this illumination (purity? passion?) undimmed in her flesh. *Lovers?* he thought, and it was not the first time he had reflected on it. *All right, then, lovers,* he thought, stabbing his own heart with the word. He wondered how she had managed it, with Colonel Roberts scenting the wind. Out of his anguish, he said:

"But I have no simple, attainable life before me. I am like a refugee in this country. I belong to nothing. Only you can tell me where to begin."

"Ah, don't say that!" Catherine Roberts cried out. The car was taking the curves too swiftly. "If you think my husband should be here with me tonight instead of you, a stranger, then say it! It's wrong of you to speak so softly, always under your breath! You should speak louder than the others, louder than any of the others, louder than the *Herr Direktor* and the *Herr Oberbürgermeister*, and louder than the brewer, because what you are saying is strangely important, like a telegram the young are sending to the old, and the sense of it must get through—"

"But I have never said anything. I have scarcely spoken," Jaeger said.

"You spoke of a nightingale giving its blood to the white rosebush. I remember that," said Catherine Roberts. "You spoke of genders, and verbs, and words that have no syntactical relation to anything in life, and the past subjunctive."

"No," said Jaeger, and he laughed out loud.

"Once you said 'There's absolutely nothing wrong with me. I've simply lost my horse.' Oh, Herr Jaeger, mine is the language of the cold white wine speaking from the dark,

dark green of the long-necked bottle!" she said. "This is the wine speaking like an eloquent sister moving in my blood. It makes it possible—no, necessary, for me to say to you that when I find Milly and put my arms around her to take her home, it will only be her flesh that I touch, and what she is will still be running away from me in silence through the trees."

"Why are you going to the *Schloss?*" said Jaeger. "How do you know where she will be?"

"Because I saw her as the speeches began, looking sideways for help or exit," she said. "And she couldn't find either, and so she went with her head lowered, to the back row with Stephany. Oh, Herr Jaeger, be Milly for an instant! I'm so afraid of that lowered head, that terrible docility! Be Milly seeking for pride—yes, I suppose pride must be a part of identity, but pride entirely stripped of medals and rank—wouldn't she run blindly to the proudest child she knew, and the proudest beasts, so where else would she go?"

"Yes," Jaeger said, slowly, pausing between each word. "Yes. Yes."

"My husband calls him a groom, a stable groom," said Catherine Roberts, and the car climbed fast. They were nearly at the archway now.

"I call him the grieving prince," said Jaeger. "He has rubbed shoulders with the elite since childhood, but what he is by this time, I don't know."

"He's still a child," Catherine Roberts said in defense of him as they drove into the courtyard. Beyond the radius of the car's lights, the stone water-basin and the cobbles could be only dimly seen, but, closer, the brocade of moss, the short fresh blades of grass, the star-like flower heads, were as bright, as phony, as the vegetation that garnishes a stage. "Perhaps you could call his name out under the window of his room, wherever the window would be," she said, and she lowered the headlights, and stopped the motor of the car.

Jaeger got out, and quietly closed the door, and as he crossed toward the stables, he was filled with a pleasurable, quiet sense of his own power. It was as if, without warning, their roles had been transposed, and now he was the figure of action and responsibility, and she must sit passive, in abeyance, until his decision was made. He did not know where Horn's room would be, but, wherever he found him, the language that he and Horn would speak would be their own male tongue, while the mother and daughter would wait, suspended in silence, until summoned from the shadows by the vigor of man's disposal of this moment in their lives. He walked across the cobbles toward the Lipizzaners' quarters, moving toward the white horses of inestimable value, as if knowing that Horn would be sleeping in a mansard room above their stalls. He found the heavy door in the darkness, and pulled it back, and he stood for a moment breathing the fragrance of the stables, harking to the scarcely audible sounds that bespoke the presence of the horses, the breath in the velvet nostril, the faintest of movements in the straw. Then he called out:

"Hello, Christoph Horn! Hall-oo, Horn!" A horse got to its feet without panic in the dark, and shook its head, and he heard the whir of its sneezing, but no answer came from the rafters. "Christoph Horn, are you asleep?" Jaeger called.

The elation still possessed him, for this was his situation as perhaps none had ever been so completely his before. There were no orders to wait for, none except those his own heart and will would give him, no voice out of any inherited past to tell him this or that was the thing he now must do. He was not *Wehrmacht* soldier, or prisoner of war, or reporter on any paper that would run this story of unequivocal decision for other men to read. In the car halted in the medieval courtyard, a beautiful, submissive woman waited, and what he did now meant either redemption or finality. However gently she might explain it afterward, he could not risk falling from a horse again. He must state in every act now a meaning so simple, so lucid, that two interpretations could not be given it. To find Christoph Horn and Millicent was not enough; he must transmute their sleeping or their waking into innocent and honorable terms. He must speak to them as if to figures in a parable of tender love, as Catherine Roberts would seek to do. Out of their fear crouching in the darkness above his head, he would make a loud, clear music that would shake the rafters with its power; out of their silence, a duet of Tristan and Isolde that would strike the trembling stars. It was certainly not the first time that lovers had lain in each other's arms in this old place while the voice of the intruder shouted from below.

"Hall-oo, Horn!" he called out, and now someone moved in the room above the stalls.

Jaeger heard the footsteps crossing the boards, heavy, guiltless steps, and when the voice came in answer, it was not Christoph Horn's, but a voice with a broad, country accent answering through a dormer window that had opened on the court.

"Horn, he took Sigmar and Neapoli out," the voice called down, the names of the horses clanging like metal on the courtyard stones.

"Took them out? Does Horn go riding at night?" Jaeger asked, and he laughed. He drew the stable door closed again, and stepped out of the odor of clean straw and horse into the sweet-scented night. In the shingled roof of the mews, no dormer was lit, and the sloping wing of the roof was opaque shadow against the lesser darkness of the sky. "When did Horn go out?" he called.

"*Ach,* maybe an hour ago," said the stable boy's voice, the pace of the words, like the movement of the thoughts in his head, labored and slow. "I'm new here," he said. "I don't know the time."

There was the sound of the window closing against the warmth of June, and Jaeger walked to the car, and leaned on the open window and, in the dimness that washed back from the parking-lights, he could see the pale, sad beauty of her face.

"Come," he said gently. "Put the lights out. Perhaps he's down at the riding-rink. We'll leave the car here."

The rink had been built at the entrance to the thickly meshed forest floor, with only a bridle path leading to it, and a bridle path leading away. He had seen it when he walked up from town to get the story on the horse show, a circular barracks whose stained wood was tangled and lost, like the wood of a hunting-lodge, in the close web of the trees. The roof of it was wheel-shaped, with the rafters the spokes of it, radiating from the hub, and a door as wide as a carriage entrance opening onto the hoof-marked path. As they walked, Catherine Roberts and Jaeger did not speak, and although only the starlight high above the path showed them the way, he did not take her hand. It seemed to him they were less alone than when they rode together in the car, and the strangeness of Catherine Roberts, or any American, walking, possessed him now as it had on the day that Snafu tossed him to the ground. Refugees, expellees, outcasts, walked; they wandered the length of the *Autobahn,* carrying all that was left to them on their backs, in search of work, or in search of families they had once known, or of wives and husbands and children that had once been theirs, or in search of the walls of houses that they must know were no longer standing anywhere. And Germans walked; they walked out of the East Zone, making for the West, the old, the young, the crippled, the hale, some on crutches, some with arms severed at the shoulder, the elbow, or ending at the wrist, like Napoleon's or Hitler's armies straggling back out of the Russian snows. Or Germans came limping back from France with the international letters stamped on their worn, grey coveralls, prisoners returning in search of what the white wine in Catherine Roberts' veins had called the mainstream of national identity. But Americans never put foot to this foreign soil, perhaps uneasy about the imprint that the Occupier must, of necessity, always leave, thought Jaeger; and now that Catherine Roberts walked through the darkness with him like the dispossessed, these others seemed to walk with them, stumbling, or limping, or swinging their torsos on their crutches, as they came.

"When you walk through the woods, do you feel your ancestors following?" Catherine Roberts said, and for a startled moment, Jaeger thought he had spoken aloud of those others who sought a *Heimat* still. "In the woods at home, it was always the Indians following me, night and day, and just as frightening, somehow, by day, hearing them following on narrow brown feet, and with them a handful of Frenchmen, in uniform, always in uniform, brought over by Lafayette, you know." The white wine gave it the quality of a dream rather than truth or history. "My father was an army doctor, gentle, bewildered, and I was born on an army post! I still don't believe it. My mother was French. I don't know what they were doing in the army, either of them. It didn't make any sense whatsoever. She knew a great many things, even that it didn't make any sense, so she became an invalid, planning it very carefully. But I didn't know this as a child, and my heart was racked, oh, racked and torn! You know, it is only mothers who matter," she whispered so that none of the others following should hear. "They can give everything, or they can take it all away. Sometimes I'm afraid to live, knowing that. Knowing, I mean, that fathers don't matter, and simply can't matter. It's only the desperate, desperate mothers, piecing their children together out of their own hopes and fears. My mother experienced it all in books, every instant of life. Think of sleeping with Flaubert, poor, shy Flaubert, and Romain Rolland, and even delighting Proust in bed! Imagine the faces of the other army wives when she brought *Above the Battle* or Jean-Christophe's insatiable passion instead of her knitting to the tea table! If they were stationed in Texas, or Fort Lauderdale, or Chillicothe, wherever it was, she always escaped. Those cream-colored, black-and-red titled, paper-back books from France were everywhere. And how could my father, so gentle, so forbearing, compete with their virility, even with Indian blood in his family history? Gently, gently, Herr Jaeger, he drank himself first to sleep, and then to death, without any fanfare at all. And you?" she whispered, for the others might be following close. "What was your father like?"

Jaeger said that in peacetime *der Alte* had served as a petty official in the city government of Niederstadt, sixty miles down the *Autobahn*, which the Americans knew only as a center of blasted factories and gutted mansions and bomb-excavated public parks. But he had grown up there and, as a boy, known it in every season and in other ways.

"When I was quite young, my father became a violent Ludendorffer, anti-Semitic, anti-Christian even," said Jaeger. "After the first war, he could no longer accept the contemporary world because it meant accepting the defeat of Germany, and that he could not take. He returned to

Wotan and Thor, to a sort of neo-heathenism, and he was always for the expulsion of the Jews, but peacefully, without murder, or arson, or argument." His father had never completed his education, and had been no more than an *Offiziersstellvertreter* in the First World War, he said.

"You hear a word like that and then you know how monstrous rank is," said Catherine Roberts, but he knew it was never a dead man or a liquidated army she was thinking of. And then the high, oblong links of light appeared, shining through the leaves, and the muted pounding of horses' hoofs shook deeply in the earth. Catherine Roberts stopped. "What am I going to do?" she whispered. "Oh, God, Jaeger, what am I going to do if Milly isn't there?"

Jaeger lifted the bolt, and the door swung wide, and a panel of light fell across the hoof-scuffed beam that served as step, and out onto the packed loam of the path. Inside, the place was lit as if for a ball, and they stepped in over the beam, and paused, bedazzled by light, on the sawdust of the entranceway. A wooden barrier stood shoulder-high between them and the oval ring, and within the enclosure of the ring, two pure white horses with silken tails passed in the disciplined gallop of the *haute-école*, the sand and the sawdust flying from under their hoofs like spray. Their necks arched, their heads held faultlessly, they moved lightly, steadily, through a silence like that interval in suspended sound when a merry-go-round revolves still, and the wooden horses rise and fall, although the calliope has ceased to play. But now another music blared out in celebration, and Catherine Roberts put her hand quickly on Jaeger's arm, for it was Milly who rode. She wore the gossamer evening-dress still, the skirt of it thrust inside a pair of breeches that hung too long over her bare feet, and her face was marvelously bewitched. Beside her rode Christoph Horn, his cheeks a little wan and hollow, his hair, under the grey *Wehrmacht* cap, pushed behind his ears like a poet's, a musician's, hair. In his sad, drab clothes and his cracked military boots, he rode without stirrups, and the fish-eyed horse, called Sigmar for short, flowed strong and pure between his thighs. But it was not the ease of their riding that made the music begin to play, but the up-roar of all that was understood between them, the curve of body, the slender, gripping legs, the hot vulnerability of wrist and breast and throat and lip, the lifting of hair from temple and brow, akin to the lifting of the horses' unsullied manes. And now the Lipizzaners as well heard the music that trumpeted in the blood, and they no longer moved in their gallopade, but floated, with forelegs miraculously poised, in unison to the measures of the air.

Catherine Roberts and Jaeger watched across the wooden barrier. As if they were spectators in a paddock, they watched Christoph Horn lead into the center of the ring, and Milly follow, and the Lipizzan horses appeared to pause there for an instant, but they did not pause, but moved into another fluid figure of the dance.

"The 'Pirouette'!" Christoph called out, his voice vibrat-ing through the rink as if he called across water to a high, far shore. And the Lipizzaners cantered lightly again, execut-ing the turns of the dance like playful ballerinas, their thickly lashed eyes on the spectators at the barrier, their bits ringing softly in their mouths. Just above the stained wainscoting of the hall, framed reproductions ran from pil-lar to post, showing the short-nosed stallions of the Spanish court performing their leaps, their ballotades, their caprioles, in the Vienna Riding Hall. In these antique copper-plates, ladies in *grand décolleté* looked down from the boxes on the horses paired below, and gentlemen of the court, with swords at their belts and fringed epaulettes, watched through opera glasses as the Quadrille passed. In the plate hanging close to the outer door, the loge of Austrian royalty was shown, with the coat-of-arms of the monarchy over the cornice, and two long-limbed warriors seated above the portrait in oils of the Emperor. But only the horses the long-dead looked down on seemed to breathe with an enduring power. Their hindquarters were etched as strong and white as life, and their necks were packed with flesh like a mackerel's side. Their shoulders were woven with muscle, and because of the great depth of their breasts, the fine Arabian heads seemed made for horses far frailer than those that were pictured, or those—their descendants—who now moved in the ring. "The 'Redoppe'!" Christoph called out, and the horses leaped with the static grace of statues flying. Over and over they made their effortless, winged leaps, with such a strange, weightless power in their limbs that it seemed as if sawdust and sand had been pulled from under them, thus giving them the appearance of soaring in the air. "The 'Terre à Terre'!" Christoph called, and no switch flicked at shoulder or croup, and no rein seemed to tighten, but once more the horses flowed into their gallopade, and at the curve fell back upon their haunches, and rose, and leaped, and then continued the parabola of their flight, and rose and leaped again.

"Jaeger, Herr Jaeger," the mother whispered. "I've never seen her belong to anything before."

"But you must have brought her up on a horse's back," Jaeger said, and he watched the girl in envy and chagrin, thinking of the horse he had once ridden called Snafu.

"But it isn't just that," Catherine Roberts said quickly, and now her hand moved from Jaeger's arm, and the clenched fingers of it beat softly on the barrier's wood. "It's more than just riding a horse. It's something no one should witness, no one at all. We shouldn't be standing here."

Jaeger could see the hollow beneath her cheekbone, and

the vein in her temple, and the tendrils of hair, dark copper, by her ear. Standing so, he could see the small face of the watch on her wrist, the hands of it marking twenty minutes past midnight, and breathe the subtle odors of her hair, her flesh. For the first time now, with a shock to his heart that was like a physical blow, he thought of her becoming his mistress, his own love, and he trembled. There would be the narrow, tilted street, and the sagging stairs, and he could even see how the dust would lie on the treads as they mounted together, and see his own hand, shaking with haste as it turned the knob of the door. They would sit on the edge of the white iron bed, and he would look at her face, knowing that it would be fixed in his sight until the last moment of his life, that he would take it down into the grave with him, fighting even in death to keep it clear of the rain, and rot, and defacement, and decay. He would be beyond speech, beyond apology for the worn places in the carpet, and for the mirror with the quicksilver flecking from it so that only garbled reflections of what they were would be with them there in the silent room. (Even the landlady's presence in the house would be obliterated by the torrent of this that poured through their veins, drowning out the whine of the voice saying that there were five women to every man in Germany, and three to every man in England, asking what had he found the ratio in America to be? "Only single men are entitled to rooms to themselves," she had said, "because men have needs that women don't have, or else don't talk about." The room would be wiped clean of her cautions concerning hygiene and decency.) His hand would touch his love's bare throat, his fingers open her blouse, his mouth close on her mouth. And then hands that were no longer his would draw the silk of her garments aside, gently at first, and then tearing them, and neither caring, neither knowing if it was midnight or dawn, or what was the season, for they would lie together on the roughness of the khaki blanket, she supple and yielding on the broken springs, he burning, mindless, naked as he had never been before in the fury of this love.

Here was her cheek, her throat, within reach of his hand, but if he had touched her flesh now, it would have had no meaning for her, for it was as if the girl rode between them, rode back and forth on the white stallion, shouldering them apart. He had not been told the entire story, and yet it seemed to him that he knew the sequence of it. It would not be just this one isolated June night, but all the nights of youth that had followed upon the hopeless, inarticulate days of youth, that the girl had gone running through labyrinths of fear. *Who am I? Who am I? Which way must I go?* had perhaps been screamed out in the German darkness as she came panting up the hill with the stuff of her evening-dress catching on bush and hedge and honeysuckle vine. *Who am I? What am I doing here?* she may have cried out to the absolute silence of this country as to the silence of the others. *Give me a drink now, God damn it, so that I needn't know! Give me a drink!* she may have shouted, she who never spoke, because drink was the only answer that had ever been offered in the tumult and uncertainty. But now she had come to a clearing in the complex of the forest, a stillness that was not oblivion, and she sat the white horse erectly, riding as straight as Christoph rode, her mermaid's eyes holding fast to him. Whatever savage mazes lay ahead, it would be different, thought Jaeger, they would all be passable, because of a stable door that had opened, if only for a little while, on a sawdust ring marked by the iron of the Lipizzaners' shoes. He remembered Borchert writing: "We are the generation without farewell. We may live no farewell, we must not, for on the stray paths trodden by our feet our wandering hearts find endless farewells." *But in the end you will have to say it to Christoph,* he thought, *and then where will you go?*

The two horses had halted side by side in the center of the ring, and now they lowered their heads and bent their knees before the spectators in the paddock, or so it seemed. But at once a clapping of hands broke out over Catherine Roberts' and Jaeger's heads, and they knew that there were others watching in the hall. The tempered applause was like rain falling gently on the wheel-shaped roof, and Christoph advanced Sigmar a step or two, and looked up at the loge, and doffed his cap in deference. But who was seated there could not be seen from the entranceway, for the loge thrust like a balcony over the heads of any commoners who stood below. And now the horse that Milly rode danced forward, but the steps he executed were never the classical figures of the Spanish Riding School. The girl rode easily, lightly, without guile, as if there was no other meaning to it, while this horse of lineage laid aside his dignity and took a step to this side and two steps to the other, ready, it seemed, to cock one foot and lean against a lamp post if one came his way.

"Neapoli's a fool. Get him out of the ring," a man's voice said in German above their heads. The tone was querulous, the accent cultivated, the pitch that of an old man's voice, a little high.

But the horse danced on like an angel debased by mortal weakness, the celestial wings lowered in the dust, the grave, intelligent countenance transformed by comedy. In another moment, he might wink one eye. And this time he danced for the two standing by the barrier, for the others in the loge above had pushed their chairs back, and their steps sounded on the wooden stairs.

"Oh, Milly, Milly," Catherine Roberts whispered, watching the girl's confession danced in shy, sly parody of the thing she had never spoken of, and could not speak of now. For she was making a clear enough statement, hamming it, playing it as burlesque, but, however she did it, still it was this that the mother had waited a long time to hear. The foolish, unbalanced look of the beast was the girl's design, the feigning hoofs, the clowning, were the stumbling, cock-eyed passages of her admission of her curse and bane. "Does she want me to say that I understand? Does she want me to say it?" the mother whispered, and there was hope in her voice, as if she believed in this instant that once the avowal was stated, then the various contrivances of redemption could be found.

Christoph turned Sigmar on his haunches, and swung him close to Neapoli, to the great, foolish, reeling stallion who had learned obedience so well that he did not question the tricks it played him now.

"Miss Roberts, be a good girl," Christoph said in his oddly perfect English. His voice and his horse were quiet as he put his hand over her hand on the reins. "Be sensible. Remember the first rule: only movements that are natural to the horse as he runs, or fights, or plays." The mask of his face was sharp and worn, like that of a child who has lived by ruse in city streets, thought Jaeger, and has eaten whatever could be filched from the refuse of the incurably rich, and, year after year, lain down to sleep on stone. "Remember there is an audience," he said hardly aloud, as the child might have said from the corner of his mouth: "Watch your step. There're cops around every corner, there're plain-clothes guys in the shadow of every door."

Their horses waited side by side, motionless, and the two riders looked into each other's faces, their eyes and mouths sad and young and more alike than other people's, but flickering now with gentle mutabilities. Christoph's hand still covered hers, and they sat as if waiting for some authority to sanction their tenderness, for Church or Law to approbate the fragrance of orange blossoms, or the length of a white satin train, or waiting merely to be granted nights without farewell. But the authorities who now stepped into the picture were neither the Church nor Law, but a lady and gentleman of gaunt, inflexible distinction who emerged from the covered stairs. They were dressed for another occasion, having clearly been routed out of sleep to make their appearance here. The lady's elderly legs were visible to the calf, and bare, and there were plaid wool bedroom slippers on her long, narrow feet. She wore a black military cloak, perhaps acquired in Italy at a time when the Axis was still solvent, and her iron hair was wrenched back from temple and brow in a chignon that any washerwoman might have resorted to. But in testimony to her aristocratic blood, a ribbed white band of grosgrain bound fast the sagging muscles of her throat, and pinhead diamonds twinkled in her ears. Her face was equine, except for the abruptly short and pretty nose. This would be the *Gräfin*, Jaeger knew; and her companion, in mustard-colored, black-velvet-collared and velvet-buttoned overcoat, would be the stiff-legged, stiff-necked *Graf*, shorn now of castle and estate, the lord in exile on his own domain, who lived on the rent of his requisitioned *Schloss* and the hiring out of his horses to those in the Occupation who sought to pass for gentlemen. (For if the *Schloss* had been turned into an Officers' Club, and no German guest was permitted to set foot beyond the ancestral doors, Jaeger knew exactly how it would be: in the entrance hall, where generations of the nobly born had laid aside *loden* capes and silver-headed canes, had unbuckled scabbards and fur-lined boots, there would be an American news-stand displaying *Time* and *Life* and *Look*, and any number of colored comic books, and a glass case exhibiting variously packeted Chiclets and chewing-gums.) The *Graf* appeared to have only a nightshirt under the shabby, three-quarter-length coat, and his polished, hairless shins were bare. But the neck, corrugated like a turkey's, rising in pride from the velvet collar, and the monocle in the right eye, were dignity enough to take the look of dishabille away. They must have been roused from sleep some time before, perhaps by the blaze of lights in the riding-rink at that late hour, or by the pounding of horses' hoofs, when all should have been darkened and stilled by night. They must have been awakened in their beds in the gardener's lodge, and stalked out past the strawberry beds and the greenhouses to see.

"Good evening," said the *Graf*, speaking a cool, disdainful English to these people he had no need or wish to know. He adjusted the glass in the socket of his eye, his ashen fingertips lingering on the black ribbon that hung from it, and Catherine Roberts and Jaeger repeated good-evening, but the *Gräfin* did not speak.

And now Jaeger felt that the situation was slipping from his grasp, and he knew that if he did not speak, the roles he and Catherine Roberts played would be reversed again, and she would no longer be a woman waiting in submission while he pounded on stable doors, and shouted out names, and shifted the wings and scenery of their stage. If he ceased to act, he would again be the Julian Sorel of the Occupation, and he wanted none of the little tutor's calculating blood slithering through his veins. For what was he before these people but merely a German, a German without the rights of lineage or culture entitling him to carry a brief-case in confirmation of his caste? He was neither lackey who groomed and trained and rode their horses for them, nor a peer who could exchange with them the acrimonious stories about the men and women who occupied their soil. He was merely a prisoner of war come home, without decorations, wearing an ersatz-wool suit, and shoes that were strangers to him still, and the knowledge of this tied him hand and foot before them, and gagged his mouth.

"The horses, the Lipizzan horses, are beautiful, beautiful," Catherine Roberts said, but no one seemed to hear her speak. And Jaeger stood with lowered eyes before the *Gräfin* and the *Graf*, and before the child called Christoph Horn, silent, because he who knew the poets of Germany, and the musicians, and the look of other countries, had failed to keep one room inhabitable in the desolate ruins of their common nationality.

As he stood there, the bloodless lips of the *Graf* seemed to shape words, as lips moved on the silent screen of a lifetime before, defining the story of what he and the others like him knew had taken place. One man, a foreigner, a housebreaker (the pinched lips affirmed, having no need of the validity of sound), one single gangster who had already served a prison term, came tramping with soiled boots over the fair earth of the Fatherland, forcing his way into the dwelling-places of the humble and the gently bred, forcing his way even into the churches, leaving a trail of filth on the sacred carpets and the hallowed graves. One man had stamped through the stately chambers of this mansion that had been Germany, through the naves of her cathedrals, screaming imprecations, execrating all that had spiritual value and cultural meaning, all that was of fine workmanship, all that he could not assess the inestimable value of, all that was beyond his experience, all that was ivory, or satin, or gold. He, a primitive from across a mountainous frontier, nurtured on envy, reared in poverty (the *Graf's* lips drew thin as a wire to say), had torn the portraits of ancestors from the walls in frenzy, for no reason that could be named except he had none to hang there in their place. He had dragged the holy images from the temples of worship, besmirching, befouling all that he touched, until, instead of the ancient Germanic forbearance and tolerance, instead of the old goodness and devotion that had, since time immemorial, lit candles at Christmastide, sent little German children singing through the streets, and brought lilies to their flowering at Easter, instead, hatred, falsehoods, and, finally, murder, became the ritual of the feast days and holidays. This murderer, this madman with a gift for oratory, had turned the ancestral halls and the churches into shrines for the anti-Christ, whose name he coupled with his own.

Yes, he murdered. He was a murderer, said Jaeger, standing silent there.

All this (said the soundlessly moving lips), all this was alien to German history. This must be considered as one chapter of the new revolution that is moving across Europe, the revolt of the ignorant and unlettered against the cultivated and wise, the revolt of the slave against the master, the assault of the homeless tramp, the vagabond, on the gentle householder as he sits at peace with his family by his hearth. It was the illiterate intruder, and those he had mesmerized into following him, who had brought war upon the country, and it was the literate, the informed men of rank, who had sought to curb him, and who went to their deaths without the medals of valor they had earned through their long service in the defense of Germany. It was the German generals, men of breeding and unflinching loyalty, whom the upstart had first blackened with his lies, and then ordered murdered in their beds, or hung on the gallows, without honor, in the name of the new doctrine of demoniacal revolt. These martyrs, said the *Graf's* tightly closed lips, went to their deaths with heads held high, stripped of their decorations, their executioners holding before their dying eyes the four-pronged symbol of hatred that was hooked even into the hearts of those who had seized power in Germany.

And what of the Jews? asked Jaeger in silence, his eyes still lowered. *What of the Jews while all this was taking place?*

There were no Jews (the *Graf*'s lips flickered on the silent screen). The Jews had been resettled. They had moved away. And now we who are left must bear ourselves as did those others who were stripped of all honor before they died. We must walk with quiet step, looking neither to right nor left, as the generals walked, not indifferent, but outwardly blind to the presence of those who, within the space of twenty-odd years, have won a second military victory over us. Is all this country's beauty, its high traditions, its carefully nurtured power, to be squandered by the money-makers on one portion of our soil, and by the Marxists on the other? The *Graf*'s eye closed for a moment like a fowl's blue-lidded eye, and the old lips shaped the final questions: *Is this our doom? Is this how we shall end?*

"Make it clear to the Americans that it is late for visitors," the *Gräfin* said in German, and she looked up with coldly armored eyes at Christoph sitting on fish-eyed Sigmar.

"The *Gräfin* says it is late for visitors," Christoph translated with gentleness to the girl.

And, at once, the riding-rink with its brilliantly lit chandeliers, its enduring copper-plates of royalty, its impermanent deposits of steaming, gold manure, was hushed for the girl to speak. And Jaeger, too, waited, having heard her voice not more than half a dozen times before.

"Yes, it is very late," she said, her tilted eyes heavy. For a moment, she stared blindly down at the *Gräfin* and the

Graf, the sight of them perhaps blurred by sleep, or drink, or love. "Why don't they go home?" she said.

And then came the whine of the police siren outside in the dark. Closer and closer it came, tentative, questioning, without haste, accompanied by the brittle uproar of snapped and broken brush as the car (a jeep, it could only have been) battered its way down the narrow bridle path. When the knocking sounded on the door, the horses remained motionless. When the American voices, young and male, rang out, the horses' ears flicked, but still they did not move. It was only when the three Military Policemen stumbled into the light that Neapoli swerved in panic, and the girl turned in the saddle and cried Christoph's name. He swung Sigmar on his haunches, and rode swiftly, casually, but with the steel of anger in his wrists and knees, across the ring, and caught Neapoli's head, and spoke to the girl and the horse in soft-tongued authority.

"We're looking for Mrs. Roberts, the Colonel's wife," said the first M.P. His cheeks were carnation pink and smooth, his eyes stark blue, and clipped yellow bristles showed under his stiff-beaked cap. He looked like a boy dressed up for this part in a school play, not at ease with the white stick they had given him to carry, not knowing whether or not to draw the revolver from the holster on his hip. "Anybody speak English here?" he said.

"We all speak English," said Catherine Roberts. "Why are you looking for me?"

"Well, orders," said the young policeman, so like a child uneasily outfitted in khaki, with a white band fixed to his sleeve, and a white stick in his raw, blond hand. "You—if you're Mrs. Roberts—and she—her," he said, the words stuttering in his mouth. "You and your daughter—if that's your daughter—we've been looking better than an hour for you. Wc got our orders to pick you up and escort you home."

"Whose orders?" Catherine Roberts said, and her lips were white. She stood there under the eyes of the *Graf* and the *Gräfin*, under the brilliant, formal lights, her color ebbing away.

"The Colonel's orders, ma'am," he said.

vi

It was
the week the currency reform took place, and, from one day
to the next, the shops that had been empty as last year's
birds' nests since the surrender were overflowing with goods
that had been hoarded in attic and cellar and warehouse for
this moment in history. At once, peasants jolted in from
the countryside around in pre-war motor cars, the women
and girls in Hessian Sunday dress, with neat white coifs and
silky aprons, and the men, the old men and the young, with
their sons exact miniatures of themselves, came dressed in
black stern enough and enduring enough to outlast endless
ceremonies of death, marriage, baptism, and countless wars.
They came on bicycle and on foot, *Omas* and *Opas*, some
hale and hearty in old age, some trembling with palsy, some
frail as autumn leaves. Plowhands, shoemakers, butchers,
and dairymen, they were, still too cautious to buy, but coming to ogle the windows of the Fahrbach stores, seeing again
the old wealth of Höhner harmonicas; gilt-stenciled accor-
dions with ivory keys; new shoes, new handbags, long fiber
stockings, rubber boots, frying-pans. They paused, stricken
dumb, but a gleam of calculation covert in their eyes, before
umbrellas with tassels of purple silk fraying on their handles,
before notebooks, both plain and ruled, and pencils, paper-
clips, thumbtacks, needles and thread that the women's
hearts had broken in half for in the long dark of the years.
They stopped dead in their heavy boots, both women and
men, on the strips of paving-stone above the cobbled gutters,
held by the sight of candles and cakes of laundry soap. No
one had seen the like of it in more than a decade.

It was like a holiday time, a time of resurrection. Jaeger's salary went up overnight, and he wanted to change the thoughts in his head as well; he wanted to take things lightly, with a wry, quick twisting of philosophy to transform the facts to his own ends, the way a Frenchman would. A new suit, another pair of shoes, might now be possible by autumn, by winter, at least by the following spring. It was as if water had been turned to wine, silver to gold, and early one morning, in the midst of this season of festivity, he took the train for Niederstadt, his heart as light as the June air. The train was one which only a defeated country would have any use for, made up of cars that had survived bombings and strafings and twenty-odd years of deterioration, coupled behind an engine that steamed at every pore. But, for him, it might have been a holiday train he was taking to glacier country; it might have been moving over mountain passes, up slopes of gentian and edelweiss, toward the world's last edge of everlasting snows. That he was on his way to the American Military Government court to cover a story was merely reality; the part of it that made him sing aloud was that he was on an excursion out of the flat country of what he had been, away from the weeping willows of his hopeless love. He walked down the corridor of the train, seeing the blur of the country through the unwashed panes, singing under his breath about "Lindy Lou," with honeysuckle yellow at her breast. He wanted a seat alone, if he could find it, and he wanted her, dark-skinned and happy, laughing hard, waiting for him in the Niederstadt station's rubble, with rhinestones glittering in her heels, and in the velvet of her ears, the Lindy Lou that Robeson's voice offered like honey to the tongue.

In one compartment he passed, there was a single traveler, and Jaeger turned back, and slid the unsteady door aside. By the long-befouled window sat a young man with black, puzzled eyebrows splashed across his brow. Only when he had slid the door in place did Jaeger see the cane between the young man's legs, and the yellow brassard, marked with a triangle of three black dots, upon his sleeve. The train had begun to move again, and Jaeger considered with some emotion that he could not name (bitterness, irritation, it may have been) that an entire division of men must have been blinded at the Russian front. God must have leaned down that winter and laid his finger on one after the other of them as they passed into the snows, saying: "This one, and this one, and this one, must give up his eyes"; not even taking the trouble to add: "What a shame for you that you've had only nineteen or twenty years to look at the mountains and fields and rivers and valleys, and so forth, not to mention the breasts of women and the faces of whatever offspring you may produce. But take comfort in the biological fact, my children, that your other senses will increase in sensitivity." For the blind were everywhere; they sat in every streetcar, in every train, in every university hall. They tapped their way to the America House of Fahrbach to listen to music, or listen to lectures, their ears sharp as traps for the sound of voices which had once read aloud to them, and might read aloud to them again. They tapped upstairs and down and along the hallways, tapping even into the projection room, for God knows what reason, where slides were being shown that they could never hope to see. Even had they not carried canes and worn the yellow armbands, and even before the scarlet, empty buttonholes of their eyesockets could be perceived, they were marked by their excessive cleanliness, their well-brushed clothing, their well-shined shoes, the hair so neatly trimmed and combed. It was as if women, all women, cherished these blind young men in the name of the children who had grown away from them, or whom they had never borne, or for the sake of the sons wiped out by war, caring for them long after they had, as men, outgrown the need, the absence of vision making them forever children for women to dress, and comb, and feed, and bathe in the warm fluid of their love.

Jaeger had eased himself into the nearest corner, scarcely breathing, for this had been designated as a holiday time, and the blind got in the way. But, however surreptitiously he had moved, still above the grating of the wheels, and the creaking of the exhausted wood, the young man in a black jacket gone too short in the sleeves, too tight in the armpits, must have heard the far sound of his beating heart, for he began to speak.

"Are you on your way to Niederstadt or getting off before?" he asked. "Are you traveling on business?" Jaeger knew the sequence of question and alerted silence, question and again alerted silence, like a wireless code tapped out to the sighted from the mine pit in which the blind were sealed. He was thirsting for talk, for sight, for life, for all things that were going on without him. Like the others, he would never be slaked, this young blind man, so immaculately shaved, so neatly dressed, sitting alert there in the misted sunlight, looking straight ahead. *Are you going to cast me the lifeline of your voice so that for two minutes and a half I may come within reach of the shore?* he might have been asking. *Are you young or old, man or woman, Social-Democrat, Communist, member of the Deutsche Partei?*

"I'm working for the *Fahrbach Presse*," Jaeger said, and now there was no help for it, and he slid down the varnished boards of the bench until he was opposite the blind man. "I'm on my way to Niederstadt to cover a story there."

"A story on the monetary reform?" the other man asked, his speech careful, precise. Whatever else his eyes had relinquished, they had kept their beauty, and they had refused to close, but stared indecently at nothing, the iris of each like a small round of black velvet, depthless, pupilless, fixed absolutely still. "Are you going to do a story about politics, or about religion? I'm interested in all these things. I'd like to know." Under the heavy, inky brows, even the eyes seemed to wait for the answer, for the weaving and knotting of the rope of words that would draw him and bind him, in the instant that he listened, closer to the world of seeing men.

"It might turn out to be political. I'm not sure about that," said Jaeger. In his hand he had the pack of American cigarettes, given him by Honerkamp two weeks before. "Would you like a Camel?" he said.

"I'm not accustomed to smoking American cigarettes," said the blind man, and Jaeger put one between his clean-nailed fingers, and waited while he lifted it to his broad, red, thirsting mouth. Then he held the flame of the match in his curved hand, and watched the blind man draw the first breath in. "Do you know any Americans?" it went on at once. "I've never had a conversation with an American. I'm a philosophy student. I'm twenty-six. My name is Heinrich Wagner. Have you ever discussed philosophy with the Americans?"

Then the questions ceased, and he waited, his eyes quite still, fixed on some point of hearing straight ahead.

"I know one or two Americans," Jaeger began, but the young man wanted to speak of the money reform, and he ran his tongue along his lip. Since the *Währungsreform*, he said, he was in a nearly desperate situation, for it had affected his life in more than a monetary way.

"It is essential that I complete my studies," he said, smoking the Camel parsimoniously. "In a sense, you are an intellectual, too, so you will understand this. Perhaps journalism and philosophy are not first cousins, but at least they are both labor of the head. But I'm in a particularly unfortunate position because I have no members of my family left to care for me. You probably have some members of your family left?" he said, making a question of it. Jaeger shook a cigarette out of the pack.

"No, none," he said.

"Good," said the blind man. He lifted the palm of his right hand that was broadened from years of closing on the cane, and the lines in it nearly effaced, and he dropped the ashes from the Camel into the cup it made. "But you still have many advantages over me. You can see to shave, and to cook your breakfast in the morning, and to clean your shoes. But me, I have no choice now but to change my way of living. I've been making my home with an old woman who prepared my meals, and took care of my clothes, and shaved me, even, and I paid her what I could. This week, the very week of the *Währungsreform*, she simply died."

"That was bad luck for you," Jaeger said; and because of the sound of reproach in the young man's voice he added: "And for her as well."

"It was the *Währungsreform* that did it, the one D-*Mark* for ten *Reichsmarks*," the blind man said. He smoked carefully, as if to make the Camel burn until the end of time. "She couldn't have managed on the money she had saved. It wouldn't have lasted her a month. So she gave up. It was a form of suicide," he said, impatient with this thing she had done so willfully, with aged, trembling intent. "She always said once the *Währungsreform* went through, old people wouldn't be able to heat their rooms, or eat more than one meal a day, so the whole generation of them would have to stay in bed. She was forever complaining about that, saying she wouldn't be serving any purpose that way. She wouldn't have been able to cook, or clean, or take in boarders, or anything, just lying there, saving her strength. Well, that's all very well for the old, I told her, but what about the young? We can't go to bed to keep warm! We can't afford to miss our classes! The university isn't going to send its professors into our bedrooms to instruct us there!" His tongue ran nervously along his lower lip that was red as the lining of an opera-glasses case, and his jaws were pocked with the eczema of these uncertainties. "And the country swarming with expellees, and East Zone refugees, eating our food, taking our rooms, taking jobs away from the kind of Germans who have first right to them! How will it end?" he cried out from the dark pit in which he lived. And then he asked the question which had perhaps been groping through his mind ever since Jaeger had come in. "What do you think of the advantages of marriage? Are you married yourself? Are we about the same age?" he asked, but he did not wait now for the answers to come. "In my present situation, I have no choice. A married man is given better living-quarters. That's obvious, of course. And then he has someone to cook for him, and if he picks out a wife of some intelligence, then she can be of use to him in his work, looking up references in my case, and keeping my papers filed. I think I will save the last half of this cigarette," he interrupted himself. He held it between his fingers carefully. "If you could tell me where to snuff it out, I have an envelope here I could keep it in."

"No, finish it, finish it," said Jaeger. "I'll give you more."

"I'm going to Niederstadt for the purpose of getting married," the blind man said with a sigh, and he put the cigarette between his lips again. "Otherwise, I would not be able to get on with my degree. I'm taking three days off, but I'm counting on making up the lost time doing extra papers over the weekend." He said he had every hope of his fiancée turning out satisfactorily. She was twenty-two, and had been brought up under hard conditions, in wartime, which was the best kind of training a woman could have. She could not cook or sew as well as an older woman, he said, but her mother was doing her best to correct these deficiencies, and, in the past month, although a day for their marriage had not then been set, her father had insisted that she shave him every day. "He works in the post office, and he has to be at his window at seven thirty in the morning," he said, "so in the past weeks he's been getting up an hour earlier so that Ursula could practice on him! It wouldn't matter too much if he went to work at the post office with a nick or two, but think what I'd look like turning up for my classes at the University with a massacred chin!" He was almost ready to laugh out loud at the figure he would cut, but there were far graver things at stake, such as the relinquishing of his privacy. He held himself fixed and rigid on his seat, as if fearing that marriage would split him in two. His palm, with the cigarette ashes in the palm of it, was extended now, and he said: "Is there some way I could get rid of these? I don't want to drop them on the floor."

Jaeger guided his hand to the half-open window, and brushed the ashes off—as wan as dawn, they looked, the handful of them in the yellow flood of sun.

"There's not much left of your cigarette," Jaeger said.

"Oh, yes, there must be a draw or two! I felt no indication of heat on my lips." And now the blind young man brought out a worn brown wallet, and his fingertips sampled the texture of the papers laid in it, and he found what he sought, and drew a photograph out. "This is the girl I am going to marry," he said. Jaeger took the photograph from his hand, seeing that even in this cheapest, most ephemeral, of likenesses, the kind that in America emerges from a slot machine in a curtained booth and in two weeks fades away, the girl's face was illuminated by the unflickering light of the promises that had been made in all the legends and fairy tales of childhood, in all the heroic novels and moving-pictures of youth, promises concerning a prince with gleaming hair and eyes a clear, Saxon blue, his flesh emblazoned with dauntless courage and tenderness and imperishable love. (Obviously, nothing had been said in the gilt-embossed book about the loss of any of his faculties, or the manner of preparing cabbage and Wurst for him, or the necessity of cleaning his shoes.) Whether the girl herself was fat or thin, dark-haired or blonde, was not revealed, for the camera had seemed to overlook the substance of what posed before it, and had recorded only the nimbus of untroubled hope. "Of course, I've never seen her. I've never laid eyes on her, as the saying goes," the young man said with an awkward laugh, but his eyes did not share in his amusement. They still waited stubbornly, perhaps fixed on the time and the place of that other uproarious joke that had blasted his sight away. "But we've been going out in the *Tiergarten* together for over a year."

(There was a lake in the Niederstadt *Tiergarten*, and rowboats moved across its surface every day and evening in the summer months, and on good Sundays in the spring. All summer, the lake was visited by iridescent dragonflies, and the silk of its waters was ripped and unraveled lazily by the rising and falling of inexpert oars. Reeds grew thick as braided hair in the shallows, and the prows of the boats nosed through platforms of water lilies, roped fast by fibrous stems to the lake floor. In one such long-unpainted boat, the blind man, Heinrich Wagner, must have drifted on Sunday afternoons, sitting upright in the stern, narrow-shouldered, pinched in the armpits by his ancient jacket, his dough-white hands holding fast to the guide-cords of the rudder; and it would have been Ursula who rowed, while he relinquished his destiny and his direction for that brief hour, but no longer, for which he had paid his nine *Reichsmarks* out. But he had actually relinquished nothing. Even drawing the guide-cords to right or left, as she directed, he held fast to the vanity of what he was. He could not see, as testified to by the yellow brassard on his arm, but what color was the insignia required to indicate that he was hard of hearing as well? Had he but given ear to it, he would have heard the silvery music of the water against the rowboat's weathered wood, and the minute collision with floating flowers and anchored vines, and heard, louder and more compelling than the thoughts in his head, the voices of other men clanging out like bells across the lake; if he would but listen, but he could not. If for two minutes he had lost sight of his past, and his present, and his future, and listened to the life stories of those who drifted in the other boats, the puzzled look would have been undone from his thick, black brows, and the eczema been sponged from his face. But, instead, he sat tense, narrow and rigid as a lath, his moist, red lips sealed fast at the entrance of the collapsed mine shaft of his life, fearing even the pliability of the reeds that bowed and flowed beneath the boat. And Ursula must have rowed docilely among the artificially constructed islands, speaking of the things about them that even sight would not have enabled him to see.

"There are a great many Americans on the lake this afternoon, a great many soldiers," she may have said to him, but it could very well have been he was counting the seconds of the minutes of the hour for which he had paid his money out, and deducting the total from the sum of Ursula's dowry, so that he could not hear so much as the whirring armor of the dragonflies. "There are German girls with some of them," Ursula may have said to him as she rowed, but he so feared the other voices clanging like metal in the sun that he would not have heard if someone had shouted out that a boat is a place for the young to lie down in and taste each other's mouths. Ursula may have added that many of them were Negroes, as their high, sweet laughter called across the water, but whatever was said, the blind man could not hear.

One afternoon, there may have been more Negro G.I.s than usual out on Sunday passes, some with *Fräuleins* in the boats with them, and some without, their khaki clinging damp to their thighs as they rowed. But whether or not there were women with them, their flesh was alive with the need of them, leaping with it, the violent satisfaction of what women gave running hot as lava from afternoon into dusk and on into the night. The tide of their alien love and lust must have come close to touching Heinrich Wagner as he sat like a small, bleak piece of granite in the rowboat, pulling the guide-cords to one side or the other, as Ursula bade him do. A piece of Artic ice hacked off by the heat or the elements and set adrift bears with it a glacial aura, and in like manner Heinrich Wagner, blind as a bat and deaf as a post, must have embalmed the surrounding air with his frigidity. His grim refusal to see or hear bore them unscathed through the waves of laughter, and through the music that echoed across the green cavern of the lake. "Oh, sugar, sugar, I love you dearly, I do take pride in you!" came the voices; and: "Oh, baby, baby, I love you, love you, love you, more and more each day I live!"; while the buoys on some deeper sea moaned in tender anguish: "Oh, God, I do love you, Helga, Gretchen, Katerina, Klara, Ingrid! I loves you, loves you, loves you, with all my heart!"

"There seem to be people talking somewhere around us," Heinrich Wagner may have said then to Ursula, a young woman with full breasts and a skin without blemish, who rowed docilely, with bowed head. The blind man had grown uneasy because of the smell of love on the air, and because of the myriad melodious voices of savages turned restless in their jungles who now swarmed across his Lutheran world of German continence. For it was the voice of Africa that now called to the blood in the *Tiergarten,* and the dark people of another continent who stretched, rutting, on the grass. What good would his cane have done him in the *Bled* of Africa, tapping, tapping, in panic past steaming beasts coupled in shameless embrace, through vegetation so pulsing, so living, that it reached out in hot possession to bind to it orchid and spreading passion-flower and rigid yucca stalk? And Ursula, smooth-throated, sweet-lipped, hearing the music that he would not hear, may have slid forward on the cross-board of the rowing-seat, and advanced one pure white, submissive leg so that her foot would just touch his. But if the blood stirred with unbearable anguish in her belly and loins, Heinrich Wagner would never have known. He sat in the stern, frozen with fear as the Dark Continent closed in on them, the spears of the warriors raised on high, the bare feet padding, drums beating, beating, beating, the rhythm of fornication unceasing, unbroken, accelerating in pace as German girls, good German girls, opened their white legs in the dusk, in the evening, to the Negroes in khaki, to pollution, to eternal shame. "Let's get out of the sound of other people's voices," the blind man may have said to Ursula. "I'd like to tell you about the subjects I'll be taking in September at the University.")

"The family has four daughters at home," Heinrich Wagner was telling Jaeger, "the other three older than Ursula, but they haven't any prospects yet. A small income goes with each of them, the largest to the first one to be married, so that's Ursula. I'm lucky to get the first one," he said, and he fitted the photograph back into his wallet again. "Besides taking care of the daily household chores, a wife helps you dress, and keeps you looking presentable. If you're writing your thesis, the way I am, she can take dictation, and that saves paying a stenographer. And then you always have someone on hand to read your reference books to you, without having to depend on friends (who can't always be depended on), or on strangers you run into in the library, who are frequently ill-bred. There's one thing I'd like to speak to the Americans about," he said. "The America House in Fahrbach ought to be better equipped than it is. A student has to go as far as Munich to get any books in Braille. Not many students can afford the trip, or the time taken from their studies, but the Americans don't consider things like that. There are a number of things the Americans could be enlightened about if they ever listened to advice." The train was traveling slowly through sunny, fertile country, and now it ground to a stop at what may have been a wayside station, although no platform, and no name of hamlet or village could be seen. "So just overnight, when the *Währungsreform* went through and the old lady died, I made up my mind and set the date." The blind man's eyebrows knitted together in the eczema-pocked area above his nose. "The only trouble is that Ursula wants to take a honeymoon, and I can't spare the time from my studies for it. She wants to make an excursion to Flegendorf to see the oil well burning there. That will cost me an extra day."

And now straight in from the open fields came a strapping young man in a wide-brimmed black felt hat, in thick black corduroys, who pushed back the sliding door and shouldered his way into the compartment where they sat. He was strong as an ox, and ruddy of face, and he carried a heavy, polished stick of spiraled wood, and a red bandana with its four ends in a knot. He said good-day in a somber bass, like the voice of a cello throbbing, and he laid his stick, and the tidy bundle of the bandana, on the rack above his head. Then he took a seat on the corridor side of the train. There he sat with his big raw hands hanging between his knees, like a prosperous farmer on his way to a country fair, thought Jaeger; except that a farmer would never have let his hair grow long before his ears, like an actor's hair, nor worn the bright loop of a gold earring in the ruddy lobe of one ear.

"Good day," said the blind young man to the sound of another voice in the compartment with them. "Are you traveling to the city? Are you going to Niederstadt on business?" he asked.

And now the cigarette was nearly done, and Jaeger leaned forward and took it from him.

"Here's another for you," he said.

"I've got an upper story to do in Niederstadt," said the man in black corduroy. From his outfit, it could be seen that he was a wandering carpenter, a *Hamburger Zimmermann*, the first one Jaeger had seen since before the war. A clean, white, collarless shirt was buttoned around his sunburned neck, and, just under the Adam's apple, a black silk tie was fixed to the shirt by a gold pin. The long narrow tails of the tie were buttoned away inside his double-breasted, white-piped corduroy. "I got word the masons are almost done with their work," the carpenter said in his deep bassoon. "I'll get the scaffolding up right away, and then the roof beams, and, after the roofing, there'll be the flooring to do throughout the house." When Jaeger held the pack of cigarettes out to him, the young man slid toward him down the bench, and his blunt, flushed fingers fumbled a Camel out. The earring shook in his left ear as he nodded, and, holding the match for him in the sun, Jaeger saw that the tiepin bore a miniature gold compass in the triangle of its head,

145

and two perfectly wrought hammers, and an infinitesimally toothed gold saw. "I've never been to Niederstadt," the carpenter said, pulling a great draught of the Camel into the barrel of his chest; "but they tell me I'm in luck to be going there. There're blocks and blocks of damage. That's what they say." His flesh looked as solid as timber that nails might be driven into and still it would not splinter or split, and there he sat with his legs spread, too big for the compartment, his outsized health almost an affront, his pleasure in the cigarette and the work ahead a rebuke to those who complained of the grief of war. "The house was hit in 1944, a mansion, they tell me it is, almost a palace," he said. "That's what my comrades in the *Bruderschaft* say. Next week the *Maurer* will get to the masonry of the private lake, and start rebuilding the swannery. It sits in a private park, so I'll be getting a lot of sun while I do the job," he said.

"So that's the kind of work you do," said the blind man. He had seemed to recoil within himself from the sound of saw in wood, of trowel on stone. "As for me, I'm a student of philosophy."

"I'm a *Zimmermann*," the carpenter boomed out. "I'm doing the years of my *Wanderschaft*. I have eighteen months behind me, and eighteen months to go!"

"A colleague of mine, a political-science major, told me yesterday that men who work with their hands instead of their heads have nothing to worry about in the future," the blind man said.

"Well, I bided my time," said the carpenter, and he laughed out loud. "I waited to take this job in Niederstadt until the currency reform went through!"

The *Währungsreform*, the *Währungsreform*, went the recurring motif of it, stated either in celebration or lament,

146

as the poem of the Lorelei might be sung, or any true German refrain. It was coins jingling in the pocket again, the *Währungsreform*, or else it was pockets turned inside out so that only the holes in them showed. It was hornpipe or requiem, cancan or dirge, depending on the zest of the musician, or his liver, and the key in which the air was played. And Jaeger was uncertain now what to do with the holiday spirit of the morning, and the careless whistling through his teeth about love.

"How long will you work in Niederstadt?" he asked the carpenter.

"Not more than six months. That's the time we're allowed to stay in one place," said the carpenter. "After six months, we're bound in honor to move on."

The blind man was suddenly flayed anew by the hunger for name and dogma and destination, for the explicitly stated direction that one man might be taking who could see with his own eyes the choice of ways to go. *Stop time, stop the recovery of the country!* he might have been crying out. *Stop the money changing in the bank vaults! It is all going on without me! It is leaving me behind! Ohne mich, ohne mich!* he might have been whispering to the rhythm of the wheels that bore them on.

"Have the *Zimmerleute* any religious creed?" he asked, and his hands moved nervously. "Have they a political party to which they adhere?"

"Nay, nay!" the carpenter's voice thundered out. "We're like no other men in Germany! We're outside of politics. We've always been. The rules were laid down for us in the seventeenth century, and we bide by them still. We're bound in honor to dress as we dress," he said. The light stubble on his chin and jaws was turned bright golden by the sun. "This necktie of mine, it's called *Ehrbarkeit*. It

147

can't be bought. Each one of us earns it through apprenticeship. It's a symbol of our honor," he said, and his fingers touched it as if it was a relic of the Holy Grail.

"How do you *Zimmerleute* look on the institution of marriage?" the blind man asked. He sat looking straight ahead.

"Ah, we're bound not to marry, too!" said the carpenter in his strong, happy voice. "For the three years of the *Wanderschaft*, we may none of us take a wife!" He was not unlike a knight, with the armor laid aside, thought Jaeger, archaic as any figure held over from the middle ages, guild member in a year when guilds must learn to die. *Where are you going, wandering carpenter?* he might be asked, and the answer would lead back through the centuries, ever further and further back through history. "We still use words that our grandfathers and great-grandfathers used, and that other Germans don't know the meaning of," the carpenter said, pride warm and simple in his face. "We're like flying birds! We wing from one place to another. You can see the birds printed there on my neckerchief." He raised one hand, with the Camel between the fingers of it, toward the rack. "They're the emblem of our *Wanderschaft*."

"I am unable to see your tie or your neckerchief," the blind man said. His brows went even blacker across his face. "But what kind of religion have you? As a man, a *Zimmermann*, what is your relationship to God?"

"We are not required to speak to others of our belief," said the carpenter, confounded a moment. "We're free men, footloose and free." If his voice had seemed uncertain in the instant that he evaded God, now it boomed out richly, deeply, again. "We carry everything we own in our neckerchiefs. What we are is stamped in pictures on it, clear enough for everyone to understand." He stood up, giant-sized, awkward-limbed, and reached the bandana down from the rack, and he turned it, knotted full with his belongings, before Jaeger and the blindman in the sun. A procession of men in flaring corduroy trousers, in broadbrimmed felt hats, or in stovepipe hats, marched single file across the red and white cotton stuff of it, across the map of Europe, and Asia, and Africa, as well. They were mighty men, bearing gnarled sticks in their right hands, and T-squares and knotted neckerchiefs under their arms, and some had the small loop of a single earring in one ear. "We've traveled as far north as the Pole, and as far as Africa to the south!" the carpenter told them in eagerness, wanting even the blind to be enabled to see the procession of men who moved, identically equipped, forever freed of the burden of disparate identity.

Jaeger wished to speak then, perhaps merely to say that he, too, was wounded, defeated man, and that he had taken America as bastille, and a package of Camels as amulet. But he did not speak, for now the train had slowed almost to a halt, and high, tangled banks of rusted rails could be seen outside the window, twisted, and broken, and cast aside, it seemed, by idiot children's frenzied hands. As if undetonated bombs lay buried still between the ties, or the area ahead was mined, the engine felt its way cautiously down the complexities of temporary track, switching to right and left, grinding over makeshift trestles (intact, and newly painted, and manufactured in the U.S.A.), over excavations of ash and slag, the wheels grinding out their protest as they turned. High on the sepulchral mounds of track lay the bodies of locomotives, cremated where they fell, and railway carriages with their roofs wrenched viciously away, the blisters from long-cooled fires unbroken on their metal flanks, their windows gaping, as they had gaped for three years now, on the chaos of cloth and bone, wire and leather,

149

man and inanimate matter, lying compounded, inextricable, within. All that had had specific meaning once, now lay meaningless around them; all that had once had function and destination was twisted into so grotesque a shape that even the intention of man seemed driveling lunacy. As the train entered the dark shadow of the station, Jaeger called it in silence the city of three shattered domes: that of the railway station, and of the opera house, and the cathedral that stood bleak against the sky.

"It is difficult to put much faith in the international summer seminar the Americans have organized at the University," the blind student said, his face puzzled under the stubborn black brows. "The *Rektor*, he has the highest hopes of what it will do for peace, world peace. But we had international seminars under Hitler, too, and even with American and English students here every year, summer after summer, it didn't swing those countries to our side when the war came."

On his way to the Military Government building, Jaeger began his letter to Catherine Roberts. He wrote it senselessly, almost without reflection, in haste, the words racing back and forth across the broken faces of the houses, and up and down staircases that led to nothing, suspended in mid-air by ropes of ivy and ladders of honeysuckle vine. He scribbled it across the scarred enamel of two or three bathtubs that hung by their pipes from upper stories, sentence following sentence (in English) over the split panels of closet doors that war had blasted into public view.

"Dear Mrs. Roberts," he began it in the soft beauty of the day, with a semblance of respect and reason in the opening lines. "Since the monetary reform some sort of national emancipation has taken place which has affected me as well as the economic system, and I am suddenly on fire with hope, impatience, and satiable desires. Something has changed overnight in the air as well as on paper and behind the barred doors and windows of banks; something has at last come to a definite end in this country which means that something else is just about to start taking place. I tell you, I have never felt so strongly in my life that a burden has been taken from me and that I have reached the end of carrying around for the rest of my life the weight of conformity my father decided to leave me as heritage out of his bag of sad official tricks. I see myself throwing everything to the winds, everything, as if they were yesterday's banknotes, preconceived notions, prejudice, obligations (monetary or any other kind). My concerns, dearest, beloved, perfumed Catherine Roberts," he wrote faster and faster across the rubble of brick and rusted girders and marble fragments, as old as Carthage in their ruin, that had been the *Landeskreditanstalt* once, "have all been devaluated, and because I no longer feel any responsibilities to any tomorrows, I want with all my furiously burning flesh to sleep a sweet, illicit sleep with you whenever I can manage it and however often it can be done. Not for a moment am I going to permit the halt or the blind or the old who have elected to stay in bed for the rest of their lives because they don't happen to like the size their pensions have shrunk to—oh, not for a moment am I going to allow them to impose their burdens on me! I have had enough of being humble and poor and—what? patronized? Is that what I have been accepting from you? Some men were made for solemn occasions, were cut out for ponderous decisions and grave reflections that followed on the ponderous decisions they had taken (or put it the other way around), and I know, since a clear wind has begun to blow around me, that I was not. Which explains why functioning as a prisoner of war suited me better than anything I'd ever done, amputating as it did the free will and relieving me of the necessity of taking a stand. Once the question came up in Colorado as to American soldiers saluting the German officers who were impounded with us, and this called for a profound searching of national (but not personal, individual) pride, for the decision reached must be based on international law and the Geneva Conventions instead of the taste of honeysuckle, and I had no base from which to spring erect and had therefore nothing to say on the subject, largely because I was accorded, or enjoyed (the word must be polite), PX privileges like any G.I., and was issued clothes and shoes. (Shoes! Do you hear that, feet?) I was as good as any member of the United States Armed Forces, if not better, and had two pairs of general-issue shoes, fatigue and dress, and if I was guilty of anything it was of not bursting into insane laughter over the timeless issue with which we were faced. Only since the monetary reform do I know that I should have split my sides over the business of a man, any man, clapping his heels together and raising his hand to his temple in acknowledgment of the presence of a man who wears a more expensive uniform than his. To raise the hand to the temple in order to put an end to things would be a saner act. Once or twice, let it be put down to my credit, I gave an uneasy smile at the sight of the crew members of a captured German submarine doing setting-up exercises, shouldering arms, submerging and emerging, in the Colorado air (thirty or forty below and three miles above sea level) with German submarine officers barking the nautical orders out. But I had not yet begun to laugh." Crossing the avenue along which chestnut trees, bomb-crippled but living still, raised the stumps of their arms to the sky, he wrote: "Catherine, Catherine, Catherine," on the wide stone steps that led to the handsomely bronze-studded door of the Military Government offices, and drew a heart around each name, and across the unscarred granite face of the building itself he continued writing: "I can probe none of the shallows or depths of your relation to husband, daughter, or foreigner, Catherine, my beloved, for all my responsibilities to other men have been devaluated ten to one, or one to ten, and become discredited currency. I have now inherited a fortune, and the new coins of it are the words I will murmur into your ears as we lie together at night in some rented room, some hotel bed, and the words that you will give me in exchange in hot, separate instants of passion, against my mouth—"

But he did not reach the end, for just inside the marble-paved entrance hall, by the imported water-cooler, a man stood, and he knew he must quiet the tumult in his blood. His features were not discernible in the first moment of indoor obscurity, but as Jaeger moved across the hall, the heavy head, the hands jerking at the cuffs, recalled a troubled incident somewhere when questions were asked and not quite answered in a room, perhaps a kitchen, that was uneasy because Catherine Roberts was not there.

"I didn't know you covered this territory, too," the silhouette said, and Jaeger knew the voice, and the convex brace of teeth. It was Overstreet, wearing a pepper-and-salt suit, chosen perhaps, it occurred to Jaeger, for the homespun look of it, at the American Clothing Store at Round-Up Circle (which the Germans persisted in calling *Bismarckplatz* still). Jaeger said he had come to cover the hearing that was just about to begin, and he would have moved on up the stairs then, but Overstreet chuckled behind his teeth. "Oh, the Irishman from Milwaukee!" he said. He went on saying in a lowered voice: "I can give you some inside angles on it that might interest you. Come into my office for a minute and I'll sketch the background in."

The door closed behind them, and Overstreet pointed

with one short forefinger to a chair, and he himself sat down on the other side of the bare desk. Canvas awnings of faded green were lowered at the two windows, and the room was cool, almost dark, with two yellow slats of outside light lying on the window sills. Jaeger took what was left of the pack of Camels from his pocket. As he lit one, Overstreet pulled open a desk drawer.

"That the brand you prefer?" he said, not actually smiling, perhaps, but the upper lip drawn back so long a time from habit that there was difficulty now in bringing it down over the glistening gum. "I've got quite a selection here," he said. He proved it by pushing five different packs across the flat top of the desk. But Jaeger did not seem to see them. He looked at the watch on his wrist, and laid the match on the edge of the ash tray. And now Overstreet leaned his elbows on the arms of his chair, and placed his small, freckled hands together, the short fingers making a scaffolding, a church spire, which he balanced against the square of teeth and gum. He began saying there was an even better story to cover than the one that was being staged upstairs, and that was the story of the oil well that had caught fire two weeks ago down near Flegendorf. He said it was burning still, and that people were driving from as far away as Munich to have a look at it, and sightseers' cars were parked for miles around. *His eyes are like that fox's eyes*, Jaeger thought suddenly; *like the fox I saw that evening from the Hochsitz, after the kill.* No white had shown in the fox's eye, but over the barricade of fingers laid tip to tip, there was in the man's eyes a rim of white, convex like the teeth, and in them, as in the fox's, the black and yellow iris was curved like the narrow body of a wasp, stabbing and stabbing its venom into the blood. "It's a story with a lot of drama and human interest in it, a local story, but one that could be blown up as big as the currency reform, if a good journalist got hold of it," Overstreet said.

"Well, we have a man down there covering it," said Jaeger. "We've been running a column on it every day. We've compared it to the Hindenburg disaster, and to the Transylvania gas-well fire in 1934, when subterranean gases burned five years or more. Our man has done quite a piece of research on it. He's gone into descriptions of how the peasants in that part of Transylvania had no need to stop their plowing when the sun went down, because it stayed light for five years, night and day. And it stayed warm, so the vegetation changed, and the migration of birds, and the lamps in that area were put in the attic, because the fire lit up the countryside. Couples used to go there on their honeymoons, the way they go to Niagara Falls back in the States." Jaeger stood up now. "I'll have to be getting up to the courtroom," he said. "If you look at today's edition of the *Fahrbach Presse*, you'll see a cut that our man dug up somewhere of Transylvania children playing in the fields, with the information that the photograph was taken at eleven o'clock at night, and that the fields were growing with rose-pink grass." He moved toward the door, aware of his height, and the bigness of his bones. "But thanks for the suggestion just the same," he said.

"I tell you what. I'll drive you down to Flegendorf," Overstreet said, and he, too, got to his feet. "It's a sight nobody should miss. It won't take any time at all. We can make it in an hour, there and back." With one small, nimble hand, he indicated the five packs of cigarettes lying on the desk. "If you had a brief-case with you, I could let you take a carton," he said, but Jaeger was already at the door.

"I'll have to get on with that story upstairs," he said.

"But that's just it: there isn't any story," said Overstreet.

He stood beside Jaeger now, the pepper-and-salt of the suit of a piece with the pepper-and-salt of his close-cropped hair, so that it was like the coat of an animal fitted neatly over his bones. "I tell you, it's the case history of a nut. That's all it is," he said, with his marmot grin. "If Legal Division sees fit to let the German press in on it, then Intelligence has to get busy. I've already had to turn three local reporters away. The Germans don't need to know about that kid from Milwaukee. He's some kind of a social misfit, a religious fanatic. He's something the German press should leave alone."

Now they were in the entrance hall again, moving side by side, the marble pavings under their soles. Before them, in a shaft of light from the glass dome overhead, was the white fan of the stairs, and high, in the four corners of the hall, were clusters of American flags, parade flags, with their gilded staffs crossed like spears, and their giddy stripes hanging in incongruously grave folds.

"This is an assignment. My paper sent me down," Jaeger said. His will had turned hard as metal in him. *So I'm afraid of these men of the Occupation*, he thought. *That's what's the matter with me. I'm afraid of these Americans whom victory has made too much like other men. They're not the ones I knew during the war. For half a carton of cigarettes, I'm expected to do exactly what is asked, and I might have done it, a month ago I might have done it, calling it by a better name, not wanting to face that defeat makes cowards and lackeys of us, or can.* "The Germans are going to read the story anyway in *The Stars and Stripes*," he said, and he started up the stairs.

"*The Stars and Stripes* isn't read by every German in Hesse," Overstreet said. He mounted as Jaeger mounted, not touching his arm, but holding him, step by step, by the persistance of his voice, his smile, not letting him get away.

"Let me tell you this." In the unabashed light the freckles stood on his forehead like sweat. "That business going on up there is typical of nothing at all, representing no race or class in America, no state in the union, either North or South. The kid ought to be in the loony bin. But Legal Division isn't Intelligence. They wouldn't know."

Into the conflict of this bounded Honerkamp, leaving behind him the shadows of the upper hall, jumping, running, fleeing down, as if the pack were at his heels. His eyes were fixed on something else, perhaps on the thoughts in turmoil in his head, and so for a moment he did not see them, and then he stopped short a step above them, his breath coming fast.

"Hi, Jaeger, hi, Overstreet!" he cried out, gay as a cricket, or so it seemed, in his unpressed flannels, his unshined shoes, his tan jacket flapping wide. But the mask of worry could be seen, fixed fierce and small on the plump young face, blighting the look of earnestness with adult chagrin. "How did you get down from Fahrbach, Jaeger?" he asked, and Jaeger told him he had come by train. "Damn it, you could have driven down with me!" He snapped his thumb and finger in annoyance. "I had Mrs. Roberts and Millicent as passengers. My driver's taken them down to Flegendorf to see the oil well that caught fire."

"That's a first-rate story," Overstreet said.

He divided the sight of his brace of teeth between the two of them, his eyes, squeezed partially closed as if with laughter, taking in Honerkamp, then Jaeger, then Honerkamp again.

"What about riding back with us?" Honerkamp said. "Can you be at the Press Club at four thirty? Just go in and wait at the bar."

"Well, the weather seems to be very nice, so I'll wait outside the Press Club," Jaeger said. He felt the blood rising under his ears, spreading across his Adam's apple, moving up over his jaws. "I'll wait on the steps," he said.

"Damn it, yes. I'm forgetting regulations again. Yes. Outside, then," Honerkamp said. He stood silent a moment, his eyes bleak, his fingers scratching uncertainly at his hair. "Look, Overstreet," he said, "I'm in the process of evading something, and I don't like the feel of it. That's why I'm running. I've been trying for a week to persuade them to let me talk to that boy from Milwaukee, but it seems I've got the wrong credentials. It doesn't do any good to be a human being. You have to be an M.P. before they'll let you in the same room with him." He gave a short, dry laugh. "I'm staying out of that courtroom now because I don't want to sit and listen without protest to what he's going to say."

"I'm glad you're with me on that, Seth," Overstreet said. "I've been telling Herr Jaeger here that there's no reason why the press—"

"Good God, no, the press has got to go in!" Honerkamp said. "The press is something else. It belongs to the public domain. I'm just an intruder from Information Services wanting to give some advice to a kid before he stands up there in the courtroom and throws whatever he is away."

"They'll give him twenty, thirty, years. He's got it coming to him," Overstreet said, the long teeth longer, almost diabolical now.

"Except there wasn't any crime," said Honerkamp. "He was shipped over too young, too soon, at the wrong time of year. The winter of 1946 wasn't pretty over here. There were skeletons, Overstreet, and there was hunger walking around, and the sound of the dying made a rattling noise in the cold. It wasn't like Milwaukee. It wasn't like anything he'd ever seen."

"When they talk about getting a lawyer for him," Overstreet said, "he shuts up like a clam."

"Something went wrong in the set-up at home." Honerkamp stood on the step above them, talking fast. "His mother remarried, and so he felt kicked in the seat of the pants by maternal love. He got over here, and he didn't want to go home again, because Germany did not hesitate to take him to her womanly breast. Germany needed him badly that year, as badly as he needed Germany, and so did the German family he got mixed up with in Niederstadt. No girl involved. Nothing like that," Honerkamp said to Jaeger now. "He wanted a home, a mama, a country he could rock in his arms."

Overstreet pulled at his shirt cuffs with his little sawed-off hands. He said:

"What kind of a picture would that give of American home life smeared all over the front page?"

"That isn't why he should be kept from saying what he's going to say," Honerkamp said, the mask gone tight and desperate now. "He's going to get up and say he wants to throw over his nationality, that he wants to become a German citizen." As he turned to look up at the courtroom door, his face seemed leavened to absurd and unexpected nobility. "The German mother and father he wanted—and had—and the three German teen-age kids he could bring his PX candy to, that was all right. And that he kept stealing all winter from the supply depot for them, stealing coal, and firewood, and flour, and coffee, and sugar, and anything else they needed—blankets even—that was all right too. And when the army caught up with him, they had no choice, they shipped him home. But by that time—that was 1947, last year—or maybe from the first day he put foot on German soil, this was his home, these were his people," Honerkamp said, "and he wasn't going to stay away."

159

"He stowed away three times," Overstreet said, and now it had become like a duel between them. His teeth bit down on his lip in sudden gravity. "Intelligence picked him up at Hamburg every time, except the last. On the fourth try, he got through."

"That must have been when you were on vacation," Honerkamp said, and he gave the short, queer laugh again, but Overstreet paid no heed.

"He got in without a passport," Overstreet said. "He's charged with illegal entry into Germany."

"And now he will get up and say under oath that he wants to renounce his citizenship, having already said it in the privacy of the stockade. And what will that do to the rest of his life?" Honerkamp said. "I tell you, it's going to echo inside him and outside him until kingdom come. There it'll be, between him and himself, between him and every man—or woman, either—who comes his way, and no sense to it. He's not a political refugee. Jaeger," he said. He shook himself as if shaking himself awake. "You'd better get into the courtroom quick and hear it all. You can write about it. I can think about it. There's nothing else we can do."

"Yes," said Jaeger in a low voice. "There's one thing. I could always exchange identities with him. I could try doing that."

"Don't speak of it lightly," Honerkamp said. "It's perhaps the closest thing to death there is. Don't you feel how close it comes?" he asked, and he touched Jaeger's shoulder gently, as a woman might, his face bemused, as Jaeger went past him up the stairs.

But the opportunity to exchange identities was never offered, for the courtroom doors of Military Government were not to be opened to latecomers once the hearing got under way. Nor was the story of the boy from Milwaukee to make the front pages of the local press, for, in the middle of the afternoon, a thing occurred which editors, despite tall stories that had appeared from time to time, maintained had no precedent in history. Photographs of those who played the leading roles in it, and factual accounts of the sequence of its incidents, replete with stories by half-hysterical eyewitnesses, packed column after newspaper column the next day. It was something that those who were passing in the street at the moment it happened would never be able to forget. It would be there like a shadow, as the knowledge that one must die casts a shadow upon the brilliant clarity of daily life, lighter or darker in intensity according to the day, the season, but fixed, immutable, forever, in some halted time and designated place. Jaeger was one of those who was passing at the instant the first dust rose.

He was on his way to the Press Club, taking it leisurely, with an hour to spare, thinking that from the paper's point of view he had come a long way for nothing at all. *You could always have gone to the Gerichtshof and talked to the District Attorney about what local Nazi trials are coming up*, he said to himself, walking past the lawns, the honeycombed glass, the stark functionalism of the O. H. Spaltenindustrie (the fortress of industry that no bomb had ever grazed, although, for blocks around, parks, dwelling-places, mansions, lay in ruins still), seeing the two hundred or more windowpanes ablaze with the reflection of the summer sun, so that this building that had been unscathed by war seemed now to be blazing from within. *Schumacher would have been pleased at the evidence of your initiative*, he thought, and he considered a feature story on the agenda of the city's conscience, German judging German in a local court of law. Instead, he had gone to the public gardens and wandered through the fragrant aisles of the orchid house, merely, he told himself, to dream in the heat, as poets dream, but, once there, he had found in the flowers the shape and texture of Catherine Roberts' face. Even her coloring could be seen in a blue-veined white orchid, its scroll as clear and lovely as a bugle call, that reached out of the jungle swelter of bracken and maidenhair. Two snickering G.I.s had stopped before this separate flower, one eating boxed crackerjack and the other hitting at the suspended, flowering roots, gnarled like sinews, until they swung crazily above their heads. When the soldiers had moved on around a bend of crisp, green orchid slippers banked in moss, Jaeger halted before this single-veined flower. The hanging, exotically leafed roots were nearly motionless again, the steam of the tropics rose from the beds, and moisture was beaded on the glass panes of the roof, the walls. "Catherine, sweet love," Jaeger whispered to the flower, and then he saw the piece of sugared popcorn that the G.I. had dropped into the orchid's open throat.

In the street now, he passed the sloping lawns of the O. H. Spaltenindustrie, the green slopes broken by formal flower beds in circles, triangles, squares (the pattern set like a child's beaded game, the texture of petal and leaf as tawdry as plastic). The short, combed grass was watered by sprays that twisted and wove like long-armed spiders, and cast bright rainbows right and left in the sun. Here was the established hub of the Occupation's life, here in this building, Jaeger knew, with American flags fixed at every turn and wing of it, and one great banner hanging high on the flag-staff that soared from a base cemented in the earth. Here the wheel of the Occupation turned as the brass sprays turned, as the glass doors turned to let those in uniform and others in civilian dress, pass in and out. A constantly revolving flow of cars moved, gleaming, up the curved drive-way, stopped briefly at the entrance, and wheeled on, completing the sphere. And Jaeger felt his own life turning and returning to the knowledge that, in one hour, less now, he would be with her, breathing the same air into his lungs that she had held in hers, listening, listening, the spell cast like a silken veil upon him as she spoke. *Whoever is sitting in the third-class carriages as the train pulls out has nothing to do with me*, he thought, *for I shall not be with them. I shall be riding with Milly, with Honerkamp, with Catherine, my love, telling them that my responsibilities to my fellow man have been devaluated, and that my solemnity has withered forever on the stalk.* He liked the sound of it, Gallic, debonair, as spirited as Rabelais, who would, had he been High Commissioner, have had engraved over the portals of the O.H. Spalten building: "Here enter not attorneys, barristers, nor bridle-champing law-practitioners; clerks, commissaries, scribes, nor pharisees, willful disturbers of the people's ease"; aware in abrupt impatience that he did not know Rabelais in French, that he did not, with any degree of certainty, know French, and that it was to be learned, it must be learned (perhaps in classes at the America House), if he was to be the wit, the poet, the multiple-tongued man. *If only for two hours on the Autobahn, I shall be rid of Germany again*, he said to himself as he walked straight toward the sun. And then he saw what had happened to the power shovel on the other side of the street.

It had been digging in the rubble, as on every other day of its life, lifting debris in its hinged jaws, chains jerking, neck rigid, pouring the calsified vomit of blasted architecture and crumpled plumbing into open trucks drawn up at the curb; until the foundations under its treads had caved in, and down had gone the heavy forefront, gone deeply into the cellar without a cry, and the heavy, rattling jaws were still. The reddish dust of pulverized brick and tile was just settling as Jaeger crossed the street, and he could see the face of a man at the window of the shovel's cab. Both doors were wedged fast in the chaotic sea of twisted girders and blasted masonry, and here was the strangely perishable face behind the glass. In another minute, the whole contraption might go under, as a ditched airplane is given its moment of respite before the sea sucks it finally to its heart. Even the weight of a footstep, the vibration of a voice, thought Jaeger, might send the whole thing down. But still he made his way over the choppy waves of tossed cement, and when he was near to the cab, he knelt in the precarious rubble, and shaped the words in a whisper in the direction of the pane.

"Try to get it open. So that you'll have air. I don't want to risk breaking the glass."

The shovel, with its reaching, retching neck, was balanced over a chasm far deeper than any cellar. To Jaeger, it seemed that the bowels of the earth had opened, and now the damp, fetid smell of the rankness of the earth rose from the entrails and rot that steamed in the dark below. From the street behind him, the voices of men called out, truck-drivers, their trucks loaded with the refuse of houses that men had built and men had destroyed, excavators, passers-by, calling to Jaeger to return, to crawl back, his life intact, across the treacherously slipping mass. But he had lit a Camel for the man trapped in the cab, and he reached over the moraine of broken fortifications to pass it to him through the inch that was open now above the cautiously lowered glass. He knelt on the raging, static surface of this tossed sea, whispering across the little distance between life and death some hastily conceived fable about the economic advantages of the monetary reform, telling with such eloquence of the miracle that had taken place in the counting-houses of Germany that the whole story seemed credible to him now. The wondrous reform of money, the freshly minted *Währungsreform*, he kept saying, the syllables like notes plucked on the strings of a harp. He talked of vacations that might now be taken, trips to the Taunus hills, to the Black Forest, men, and their wives and their children with them, the words whispered in promise to the face behind the pane, offered as reward to the working-class of Germany if one man would agree to expand his lungs and take in the air of June while it was still available, and hold on to it even if the craft went down. It might be that the prosperity of the country depended on one frightened man's determination to survive.

And then the crowd parted to let the police pass. After them came the wailing ambulance, and a fire truck clanged to a halt. The wrecking-crane came late, feeling its way along the curb, across the sidewalk, like a primordial beast, its grappling-hook swinging right and left. It established its position on the mounds of chaos, and extended its yellow iron neck. The crowd stood quiet as the hook began its descent. The chains that held it reeled and unreeled, and it hung there a moment, immediately above the cab, and Jaeger and the helmeted police drew back from its reach. Down it swung, curved fingers extended, seeking above the rubble as a hand might seek, and in the instant before it closed upon the cab, the shocking thing that could not happen now took place. Out of the cellar's, or the earth's, dark, fetid depths came a figure. It moved like a spider caught in its own web, like a broken crab, clawing its frantic way up through the rusted girders and disjointed stones. Wild as a scarecrow in the wind, it came, far wilder because of the threshing of its arms and legs, robbing the man trapped in the cab of his claim to drama, reducing his situation to merely another facet of the human predicament, as it scrambled into the light. It emerged in all its panic and frenzy within touch of Jaeger's hand, dislodging fragments of debris that rippled in small avalanches back into the depths, and

Jaeger stood astounded only because he knew the entire story, had read it in newspapers half a dozen times, and dismissed it, and now must watch it taking place.

Exactly as in every account, whether from Danzig, or Munich, or Warsaw, the rags of a *Wehrmacht* uniform clung to the figure's bones, the sleeves, the trousers, hanging in shreds, slashed back and forth and up and down by outraged time. A soiled, discolored beard hung to its waist, and the long, greenish locks of hair on its head mingled upon its shoulders with epaulettes of dust. Filth rendered indecipherable the insignia that had once designated rank, and blackened the medals that had testified to the valor of an individual or a regiment. There it stood, an emissary from the earth's exuding heart, a revenant from a war lost three years before, swaying, babbling, shaking, gesticulating, saluting, seeing nothing in the bright blaze of the lowering sun. The story enacted now was no more than a rumored tale, like that of the Indian rope trick, never quite seen and never once caught on photographic film, although countless camera lenses had snapped open and closed before it. As the hero of it balanced upright above the rubble, a murmur of horror rose from the throats of the people gathered in the street.

"Russians? Comrades?" the voice croaked from the boneyard of the hero's breast. He raised his fleshless, bleached arms on high, his hands held weaponless above his head. "I surrender! I surrender!" his voice echoed hollowly out of the long unbroken silence of the tomb.

This was the story the papers carried under banner headlines the next day, if only because myth had been given the flesh of reality before a population's eyes. They had read it as they read the items printed from time to time about a rain of small frogs falling, or clouds of locusts darkening the sun, but now it had actually taken place in a street they knew in the week of the resurrection of the currency. Before the scarecrow was carried off in the ambulance (usurping the rightful place of the man in the power shovel's cab), he said this much: there had been five of them in the air-raid shelter that April morning in 1944 when the bombers had come over, and the falling houses had sealed the five of them in. And then the tears poured from his eyes, and he wept uncontrollably as the interns helped him the long way across the rubble to the street, even his slobbering mouth seeming to weep its own mad tears. The others had died, two in the first year (or so the survivors had calculated it), and two much later. Not of hunger, for the shelter had been a food reserve, and the shelves in the endless passageways of it were still not empty even as he clawed his way up into the light. One corridor ran as far as the opera house. He was sure of that, for once in the daily, interminable walks, he and the others, scratching for exit, had found a cello bow, and the bones of fingers interred with it above their heads. The halls contained drums of water, bottles of *Schnapps* and vinegar, tins of oil, all still untouched; and barrels of flour that he had eaten in handfuls with the rats—and eaten the rats when he could get them. Once he had had a tooth-ache, and he had dug the tooth out of his jaw with his army knife, he said. Then the ambulance door closed on the filthy, wooden clotheshorse that he was, lying shaking and sobbing on the snowy pillow and pallet, between the interns in starched white coats.

Jaeger stayed until the crane had raised the power shovel and the scarcely remembered driver had been freed; waited until the ambulance had returned to bear him off, and then he walked away. He followed the streets that led to the station, and in the anonymity of its destruction he sat down to write the story while he waited for the Fahrbach train. It was not that he had made a choice. It was merely that the

Press Club had gone from his mind; that Americans were waiting for him to ride with them was now effaced. He wrote methodically, in a kind of benumbed, halted grief, saying that each of them, every German, must claw his way out of the depths of what he was, letting the faded, filth-encrusted insignia fall from him, and the medals for military valor drop away. When the time came, Jaeger went like any other German into the destitution of the third-class carriages. After a while, as the train moved up the valley, he slept, and when he awoke there was dark at the windows, and on his heart, like a weeping woman, lay the terrible burden of Germany.

VII

This time it was a larger hunting-party that set out at ten o'clock on Saturday morning in the hard bright sun. There was the Colonel at the wheel, and Stephany beside him, and Milly between Jaeger and Honerkamp on the seat behind. Jaeger had been summoned by telephone to come, and no word was said of Catherine Roberts; but now, as they drove through the flowering country, Honerkamp spoke uneasily of Paris, seeming to fear even the sound of the illicit, Gallic word in his mouth. Without him saying the rest, Jaeger knew from the stillness of Milly's profile, from the authority in the Colonel's shoulders riding ahead, that Catherine Roberts had gone—gone to meet her brother, to buy new clothes, to stay for a week in Paris and forget the taste of Germany, Honerkamp said little by little, in intervals, as they drove. Her going might have been the signal given at last, for the Colonel had lost no time in planning his campaign and mobilizing his men. The force he had mustered was to spend the entire day at Ober-Pastau, mapping out the lie of the land in the daylight hours before the maneuvers of the evening would begin. By the time dusk fell, he said, driving fast through the metallic sunlight, every cow-path out of the village, every entry to the forest, would be patrolled.

"We'll draw the net tight around the bastards at last," he said.

"Referring to civilians or beasts, sir?" Honerkamp asked.

"Referring to both," said the Colonel, his tone genial and light despite the color smoldering, not flaming yet, in the flesh packed in his neck. "This time we're after renegade hunters and renegade swine. I've had enough of both," he

169

said, pleased beyond measure with the look of things ahead.

"That boar who stampedes through the village streets sounds like something out of the stone age," Stephany said. Here he was, the cheerful young subordinate, his mustache and hair agleam with life, turning now to inform the others of what the Colonel already knew. "Knau called me yesterday. He said it was seen in the fields on Wednesday night, big as a bull. Not having any guns, they set the dogs on it, and it tossed one—tore it open, they say—before it was driven back into the woods."

"Oh, I've been reading about the mythic beasts!" Honerkamp said, leaning forward in the car. "There's a tremendous one in Irish chronicles who was fattened for seven years on the flesh of fifty cows per year, and it took the strength of sixty men to lift its tail."

"The common or garden variety of boar is not carnivorous, or so I've been told," the Colonel said pleasantly, forbearingly, for nothing must spoil the established mood and plan. "Is there any information available in your books, Seth, as to the date when the boar took up eating chestnuts and truffles and gave up his diet of steak?" When he put the next question to Stephany, the sarcasm was gone. "What nights did Knau say the jeep had been out?" he said, wanting fact, not fiction, in the briefing of his men.

"They set a record this week, the deer-jackers," said Stephany, half turned in his seat to say it to the girl. "They came out twice, and the tommy-guns were blazing. Whenever Knau was nearly up with them, they moved on. Thursday, the stream was streaked with blood, Knau said, and yesterday morning, early, he found a dying deer."

"I've had enough of it," said the Colonel, keeping his shoulders quiet, however much they wanted to toss and turn under the weight of man's violation of this terrain held under the Occupation in his name.

170

In the courtyard of every house in the village was a manure pile, liquid as a bank of moss is in the spring, but golden in color, and each courtyard was identically bounded on three sides by house, and stable, and granary. The cobbles, the benches by the doorsteps, the besoms of cut brush, all were alike, and in the shade of each stable's overhanging eaves cattle could be seen, stall after stall of them, in the light-dappled quiet beyond reach of the sun. The pigsties were placed between cattle and granary, and in them great, long-legged pigs grunted and throttled on their fat, their ears erect as they shouldered their way to the soiled picket gates to watch the car rock past. Only the tints of the geraniums in the window boxes varied, or, at times, the mesh of the crocheted curtains behind the dollhouse-sized panes. And only the forester's house had glazed tiles set along its cornice, picturing in primal colors the flowers and grains of the crops that followed one upon the other from spring, through summer, into wealthy autumn. They who came in the emerald station wagon had nothing to offer to men who lived in this enduring prosperity—nothing, thought Jaeger, but the fleeting gift of three rounds of ammunition and the night's loan of a gun. Yet it was for these modest dispensations that Knau jumped up from the kitchen table when the Colonel brought the car to a halt between the manure pile and the door.

"Many cows, much milk and butter," Honerkamp said in his brash German to the forester. He and the others had stepped down onto the courtyard cobbles in the sun.

"*Ja, ja,* but no horses!" Knau cried out in complaint. On the doorstep behind him, a silky-haired dachshund, with a face as lively as a lawyer's, watched the strangers with bright, humorous eyes. "They took the horses away during the war, and paid us half of what they were worth. I had four of them. Good horses, too! And then they expected us to join their Party and fight their war for them!" he said.

He stood shaking his head at the effrontery of it, his black felt hat set low, sealed permanently to his brow, it seemed; as much a part of him as his black-haired ears, and no more to be removed than were the ears, either for bath, or bed, or love-making, or church. Behind him, the dachshund slowly fanned its blond, silky tail, and the mesh curtains at one window moved. There, the faces of two children watched through the geranium stalks and leaves, their grave eyes on the strangers and the car.

"There's going to be a horse fair in Kneith in September. The first since the war," Jaeger said in German. And now, perhaps because the talk was of horses, he glanced shyly at the girl. She was standing beside the Colonel, her head lowered, and when Jaeger repeated the words, tentatively, in English to her, she looked up across the bold, Germanic sunlight at him, but neither of them gave a sign. Whatever they knew of horses, and the rage of loneliness, and love, it was a knowledge they must share in secret, for the others standing in the courtyard could not know of the tenderness that filled their hearts. *Christoph!* she may have wished to call across the tide of sun to Jaeger, but her lips did not move; and he may have longed to ask her in his pain: *Why did she have to go to Paris? For God's sake, what is she doing there?* But, instead, he went on saying in English: "The peasants have never wanted for anything."

"There's a fatted bull in there, too heavy to stand," Honerkamp said, shading his eyes to look across the courtyard to the stalls. "The entire village will have to carry it to the cattle fair and prop it up against a wall."

"It wasn't easy for a man to know what to do," Knau said to Jaeger, for all of them had turned their eyes now to the monstrous, sleek-coated beast lying in an angle of sun on its bed of straw. "There wasn't any sense in putting him up for sale before the *Währungsreform*," he went on in loud, bleak complaint. "It would have been throwing so much money down the drain." The sun smote their brows and blinded them with its impact, and Jaeger's mind reeled in confusion in the heat. Each thought in his head seemed like a rudderless ship adrift on the unrippled brilliance of the courtyard; and one thought was that it was not like the Colorado sun, for this German sun halted against the boundaries of wall, or roof, or measurable distance, while the sun in Colorado went racing up cliffs, blazed its way over mountains, careened down canyons, leaped rapids, with a transparency that drenched the heart. Another thought was that German painters who escaped, by some miracle, to the south of France, or to Italy, or Spain, or Greece, could not accustom their eyes or senses to the ephemeral light, and could not put brush to canvas in their uncertainty. And still another of these thoughts that drifted without direction was that race horses, when taken to other countries, for the first long week cannot gauge the slope of the land or the height of hurdles, and stumble and fall and break their necks in the foreign light. There was a bland finality to this German sun. In the courtyard now it was like a door of solid gold that closed them in. "They held up their *Währungsreform* so long that the bull is nearly dead of overeating," Knau said. "If he can't stand up, what kind of a price am I going to get for him? It's hard in times like these, I tell you, for a man of conscience to know what he's to do."

And now Knau's wife, in her Hessian peasant dress, had come to the door with a pail of freshly washed potatoes in her hand. She was young, not more than thirty-five, perhaps, and her tan hair was drawn up in a tight, smooth topknot on her head. Her pale cheeks were polished like wax, polished by cleanliness, physical, spiritual; and by the light of devotion to principle that no word or act could dim, by faith in an acceptance of God that was pure as a nun's (a Protestant, puritan God, Jaeger knew, colder than any winter). It was there in the iridescence of her eyes, and in the gold cross on the chain around her neck. The dust-colored wool of her skirt fell, heavy and full, in open pleats, below her ankles, and the stiffened bodice was laced by a velvet ribbon high beneath her breasts.

"The wife, she and the children saw the pig on Wednesday night," Knau said. He took a handful of poppy-seed pods from his trouser pocket, and he split one pod with the black nail of his thumb. As he spoke, he offered the seeds to them in the hollow of his palm. "A ewe lamb strayed off a week ago, and after supper now in the evening, the wife takes the children and walks down to the stream. She thinks the ewe lamb might come back at sundown to drink," he said. With the stiff hat fixed immovable on his brow, he shook his head at this simplicity. "On Wednesday, there was the boar standing his ground in the marsh, on the other side of the stream, close enough to have killed the lot of them!"

"His eyes were red, like coals," his wife said quietly. With one open hand, she smoothed the darkly flowered apron at her waist.

"What in God's name are they talking about?" the Colonel asked, but genially, patiently, determined to keep it well in hand as he looked from one to the other in the sun.

And now a tall boy stood behind the woman at the door; a boy in outgrown corduroys standing with his small head drooping forward on his strong, narrow neck, and his wrists hanging long and bony from his sleeves, flesh and bone of both of them, but already taller than either one. In his dreaming face, it was the mother's wide, grey eyes that observed the hunters, but from under Knau's black, glossy brows. His neck and hands were weathered like the man's, but his lips were delicate and the palest coral, and his hair

174

was the color of a wild hare, with white flecks at the temples such as touched the mother's hair. As she and the boy left the wooden step, the younger children watched covertly through the curtain's mesh, watched the tiny, weightless woman who now followed them, no larger than a child herself, but she and the mother dressed identically, except for the *Oma*'s white coif on her head. The women moved to a bench below the kitchen windows in the sun, and rolled their heavy sleeves back on their forearms, their motions, too, identical. The boy, in strange variance with the gentle look of the prophet in his face, crossed the cobbles to brood in wonder at the guns lying on the station-wagon floor.

"Walter, here, he saw the jeep both nights with me," Knau said, the poppy seeds between his teeth. "We went after it together, carrying sticks. Two of us on foot, and without guns! We might as well have been trying to catch witches!" he roared at the absurdity of what was asked of them.

"Let's get along to the area at once," said the Colonel briskly. His patience was raveling out. With a gesture of his hand, he disposed of the hogs, the geese, the hens, the cattle, dismissing the sound of Knau's complaining of he knew not what, and the sight of the women with their bright, quick knives peeling the clean potato skins away. All this was background scenery, like the funeral pyre of manure intricately laced with smooth filaments of straw that had been dyed by urine to the purest gold. "Lock up the car, Stephany, so they can't get at the ammunition," he said, jerking his chin toward the tall boy. There was a reckless note in his voice now, perhaps the sound of his willful abandonment to circumstance, as if the adventure that lay before them was as pleasurably hazardous as war. "Come, Milly!" he called. "You and Stephany fall in together!" And then he led off down the village street, his ruddy flesh packed firmly in his khaki, a paratrooper's silken scarf, mottled olive and sand in camouflage, knotted at his throat. And Knau, his back and shoulders as stiff as wood in the old, ceremonial black of baptisms, weddings, burials, kept pace beside him. The dachshund's short, bowed legs were hung with champagne-colored hair, and a flexible, twisting part ran the length of her spine, with the hair falling in two ways from it, as she followed in obedience at Knau's heels. Here and there, a chicken that had bedded down in the dust between the cobbles fluttered up in panic, and fled with its quick, rolling, yellow-footed gait from the sound of their boots ringing out on the stone. From one courtyard they passed came, hissing aloud, a string of geese as white as swans, and their necks as long, but their vicious acceptance of the limits set by gutter and dung, and their gaudy, clown-like feet, took any title to the beauty of swans away.

Whatever else the Colonel cast aside as irrelevant to this totally male safari, the girl had never been discarded. She was there, bare-headed, bare-legged, in her green dress, neither hunter nor hunted, so self-effaced that each could endow her with his own choice of identity. Her presence gave a liveliness to the Colonel's step, and a knightly gallantry to this role of defender of the villagers which he had chosen to play. She walked docilely beside Stephany, her russet head lowered, a reluctant bride, thought Jaeger, approaching the altar beside a bridegroom whose flesh she cannot bear. (But *what bride, what bride?* he asked himself, walking behind them. The name he wanted for her seemed on the tip of his tongue. "On earth I was a Virgin Sister," he remembered a fragment of the poem; ". . . and this which seems so low a post was given to me because the vows I took were broken, or rather complete observance was lost. . . ." He could see the bride clearly, but like a flower whose name he could not remember, that delicate spirit whom Dante had asked about in Purgatory as he passed through—asked about as casually and colloquially as a man might ask at the corner drugstore about a girl he had taken to the movies one summer night —and whose face Dante had recognized among the ghostly ones that pressed about him in the Heaven of the Moon. And then Jaeger found it. "Piccarda, Piccarda!" he had to keep himself from crying out, and he saw the girl who walked before him as lost, as damned, as violated, as the thirteenth-century Piccarda, with no one to stand between her and the purgatory or inferno that lay ahead.)

"I was thinking of Dante in the *Paradiso*," Jaeger said, his voice lowered so that Honerkamp, walking beside him, cupped one hand around an ear.

"Even the infantry, even marching in formation," Honerkamp said, "can retain for a little longer the right to think. But not indefinitely, oh, Jaeger, not as far—I should think— as the threshold of the next war!" With his eyes on Milly and Stephany, he went on saying that he didn't like the Colonel's military strategy. "I don't approve of his deployment of his men," he said. Jaeger wanted to speak to him of Piccarda Donati, who had dedicated herself to silence like the girl who walked before them in a dress the color of fern frond, of inchworm, of *Paradiso* (for now the Florentine Beatrice and Catherine Roberts, like Milly and Piccarda, had become interchangeable to him, and he and Dante were abruptly one. He saw himself condemned to live, as Dante had lived, with no knowledge of the loved one's flesh. *Ach, Gott, must I make literary personages of the bone and blood of these women?* he cried to himself. *Let me get them, Beatrice, Catherine, out of the pages of a book, and hold them hard against me, like a man!*). But Honerkamp was saying as they walked: "Already, the first time we met, she made a choice. But now, perhaps tonight, she will have to act on it, for the Colonel is asking for action from us all. It may be as close as that, the showdown. It's so present that I can taste it, smell it, on the air."

The village street was like the trough of a dry stream's rocky bed, and it now turned abruptly steep under their feet. In the spring, thought Jaeger, it must be transformed to a muddy, roaring torrent from the rains cascading down. Even in desiccation, it had the drained look of a cobbled moat, and the last bend of it brought them past the blacksmith's forge. In the dark gap of his barn door, the forging-iron burned, white-hot and visible in its own right beyond the threshold where the outside heat and sunlight ceased. A speckled grey horse was tied to a ring in the door's weathered frame, his loose lip hanging, leathery and blue, his limbs trembling in fright as the smith cradled his hoof in the leather apron spread across his knees. Two by two, the Colonel's entourage passed by, the elite in olive drab, and the others following in humbler dress, leaving the village behind and taking the footpath out through pasture and cultivated fields. Here the land advanced blade by incredibly green blade of rye, by small, hard, white shoulder after shoulder of winter beet under separate canopies of blistered leaves, proceeded stalk by stalk of moon-petaled poppy, and the bleached embroidery of Queen Anne's lace, to the far edge of the forest, shadowed already by the secrecy and murder of the night.

Now Knau stopped short.

"The big pig came down this far last Wednesday night!" he shouted back at Jaeger. "*Mittwoch Abend!*" he roared, and the dachshund called Hexe listened sharply to him. Her ears hung in long auburn locks on each side of her sunken face, and the pointed wafer of her tongue showed in her mouth. If Knau had asked it of her, she would, in her eager courage, have sought out the wild boar now and driven it from ambush for his delight. "Right here, he stood!" Knau shouted to Jaeger. "The wife and children had to run for their lives back to the house!"

"Before dark, we'll leave a man here where the footbridge crosses the stream," said the Colonel. "Seth, that will be you. You'll get here on foot. The rest of us will drive out the lumber road. And there, out there, where the path joins the road," he said, his arm pointing the way, "we'll drop Stephany off. We'll go on as far as we can by car. You're to keep out of sight, Seth, and keep upwind. Your job is to let Stephany know if anything's coming his way. If you hear the jeep coming out from the village along the road, double-quick it ahead, and close in with Stephany. You're to shoot—both of you—at the tires as it goes by."

The world was so armored with brilliance that the blackness and contraband of the coming night had little meaning. The time for its peril to move out of the forest and across the shining fields seemed a hundred years away. Yet Honerkamp must have glimpsed some sight or smell of it as he stood, halted, his fingers combing quickly through his curly hair.

"I think I can cope with the jeep, sir," he said. They were standing closer together now, so there was no need for him to raise his voice. "Man and his possibilities are my terrain, I suppose. But a better hunter than I am will have to brief me on the boar."

"Just shoot for the heart," said Stephany. He raised both arms, as if handling a gun, and mockingly took aim, and closed one eye.

"That's all. As if you were courting a woman," the Colonel said; and he added: "Jaeger here could probably show you how."

"Aim for the heart in total darkness?" Honerkamp said.

179

"You won't have any trouble. Their eyes are luminous," Stephany said. He rubbed the back of his forefinger under the clean hairs of his mustache, effacing the smile.

"Jaeger, you'll circle the woods on the left flank," the Colonel said. "Knau and I will keep circling to the right. We'll have five guns among us, provided Milly wants to carry one."

"Five," the girl said, speaking for the first time now. It might have been a question that she asked.

"Jaeger isn't a forester, and he doesn't happen to be an American. If you're going to have regulations, then they're to be respected even with no one looking on. At least, if I'm around, they are," the Colonel said. "Milly, you're under orders, too, tonight. I don't want to have to worry about rounding you up. You'll stay with Stephany."

"Yes," the girl whispered. Her head was lowered. "Yes. But I'll go without a gun."

"It's the size of this boar that I'm concerned about," Honerkamp said. He went on talking quickly, eagerly, as if the Colonel's words had not struck his heart their separate blows. "*Hylocherus meinertzhageni*, they say, is the largest known, measuring six feet, and found only in the densest forests. But, according to legend, there was a boar hunted by King Arthur that measured sixteen feet, and that had blue-black bristles, like stunted pine trees, down its spine, and the foam on its mouth when it was ready to attack, the books say, was like the spume of a mighty waterfall."

"The German variety's slightly smaller," Stephany said, keeping the sound of laughter back.

"Ask Knau about the size of this local pig," the Colonel said to Jaeger, and he waited a moment, impatient with the German words. "Well, what does he have to say?"

"He says about the size of a large dog," Jaeger translated.

"Thank God, my wife isn't here!" the Colonel exploded with a show of joviality. "If she heard that, she'd come right back from Paris and take it home as a pet! She's always befriending the outcasts, the lame ducks, the maladjusted. That's why I gave her a week's leave," he said. His blue eye was colder than metal as he looked at Jaeger. "I would say this particular boar was maladjusted, wouldn't you, Jaeger? I would say he was introverted—you know, unable to mix with his own kind. Ask the forester's opinion on that sometime," he said, his shoulders tossing, and now he set off again with Knau beside him, keeping the lead. And this time Honerkamp got out of line and caught up with the girl.

"I dug up a recipe for stuffed boar's head," he began saying to the right side of her face. On her left walked Stephany, and she looked at neither of them, but walked as if alone. "First, you take the skin of the head off carefully—"

"Let's skip that phase of the operation," Jaeger heard Stephany say; and Honerkamp went on:

"—and then a mixture of minced pig's liver, chopped apples and onion, rosemary and sage, is molded into the empty hood, restoring the boar's head to its normal shape. Then a second stuffing is placed inside the first, consisting of sausage meat, ox tongue, truffles, mushrooms, nuts and apples, the lot of it saturated with Calvados. And once you've got the head packed solid, you wrap it up in a linen cloth, sew it in—"

"That would be a shroud," Jaeger, walking alone, heard Stephany say.

"—and you place it in an iron receptacle, and cook it over a slow fire for—good God, I'm hungry!" Honerkamp broke off, and the Colonel turned quickly on his heel.

"Seth, keep in formation!" he called back across the light

of noon, his voice still equable, but the blood igniting slowly in his jowls.

So Honerkamp walked with Jaeger again, and as they came to the lumber road, Knau could be heard speaking of foxes, shouting the words out louder and louder, as if the sheer volume of his voice must crack at last the Colonel's resistance to what was being said. Knau was saying there was a fox burrow that ran in and out of and under the rocks on the first slope behind the clump of oak trees just around the turn. They would be in sight of it at once, he said, his arms threshing like a windmill's in the direction where it lay. The foxes, the foxes, he shouted, as if in argument with the Colonel, and Hexe lifted her silky, auburn ears and watched his face. There were half a dozen fox cubs who played there in the early morning and early evening, said Knau, and he wanted to wipe the marauders out.

"What seems to be on his mind?" The Colonel had turned again, and he called the questions back to Jaeger. "What's he trying to get at?" he said.

But once they had passed the compact island of trees, even the Colonel could see. For now it was Knau's campaign that was getting under way, and it was he who designated the positions to be held. A man must stand in readiness at each of the far-flung exits, while he took for his own the main door hollowed in the tangled roots of the oak trees. The sun poured over the stones and the scorched earth of the foxes' burrow, but halted abruptly at the dark line of the forest's midday shade. Within that shade, among the lacquered leaves and fern and the rot of fallen branch and bark, Jaeger saw what he took for a moment for a wreath of delicate, blanched flowers. But it was not flowers, and what had seemed a wreath was the circular stampede of death as fox teeth tore the white plumage in frenzy from a still wildly fighting chicken's flesh.

"Get them hard on the back of the neck as they run out," Knau was directing them, his eyes stubborn and black under his hat brim and his brows. In the absence of firearms, each man was equipped with a branch wrenched from the forest's intricately laid floor, and they moved to their positions, testing these in their hands. But to the girl and the Colonel, Knau gave no orders. They stood apart in the dappled sunshine by the clump of trees. "I've counted six of them, six young, mornings and evenings when I pass. If the old ones are out in the woods, we'll have no trouble with the cubs," Knau said.

Now the men were ready, and Knau spoke the single word to Hexe, and she went flat on her belly, her pointed tongue out, her lips half smiling, the champagne-colored silk of her tail visible an instant, as she entered the sloping tunnel of the fox's hole. The threshold of the hole Jaeger guarded might well have been the playground of the cubs, for the earth before the opening was strewn with small, brittle bones, some leg, some rib, and with the tiny, desiccated hoofs of fawns, of lambs, and even the fan-like frame of a stripped wing, like the paraphernalia of games discarded at the sight of something marvelously new. Stephany's exit was to the right, and he, too, stood poised, the handsome, unresolved face above the olive of the army shirt now flushed and set with the heat of his intent. On the left, Honerkamp had something else on his mind, for his head was thrown back, and his eyes were squinting at the sky above his head. Although Jaeger stood weighing the club in his two hands, he knew that the day was too clear, too bright, too unsullied, for the dealing of violent death.

"Jaeger," Honerkamp called suddenly, "I've just worked something out. Once, just before dawn, I flew up this valley, and, damn it, I can hear the steel hearts of the bombers now. This morning, today, as we drove out, there was a road sign outside Ober-Pastau saying Kastel is a hundred kilometers to the north, and I knew it must have been these hills I crossed. Kastel," he said. "You may have been there since. We brought such annihilation on that one town that they tell me what's left of it even now bears no more relation to reality than the hushed, volcanic twilight of Pompeii. We hit all targets. Nothing was taboo," Honerkamp said, still looking at the high, luminous sky. "Sometimes I persuade myself that Kastel can be dismissed now, written off, as classical ruins have been written off in silence—those ruins produced by act of God and not by man, and somehow salvaged by their own irrevocability. Nothing was taboo," Honerkamp repeated. "Not like Niederstadt. We could hit the opera house there, but not the O. H. Spaltenindustrie. I like to believe it was because we knew we would need the administration buildings when we moved in. Only for that. Not because we, as a country, were protecting something we still had capital invested in. Music, and those who listened to it, could go," he said, "but not the O. H. Spaltenindustrie."

"The opera house," Jaeger said, not loud. *The opera house. And this man, close as a brother, had his part in it.*

"One night in April, the music stopped playing, and the singers no longer sang," Honerkamp said. "I had done my bit. . . ."

And now the muffled yapping of the dachshund sounded in the labyrinth of tunnels, the frantic, strident cry of her pursuing sounding underground, now near, now far.

"Get ready for action, boys!" the Colonel cried out, and a tremor seemed to pass from the screaming earth beneath their feet into the bodies of the waiting men. "Get ready, boys!" the Colonel called, his voice strangely choked with his delight. At once, a wild, blind passion ran headlong in their veins. Hot and panting, it ran, like rabid dog or fox, and no way out for it, no exit, no escape, unless they raised their clubs and struck. *Ah, but I won't, I won't!* Jaeger told himself, but he was trembling in the sun. *Ah, but you'll see, I won't!* he said with a craftiness designed to outwit at the final moment the hot, bright, violent desire to strike down all that ran and shrieked and bared sharp, vicious teeth at death, to deal blow after frenzied blow on all that snarled and spun and clawed at life, to strike over and over, end-lessly, until the lust was drained out of his veins. "They're going your way, Stephany!" the Colonel shouted, and a coarsened, heavy look hung on Stephany's mouth because of the fury of this thing he was prepared to do. But the outcry of the chase swerved right, then left, and for an instant it seemed that the pursued turned on the pursuer, for the dog's voice no longer yapped, but fought savagely for life.

At what moment the girl had turned from the sound of it and walked away, Jaeger did not know. For a time, she was there by the oak trees, and then she was gone, already quite far, her back turned to them, going alone in her green dress through the varying greens of the countryside, follow-ing back the lumber road. In the foxes' tunnels, the pack ran screaming still, and because of the fire in the Colonel's blood, he did not seem to know that she had gone. She walked steadily away, walking, it might be over and through this country and into another, not looking back, or looking across the fields that lay on either side, but following the lumber road until it turned into the village street and then into the highway, walking until it crossed the frontier be-tween this country and the next, between Germany and France, by some bridge across a river, or some quiet wood where gravestones stretched endlessly, not stopping at the customs because she didn't have any baggage with her, having nothing but absolute silence to declare. She would walk through France, bypassing the towns, walking on through fields and brush as she walked now, because one got to Paris quicker like this, the way a crow or a carrier pigeon flies. The sun struck brightly on the crown of her head, so after a while only the russet of her hair could be seen glowing against the separate greens as she went on, walking through the Porte d'Orléans, crossing the Champ-de-Mars and the Seine to the Champs-Elysées, walking up under the *marroniers* to where her mother might be sitting on a café terrace, walking in absolute silence, slender, erect, out of the territory of Germany. *All right, but what about Christoph?* Jaeger wanted to call out after her. *You can't go without him, you can't leave him here without—without what?* He paused a moment. She was growing smaller and smaller, green against the varying green, even the shining russet fading now. *Without love!* he wanted to shout before she had gone beyond recall.

"They're bearing your way, Seth!" the Colonel was crying out. But Honerkamp suddenly flung his stick behind him into the underbrush. "What in God's name are you doing? The foxes, damn it, the foxes!" the Colonel cried.

Honerkamp looked at each of the men, his face closed tight as a fist against them, and then he began to run, his tweed jacket flying open, his grey flannel trousers flapping above his tennis shoes, running swiftly and lightly, for all his weight, down the slope to the road, jumping sideways over rocks and roots, after the small, far figure of the girl. And the Colonel stumbled, cursing, toward the mouth of the unguarded hole. From it, the tumult of yapping now issued, high and clear. He fell on his knees before it, groping frantically in the underbrush at the forest's edge for the discarded club, the stick, the bough, any bough, any branch, any stone, that might serve as weapon to clobber the fury in his blood; and louder, sharper, wilder, racing closer to the surface, came the snapping and snarling of the foxes and the dachshund's piercing cry.

"Stop them, stop them!" the Colonel roared. The whites of his eyes were shot with blood, and the irises blazing with blue fire. "Get over here, Stephany! Get a stick for me, Jaeger!" he pled. "For Christ's sake, Jaeger, get me a—"

Empty-handed, he reeled to his feet, his fingers working, reaching, as if he would strangle the life from the foxes as they came. And, one by one, they shot from the tunnel and between his legs, six of them, six separate flashes of red, with Hexe close on the brush of the last one, but not close enough to seize it in her foam-flecked jaws. Off into the woods the lot of them went, the sound of the chase heard a little longer, but fading, and then the dark door of the forest was closed on the clamor of their flight. For a moment, the dachshund's voice soared in one faint, distant note, almost musical, and now strangely touched with sorrow. She had given her bright, unquestioning courage to this that man had asked of her, and if she had failed it was because man, too, had failed. When she returned, she walked in shame, her eyes lowered, her tail dragging in the leaves.

Jaeger had wanted to laugh uproariously in the instant the foxes flashed through the Colonel's legs, but now in the silence of his defeat there was no humor in it. Everything had escaped the Colonel's grasp—at least so it seemed for this moment in the sun; not only the meaning of boar and jeep, and silence and speech, but the ebony-nosed, murderous little foxes had now eluded him, gone as artfully and irretrievably as his wife and daughter, leaving him standing baffled here.

VIII

In the middle
of the afternoon, they sat down at the round table in the
forester's kitchen, Milly and Honerkamp side by side on a
bench set against the paneling of the wall, and Knau on
Honerkamp's left hand, his back and shoulders rigid, his
square face as inflexible as wood under the black hat's rigid
brim. Then came the *Oma* (her white coif no larger than a
paper drinking-cup, and she no larger than the child beside
her, but a figure of unassailable dignity because of the carriage of her head and the history of consecration to God
and man that was written on her brow). Next came Frau
Knau, with the blond children seated low on stools on either
side of her, their eyes just visible above the tablecloth. The
Colonel, and Stephany, and Jaeger, and the stooping, dreaming boy completed the circle, the boy last, sitting at Milly's
right hand. The Colonel opened the neat cartons of sandwiches his cook had prepared, laid the waxed paper back,
and distributed hard-boiled eggs and paper napkins, the
good officer, the official provider, the situation well in hand
again, sacrificing nothing of rank or discipline, but sharing
the available rations and quarters with his men. He had
nothing at all to say to Honerkamp, and no glance to give
in his direction. In betraying men who hunted, it might be
that Honerkamp had betrayed country and countrymen as
well; and the girl could have been dead and in her grave for
all the attention the Colonel paid to her.

A great wheel of brown bread had been placed in the
center of the table, one of twenty Frau Knau had baked in
the village oven at the end of the street. They had seen the

others, stacked on shelves and covered with unbleached muslin, in the damp of the woodshed behind the house. Knau held the dark, dusty wheel against his black vest now and cut thick slabs of it, and offered each slab on the point of the knife, to the women last, once the children had been served, but offering it first to the men. And Jaeger ate hungrily, spreading sweet country butter on the bread, and drank the good coffee that Frau Knau had poured into their cups, aware that this wealth of food belonged only to the peasant, and to the Occupier of his soil. The rest of the country queued up on shoe-leather worn thin, in clothes gone threadbare a long time back, and paid their coins out carefully, one by one, on the counters of the stores. He thought he had never tasted butter as good as this, and the sugar in the flowered china basin was Jack Frost sugar, the very finest, poured from the American five-pound blue bag of it that Frau Knau kept with the other bags, and the tins of coffee and cocoa, out of sight of the curious in the cupboard underneath the stairs.

American and German hands alike reached for the sandwiches, the prophylactically bleached slices, cut in America before traveling overseas, and spread now with potted ham and chicken, with synthetic liver-paste, with processed cheese, no tastier than wax, with cream cheese studded with olive and pimento, all from the groaning shelves of the American Commissary that stood under Fahrbach's horse-chestnut trees, to which no German had access unless he served behind the counters there. Only the girl did not eat; she took the half-moon of a bite from the corner of one sandwich and then laid it on the cloth, waiting, it might be, for the moment when she could put a cigarette in her mouth, or hold a drink in her hand, seemingly benumbed, almost effaced, knowing some inviolable pattern would be

189

broken if she did either here. She sat, her still face masking whatever furious demands clamored within, watching the blond children across the cloth.

"Here you are, kiddies-o. Here's something you'll like," the Colonel was saying in a loud voice, and the children sank lower and lower on their stools at the sight of the bananas he now brought out.

"We didn't have bananas during the war," Knau said, the inflexibility giving a little. He picked one up in his black-rimmed fingers and drew the yellow skin back to show the children how it was done.

"Maybe they won't like the taste," the girl said scarcely above a whisper. And they did not like it. They drew the backs of their hands across their mouths and turned their faces aside. It was the *Oma*, her lips working fast as a monkey's, who ate the waxy pieces that they left beside their plates.

But however the military ostracized him, still Honerkamp would have his say about music, and he leaned one arm in the tweed jacket on the table and talked his reckless German eagerly to Knau. While he talked, he ate rapidly, furiously, saying, chewing, that to replace the military tradition in this country, the tradition of music, German music, must be brought into the ascendancy. Military strategy must be rejected for the polyphony, say, of Mozart, he said, rejected even for one Austrian who died too young, and the figures who stood massive and immobile in German history must no longer be Frederick the Great, or Bluecher, or Moltke, or Bismarck, no longer Ludendorff, or Hindenburg, or whatever others there were who stamped out the measure of the booted, belted, homicidal dance. But, crowding the national stage until they became the corporeity of man's belief, should be Bach, Handel, Haydn, Beethoven, Schubert, right up to Orff, and not stop there.

"I see them, and all the others, poets, musicians, I haven't named," he said, or he was trying to say, having trouble with the tenses of the verbs; "I see them with hands reaching out to touch the hands of other poets, composers, reaching out of the past, through the critical interval of the present, into the indefinite spaces of time ahead. I see them as links in a chain—not any kind of shackles, but a living chain to which free men can cling for life—and not one single poet, not one musician, is to be discarded or overlooked, none, for the chain must stretch unbroken, link by link, from time long past to time immeasurable ahead, if Germany is to fulfill her destiny. They are to be cherished, these poor, longing men, in the same proportion and with the same national devotion with which every military figure has been cherished until now. They are all to be revered, and when this has been understood, then every military figure will be rejected as unworthy to speak and act in the name of the true dignity of man." He paused a moment, his features tense and small, chewing fiercely at the bite of brown bread in his mouth. "The hands of the musicians, the poets," he went on finally, "the hands of these men who attest to the only absolute truth we know, must reach out and grasp one another's, stretching from one century into the next, from death through life, stretching into the only kind of afterlife of which we can be certain. You see that, don't you? You understand that, don't you, Herr Knau?" he said.

"*Ja, ja,*" said the forester. "*Ja, ja,*" and gravely, wisely, he nodded his head.

But in his eagerness, Honerkamp could not say it all as he wished in German, and he turned suddenly to English, asking Jaeger to put it into better German than he was able to for Knau.

"At the America House I'm setting up courses that I think would interest you, Herr Knau, to come into in the

winter when the farm work slackens off." He reached for a
sandwich now, raised one corner of it with an expert finger
to see what lay within, and then folded it into his mouth.
As he chewed, he listened to Jaeger putting the words into
German for Knau. "I'm getting a course into shape on the
recognition of the creative identity," he said, and Knau listened to the sound of it translated to him, and gravely
blinked his eyes, and gravely, gravely, nodded. "I want to
undertake some sort of study of the *Befindlichkeiten*
of man, of musical man, as a beginning," Honerkamp said,
and the Colonel and Stephany looked across the table at
him with jaundiced eyes. "Now that armed conflict is done
with for the moment, another kind of conflict has got under
way. And this time it's going to be a battle to the death,
and not only here in Germany, but all over Europe, the Far
East, right across your world and mine, Herr Knau." Honerkamp's features were gathered close and small to a focal
point in the center of his face, fixed there by the fury of his
chewing and his speech. "We've got to take part in the sur-
vival, whether it be as civilian or military man; the potential
defender, that is, of individual integrity or the defender of
national boundaries. That is the choice," he said.

"*Ja, ja*, said Knau; "*wahrlich, wahrlich*," his eyes bleak
with bewilderment as he got up from the table. "*Ja, ja*," he
said, and he walked to the cup closet by the stove and took
the bottle down. He bore it back to the table, his fingers
fast around the neck of it, as if it was a living thing. In the
other hand he carried five squat, greenish-colored glasses,
their thick bottoms nestling in his palm. Honerkamp's voice
ceased as the forester stood looking at the faces of the men.
"Would they like a little drink of *Schnapps*?" Knau said to
Jaeger, and he set the glasses down before them: one for the
Colonel, one for Lieutenant Stephany, one for Honerkamp,
one for Jaeger, and the fifth at his own empty place.

They watched in silence as he poured the liquor slowly out, filling each glass nearly to the brim. And even though there might be no more than the promise of one burning swallow in each glass, still the presence of drink was like dispensation given, and the Colonel looked quickly at the girl. Then he pushed his untouched glass toward her across the cloth.

"Let's have one more here," he said to Jaeger.

"So the daughter drinks *Schnapps*, too!" Knau said, and he gave a laugh.

The women watched her, their eyes clear and uncondemning, not judging her for this any more than for the red on her mouth or the indecency of her naked arms and legs, observing without astonishment or censure that this was the way things went in another country, that this was American, acknowledged like the powdered substance in glass jars that turned to coffee at the touch of water, and was called, for no good reason, by an American general's name. Now that life had taken on another look, the Colonel was smiling at Milly, and he lifted his brimming, doll-sized glass in her direction.

"Here's to your mother's trip to Paris!" he said. The fires of warmth, of conviviality, were lighted in their blood again, and all that had taken place in the morning, all that was to transpire after evening fell, was bearable now, was funny, almost. A different light had been shed on everything. "Here, fill them up again," the Colonel said cheerfully. "Now that you've brought the issue of civilian and soldier up," he said, his good humor embracing Honerkamp as well, "I'd like to point out that, provided, of course, I have any say in the matter at all, I'd prefer my daughter to marry an army man. Selfish, you think? Well, perhaps it is. He'd have to take orders from me, all right." He looked around the table, and jerked his shoulders, and laughed. "Why not? Doesn't experience count for anything? Aren't the benefits of it—twenty years of it, in my case—let's say the experience of dealing with all kinds of men—isn't that good enough to earn a son-in-law's respect?"

The girl was smiling, too, looking straight into her glass.

"I think it will shock you terribly when I marry," she said in a low voice.

"Shock me?" the Colonel cried out, his eyes quite startled. "Here, Jaeger, have Knau pour us a little more." He pushed the drained glass forward with his fingertips.

"Yes, terribly, terribly," the girl said. She watched the liquor slowly filling their glasses again. "Because I will marry someone you would consider inferior. You know," she said scarcely aloud, but smiling still, "the way you consider me inferior."

"Consider you—? Consider what?" the Colonel cried out. "You, inferior? My God, what's the matter with you, Milly?"

His hand pulled at the scarf at his throat, seeking to loosen it, as if it were its mottled silk that choked him now.

"But, yes, you do," the girl said, her voice quiet, but her hand trembling a little as she lifted the glass and took another swallow of the *Schnapps*. "If I married an army man, then I would take on some kind of standing—you know what I mean. There would be rules to obey, and things like that, and you think that would raise me to a sort of standard. I mean, officially. But I'm going to marry somebody quite different from an army man. I know exactly who I'm going to marry," she said, looking down into the little glass.

"Oh, you do?" said the Colonel. "So you know who you're going to marry?" His voice was dull now, and he spoke slowly, the fire in his blood extinguished. There seemed no anger left in him as his eyes moved to Honerkamp in awful recognition of what was taking place. "So you know already. I suppose you could even tell me his name, and the date that you've fixed for the ceremony," he said, looking dully at the girl. "This is extremely interesting. I suppose your mother knows all about it. I suppose she's gone to Paris to pick out the trousseau," he said.

But now Stephany came abruptly to life at the table. Under the smooth, glossy line of his mustache, his teeth seemed extravagantly white, his closely shaven jaws, the olive of his shirt, the cloth of his battle jacket, extravagantly clean in the glare of the indoor sun. The Colonel's bereft eyes were turned to him, given respite for a brief moment by a look of hope, for Stephany, his hand playing with the fork beside his plate, had begun to speak with a new power and authority.

"Aren't there established rules for any well-regulated game or life?" he said. His handsome, well-groomed head was cocked sideways at the girl. "I was surprised this morning to see how you reacted to rational decision, and I would have said that it was a feminine and irrational reaction, except that Honerkamp took your part. Here you have poachers—I'm speaking of the foxes—and you can't face up to the logical disposal of them. In failing to do that, it seems to me that you and Honerkamp are putting yourselves on the side of the men who drive out here and machine-gun the deer." His hand played indolently with the fork still, and his mouth was quizzical under the line of his mustache. "Do you think we're all entitled to make our own personal rules as to procedures?" he asked, leaning back in a leisurely, almost arrogant, way in the hard, wooden chair. The Colonel had seemed to close his ears to the sound of it, and he watched him with drained eyes. "For instance—to give you an extreme supposition," Stephany said, "do you think any army would have the right to go into battle with a two days' growth of beard—"

195

"Yes," the girl said, not looking up, her voice not loud. "Yes. Armies have done that, and sometimes they won."

"They won because they hadn't shaved?" said Stephany, the smile pulling at his soft, twitching mouth. "Well, of course, you may be perfectly right. But I think you should give us names and dates, then. I think Colonel Roberts would agree with me on this. I think you would, sir," he said, turning his head in deference to the Colonel now. His fingers ceased playing with the fork, and he reached absently for the half-empty glass before him, and, scarcely seeming to see it, drank the hot liquid down. "I know the Colonel has confidence in a system that tests a man's quality by his endurance, as we do in the field, for instance, by taking a team of four men, and putting each member under a thirty-pound load, plus ammunition and rifle, and keeping those men going over rough terrain on an average of forty miles a day. I think—I feel pretty certain—that you would agree with me, sir, that officer material, and I say quite frankly that I don't think there is any better material—"

"All right," said the Colonel testily. "All right, Stephany, let's forget it now." This was never the love song that would woo her. This was never the music that she would want to hear. "I believe it when you don't say it, if that makes any sense to you," he said. He looked at Jaeger. "Tell Knau to open another bottle," he said.

"Now this morning, out in the field, Honerkamp," Stephany said, keeping the offensive still, "you spoke of taking aim in the dark, and I think the information we have on that would interest you. Only in the training of the military man, as you call him, have we worked out a method of muscle and eye co-ordination that makes it possible for the well-trained soldier to get his target three times out of four in total darkness at a range of fifty yards."

"My God, Stephany," said the Colonel, "I didn't know

you would be going intellectual on us, too! Let's drink up and get out in the field and see some action for ourselves," he said.

(At this moment, Jaeger's mind, or perhaps merely the cranium that housed it, became a square room, bare of furnishings, lit by the single hot bulb of the *Schnapps* he had drunk down. In this uncluttered space, Jaeger saw several Stephanys; saw him as child, black-eyed, black-haired, white-skinned, emasculated by all that swaggered in him in uncertainty; saw him as cub scout, boy scout, the uniform always fitting well, the oath of allegiance given, even if only to himself, with photogenic gravity; saw him beloved of family, but always, at any age, a drop of bitterness in the sweet draught of the love borne him, always a stale crumb of betrayal in the fresh leaven of the bread of every day; saw him fearful and alone because not valued by peers or teachers, never cherished as friend, and yet almost getting by because he could counterfeit all parts for short duration; driving the family car, recklessly, heedlessly, at fourteen, beloved for brief weeks by the wrong girls, irresolute, not quite reliable in any place, at any time, in any role, the scarcely audible sighs for what he failed to be misting the brightness of the committed hearts; saw him, ever since boy-scout days, wanting to make it with someone others coveted, someone with a name in movies or on the stage, trusting no choice, no decision, unless it had been popularly confirmed. There he stood in the clinical light of Jaeger's square room, with nothing but vanity to cover his stripped, quaking bones. He had been summoned out of the darkness of one night in the early spring, summoned by gossip which said that he had tried to shoot a fellow officer—both of them roaring, blind, fit for the guardhouse, the story went at the *Fahrbach Presse*, but spared because of rank—and now he faced in Jaeger's cranium the poor truth that, even unconscious, it must never be your own kind that you betray. He had tried to shoot a fellow officer outside the Officers' Club, for the sake of a German waitress smelling of American detergent and German *Kraut*, whose bed he had shared the night before and wanted to share again. It was the Colonel who had shouted "Hush" louder even than the shots Stephany had fired, a "Hush" so loud that the M.P.s weren't certain they had heard the shooting down the hill; and the Colonel it was who silenced the accusations of the other officer before seeing him transferred to Austria, leaving only the screams of the German girl to ring uncomforted across that April night. This the Colonel had done in brusque indulgence of Stephany, having marked him, if marriage ever threatened Milly, for his own. He was his handful of clay, to be molded, punished, dressed, and decorated, year by year, not only into the figure of a son-in-law shaped by his will, but as well into a figure of a man. But always there was a sense of loss, a missing dimension, always the knowledge that he would not quite do, weighing on the longing, loving, sighing hearts that would enfold this Stephany. However he moved in Jaeger's bare, square room, and smiled under his mustache, however he pled that he needed the Colonel's daughter to salvage his future and his pride, still he had the grace to turn his face away a little so that no one need feel the obligation of looking into his eyes.)

Before they had sat down to eat, Honerkamp must have gone from top to bottom of the house, for he had seen the miniature organ closed in the parlor, and it was this he spoke of now. Knau told him it was the son who played the organ every Sunday in the village church, and who played the family organ here. And after a while, Honerkamp had it out of them that music had given their courtship its flavor and shape. Knau had his viola in the attic still, and Frau Knau had sung, as a girl, in the church choir.

"But now I am too old. I have too many duties," she said, and the color rose in her smooth cheeks as high as the half-moons of shadow under her eyes.

"She's out picking potatoes instead of practicing her hymns!" Knau said, and he laughed. But his eyes were soft and warm as he looked at his wife, and he pushed his hat off his brow for a moment with the back of his hand.

It was to Honerkamp they spoke, offering the memories of what they had once been to him alone. In the end, Knau rose from the table and crossed the hall, and opened the door of the parlor, and beckoned to them to come. Like Sunday, it was kept apart from the light and air of every-day, and this was an honor he conferred now, ushering them a day before the Sabbath into the hush of the apple-scented room.

"We haven't much time to spare," the Colonel said in a whisper.

"You're right, sir; we haven't," said Stephany. He looked at the time on his wrist.

But now Knau had brought his viola down, and he wiped the dust from the worn brown leather of its case, and he took it out, and laid it on the folded handkerchief under his chin. While his forefinger plucked at the catgut strings, and his dark ear listened for the "a," the "g," the "e," the boy sat down before the organ and spread his fingers on the keys. The others, civilian and military alike, were crowded behind them, the Colonel and Stephany near the door, their arms crossed over on their breasts, breathing uneasily the odor of sanctity that hung on the parlor's consecrated air. As the gasp and wheeze of the organ began, Honerkamp opened the pages of the hymnal that had stood on the music rack, and the boy closed his eyes, and raised his face in humility as if to receive the benediction of some mystic light. But to Jaeger, the Colonel's and Stephany's distaste for Honerkamp seemed stronger than faith and louder than the music of voice and instrument that began to fill this dedicated shrine.

"*Ein' feste Burg ist unser Gott!*" sang Honerkamp, and, beside him, Frau Knau sang too, her Ingres-like hands clasped on her apron, her rounded, golden throat filled with a smooth column of sound. "*Ein' gute Wehr und Waffen!*" they sang. The righteous, Protestant words of Luther thundered now against the ceiling of the little room, while the music of organ and viola cried yea, and yea, and yea. The boy's fingers pressed the keys, tenderly, urgently, pressing and pressing a fervent music from the organ pipes that sighed and trembled and fought for breath, but never quite expired. "*Er steht uns bei in aller Not!*" the voices declared in approbation of all that was finite and absolute, all that was uncorrupted, all that was as cold and unforgiving as stone.

Knau sawed the flat of his bow from end to end across the strings, his shoulders square, his arm beneath the instrument unshaken, his black-rimmed fingers closing like traps on each separate note and holding the handful of them fast. On one side of Jaeger stood the girl, humming under her breath, and, on the other, the *Oma*, her hands folded on the dusty pleatings of her skirt, her foot tapping steadily, her voice keening perilously high.

"*Wir treten zum Beten vor Gott den Gerechten!*" the organ pipes trebled, and the voices rose in celebration; and so illumined was the boy's raised face that he seemed to be seated below an altar, with the refulgence of peopled-and-chronicled glass windows shining down upon his brow. "*O Herr, steh uns bei!*" Frau Knau and Honerkamp sang fervently, and the *Oma* keened on her single note, mourning because of the potatoes still unpeeled, the socks still not darned, the new cabbage not brought in from the fields, the dishes not done, the fire, it might be, dying in the kitchen stove; improvident, improvident, this lost half-day that was not the Sabbath, and the vegetables for the evening soup still in the soil. Under Knau's chin, the viola spoke with a broad, country accent of the fatted bull that could not get to its feet in the stable, speaking in complaint of the menace of boar and unlicensed hunter, and the need of a horse in place of an ox behind the plow. It was clear that only the boy was pure enough to receive God's illumination on his flesh; only on him, as he played, did the pale light seem to fall. *"Aber heute ist Sonntag, und alles ist vorbei!"* the voices stated with conviction, and even if this was not true, still they sang in commemoration of this day when the Occupiers, for once, came as friends would come, by daylight instead of furtively in the twilight of evening or at dawn, or to stalk the woods like outlaws under cover of the dark.

And now the Colonel and Stephany moved aside in relief, and the *Oma* ceased to beat time with her flexible-soled shoe, for one of the blond children, pushing a doll carriage, had come through the parlor door. In the doll carriage lay a soiled white hen, its head on the pillow, a pink doll blanket tucking its ailing body in. The hen's bright, avid eye was turned sharply on the lot of them, and its beak seemed ready to open in venom and hurl a curse upon them all. The *Oma* stooped to settle the blanket closer around its scrawny neck, and "Squawk!" said the hen in such coarse abuse that the boy lifted his fingers from the organ keys, and Herr Knau lowered his bow, and the singers' voices died.

That was late afternoon, and at once the party set out as the Colonel had planned it, except that the boy went with them. He had just turned sixteen, this son called Walter, Knau had said, and it was time he saw a full-scale hunt. Knau and the others got into the station wagon with the guns and rocked away, and Jaeger and Walter set out on foot. At first it was not easy for them to speak, for Walter's dreams, or the presence of the hymns, or the assemblage of thoughts in his head, were like a veil between them. His long fingers wove and unwove, and wove again, the string of a cat's cradle as they walked down the village street, and then drew the cradle taut in his spread hands. But when he began to speak of the oak that had been planted at the gateway of the forest on the day of his birth, the words came easily. Gateway, he called it, as if the oak would swing back on iron hinges to let them pass, and he watched the cat's cradle as he spoke. An apple tree had been planted in the orchard for his brother, and a pear tree at the birth of his sister, and his was the oak, he said. If they entered the forest at the place where it stood, then the witches would let them be.

Now they were skirting the fields, and the voices of larks could be heard high above them, and around them the separate and minute evening celebration of the myriad birds. Walter moved, long-legged and vulnerable, like a young giraffe, beside Jaeger, watching, watching, for what might be taking shape in the grass.

"I've always taken good care of my tree, and now it has grown taller than I am," he said. "I covered its roots with fresh dung when the winters were cold, and I carried it pails of water every evening of the summer drought. That was last year, and the cattle were dropping dead in the fields, struck by the sun." He said the apples on his brother's birth tree were riddled with worms one summer, and his brother had come down with worms; and when his sister's pear tree had lost its blossoms in the wind one early May, her hair had fallen out in handfuls the same week, and not grown back until the tree was putting forth its buds again. Be-cause of the light that had seemed to fall on his face as he played (the poet's, the prophet's, the saint's illuminated face), there seemed nothing strange in all these things he said. He rolled the string of the cat's cradle with painstaking care, and put it into the pocket of his corduroys. "The witches come out in the early morning and the early evening," he said, and his voice was low.

"Oh, the witches!" said Jaeger. "I tell you, in our country there's always some kind of menace." *Our country*, he had said. *Our country*. "There always has to be. At this moment, I'm more worried about the boar."

"Hush, now," said Walter, the loping, tentative, giraffe-like stride bringing him closer to Jaeger. "You don't have to say it so loud."

The faces of the summer flowers had become as luminous as stars in the tall grasses on either side of the path, and now the precarious clarity of evening opened wide about them. Jaeger thought of the wild things that would stir, unseen, in the long twilight, that were even stirring now, and he was impatient with his own anxiety.

"I don't know much about witches," he said, "but they tell me there's nothing as tenacious about life as a boar. They can endure more than expellees, more than refugees, if you can believe it, more than Jews can, even, these German boar," he said in abrupt irritation with them because they would not die. "Even a shot straight through the heart or the head won't finish them off, nine times out of ten. That's what hunters have told me. 'Unyielding courage' should be written on their coat-of-arms, for enough of it endows men and beasts with a kind of second life."

"Does it?" said Walter, his voice wondering. "Does it? Is that really true?"

"Oh, yes," said Jaeger. "You can outwit a witch by the way you take into the forest, but you're not going to fool a boar."

"Hush," said Walter. "Hush," his face as white as the flower faces around them in the dusk.

"But we have to have them, just as England has to have her constant scourge of rabbits, bunny rabbits nibbling her vegetables away," he went on, trying to make it funny for the boy. "In our forests, in our eternal dark underbrush, we have these brave, stubborn pigs." *Our forests, our underbrush*, he heard himself saying. He did not remember when he had spoken like this before. "They are shy as maidens, that is quite true, but they are also as fierce as tigers. They'll battle the dogs when they're cornered and shot—as the Jews fought tooth and nail for their lives," he added without warning, not knowing that he would say it or why it was said. He did not remember having spoken that word to any German since the war. "They tell me they never cry out, but with bullets pumped through them and intestines ripped open, they'll leap to their feet and shake off the pack, and thrash out at man—"

"The Jews?" said Walter, his voice wondering still.

"Yes. Well, yes," said Jaeger. "But I was speaking of the boar."

"I can tell you a story about Jews," said Walter, and then he stopped speaking. They had come to the edge of the forest, and in the stillness that hung in a bluish veil, and yet flooded like water over the country, Walter reached out and laid his hand against the bark of a young tree. "This is my oak," he said. Behind them, the open land was going dim, and here, at the threshold of the woods, an even more impenetrable shadow was cast on leaf, and rock, and branch. "You touch the tree, too, and then there will be nothing to fear," said Walter, and Jaeger pressed the cool side of the tree an instant with his open hand.

Then they moved cautiously into the area of trunks and brush, keeping to the left flank, as the Colonel had ordered; and here a path was worn in the rich, ancient earth, perhaps by Walter's feet alone on the journeys he made to his rooted, tough-leafed identity. And now that his being had been purged by ritual, wiped clear of all images, all faces, all sounds, except those of the story he wanted to tell, he began speaking of it again.

"I knew a Jew last year," he said, "but she was not like a Jew. She was not the way they say Jews are. In the war, she'd been in a place where people died, and when the war was finished she went to another place where all the lost children were. She was ten years old when she came to Ober-Pastau, and she lived a few months with a family in the village, waiting. She was waiting for them to find her mother and father for her, because they got lost during the war. She used to come and sing when I played the organ, but my father didn't like her to come because sometimes Jews carry diseases. That's why they had to put them away together during the war. So she and I used to walk down to my oak tree all that summer, and I showed her the way to enter the forest," Walter said. Before them, the small voices of crickets fell silent, and spoke tentatively behind them again when they had passed. "One night she climbed out the window of the house across the street from us where she was staying, and no one ever saw her again," Walter whispered. "She must have got tired of waiting. And I cried; I cried for a long time after she was gone. She could have got lost in the forest. But nobody knows. She could have got caught, you know—caught, and turned into something different from a girl."

There seemed nothing strange to Jaeger in the story that Walter now began to tell, and nothing to wonder at that he wanted to tell it as they moved through the faintly breathing, faintly murmuring, beginning of the dark.

IX

It must have been country like here in Ober-Pastau, Walter said, and although it was June now, Jaeger could see the snow lying over the hills, and the wind sweeping it off the surface of the roads, baring the black ice underneath, and moving on across the fields. He could see the entire world armored in ice, for Walter said that when the story began, the month was January, and the year was 1947, and everything had died of the cold that month, that year. Trees were frozen upright, without so much as a crow to give life to their branches, and nowhere was there any sign of flesh and blood. *Flesh and blood. Flesh and blood.* If you had said these words aloud then, they would have begun to steam like fresh dung on the air. Everything that lived seemed to have fled from this country that had lost the war; except the small figure of a child could be seen walking along the road.

"You knew it was a girl because of the pieces of hair that lay on the collar of the overcoat," Walter said, each detail as clear in his mind as if he had watched through a window as she came. "They hung out from under her hood, the pieces of hair, and the hood was knitted wool, so you knew it belonged to a girl. But the rest of the clothes were men's clothes. I saw them. She was wearing them still when she came here in the summer," he said.

The sleeves of the overcoat were turned back nearly to her elbows, and still they were too long for her, and the coat was buttoned down tight below her knees, and someone had cut the rest of it off to make it the right size. Strips of sacking were bound around her feet, but they didn't keep her feet warm. But she had been walking a long time with hunger and cold as her companions, and she didn't want to argue with them any more.

("I'm telling you the story exactly the way it was," said Walter. "She told it to me so many times that I know. She didn't have the sacking around her feet in the summer when she came here, but I'm talking about the winter when she was walking still. I never could understand the story very well, so she told it to me over again every time we walked down to my tree together. She said the coat weighed too much, even in the winter, and so did the *Wehrmacht* trousers they'd cut down for her, and so did the grey canvas bag on her back.")

She knew she couldn't carry these things much farther, but she didn't want to give up now when she had come this far. Her head was lowered against the wind, and when she came around a bend in the road, she looked up, and there she saw the houses huddled together. Icicles as tall as men hung from their eaves, and there were frost flowers on the windowpanes, so she knew it must be warm inside them. The ends of her fingers had come through her gloves, and she looked at the white tips of them as she knocked at the first door, and then she put her hands quickly back in the pockets of the overcoat again. The woman who opened the door didn't open it very far, just enough to hear the little girl asking where Hoffnung was, but not enough to let the cold enter like a wolf into the house. The woman pointed to the sign at the turn of the road ahead, and the little girl looked across the snow at the words of direction written in Polish as well as German, for she could read Polish as easily as German now.

("But they weren't her languages," Walter whispered to Jaeger as they walked. "She had another language, but she couldn't remember what it was. It had been too long ago.")

"You'll find stone sentry boxes marking the entrance to

the camp. It used to be an S.S. camp," said the woman. Behind her skirt, the little girl could see a red strip of fire where wood burned in the grate of the stove. "It used to be very well kept up, with soldiers in fine winter uniforms, but times have changed. Now there are twenty or thirty thousand foreigners up there in Hoffnung. People who have no homes," the woman said in blame.

"Yes. Hoffnung's the place," the little girl said. "That's where I want to go."

"So you're a foreigner, too?" said the woman.

"I'm not sure what I am," the little girl said, "but I think I'm going to find my mother and father up there, and then I'll know. I can speak Polish very well now. I learned it on the way."

"So how long have you been 'on the way'?" asked the woman. She closed the door a little more so that the heat would not get out and the cold would not get in.

"It was summer when I began to walk," the little girl said. "I wanted to get to Hoffnung because they say that's where the parents are waiting for the children to come."

("The story is hard to understand," Walter interrupted the murmured telling of it. "Sometimes when I think of it, I don't understand it at all, and other times it's almost clear." And so he went on telling it as explicitly as if it had happened to him, and more than that: as if nothing else that had ever happened in his life had the same hard, indisputable veracity.)

"Where have you slept every night since the summer?" the woman asked, perhaps believing nothing that had been said.

"Sometimes people gave me beds, and sometimes I slept with the cattle. It was better with the cattle," said the little girl. "It was warmer there."

"Ah-ha!" said the woman. "That's what I thought! If it

was summer, you wouldn't have worried about being warm. You haven't been walking that long at all."

"Yes," the little girl said. "When I slept with the cattle, winter or summer, it was better. It was not so lonely there."

"But you didn't learn Polish from the cattle!" the woman said, closing the door until only a thread of warmth was left.

"I learned it from the Polish people who walk on the roads," said the little girl.

"Well, you'll find enough of them up there!" the woman said, and she closed the door all the way.

The little girl passed the empty sentry boxes, and came around the shoulder of the hill, and she had trouble putting one foot before the other because the snow had drifted with the wind, and here it was above her knees. When she saw the first grey stone buildings, she thought maybe the faces she had known a long time ago were waiting and watching for her at the windows, and then she saw the military cars drawn up and hooded with snow before the steps, and she went on by. It must be higher up, beyond, among the twenty or thirty thousand others, that the parents would be, for she could see the smoke of the kitchen fires rising above the needle trees. And, at the top, she came to snow-packed streets that were like the streets of a familiar village, and windows were already lighted. Evening was beginning to close its arms around the world again.

("It was about this time of day," Walter whispered, for the wild game in the forest must not hear them coming; "except it was January instead of June. The dusks are short in winter, not like now." He had scarcely finished speaking when a faint, weary bleating could be heard before them in the undergrowth, and they halted. It seemed to be there, just ahead in the tangle of the forest floor, and they moved again, feeling their way toward it in the dark. "A week ago, we lost a young lamb, and Mutti goes to the stream with the children in the evening and watches for it to come to the water to drink," Walter said.

Jaeger was kneeling on the ground now, and his hand fell on its matted coat, on the small skull crowned with burrs and thistles; and the lamb's mouth nuzzled and sought for the ends of his fingers, and frantically began to suck.

"It might not be a true lamb, but a witch that has taken this shape to put a spell on us," Walter whispered. "It spoke my name. I heard it." He would not come any nearer. "It cried 'Walter, Walter'!" he said.

"Witch or not, I'm going to tie it here so that we'll find it on our way back," said Jaeger. "We can't carry it with us. Its bleating would scare things off. Give me the string you have in your pocket," he said, and Walter reached out from where he stood and put the string of the cat's cradle in his hand.

For a while, the lamb's voice called after them, called piteously and grievously, and the farther they went, the less it seemed a lamb's voice, and more the voice of a child that cried for succor through the trees. As if to efface the sound of it, Walter went on with the whispered story of the little girl, until wandering child and wandering lamb became interchangeable to Jaeger, and he did not want to think of them in the man-ridden and fox-ridden night).

"In the first street she came to, there were people walking, just like in a village," Walter was saying.

He said there were women with market baskets on their arms, perhaps going home to make the soup, and men in work clothes, going home at the end of the day. When a group of children came by, the little girl began walking with them through the twilight, walking toward warmth and food and the parents, for this was the direction that children would know. But one girl cried out in Polish:

"We're not to go back to our houses now! We're to go to

the entertainment hall first! There's something happening there!"

The children were happy when they heard this, and the little girl thought that perhaps in the entertainment hall all the mothers and fathers would be sitting on seats like in a theater, and the children would go rushing down the aisles. They would take the red plush seats the parents had saved for them, and the smallest would be taken on the parents' knees, and they would watch the stage with their mothers' and fathers' arms around them, and after a while the music would begin. It had happened to her somewhere before, in another country. She could remember the height of the ceiling, and the light dying in the chandeliers, and the people seated on red-cushioned seats, and the curtains parting. But she did not know the name of the city, or the country even, where this had taken place.

"Appolina, Teodor, Antoni!" the girl who had spoken called out to the younger children. She was a thin, beautiful girl, with sad eyes, and she wore a blue handkerchief tied over her head. "Izabela, Ryszard, Sofia!" she called to them, the way a mother would call out to her children.

Now they came to a building with long windows lighted on the snow-filled square, and although the small children waited at the bottom of the steps, the big boys stopped making snowballs and ran boldly up and turned the handles of the double doors. The light that poured down the steps made a passage through the cold, and the tall girl led them up this corridor, the wood of their boot soles ringing out like the boots of an army on the stone.

"Sofia, Antoni, Izabela, Teodor, be quiet now!" she said to them, and they did not talk or laugh any more after going through the doorway of the entertainment hall.

("Twice," Walter interrupted himself again, stopping now in the dark, "I saw a stranger in the woods, once in

May by my oak, and the second time right here. Right where I'm standing now," he whispered, "maybe two weeks ago." The first time, he had kept his hand on the trunk of his oak, and nothing had happened to him. The man had simply walked by, with a gun on his shoulder, but whether he was tall or short, native or foreigner, he could not say. "The first time, I stayed so quiet by my oak that a spider spun her web between the sleeve of my jacket and my tree," Walter whispered, "so that kept me from any harm. But the second time, I saw the ferns and violets right through his legs." *So he could have been made of mist, or glass, or running water.* "It wasn't quite dark, and he passed so close that I saw the blood of animals underneath his nails," Walter said.)

Then they went on, walking softly, and Walter took up the story of the little girl again, saying she had gone into the hall with the other children, and it was not like a theater, for there were no red plush-covered seats, and no stage, and no curtains that would part or rise. There were benches set in rows before a platform with a table on it, and there were no mothers and fathers sitting there. There were only children, hundreds of children, some scarcely able to walk, with older brothers and sisters beside them, and others with schoolbags on their backs, and the little girl walked down the aisle and found a seat, and slipped the straps of the canvas bag from her shoulders, and sat down. There was no music playing, and none about to play. But two men in uniform had climbed up on the platform, and one began to speak.

"Some of you here this evening will remember me," he began saying, speaking in Polish to them. There were colored ribbons and medals on his breast. "You will remember that I came here two months ago and spoke to all the children who have no parents in the camp. Poland still needs those sons and daughters who remain abroad."

"Is he St. Nicholas?" the little boy called Ryszard whispered.

"Maybe he's God," said the little boy called Teodor.

"Hush, children," the tall girl said.

"Perhaps you will remember the nice trip we offered to every child," the officer said, clearing his throat. He was dark-haired and young, and he gave a wide, friendly look to the hundreds of children before him in the hall. "And now I want you to know that we are offering the same thing to everyone again. You may remember that I spoke about a train, a special children's train, with all kinds of things in it that you would like, very different from any train you've ever seen. I know many of you came to Hoffnung in trains, but they were freight trains, they weren't special children's trains. You had to stand up in the cars you came in the way cows and horses do when they go for a trip." He smiled out across the rows of benches, wanting them to laugh at this, but they did not laugh. "This train, this special train," he went on, "has beds in it, real little beds that you can climb into and go to sleep in, and it has real sheets and blankets that you can pull up over your heads."

The children had begun to talk among themselves, and the boy called Antoni turned in his chair to the tall girl who held Izabela in her lap.

"Stanislawa, what are sheets?" he asked her.

"Hush," she whispered, leaning forward. "They are white linen coverings for beds. They come between you and the blanket, and between you and the mattress, very clean and nice—"

"And in this special train that was made just for you,"

213

the Polish officer was saying, "there are bright silver basins with spigots that you turn, and water runs out of the spigots into the basins." The children murmured aloud at this, and then they listened again when the officer spoke of the pillows they would have to put under their heads. "You climb into these beds in the train, and you go to sleep," he was telling them, "and when you wake up a wonderful thing will have happened. It will happen to you just as it happened to all the other children who left here with us two months ago. When you wake up, you will be in your homeland! After the terror of the German Occupation, after all the years of moving from place to place, you will be back in Poland. You will be home again at last!" He stood smiling at them from the platform, while the other officer looked down at his papers on the table, and shuffled them, getting ready to speak. "Last time I was here, the children ran out of the hall and packed up their things," the first officer went on, "and they were able to go off the next day in the special children's train. This much you know, but you do not know that just before the train went off every boy in it was given a game and a picture book, and every girl was given a doll, that they could keep. These were new games, and new books, and dolls, and they never had to be given back. That was the first train to leave Hoffnung, and tomorrow the second train will be going, and it will be a finer one than the first train, for this one has a dining-room in it, a dining-car, and you can sit down and have your dinner at little tables, all of you, tomorrow night."

("I'm telling you the story the way she told it to me. Whenever we went to my oak, she told it," Walter whispered to Jaeger. "I've never told it to anyone before.")

The other officer picked up his papers from the table, and he straightened his shoulders, for now it was his turn to speak.

"You have heard all about the children's train, so now I will tell you about the special things that are waiting for you when you get back to Poland," he said. He was an older man than the other, and he spoke sadly and gently to them, glancing down every now and then at the papers in his hand. "The place where you will go is not a large settlement such as you live in here with thousands of grown people from different countries in it. It is a camp that has been arranged, just as the train has been, especially for you, especially for Polish children. There are playgrounds waiting for you there, and there are many unusual attractions," he said, referring to the paper he held. "There are, among other things, sand piles, swings, slides, and a swimming-pool. And that is not all. For the older children, there are many opportunities offered for education. There are trade schools for girls as well as boys, special training-courses, and many other unusual—" He sought for another word for a moment, but could not find it, and so he repeated: "attractions. You can learn to be carpenters, masons, plumbers, skilled factory workers." His voice droned on, filled with a singular sadness, as if his heart was somewhere else. "Poland needs engineers, technicians, doctors, lawyers, teachers, and professors, clerks, officers, priests, and men in other walks of life. Each young person is free to choose the work he or she wishes, and to follow the courses which seem best suited to his or her abilities. Warsaw is rising from the ruins. . . ."

There was a stir of unrest in the hall because of the monotony of it, and because suppertime was near, and the young officer interrupted the other with a smile.

"Before you go on, Captain," he said, "may I speak to the children of one other aspect of the future? May I just mention the children's families who are waiting in Poland?" The children's faces turned at once to him, and silence fell on the benches; no piping, childish voices asked to leave the hall now, and no fretful cries were heard, for the hope and the longing that mingled in the memories of the older ones had been transmitted magically to those they held on their knees. "Now, I know all of you," the officer said in his pleasant, friendly voice, "would like to have news of the parents you have been separated from for so many years. Well, that is another thing we are ready to promise you. Here you have been living with guardians, with people who have befriended you, but who are not people of your own blood. In many cases, you have become very much attached to them, for they have been kind to you. But what future awaits you if you stay abroad? You will have a difficult life among strangers, among those who can never be the same as your mothers and fathers, while at home you will find a hearty welcome, and the love of those nearest and dearest to you, and the future will mean working for the well-being of your own land." The smile was fixed, immovable, on his lips now as he walked back and forth on the platform, looking up and down and backwards and forwards across the hall, his eyes moving swiftly across the rows. "So when this meeting is over, stop at the door on your way out—all of you—and show your identity card to the officer who will be waiting at a table in the hall. He will write down in his book your names, and the names of the towns where you were born, and that means you will be put on the list of the children who are going home tomorrow on the special train. This is your own decision to make," he said, and, although he smiled still, his face seemed to darken. "Do not let others change your minds. Special food rations will be given to every repatriated child, to every boy or girl who decides to go home to the towns where they were born." The shadow that had fallen on his handsome face lifted now as he went on saying:

"There is therefore no reason for further delay. Return to your homeland tomorrow! Your names will be sent ahead of the train by telegram, so that all the towns will know!"

It seemed to them, then, that this was the way it was going to happen. In that moment of quiet when the officer's voice ceased, they believed that their names would run like messengers before them, and that the syllables would be called out from street to street, from rooftop to rooftop, of the towns of their own country; and as the sound of their names rang out, the people they belonged to would spring up with cries of recognition, and would come hastening to the stations at which the special train stopped, and crowd upon the platforms as the cars pulled in. "Antoni, Ryszard, Sofia, Izabela!" the voices of the mothers and fathers would shout down the years. "Stanislawa, Teodor, Appolina, Josef, Waldemar, Antonia!" These imperishable names would be heard above the whistling and rattling of the special train, and even above the fierce denial of memory, the voices of those who had given the children their flesh, their blood, louder than the clamor of any church bells at Christmastime, and than any organ music thundering across the winter air.

All this went undisputed, filling them with wonder, until a dark, thin boy jumped to his feet in the middle of the hall. A purple scarf was wound several times around his neck, and the thickness of this scarf made him hold his head up as if in pride. His hair was black and curly, and uncombed, on his skull, and he faced the Polish officers without any sign of fear.

"No. That isn't true," he said in a strained, high voice. "Our parents are not there." The children's faces now turned to him, but almost in impatience, seeing his hair was too long, his cheeks too hollow, not wanting to hear the things he said. "My father was killed in 1940. I saw him

217

killed," he was saying. "The Germans shot him against the front of our house. My mother died in 1944 in a camp where we were together. I wrote the date down." His voice was thin and high in the silence of the entertainment hall. "This boy, here," he said, and when he gestured it could be seen that the jacket he wore was too small for him, and that his wrists hung long and red from the tight sleeves. ("Like my corduroy jacket," Walter whispered, not saying: *The wrists could have been mine, couldn't they, Herr Jaeger? The voice could have been mine. That's why I don't understand it. I don't understand why they weren't mine.* "My corduroy jacket's getting too small for me the way his was," he said.) "He and his parents were brought into Silesia by the Germans," the boy went on saying in the entertainment hall. "His mother and father worked in an ammunition factory, and he saw the factory bombed, burned down, wiped out, you understand? That was three years ago, and he saw it, and now you tell him he'll find them again in Poland! In some of us there is perhaps a little hope, not much hope, and not in many of us, but still a little hope is left to us who did not see them die!" His voice had gone thinner, shriller, and now, without any warning, he flung at them the words of furious, adult obscenity. When that was done, he became a child again, and cried: "How can you make these promises to us when you do not know?"

And now the situation must be saved, for the sake of the children it must be saved, and the tall girl called Stanislawa put Izabela onto the lap of the next child, and stood up from the bench. The young officer moved uneasily on the platform, and the older one reshuffled his documents, his eyes lowered under his grey brows. Stanislawa curtsied to them before she began to speak.

"Oh, believe me, sirs," she cried out across the children's

heads to them; "believe me, all of us here wish to go home!" She stood like a statue, a monument, above the seated children, and on the tide of their bewilderment, their faces drifted helplessly toward her. "But where is there for us to go back to when we remember—we who are old enough— we remember everything? You ask us to return to a special camp where there will be playgrounds for the children, and schools, and swimming-pools, and to wait there until our parents come. But our parents will not come for us, never, never. They cannot come. It is no longer possible for them to come." She looked with anxious, despairing eyes around the hall, but whatever had been ready to break in her voice faltered only for an instant, and then she went on speaking clearly and strongly again. "My brothers and sisters who are here with me do not remember. For six years, they have been my children, Ryszard, Antoni, Sofia, and Appolina," she said. "Whatever they saw six years ago, they have forgotten. Believe me when I tell you, sirs, that there are no parents left for us to go back to, not for any of us here!"

And now, one after another, the children on the benches began crying, but unlike the way in which children cry. It happened like this: a child in the back of the hall would cover his face with his hands, and then another, and still another, would bow his head, until it seemed to the little girl that whichever way she looked there were children crying silently. But this crying made no demands, shouted out no accusations, asked for nothing, not even to be heard, voices and tears having been separate so long a time that neither was part of the other any more. The older ones— those who did not have the right to succumb—bowed their heads as well, and covered their faces with the ends of their scarfs, bit into them, even, to keep the sound of crying in, while their bodies shook as if their hearts were tearing slowly apart inside their breasts. Even Stanislawa had failed them now.

The little girl closed her eyes so as not to see them, and the hard, dry pain came into her throat. *If you don't let your mouth take the shape of crying, then you can't cry,* she told herself. But she had been walking a long time, and she had not eaten since morning. She had come a long way to the place called Hoffnung, and it did not seem to be the place, after all, where the parents were waiting.

("I don't understand the story," Walter said again.)

The fluid night had closed like water on their mouths, and sealed their eyes. They were the only two swimmers left in the current, greased and masked with black for a channel crossing, their feet insensible to the feel of the forest rot, inasmuch as all foothold was illusion, they being swimmers, not walkers, swimmers drifting out of the reach of each other's hands, almost beyond the reach of the ever-widening lassos of each other's voices. They were alone in a black sea, so far from other men that the sound of the gun firing far to the right did not concern them, and Jaeger felt no shame when the tears came to his eyes. (*Oh, God, why tears, tears of pity for what, self-pity, Walter-pity, pity for all men whose loves have been denied them, pity because there is only one co-citizen humble enough to swim with me through the black waters without foothold or destination or estimate of the distance covered, without passing verdict on those who have not undertaken the crossing from the familiar mainland of hearth and home, from the unalterable names of table and chair, to the floating continent of mythical foliage and beasts that speak man's name aloud? The tears are not for the children in the story, Walter, for if you cannot understand it, it is for the same reason that I will not understand it, for we know it is not the*

story of a child who walks the roads of a country seeking
the flesh and blood of his people, but that the child is man,
his heart lifting in hope at the smell of honeysuckle or the
sound of a singer's deep voice, man seeking his own per-
jured identity, either wandering a country road, or groping
through a forest, or at a copy desk, feeling his way from
word to word; and who the officers on the platform of the
entertainment hall may be, I cannot tell you; perhaps
merely the givers of easy answers, or wrong directions,
merely the false prophets offering their meaningless jargon
to harassed man.)

And then the second blast of gunfire came, closer to them,
splitting the night wide open. It was, again, a single shot,
but this time the reverberation of it ran a crooked course,
carving like a scalpel of lightning through wood and stone.
The swimmers who had lost their footing when the deep,
still night poured over them were fixed to the earth now,
rooted like trees, the sap halted in them.

"That was on the other side, down near the lumber road
this time," Jaeger said, whispering it, although the need
for silence had been shattered with the night.

"*Ja, ja,*" said Walter. His fingers closed, cold and shaking,
on Jaeger's hand. "Let us get back to my oak. Let us get
there quickly," he said.

Jaeger led the way, drawing the boy on with him, seeing
nothing, the mere acquiescence of the earth underfoot
confirming that this was the path by which they had come.
In another moment, the lamb would bleat, and they would
kneel in the underbrush and grope for it, and the blunt nose
would nuzzle for comfort against their hands. Jaeger would
untie the string at its neck, and lift it, weightless, as the
starving, the dying, are without substance, and he would
button it inside his coat. They would pass the oak, pressing
it with their open palms, and move along the edge of the

221

marsh, talking as loudly as they pleased now that death had been dealt by the hunters and authorized the wide, dark night to speak. (*While I walk, the oil well at Flegendorf is still burning*, thought Jaeger, *giving the fields around it the color of flesh and blood; the blind student is talking still of the Währungsreform as he taps his way down the halls of learning; the Zimmermann upholds his honor with eternal hammer and triangle; the Lipizzan horses still leap to the sound of Christoph's voice in the ring; the Herr Graf speaks unceasingly of the revolt of the ignorant and the unlettered that is moving across the face of Europe; of all my countrymen, only the Wehrmacht soldier has changed his role: he no longer scratches and claws for freedom in the sealed halls of the air-raid shelter, no longer surrenders to the Russians, having surrendered to death in the ambulance that was bearing him toward life. What irony, eh, Walter? After surviving four years of entombment, what arrant effrontery!*)

Indeed, the night was authorized to speak, but they did not know it would suddenly cry out in terror. They did not know that teeth would be sunk into its throat, tearing from it scream after dying scream. The sound of it stopped them short in the dark, and Walter stood moaning, swaying against Jaeger, his hands covering his ears so as not to hear this brutal ravishing and murdering of the night. Jaeger put an arm around his shoulders and held him fast, feeling his own heart trembling in him. And then it was done; it was completely over; there was nothing left but the flight of airy feet through the leaves.

"The lamb. He got the lamb," Jaeger said. The stench of fox was drifting, as smoke drifts, slowly rising, unfurling, on the windless air.

"*Ja, ja*, but it was like a child screaming," Walter said. He moaned the words through his closed teeth, and he could not stop his shuddering. "We should have taken it with us when we went. We should have known, we might have known that . . ."

"Yes," said Jaeger. He wanted the night to breathe and murmur again, to speak with the small, bright voices of crickets. "I should have carried it inside my coat," he said.

They did not see the lights of any car on the lumber road as they walked back to the village, but there in Knau's courtyard stood a handsome green station wagon, only it was not the Colonel's car. It was parked by the dungheap, its lights extinguished, the faint wash of lamplight through the kitchen windows turned bright and garish on its chromium armor and its Simonized flank. The rear door was open, and the short figure of a man bent in the shadows, busied with what lay within. At the sound of footsteps on the cobbles, he straightened, and they saw the silk of his summer jacket take the light, and the neat, tan-colored straw hat that was set on the side of his head.

"Well, hi, Herr Jaeger!" the opera singer's voice called out, warm as a friend's, after the first instant of recovery. He took a step forward, and then thought better of it, and took a step back. His mouth was smiling, but not quite with ease. "It's a pleasure, but an unexpected one, to see you here!" Dardenella said. He placed the hat, with its smartly pleated, flowered band, at a more casual angle, his hands decked out in short, yellow gloves, unbuttoned at the wrists. "It was such a pretty night for Germany that I drove out to get some country air. *Guten Abend*, Walter. Walter's an old buddy of mine," he said, standing between them and the station wagon's open back door. "Gee, I remember when I was a kid, wanting to get that two weeks of camp, waiting around for the word to come, waiting like crazy every summer, and a couple of summers it didn't come through! I remember that! And there I was stuck in a place called Brooklyn where only one tree grows!" He was laughing as he crossed his arms over, the links of the bracelet light and loose on his wrist. He leaned against the end of the car, one foot cocked in its neatly fitting suede shoe. "Are you doing some kind of business out here, Herr Jaeger?" he said, his voice filled with kindliness and warmth, wanting to be on Jaeger's side, asking for nothing but just that in return.

"Yes. Interpreting for the Colonel," Jaeger said. Whatever was taking place, he wanted to make it explicit for this little man with his dark, yearning eyes lashed so luxuriantly, richly, like a horse's eyes. "We left the rest of them back in the woods, lost track of them. There was shooting, so they may be bringing a roebuck in—the Colonel, Miss Roberts, Lieutenant Stephany, and Honerkamp, and the forester, Knau."

"Oh, a party! I wouldn't want to intrude, then," Dardenella said. "I'd better be getting on my way." The Colonel's name had changed the look of things, had altered the sweetness of the evening air, and Dardenella turned quickly now, and closed the station-wagon door. He twisted the key, and drew it out, and tried the handle. Then he dropped the key in his jacket pocket, and dusted off the palms of his gloves. "Herr Jaeger, I'm not fooling about the country air," he said, "but I'd like to give you the straight story of what I'm doing here." With the side of his left shoe, he scraped a farmyard deposit from the other sole, looking down, smiling uneasily. "Once a week, I drive out here to pick up first-class feed for the horses, for my Lipizzan babies. I come out and pick them up good meadow hay—fescue, and crested dog's-tail, and rye grass, and yellow oat grass, and cocksfoot, and sweet vernal. I know them all. I've studied the books," he said, still smiling. "I come out here, and I don't know whether it's a black-market deal I'm putting over, or what it is, and I don't want to know. I just want the best I can get for the two of them, for Neapolitano Virgilia and the mare. I guess I don't care if I'm breaking some kind of law, Herr Jaeger. I guess it's come to that." He moved away from the station-wagon window, and he laid his small, gloved hand on Jaeger's forearm. "Just look inside there and you'll see the hay. You can see it, can't you?" he said. He had drawn Jaeger forward to look through the glass at the greenish sprays that lay on the station-wagon boards. It was hay, Jaeger saw, it was certainly hay, but scarcely enough for a week's feed. "Maybe you heard about the horse fair they're holding in Kneith in September," Dardenella said, almost laughing in his eagerness. "Christoph Horn and me, we're going down. There may be a Lipizzaner up on the block. We got a tip. I don't want to say too much, but we're going down to have a look. That would make three."

"But a horse like that, a Lipizzaner," Jaeger said. He sought the right American phrase. "It would cost you a million."

"Yes. A million, a cool million!" Dardenella said, and he liked the sound of it so much that he stood there laughing, looking up at Jaeger from under the tilted brim of the tan straw Stetson, his soft mouth warm and dark with his secrets, his teeth clear white as he laughed. "You see how it is, don't you, Herr Jaeger?" he said. "You understand about the hay. Only, you understand, I wouldn't want the Colonel to know."

There was no question that it was hay. Jaeger had seen it in the square of light that the kitchen window cast on the station-wagon floor. But when Dardenella had driven away, there was something else: Frau Knau was busy in the kitchen as they came in, bearing the tall, brown, commissary bags in her arms, lifting them from the table and carrying them one by one, because of the weight, to the closet underneath the stairs.

"*Guten Abend*, Herr Jaeger," she said, her voice and face entirely serene. "Come help me, Walter, to clear all this away."

There was no sign of it left by the time the Colonel's party drove into the courtyard. Frau Knau and Walter had gone upstairs to bed half an hour before the twin stream of the headlights moved across the windows and swung, like the shafts of a lighthouse beacon, toward the pigsty and the cattle stalls, and then went out. Jaeger had sat alone in the kitchen of the waiting, silent house, and now he put out the end of his cigarette, and stood up from the table. It was not quite ten o'clock as the Colonel and Knau came through the door.

"There's been some trouble, Jaeger," the Colonel said shortly. "Can you tell me where my daughter is?"

It might have been something to laugh at, the fact that she was gone again, if the look in the Colonel's face had been different. But the flush of drink, the fire of energy, were gone from it, and he stood there, haggard, brooding, old. Behind him, Knau closed the door against the warmth and the involvement of the outdoor dark, his shoulders wooden as he moved, his eyes, under the black hat's brim, blinking numbly in the light.

"She was with Lieutenant Stephany," Jaeger began, but the Colonel cut him short.

"Yes. That was five hours ago," he said. "Somewhere, during that time, she gave Lieutenant Stephany the slip. He doesn't even know which way she went." Jaeger watched a pulse beating in his left jaw as the Colonel felt in his trouser pocket and brought out a handful of crumpled bills and coins. "You gave my wife some German lessons. I don't remember how many, but take what I owe you out of this. I'm wiping all my blackboards clean." When he threw the money down on the table, two or three coins rolled over the edge and across the floor. "Take out for the interpreting, too," he said.

But nobody moved; nobody spoke. Knau dared not cast so much as a glance at the coins on the floor, sensing, it may have been, the presence of something more final than money in the kitchen with them now.

"I'll go upstairs and ask the wife," he said.

When he moved, the Colonel did likewise, following him up the narrow, ancient stairway, mounting vaguely, almost will-lessly, where the forester led, perhaps for no better reason than because he did not know where else to go. And Jaeger, not having relinquished yet the interpreter's role, followed after them. The upper hall was lit by one hanging, unshaded bulb, and they passed under it in single file, Jaeger stooping a little so that he would not strike it with his head. Knau, his back and shoulders rigid, turned the knob of the first door. Even when he entered the bedroom, the Colonel followed him doggedly, blindly, his mind and anger somewhere else, his step that of an older, broken man. Jaeger paused only an instant on the threshold, and then he followed behind the Colonel into the room. Knau had switched on a light on the dresser, and, along the east wall, the beds could be seen now, four of them, to judge from the wooden headboards, but the four of them pushed together to form a high, snowy plateau. On it, four pure white featherbeds ballooned in the half-obscurity, and long white bolsters propped the sleeping heads.

Frau Knau's was first. She lay a little in from the edge, leaving space, it might be, for Knau to lie beside her. When his labors would be done, he would take off his boots, and lay aside his ceremonious black, slip the suspenders free from his shoulders, lay his pants across a chair, and, with no more than this as preparation for the night, he would enter the clean white bed. Her braids were unpinned now, and one of them, tapering like a serpent's tail, lay long across the laundered casing. The gathered shoulders of her heavy nightgown could be seen, and the buttons fastening the neck. Next to her lay the side of Walter's face, restored to childhood as he slept, his ear and cheekbone flushed. And then came the *Oma*'s neat, gnome-like head, encased in a nightcap, the white ribbons of it tied under her fallen chin. Beyond them—and nearly beyond the reach of the lamplight—the blond children lay, their heads turned dark against the bolster's white. The shadows of the far corner had fallen like wings across them, so that for a moment the men did not see the third head there. It lay between the children's heads, the hair fanning wide behind it flexible as satin, the brows more beautiful than Jaeger had remembered, the mouth, in sleep, pale as a flower, neither smiling nor grieving, merely untroubled, asking for nothing at all.

"My God!" said the Colonel. "There's Milly over there!"

It seemed to Jaeger that he saw her for the first time now, the delicacy of her temples, her ears, the long, suave tilt of the closed eyes, the point of hair on her forehead as fine as the tip of an artist's brush; this face she always turned from them in misgiving now redeemed by sleep. It lay quite calmly on the bolster, as if soothed by an invisible hand. The Colonel might have been seeing her clearly for the first time, too, for he held his breath as he tiptoed toward the bed. Just once he turned to look back across his shoulder, as if asking for help, and Jaeger saw that a glaze of tears lacquered each blood-shot eye.

"Tell him he'd better wake her and get started for Fahrbach," Knau said to Jaeger, not speaking loud. "He'd better get the man to a doctor now he's found the girl."

228

"To a doctor?" Jaeger repeated. He looked at Knau. "What man?"

"Out there in the car," Knau said, but he did not finish, for the Colonel had begun to speak. He stood in the far corner of the room, looking down at the girl.

"Milly, wake up. Morning time!" he was saying, perhaps in remembrance of some childhood game they once had played. When she did not rouse, he spoke louder, and Frau Knau sat up, drawing the white case of the featherbed high under her chin. "Milly, wake up!" said the Colonel, but it broke his heart to do this. "We have to go quickly, Milly-kins. There's been an accident. Honerkamp, he was shot. He's bleeding like a stuck pig in the car."

"Honerkamp?" Jaeger's mind went blank and cold. "Honerkamp?" he said.

"There was somebody else out in the woods tonight," said the Colonel. He straightened up and threw his shoulders back. Across the room, his eye met Jaeger's eye. "Knau shot once. I say it was a roebuck we saw, he says a boar. He wanted to keep on through the forest after it, even without the dogs," he said, "so I let him go. Just before I hit the lumber road, coming back, somebody started blasting away."

But Jaeger did not hear the rest of it. He was running down the stairs. In the courtyard, Stephany walked up and down, up and down, impatiently, moving between the dungpile and the car.

"Honerkamp, good God, poor Honerkamp," Jaeger said as he opened the station-wagon door.

Honerkamp lay on the back seat, his face, in the light from the kitchen window, sapped of color, his mouth strangely dark and small.

"It's nothing, Jaeger, nothing," he said, his mind, his thoughts, on something else. "Did you find Milly?" he said.

229

"She's upstairs. She's asleep," said Jaeger. He was kneeling beside him on the floor. On Honerkamp's right arm, below the shoulder, was a tourniquet fashioned of the Colonel's mottled scarf, and the wound in the forearm was bound by a stained cloth. The hand that lay on his chest was cold. So passive was this hand now, not leaping from plate to plate for food, from book to book on a library shelf, the fingers of it not scratching in eager turmoil through his hair. "You're cold," said Jaeger, and he took off his coat, the brown jacket of ersatz wool with its slick undersleeves and its fraying cuffs, stretching it wide over Honerkamp's shoulders and the beating of his heart.

X

It was Monday morning, and Jaeger sat in the train that would carry him northward, a man again bereft of women, getting on now with the work there was to do. In the cellars of Kastel, the theater was coming to life, the political *Stuben* were satirizing Occupier and Occupied, and Borchert's *Draussen vor der Tür* was being played. It would make an article for the midweek edition, he thought as he looked through the window, his eyes seeing nothing, not even the beads of rain that merged into water snakes and writhed down the soot-fouled pane. The piece could be a deposition in his own terms concerning the dead and buried youth of Germany, and a salute to the violently alive who leaped, as if out of the grave, to the boards of makeshift stages now, to shout out their challenge to God, and nation, and official man, in uproarious travesty. At two, he would interview Fritzludwig, actor and producer as well, in a *Weinstube* off what remained of Kastel's Hindenburgplatz. He would meet at five with the players of two political cafés as they went through the pages of the Hamburg and Berlin daily papers, and *Der Spiegel*, for news not yet twenty-four hours old to give fresh barbs of meaning to their acts. At eight, there would be Borchert's comi-tragedy, acted under canvas stretched over a reconstructed stage, with the arches, and lobbies, and galleries of the demolished theater kibitzing in chaos from behind the audience's back. And after the final curtain, he would make the rounds of the night-club *Stuben* that had been air-raid shelters once, where, under the debris of a ruined city, the lively farce of the Political Passion was being played. But now it was morning, the train had begun to move, and the houses of Fahrbach were slipping away. And then Jaeger heard the compartment door grind on its runners and cry out in protest. When he turned his head, he saw Catherine Roberts seeking to open it from the hall.

"Jaeger," she said, her lips shaping the name against the glass that stood between them.

He had got to his feet, but his knees were stricken. He scarcely dared lift his eyes to see her, or breathe the air because of his fear of her scent.

"You're in Paris," he said in a low voice as he jerked back the door. "You can't be here."

"Yes, yes, I know," she said in confusion. She sat down, not looking at him as she spoke, but at the white fingers of the glove that she drew from her trembling hand. "Ephemeral, like the brewer," she murmured. A half-inch of varnished wood lay between the light linen of her dress and the brown wool of his trouser leg. "I took shape last night, in time to be there for the official questioning," she said, talking quickly, smoothing out long and straight the fingers of her glove that lay on the woven handbag on her knees. "It took place in Seth Honerkamp's room in the hospital. We walked every step of the way through the forest, walked it over again, I mean, looking for the stranger, the armed marauder, who was there that night. Each of us sees him in a different way—according to our prejudices, according to our tastes." The damp of the rain had burnished her hair to copper, and she seemed then more beautiful than any woman man had dreamed of, purer, more delicately colored, than Botticelli's Venus, but fashioned and destined for man's single purpose like Cranach's Eve. *Ah, but something has happened to her in those days and nights in Paris!* Jaeger thought. His eyes moved in anguish over the pale shell of her ear, across her unblemished cheek,

232

down the milk-white satin of her throat. Something had taken place that gave each hair that sprang from her temple and brow, each pore of her skin, a sun-struck lambency. *Some man held her in his arms, and kissed her mouth, and touched her breasts,* he thought in grief, listening to her speak of the stranger who had come and gone in the darkness of the woods. *Ah, yes, in darkness!* he thought savagely. *In the darkness of a hotel room!* Once, in his late schooldays, at a time when he knew nothing of America, he had written an essay placing the blame for the lack of moral values in American life on the collapse of the scaffolding of tradition that kept the social orders in their place. He remembered the simile well. Modern divergencies, he had written in young pomposity and ignorance, such as canned foods, had brought about the degeneration of the American people. They corrupted values according to their whims, the Americans, he wrote, allowing a workman to become a senator, a businessman a general, a miner the owner of a mine. And sitting there in the train, it seemed to him still that they split tradition up like firewood, condoning it if a married woman, a mother, an officer's wife, went to Paris and walked the streets in search of love, and found it, and carried the memory of it back like a lamp lit in her flesh. "It could have been none of the men who carried a gun that night. My husband checked every gun, and the ammunition," Catherine Roberts was saying. Her head was lowered still, the shallow white cup of her temple level with his shoulder, the tapering of her eyebrow glossy and supple as a swallow's wing. "Only the forester shot higher in the woods. You were there. You know that, too," she said. "I see the man as a German, a peasant, who didn't turn in his arms at the surrender. My husband and Stephany see him as American, a civilian, of course, and, of course, of foreign extraction. My husband has a long list of civilians he would like to see taken into military custody." *But Paris*, thought Jaeger. He could no longer bear to look at her. He thought of a shoemaker he had known in Colorado, an old man who had left Germany while still a boy, promising his father and mother and priest that, wherever he wandered, whatever his destination might be, he would never at any time, in any year, pass through the cesspool of all that Paris was. He had emigrated by way of Italy, believing then, and still believing it sixty years later, that because he had never breathed the air of Paris, his flesh and his soul had not been branded by iniquity. *Perhaps that belief lives in every German, in every one of us*, thought Jaeger, and his heart went bleak with the knowledge of his own damnation, and the woman beside him seemed bright and hard as a pillar of salt, and her purity a spurious thing. "Only Seth showed no interest in tracking him down," Catherine Roberts was saying in a low voice, "and it seemed to me it might be because he knew, or thought he knew." Her eyes did not move from the woven straw of the handbag on her knees, and her hands moved quietly, not trembling now, smoothing out the empty fingers of the gloves with care. "My husband has never for a moment forgiven Seth for having got the Officers' Club away from the army, and for having turned it into the America House. Never, never, waking or sleeping, sleeping or waking," she said. "Seth was being serenaded last night from the hospital garden below his window, by oboe and flute and violin, it must have been, and he was more interested in that than in finding the man who had tried to take his life; and interested in what you had written." The low voice went on speaking quickly, refusing to stop for breath. "He read me the article on the *Wehrmacht* soldier caught in the ruins, translated it word by word from the newspaper, and the one on the boy from

Milwaukee who buried his passport at the frontier, and his dollar bills with it, before walking across the border into Germany, expecting what flowering bush, what high tree, to grow there nobody knows. I think that is the way you wrote it. I think those were the words you used," she said.

"And Honerkamp told you I would be going to Kastel today?" Jaeger said. If the words she had spoken were music to his ears, still he had no wish to hear them now. "Honerkamp told you that it is a city that has been nearly totally bombed, and that it was a place every American should see. I hope you brought your camera with you," he said, his voice gone strained and evil in his mouth.

"We didn't speak of Kastel, we didn't mention Kastel," she said, and now her hands had ceased to move. "I telephoned the newspaper. I wanted to tell you I was back, back sooner than had been planned, and to ask if the German lessons could begin again. They said you were at the station, going away, and I got dressed, just throwing things on. That's why my hair looks the way it does." When she lifted her hand to put the shining tendrils back from her brow, her bare white forearm passed close to his mouth. "I couldn't find you in the station, so I got on the train. It happened to be the only one there," she said, saying these things quickly, breathlessly, as if fearing the other things that might be said.

"As for the lessons, that might be difficult. Your husband, the Colonel, he feels you have learned enough," he said, his voice still venomous.

"Yes," Catherine Roberts said. "I know."

"And still you telephoned the newspaper to ask that we go on with them?" said Jaeger.

He was outraged by her perfidy now. *Ah, God*, he thought, *to see the Seine polluted, to hear the chestnut trees on the boulevards go down screaming under the teeth of the electric saw! To see every bed in every Paris hotel dragged from the red plush and yellow satin upholstering of the rooms and burned in the Place de la République and the Place Vendôme, and any other Place, to make a public spectacle of it! To slash to a thousand ribbons every divan where she has lain with her lovers, to rip out the springs and guts of beds and men with my own hands, and leave them in the dismantled rooms, never again to reek with her scent, or groan beneath the ecstasies of her love!*

"Yes, still I telephoned," Catherine Roberts said, whispering the words scarcely aloud. "I could not bear it any longer—I mean, I did not wish to live any longer without seeing you."

He did not know if it was he who was the first to move, or whether it was she who turned her head to him, but suddenly his hands were on her shoulders, and he drew her against him more fiercely, more tenderly, than he had ever done in dreams. Her bag, her gloves, slipped to the floor beneath their feet, and his mouth closed on the soft, moaning music of her mouth. A quivering tide poured through their nostrils, filled their lungs, suffocated them, so that each breathed only with the other's breath. Now they were lost, borne farther and farther from all that had foothold in reality: the moving train, the falling rain, the unalterable demands and meanings of their lives. And even as he perished, Jaeger cried out in incoherent rebuke:

"Oh, Paris, Catherine! Those days, those nights!"

"No, no!" she whispered. "You are Paris, Jaeger, and all the nights and days," the words as soft as her lips, her breasts, her body dying in his arms. "There has never been anything, anyone, before. . . ."

They did not speak of a future, or a room, or bed, or years, they might share together, as if this was accepted beyond speech, beyond conniving, as how things were to be. They walked hand in hand out of the devastation of the Kastel station, and saw that the rain had drawn aside for a moment, and this seemed like a promise made them, and they smiled. A perpendicular ray of sun, metallic as moonlight, fell like a blade through the somber grisaille of afternoon —it was just after twelve—and they stood looking across the stripped square for the sight of one hotel left standing above the rubble beyond, but the word "hotel" was not pronounced. It leaned there in memory, as pictured on postcards of Paris, or on theater backdrops, and in tinted illustrations: the *Hôtel de l'Univers et d'Angleterre*, or *du Commerce*, or *du Nord*, supported on one side by the *Hôtel du Vingtième Siècle*, or *du Terminus*, and on other by the *Hôtel des Voyageurs* or *de la Gare*. But no sign spoke out to them across the ruins. Only a faint mist rose from the dump heaps of men's lives and habitations, steaming a little in the rain-washed air, so that they seemed to smoke still, as if the bombs had fallen only the night before.

"It has a terrible kind of beauty," Catherine Roberts said, for now even the look of tragedy had been transformed into a spectacle for them, and they smiled at the miracle of each other's faces. "Like Carthage," she said, ready to laugh out loud.

"There were crashed fighter planes lying in the fields even there," said Jaeger, "around Carthage even. And the two-thousand-year-old stone plows still drawn by oxen, detouring around them, going on turning the soil as they had in every other century, in every other year." He held her arm hard against him, her hand fast in his hand. "We could take a walk through the streets, if you're not tired," he said. In all his life, there had never been anyone to care for before.

"Tired?" Catherine Roberts cried out, appalled by the mortal insult of it. But in each of their minds, the dark, narrow lobby led in from the shattered street to the worn desk, the counter, on which the register lay open, and the cage of the elevator mounted uncertainly to the dusty strip of carpet and the closed doors of the upstairs hall. Outside each door, the pairs of shoes stood, the man's shoes and the woman's side by side, the woman's leaning, it might be, against the man's, and none of them polished yet, but still marked with mud because they had walked a long time through the rubble in search of a place where a man and a woman might lie down together in the embrace of love. "How could I be tired?" Catherine Roberts cried. She stood smiling, looking up at him. "You are wonderfully tall," she said, and although there was no humor in it, still they laughed.

"Would you take your high heels off?" said Jaeger, his voice hard and fierce, his hand nearly breaking the pliable bones in her hand. "Would you take them off here so that I can see how really small you are, your head hardly reaching my shoulder. I want you to do it here, in front of everyone," he said.

"Everyone?" she repeated in wonder. She looked around her, amazed.

And now that they took their eyes from each other, they saw that, despite the plague-stricken look of the square, there were others moving out of the station, some carrying brief-cases, bags, some with umbrellas raised although the rain had ceased to fall. But none of them stopped to hold each other's hands in love but crossed the square, knowing exactly to which black gaping entranceway, which crumbling mass, their business took them, going, with lowered heads, toward the halted heart of the town. In the first street that Catherine Roberts and Jaeger took there was no house left standing, and the hallway of no hotel tunneled through the craters, but still they believed that in a moment they would come upon it, perhaps just beyond the next broken façade, on the other side of the next rampart of debris, at the end of the next shattered arcade. And although in the second street, and in the third, there was still no sign, still their hearts were no less certain, and they put their concern with it aside. As they walked, they spoke of America, arm pressed in arm, the sound of the name filling them with elation, as if that was the next door that would open into the widening hallway of their lives.

"Most of Florida has been ruined, but still there are parts where the land and the vegetation have not given in," Catherine Roberts said, her head lowered, watching their feet walking side by side. "You can fight your way through that wilderness, or you can skim your way over the surface of it in special boats, air-boats, they call them. I can't tell you how fearful the place and the flying is." Their eyes sought the length of another street they had turned into, and came back gently, shamelessly, to each other's faces again. "We were stationed at Fort Lauderdale before the war, and the pinelands, the cypress swamps, the trees hanging with Spanish moss, were stranger than any foreign country I've ever known. Flocks of white herons, and blue herons, and red-necked vultures, and everywhere that jungle moss," she was saying, giving the tropical look of it to the bleak stretches of death that lay before them, and lay behind them, and on either side. In the next street, or the one after that, there would be the door they could close, the key they could turn, and the bed that had opened wide for other lovers would open wide again for love. "Even in America there are lonely places," she said shyly, almost in apology. *Is it possible that we might be permitted to begin again?* she did not say aloud to him. *Is it possible that we might sometime, somewhere, in another country, take all the first steps, say all the first words of love over and over,*

*not just once, not just today in a hotel room, but somewhere
forever?* Aloud, she said: "Sometimes I have wondered if
you would like to become an American."

"Then listen," Jaeger whispered, and he lifted her hand
against his mouth. "I am whatever you are, whatever nationality that might be called, whatever name it could be
given."

"No, no!" she cried out. "You must not be humble!"
Her lips embraced his fingers now, saying to them: "It is I
who wish to become exactly what you are."

The rain had begun to fall again, gently shedding its grey
tears over the graveyard that was Kastel, falling gently on
their hair, their eyes, but hope had no intention of dying now. There were other sections to this town, other
streets to follow, and the portal, the long hall, the gloom
of the lobby, the open register in which he would write their
names, would be suddenly there before them, startling them
by its accessibility. But down the uneven path of the pav-
ing-stones, moving rapidly toward them, came now a clot of
singularly abbreviated men. They did not stand upright,
nor did they sit, for the torso of each had been strapped
erect to a small wooden platform, homemade and mounted
on castors, and on these platforms they sped forward,
propelled by their knuckles, which were cushioned and
bandaged with leather pads. There were four of them, with
the beaked caps of the *Afrika Korps* worn jauntily on their
heads, although the insignia, and the braid, had been deleted with the honor a long time before. On the tan military
blouse of each was a single, identical decoration: a tin mess
cup that hung, empty for offerings, around each man's
neck on a knotted string.

"*Guten Tag! Guten Tag!*" they called out in greeting,
and they swung their platforms to a halt. They hooked arms
instantly then, and blocked the way, and a kind of wit or

humor passed, as tough as rope, from one to the other of them, as they waited there on their wooden mounts like dwarfs, like freaks, for some sideshow to open so that they might cash in on their eccentricities. But they were not dwarfs, for, down to the hips—which was all there was of them—they were handsomely proportioned men. Their faces were ruddy with health, their necks weathered with an old and enduring burn of wind and sun, as blazing as the desert underneath the falling rain. Their eyebrows were the color of sand under their caps, and their eyeballs, as white as porcelain, were marvelously diffused with blue. They might have been mountain guides seated at a table; for they had the look of men who came from high glacier country, and not as if they were fragments left over from the battlefield, alive still only because of a surgeon's ingenuity. "*Guten Tag!*" they said, with no respect for woman or man, and no courtesy, in the sound of it. In a moment, they might forget there had been a war, and jump to their feet, and flick their ski-poles under their armpits, and go twisting and turning down a mountainside, their mouths roaring and yelping with their yodeling, the snow winging behind them in sails of spray.

"Would the *Gnädige Frau* and the *Herr Gemahl* have a little *Trinkgeld* to spare?" asked the first man on the left of the row of them, his voice mimicking the craven, the beaten, the poor. In the worn leather cushion that bound the knuckles of his hand, he held his tin cup out toward Jaeger. "*Eine Kleinigkeit*," he whined.

"A *pfennig* or two for the needy!" puled the first man on the right of the line, his head cocked sideways to look up in sweetest mockery at the gentry standing there.

"We're collecting funds for the next war," said one of the others in a pious voice, aping the undefeated of Germany.

"It will have to take place on foreign battlefields,"

said the first man, and he shook his head. "We've used ours up. The scenery is falling to pieces everywhere."

"And, you know, this war, it will have to take place without me," said one of the two men in the middle. He looked up at them as if in true regret. "*Schade*, and me such a patriot," he said. But for all the comedy of these lines they spoke, still their eyes were sharp, their ears were peeled. They were watching for the audience before them to declare itself as well. "The whole bloody business will have to be undertaken *ohne mich*," said this man who appeared to be older than the others, the lines carved more deeply around his mouth and between his eyebrows that were bleached to golden bushes by a sun that had shone on his flesh, and his medals, and his equipment, in another country, a long time before.

"And *ohne mich*, if you can believe it," said the first man, sighing deeply.

"And, by coincidence, *ohne mich*," echoed the man on the right.

"*Ohne mich* as well," said Jaeger, his voice modest, low.

At once, the four men threw back their heads on their strong, weathered necks, and their platforms rolled this way and that.

"But, look here, you're still tall enough! They could even make two out of you to swell the ranks!" the first man said, and the platforms rolled on their castors, and the men laughed under the falling rain. All about them was a dying, grieving, somber world, and they as warm, as rich, as bulls or stallions, their flesh refusing the backdrop and wings of bloodless, broken stone. "Let me tell you that we could still serve, in case of need, set up in the turret of a tank!" the first man said, and still they laughed.

When Catherine Roberts and Jaeger put money into their empty cups, the men's blue eyes went sharp with acumen. And now, as the castors bore them swiftly away, they began to shout a marching song aloud in furious blasphemy. *"Und wir fahren, und wir fahren, und wir fahren gegen Eng-e-land!"* they sang, their voices loud, fierce, ironic. *"Heute gehört uns Deutschland, morgen die ganze Welt!"* rang the echoes far in the wrecked quarries of what the city had become.

When the interview with Fritzludwig was done, thought Jaeger, there would be time and to spare for love. If it was not to be allowed them in one long, sweet stretch, then pieces of it could be whittled from the end of the afternoon and the beginning of the evening, from today and tomorrow, and the days after that, from the quick minutes, the split half-hours, out of the hot nights of the unending summer that lay ahead. For this was the beginning, the tenderest season, for which all things with blood in the veins or sap in the stalks eternally waited. The calendar stood arrested at the first bird's call, the first blue lilac branch that flowered at the open door of spring.

"I am hungry," Catherine Roberts said as they walked, and now that they sat at a table against the wall in the *Weinstube*, held in the bower of the polished, high-backed seat, she said again in a low voice: "I am hungry and thirsty, Jaeger."

It was no more than a great stone cave, this *Weinstube*, hollowed two flights below the street. Around them in the half-dark the tables stood empty at this hour of the day. And to Jaeger their roles seemed singularly altered, for she was no longer a woman of subterfuges, girded with the national armor of American candor and American naïvety. (He had known it on men and women alike, that coat-of-mail of forthright innocence, so familiar to him now that he wanted to laugh out loud in pleasure at the thought of

243

it.) She had become uneasy as a child, a stranger in this place, and he must provide comfort and food, and interpret the meaning in men's faces and their voices when she looked at him uncertainly. He was the one who talked, telling her that people came here in the evening, or after the theater at night, and that a gypsy orchestra wandered among the lamp-lit tables then. It was as if she, who had always spoken so quickly, so easily, did not know the simple vocabulary that was required of her now.

"Yes, we shall eat," said Jaeger. There was only a middle-aged woman in an apron, her hair wrenched up in a fierce grey knot like a man's fist laid upon her head, who moved in the room, switching on the table lamp, setting the *Speise-karte* wearily before them, wiping the black oak of the table clean. "There is boiled hen. Do you like the sound of that?" Jaeger said softly to Catherine Roberts, softly, softly, as if he was speaking of other things.

"Do you ever eat enough? Do you sleep enough?" she whispered, hesitating over the words. She could look at nothing but his face.

"Now I shall eat enough, now I shall sleep enough," Jaeger said. It was still the beginning of spring.

As they waited for Fritzludwig, and waited for the food to be set before them, they held each other's hands in si-lence, hearing a man's voice in the kitchen exhorting the sad woman in her apron to jump higher, run faster, to get the carrots, the potatoes, the breast of chicken, the bread. They had begun to drink from the long-stemmed glasses when the woman returned to the table again and stood there, rocking a little, seeking gravely to keep her balance as does an unaccustomed ocean-traveler as a ship rolls out to sea. (*I have come to the end*, the woman was certainly saying, although her grey lips failed to speak the words aloud. She held to the table, the longish hairs on her upper lip trembling in the lamplight, her squat, manlike body reeling a little under the weight of all that life had been. *You might think it would be getting better now that the prisoners have begun to come back from Russia*, she might have been saying in the hush of the *Weinstube*, but that, too, was not without its awful depths of irony. Whether she told the story then or later, Jaeger did not know. It could have been articulated merely by her presence, and yet the date was somehow established in his mind. Her son-in-law, her daughter's husband, had been missing since 1942, and then last month, in the beginning of June, word came that he was on his way back with a shipment of them. Her face was as grey as granite and sober as a judge's, but she held to the table as if the room were swinging and swaying from right to left, and looping the loop as she talked. It might have been cattle, this shipment of which she spoke. *We were bombed out twice*, the story went on, without any drama to it. *My husband and two sons, fifteen and sixteen, killed the same night. And just last month, this other thing, as if we hadn't had enough.*)

She shifted her left hand to a chair now, and pulled it out, and sat down facing them. In her right hand, she still held the rag to wipe the table clean. She took the first swallow of white wine from the glass that Jaeger had put before her, and looked across the table with distant, absent eyes.

"My son-in-law, he'd never been much of a worker," she said. " 'Missing' was the right place for him to be." She stared at the wine that lay like moonlight in her glass. "Back in 1943, my daughter took up with somebody else, a good man, a butcher. She had to think of the children," she was saying. "And five years later, her husband takes it into his head to come home again. I tell you, I've had more than enough of the goings-on of this life and the kind of tricks that God thinks He can play."

She took another swallow of the wine, looking sternly from under her grey brows, even the whites of her eyes soiled and cold as iron in her face. And now the man, the chef, the proprietor, or whatever he might be, appeared in the top half of the swinging door, and he shouted out her name.

"This isn't the time to sit down and start drinking again, Frau Klingelhöfer!" he shouted out. She got to her feet, leaning wearily on the table a moment before she moved away.

Then she bore the tray of food back balanced on the flat of her palm, walking cautiously, the other hand outstretched to grasp the rail if the ship should wallow and fling her, reeling, from her course. On the dishes she set down was boiled fowl, milk-white in its yellow, wrinkled skin, and carrots with broad, orange hips, and *Salzkartoffel* laced with the green silk threads of leeks. There were white stalks of asparagus, bloated like the fingers of the drowned, different from the delicately seeded ferns that Jaeger had known by the same name in America, and that tasted of spring all summer there. When the woman had served them, she sat down with them again.

"Every time a prisoner comes home, you know how it is, they start decorating the street where he lives, and the front of his house," she said. "They string up flowers all over the place. So they did this for my son-in-law." Jaeger had filled up her wineglass again, and she sat looking at the cold, misted substance he had poured, her eyes seeing the vision of her own life as they ate. The *Weinstube* was quiet, the knowledge of the rain gently falling outside, muting the air, closing them in. Fitzludwig had still not come. "But nobody felt very good about my son-in-law coming back from Russia like that," the woman said. "With the shortage of meat there is, and the price of it, the butcher's the best man for anybody to know. Some people were saying that my daughter could divorce her husband after a while, and marry the butcher, but for the day he came back they had to dress the whole place up for him. It's always the custom. It had to be that way."

"Bring out the plates and the silverware, Frau Klingelhöfer!" the proprietor shouted after a while. "You leave the guests sitting there before their soiled dishes! They want their *Nachspeisen* and coffee now!"

The woman rose, and began to stack the tray again, and the kitchen door swung closed. When she came back with the *Strudel* and coffee, she said her grandchildren couldn't remember their father. The butcher was the only one they knew. And the butcher and her daughter had talked for a week, and even the mayor and the doctor had come into it, and the neighbors had all had advice to give, but nobody knew what to do.

"All I could say was that she had a good man in the butcher, and that she had the children's future to think of," the woman said. With the ends of her fingers she pushed her empty glass across the table toward Jaeger, and he lifted the long-necked bottle—the second, this would have been—and poured the cold wine slowly, carefully, in. "All I could say was," she went on saying, her face unrelenting even now, "that here was a man coming back with nothing to offer, even his medals and citations worthless, after six years of being away."

When her daughter had gone to the station to meet the train of prisoners coming through, she'd been crying night and day for a week. The butcher closed up shop for the afternoon and went for a walk so as not to be anywhere around when the other one came up the decorated street. And the woman had dressed the grandchildren up in the best they had. For the first day he came back, she said, there was nothing else to do.

"And then when the train came in, my son-in-law wasn't on it," she said. Her eyes were those of a hopelessly defeated man, asking help or pity of no one, committed to nothing now save the white wine in the glass. "They told her the train was running in sections, and maybe he'd be on another section, and so she waited. She waited until all six sections had passed through. She was four hours at the station before the Red Cross told her he'd died on the way, the night before, and they'd taken the body off in Nürnberg. Tuberculosis. He'd contracted it over there where he was. And that would have been all right," she said, her voice and her face as cold as stone. "That would have been a way out for her. But the butcher—before she got back from the station, the butcher had hung himself on a tree. That's how it was." She was sipping steadily at the wine now, running her tongue along the grey line of her lips. "Four women to every man in Germany, they tell you, and she lost two of them the same day. And the flowers, the decorations." She broke off for a moment, and sat twisting the stem of the wineglass in her square, worn fingertips. "They took them down from the front of the house, and took them off the poles in the street, and they covered the butcher's coffin with them, and they covered his grave with them. That's the purpose they served," she said, and she drank what was left of the wine in her glass.

And now she got up from the table, for the man they had been waiting for came running rapidly, eagerly, down the stairs from the street, turning his jacket collar down again, and smoothing the rain from his hair. He came past the empty tables, through the shadows, straight to Jaeger, his teeth and his eyeballs white in his dark-skinned, narrow face.

He had the look of a bullfighter, with the warmth and color of the Spanish sun still staining his skin, and what business he had in a Nordic wine-cellar could never be explained. He had been held up at a rehearsal, breaking in an understudy to God, the regular God being out with a liver attack, he said, his dark face scarred with his smile. He was a young man, tough as a root, with a black lively pompadour of hair, who bore a dynamo of hot magnetic vigor in his flesh.

"Perhaps you've read the play?" he said in excellent English as he bowed to Catherine Roberts; for he, too, had been a prisoner of war, but in England. He and his colleagues had got a theater group under way in prison camp. " 'Colleagues' means fellow Germans in this instance," he said. He had sat down across the table from them, and now his black-lashed eyes moved from wineglass to dish, from pack of cigarettes to Rhine wine bottle, his ears and eyes alert, his head slightly cocked for whatever Catherine Roberts might have to say. They had put on Ibsen, Shaw, O'Neill, even Joyce's *Exiles*, he said, and when they came back and found nothing waiting for them here—"no customary roof on the house, and no front door, no mother-machine rocking on the hearth—indeed, no hearth," he said, his face scarred quickly, briefly again—they had decided to stay together as a theater group in Germany. "You'll see Borchert's play here tonight with Herr Jaeger," he said, for Catherine Roberts had answered timidly that she did not read German well. "*Ja, ja,* I'll have *Strudel,* too, and coffee, and wine, *ja,* wine," he said, leaning back in his chair to smile up at the serving-woman who stood, rocking a little, holding to the table for support.

"Please," Catherine Roberts said shyly, "what is a 'mother-machine'?"

"It's the opposite of a 'father-machine,' " said Fritzludwig, his face almost painfully distorted with laughing now.

"It was invented in April, when spring began to take its casualties, by the father-machine who directs the Niederstadt zoo. He made it for the baby monkeys so that their mothers could lead their own lives without appendages when they felt that way. It was made out of an ironing-board padded with hot-water bottles, all wrapped in an army blanket, with baby bottles set at regular intervals down the front. The frightening discovery was, at least for mothers, that it worked as well as the original," Fritzludwig said.

"Another bottle of wine," said Jaeger. He lifted the empty one to show the woman in her apron as she set the plate of fresh *Strudel* and the coffee down.

"Your articles," Fritzludwig said at once to Jaeger; "I'd like to see the ones I've read collected."

"In a country with a paper shortage?" Jaeger said.

"*Ach Gott,* isn't every creative man a prophet, and isn't the soul of this country crying out for prophets now? Is Borchert to be the only one we are allowed?" Fritzludwig said. He looked at Catherine Roberts, wanting to state the verifiable, unembellished facts to anyone who could understand the passion and tragedy that had replaced the legal terms, the lawyers' jargon, in this testament of the young dead. "He wrote the play in a few days' time, in 1946, calling it a play that no theater would produce and no public would want to see. He died at the age of twenty-six last year," he said. "And the day after he died, his play was played. Irony?" he said, and his teeth showed white in the lamplight as he smiled at Catherine Roberts. She was no more than a member of the audience, on the wrong side of the footlights in this theater in which the comi-tragedy was played. "The young have become accustomed to irony. They can deal with it the way another generation can't. Twenty-six," he repeated. He looked at Jaeger. "My age and probably yours. He died from the months of sickness and starvation in the Russian campaign, and the months in Nazi military prisons. He'd been under sentence of death for the letters he'd written home. He died, but we were smarter. We stayed alive, eh, Jaeger?" he said, and he laughed again. The American woman who sat at the table was merely a stranger who had bought a ticket and come in late to the darkened house, excluded from everything they were. As long as he spoke, there had been no reason to look down at his hands, but now that his voice had ceased for an instant, it could be seen that they were mutilated. They lay, grotesquely clasped, at the edge of the pool of light on the black wood, three fingers gone from the left hand, and the thumb and forefinger from the right. Even when the woman set down the bottle of wine and the fresh glasses, he did not move them, for he had undertaken the audacious role of being ashamed of nothing that he was. When the wine had been poured, he picked up his glass expertly. "Let's drink to irony," he said, and once he had drunk, and drawn the serving of *Strudel* before him, he went on saying in his easy English that a translation of the play would appear in the autumn on the Third Programme of the B.B.C. It might all have been a subtle joke he was telling them, the wineglass in his mutilated hand, the bite of apple cake sweet in his mouth. " 'Your windows look so warm from outside,' " he whispered the lines of it across the table. " 'I just wanted to feel again what it's like to look through such windows. But from inside, from inside. Do you know what it's like to see such warm lighted windows in the evening, and be—outside?' "

And now Jaeger cleared his throat and took up the cue.

" 'You know, I have a strong impression,' " he quoted softly, in German, " 'that you're one of those whose minds and ideas have been a bit confused by this spot of warfare.

251

Why weren't you commissioned? You'd have had entree into quite different circles. You'd have been quite a different person. Why weren't you commissioned?' "

"That's the Colonel speaking," said Fritzludwig in delighted explanation to the audience. His unstained eyeballs, his teeth, were clear white in the lamplight.

"I've never seen it played. I've only read it, but over and over," Jaeger said.

"Well, tonight you'll hear me answer: 'Then they move in, the Gladiators, the Old Comrades!' " Fritzludwig cried out. " 'Then they rise up out of their mass graves and their bloody groaning stinks to the white moon. That's what makes the nights what they are. As piercing as cat's dirt. As red as raspberry juice on a white shirt. Then the nights are such that we can't breathe.' " The quality of his voice changed now, rising a little, tightening, as if fingers had closed upon his throat. " 'Then we smother if we have no mouth to kiss and no spirits to drink. The bloody groaning stinks to the moon, sir, to the white moon—' "

" 'Nonsense,' " whispered Jaeger, and the whisper itself seemed cold with fear. " 'Of course, the moon's yellow. Always has been. Like honey bread. Like an omelette. The moon was always yellow.' "

" 'Oh, no, sir, oh, no!' " Fritzludwig cried out, his head lifted. " '. . . No, sir, the moon is white on these nights when the dead walk. . . . They rise up out of their mass graves with rotting bandages and bloodstained uniforms.' " The strong voice, the German words, filled the *Weinstube* now, each syllable striking against the wainscoting, beating the rhythm of marching feet from dark wall to wall. " 'They rise up out of the oceans, out of the steppes and the streets, they come from the forests, from the ruins and marshes, frozen black, green, moldering. They rise up out of the steppes, one-eyed, one-armed, toothless, legless, with torn entrails, without skulls, without hands,' " beat the steady rhythm of marching feet, " 'shot through, stinking, blind. They sweep up in a fearful flood, immeasurable in numbers, immeasurable in agony!' " Fritzludwig's hands seemed whole hands now, and he himself a tall, powerful man seated in the chair, the strength of his deep, suave, knowledgeable voice summoning the dead to walk through the *Weinstube* door and take seats at the empty tables. But now the rhythm of the marching ceased, and Fritzludwig spoke in a conversational, almost casual, tone. " 'And then the General with his stripes of blood says to me: "Corporal Beckmann, you'll take responsibility. Number off." And then I stand there,' " Fritzludwig said, playing out one man's modest bewilderment, " 'there before the millions of grinning skeletons, the wrecks and ruins of bone, with my responsibility . . . but the fellows won't number. Their jaws jerk terribly, but they won't number. The General orders fifty knee-bends. The rotting bones rattle, lungs squeak, but they won't number. Is that not mutiny, sir? Open mutiny?' " he roared the Corporal's misery out.

" 'Yes,' " whispered Jaeger in the same cold, fearful whisper. " 'Yes. Open mutiny.' "

Catherine Roberts sat close beside him still, their shoulders, their arms, their knees, still touching, but all that Fritzludwig had summoned to life by his eloquence, his unmutilated virility, had come between them now. Jaeger felt Catherine Roberts' fingers slipping from his, her warmth and tenderness receding; felt her turning in silence from him, leaving him to the dead and the living men of his own country, and to a language that seared like a branding-iron upon his dual self.

"Jaeger," she said so softly that she might not have been speaking at all; "I shall have to telephone. I shall have to let Milly know where I am. It's after three o'clock. She may be beginning to worry. Nobody knows that I came, that I took the train, even. Nobody knows I'm here."

"But the play," Jaeger said; "it won't be over until eleven." She had got to her feet, and the men stood, too. "Can you tell her that we'll be getting back late, very late?"

"Yes, yes," she murmured, her face turned from him. "But I can't say that. I can't tell her I'm here with you."

She was gone then, and Fritzludwig and Jaeger sat down, two Germans alone, and at once a feeling of relief lay on the air. They talked of Fritzludwig's plans to take his company on the road, and the skits in the political cafés, and the need for articles, critiques, explanations, to appear.

"When we put on Zuckmeyer's *Devil's General*," he said, his high forehead webbed with lines under the coarse, black pompadour, "we advertised for *Luftwaffe* uniforms and Nazi armbands for the actors, relics which had been ordered turned over to the authorities three years before. I tell you, in twenty-four hours we were swamped! We could have fitted out a new air force and sent a regiment into battle with the old insignia on their sleeves! Our good townspeople had laid these treasures away in lavender with their wedding veils and their wedding tails and their tear-soaked memories!"

He was standing, ready to be off again, when Catherine Roberts came back through the shadows of the room.

"I must be leaving too," she said in a low voice, not sitting down. She looked at Jaeger, her hands closed tightly on her gloves and the summery straw of her woven bag. "Something has happened to Christoph. He's very ill. Milly wants me there."

At the station, there was a quarter of an hour to wait, and Catherine Roberts tried saying again to him the words she had sought to say as they hurried through the streets. They stood together on the platform, out of the thin mist of rain,

and the side of her face was waxen, her voice so low that
Jaeger must bow his head to hear. She spoke of the cafés he
would write about, and Fritzludwig, and the play. *Because
this is your life,* she might have been saying to him, *and I
am an intruder in it. If I must go back to Fahrbach to my
child, then the same inevitability must keep you here.*

"But I want to go back with you," he said, his lips moving
across the dark fire of her hair.

"For a thousand reasons, you must not, you cannot," she
said. "My husband will meet me at the station. You see
how impossible it would be."

"Just before the Fahrbach station, there is a level-crossing
stop," said Jaeger. "I have got off there before."

"And then there is this," she said, not seeming to hear
him in her concern for what she had to say. "Those lines of
Borchert's. You must not be a man outside looking in
through the warm, lighted windows at the others. I do not
know how to say it. This is your language. You belong here
with these men." *Just a few hours ago did we speak of beginning life over again together?* said the silence between
them now. *Did we talk like fools of the places where the
land and the vegetation have not given in? Did we mention
the vulture's defiance, the heron's flight, the pineland's refusal to surrender, forgetting the craven surrender of men?*
Now they could hear the train approaching through the
open fields, over the scorched earth of the forests. They
could see it now, taking the bend. "I think I am trying to
say that I cannot, that I do not want to, that I have not the
right," she said, but she did not finish. "Tomorrow— I shall
telephone, at the office tomorrow." He could scarcely hear
her voice above the sound of the train coming in. "We shall
see each other tomorrow, Jaeger—"

"Yes," he said, "yes." He took her in his arms and kissed
her mouth. All July, all August, lay ahead of them. "Yes,

tomorrow," he said, the words blurred, his love for her like a spear entering his flesh.

Then he stood alone on the platform, and the cars began to move slowly past. For a moment, he walked beside them, seeking to keep abreast of the window where her face might appear, hurrying as the train increased its pace, in the end almost running beside it through the gently drifting rain. Then he could keep up with the turning wheels no longer, and he dropped back, and the cars moved by, leaving him with his heart gone desolate in his breast. And then, as the last car sped past, he flung himself toward it, as if knowing suddenly, in desperation, that no July or August waited for them, that the brief two hours of this journey were all that was to be allowed. He grasped the hand-rail of the steps on the last platform and swung himself up, his trembling blood stampeding at his temples and wrists, crying out in his veins: *Catherine, Catherine, my love!*

XI

Honerkamp was
back at his desk at the American House the next day, his
face gone paler, the curls lying tight and classic as a statue's
on his head. Jaeger and Overstreet had met at the door, and
now they sat in the tabernacle of the music room with him,
stretched at ease in the low-slung, steel-tubed chairs. Beneath the busts of Wagner, and Beethoven, and Brahms,
set newly beside the others, the voice on the record-player
sang with velvet flexibility of another state of mind, another
climate. Honerkamp had turned the music low so that
they could speak together, and the singer's voice flowed pliantly, making no mention this time of the smell of honeysuckle under the moon, but pronouncing tractably, softly,
as if behind the closed door of another room, words of sentiment so plain that Jaeger's heart was moved anew. "The
house I live in, the goodness everywhere," sang the voice
that, because of its depth and weight, should have been
cumbersome, but was not. Overstreet leaned back in the
green canvas hammock of his chair and laid the spire of his
fingers against his smile.

"And so you were typing all night at the office?" Honerkamp said. He passed Jaeger an open pack of cigarettes. "I
stopped in, looking for you this morning. Old Schumacher
said you hadn't had any sleep."

"I got in an hour or two on the office couch, once I'd got
the piece on the theater done," said Jaeger.

"Tell old Schumacher to keep his columns open," Overstreet said. "There may be a big story coming through tonight." Jaeger looked over the flame of his lighter at the yellow wasps of Overstreet's eyes, curved insidiously to the

eyeball, stabbing the venom in. "I came to you two for some supplementary data before we break it." The short upper lip sought to descend over the bared teeth, but could not. Jaeger closed his lighter, and leaned back again, and looked at the small, freckled hands, the long-toothed grin. On the record-player, the voice sang: "The worker and the farmer, the sailor on the sea," and Jaeger stirred like a sleeper not wishing to waken from his dream.

(Honerkamp's attention was somewhere else, held perhaps by the light from the chandeliers in the Colonel's house that had once polished Schumacher's bald, modest head like a beacon; by the thick lenses of his spectacles touched by the same impartial sheen that glinted on the goblets of wine, the glass beer-mugs, the silverware, and the medals of the military; Schumacher wearing the tails his wife had kept in camphor for the thirteen years the Nazis had closed him away; or held by the sight of Schumacher eating Wurst. "There are," Honerkamp had said one night, or was in the process of saying now, or was just about to say, "not more than two ways of eating Wurst. I tell you, I've made a study of it. Either you rape it with lust, your breath coming in jerks, either you rut as you eat, or eat as you rut, and in this event it should be done without witness. And then there is the other way. There is the way that Schumacher eats Wurst, tentatively, but certainly not timidly, afraid of nothing except that he might be depriving somebody of it who wanted Wurst, needed Wurst, more than he himself who wanted nothing with concupiscent appetite or passion except respect for the dignity of man. Ask him how he maintained that dignity through the nightmare years!" Honerkamp was perhaps asking this of Overstreet now, or was just about to ask him, while the singer's voice turned pliantly, like the heavy, somnolent body of a snake unwinding on the record-player, singing from a great distance away: "The words of old Abe Lincoln, of Jefferson, and Paine"; "and Schumacher will answer: 'For many of us, maintaining dignity depended on the women we were married to.'" His bald head was as good as there in the music room with them, modestly taking what sunlight could be spared from the brooding presence of the great Germans set high on the shelf, and when he began speaking, Honerkamp rose from his chair and lifted the mechanical arm and with it the jeweled point from the record's groove so that they could better hear the words Schumacher said. "During that time," he began saying almost shyly, "my wife advised me to speak and act in accordance with my beliefs. But there were other women who loved all that was theirs as well as my wife did—loved their children, their husbands, their country, just as well—yet saw their duty differently. They would kneel down before their husbands and cry out: 'We are not Nazis! God knows we are not Nazis! But for the sake of the children, for the sake of your life and mine, what else can you do?' That made it harder for men not to join up. That made it difficult," Schumacher said. "I did not have to contend with appeals made in the name of expediency. First they put me away for a year, and the next time it was longer. It was for three years." His eyes were magnified, swollen, like the eyes of a grasshopper, behind the thick lenses of the spectacles, as he stood there stating these things with the greatest modesty. "When I came back, each time in those intervals my wife said: 'Karl, just go on speaking and acting in accordance with your beliefs. The children and me, we can always get on. We've got on before.' The last time was for nine years," he said. He seemed to be apologizing to them for the trouble he had caused, and the length of time that trouble had endured. At the Colonel's, he had stepped aside from the platters of *Weisswurst* and *Bratwurst*, from the *Knackwurst* and the *Blutwurst*, and even from the *Speckwurst*, out of deference to those who wanted *Wurst* more than he could ever want any food again. Rather than relish the juices running through his jaws, he had spoken of extermination camps at gatherings where such references were looked on as a breach of etiquette, and spoken of the gas chamber before those, German and American alike, who were embarrassed by his lack of delicacy. If Overstreet had begun to ask the questions he had come to ask, Jaeger did not hear him, nor did Honerkamp, who was walking up and down on the stealthy soles of his tennis shoes in agitation in the room. "I believe we are doomed, Germans, Americans, all of us, and that we are just beginning to recognize our doom," he was saying, or had once said to Overstreet, or was on the point of saying to him. "I believe that when a species becomes totally involved in the processes of its own destruction, then its termination is already defined. We have accepted to crowd ourselves or blast ourselves from the earth. We will squander our water supply until drought chokes us, and we'll splinter our forests into kindling wood so that there will be no refuge left us from the sun. In exterminating those whose politics or God differ from ours, we shall end by effacing the image of man. If the birds of the air and the beasts of the fields require an expanse in which to roam, does not man too need to know that vast, uncontested areas are his from which to draw strength, in which to go on drawing breath? Whether he ever lays eye on it or not, must he not know that he is nourished by an earth lavishly watered, ripe with grain, held firm by deeply rooted trees, abundantly stocked with cattle and crops, not plundered, murdered, usurped, defiled? The buffalo perishes behind bars not only because he is deprived of liberty, but because he senses in his savage blood that the plains he has been taken from have also been taken from him, that they are now the highroads, the main streets, the back alleys, of man's enterprise, and no longer stretch to the farthest horizon of eternity. He cannot live, any more than man can live, knowing that progress means the power of man to engrave his human swastika, indelibly, on land and water and sky." The small, concentrated mask of worry hung on Honerkamp's face, and, as he walked, he nursed his wounded arm against his heart. "I'm afraid that man was not ready yet," he said. "In spite of all his military victories, I'm afraid he is simply not going to win.")

And now Overstreet spoke louder. "Seth, I wanted to ask you about the other evening," he said. *Evening*, he put it, as if it had been a casual business between two after-dinner strollers. *Night* would have given it an ominous sound. "I have a kind of left-handed report that you know who it was who winged you, some fumbler who couldn't tell the difference between man and roebuck and deer."

"It was black as your hat that night," Honerkamp said, having no time for it.

"We've got a suspect under arrest," Overstreet said. His two forefingers, with the tips laid together, tapped lightly against his teeth and lightly drew away. "A guy who disposed of nine thousand pound-tins of coffee over a two-year period, plus sixteen thousand cartons of cigarettes. His dealings in sugar, cocoa, chocolate bars, and sundry articles, have not been tabulated yet. Perhaps the adding-machine doesn't go that high. A big-time operator," he said, the marmot grin like a showcase on his mouth. "He passed counterfeit scrip, falsified the entries, played every trick in the pack with the PX accounts."

"The PX accounts?" Honerkamp said. He had stopped walking in the room. His fingers ceased combing through his hair. "You mean— Whew, what a story! Dardenella? Is that it?" he said. He ran his tongue along his lip, watching Overstreet's face. "Oh, damn it, the poor guy!"

"Poor?" said Overstreet. "You mean, *poor?* He had fifteen suits of clothes in his billets, and twenty-three pairs of shoes. He's got a couple of pedigreed ponies up at the *Schloss.* He wasn't caught with any *Reichsmarks* in his pants when the money reform went through, not him. He'd paid the board for the two horses in advance the day before, so it was the old *Graf* who got short-changed," he said.

"The coffee, the cigarettes, all the rest of it, all for the Lipizzaners, for a pedigreed identity. Yes, it could have been." Honerkamp said it to himself as he walked back and forth again in the room, the empty eyes of the three musicians high on the shelf watching him turn through the bars of shadow and bars of sun. "And if he did it, I would say that it has a shape and size to it that is not to be judged by customary standards or measured by any customary scale." As he walked back and forth, his right hand scratched painfully, but heedless of the pain, through the close curls of his hair. "I would even say that it has a kind of nobility."

"Even taking a shot at you?" Overstreet said.

Honerkamp stopped short.

"For God's sake, what's Dardenella got to do with that?" he asked, his face blank, motionless.

"He was there. We've been watching him. The M.P.s followed him out. They kept out of sight, but they went through the cellar once he'd gone. Knau's cellar," Overstreet said. "It was nicely stocked. Knau's been forking out German currency to him for six months, a year. He's been selling American produce for him like crazy to the peasants all around. Twenty-two marks for a carton of cigarettes, fifteen for a pound of coffee. That's being conservative. Knau was the middleman. He got his cut." Across the spire of his fingers laid tip to tip, Overstreet looked at Jaeger now. "You saw Dardenella in the courtyard that night. I hear you talked to him," he said. "The M.P.s are interested in what he had to say."

"He'd driven out after hay for the Lipizzaners. Special kinds that he wanted," Jaeger said. It was not a good story. He didn't want to take notes on it or write it up. He didn't want it to be happening like this. "He showed me the hay on the floor of the station wagon while we talked."

"And maybe," said Overstreet, grinning behind the barricade, "the gun was under the hay."

"I tell you Dardenella's never set foot in the woods in his life," Honerkamp said, walking impatiently again.

"He was in Ober-Pastau. He was at Knau's. That's near enough," Overstreet said, the tone easy, placating. "We've got him booked on black-market deals. Once you've identified him as the man who took a shot at you, we can snap the whole case closed."

"Except that he couldn't anywhere, at any time, blast the life out of beast or man!" cried Honerkamp; "or even try to, or fumble while trying! I've known him two years. I've never seen him touch a gun."

"And maybe sometimes," Overstreet went on saying in the same calm, plausible voice, as if addressing the hopelessly insane, "maybe every now and then in those two years, you had reason to suspect his activities. So maybe from his point of view, you had known him about long enough."

Whatever Honerkamp may have been about to say then, he did not say. Instead, he swung around on his tennis shoes to answer the knock on the door. And there stood the blonde German secretary in the hall, her hips in the tight brown skirt, thought Jaeger, broad enough to bear an entire race of big-boned, Nordic men.

"There's an urgent call for you in the office, Mr. Honerkamp," she said, her voice as brassy as if it came without

263

transition out of the middle-west, aping the English syllables with fearful accuracy. She lingered a moment in the doorway after Honerkamp had gone, her eyes seeking Jaeger's and meeting them at last, the look in them stating without subterfuge: *Anywhere, any time you want, standing in a closet, or lying in the grass by the river at night, if you want it that way. My blouse comes from Sears Roebuck. It's easy to open. Oh, he didn't send away for it, not him!* Her mouth twisted in bright, brassy contempt for all that Honerkamp was. *He's not that kind. But you're different, Herr Jaeger. I've watched you every time you've come. You can have it anywhere, for as long as you want it.* In the silence of the music room, the breath died softly in her mouth.

Afterwards, Jaeger knew that the eight or ten minutes which followed the closing of the door already spelled the end. But when Overstreet's high, nasal voice began speaking to him, he did not recognize the sound of doom, or know that the loss of one night's sleep was to seem an instant of celebration allowed him in the long stretch of sleeplessness that lay ahead.

"Honerkamp would appear to be doing a pretty good job here in the America House," Overstreet was saying. "Being energetic, he gets on with the program; and, being young, he gets on with young people well. But in the steering-committees, the question is always coming up as to what is representative, and what isn't representative, of America, and there's a lot of concern about what might do harm to the general picture, throw it out of focus, as it were." Jaeger watched the small, freckled hands indicating the vast dimensions of that picture. "We want the straight story to be told about America. You see what I'm getting at?" Overstreet said. "The men in the individual America Houses are given a pretty free rein, and nobody interferes too much. For in-

stance, Honerkamp up here in Fahrbach will give a lot of
play to some singer, some writer, that maybe the man we
have down in Heidelberg wouldn't touch with a ten-foot
pole. What we're interested in at this point is the German
reaction to what they're being fed. Have you heard any
comments from the German side?" the nasal voice asked.

"Comments?" repeated Jaeger. He was thinking of Dardenella, thinking of sleep, not knowing yet that the sentence
had been passed. For a moment, he dreamed of Catherine
Roberts' face, and his heart stirred in him. "Comments
on what? What kind of comments?"

"Well, let's begin with the music, the records," Overstreet
said. "Would you say they're the kind the Germans ought
to hear? I've been compiling a sort of informal report on the
America Houses, the books, the records, all that. My pre-
liminary findings are already being studied in Washington.
But recently I've noticed one or two things: for instance,
University students walking around with that book about
Hiroshima under their arms, that book by Hershey. They
say he's some kin of the chocolate-bar people, and that's all
right by me. But I'm trying to take a kind of Gallup Poll
of what the Germans themselves are saying about the book.
This is my particular baby, literature, the power of the written word. I'm trying to fit the pieces of information together
as to whether or not it's good policy to have the Germans
reading about the effects of our bomb written from the
point of view of the enemy. Victims have a tendency to
take a one-sided view." His thumbs were hooked under his
muskrat chin, his forefingers tapped softly against his
bright, moist gum, as he smiled at this. "And then again,
up in the periodical room I came across a very fancy book
of photographs, de luxe, arty photographs, blown up a foot
square, showing lynchings in the south. It's a sickening
kind of thing, and I don't know why Germans have to

look at it. Here we get up and preach about their concentration camps, and then we turn right around and hand them a roomful of slanted stuff about things that used to happen every now and then in the sticks back home. I'm not sure that there isn't something going on in the America Houses that none of us knows about, and it's on the record in Washington exactly what I think. It may be that books are being slipped on the shelves on orders coming from somewhere else. That's what I'm interested now in finding out. I was looking at some of the titles the other day, and they'd surprise you. I can tell you that. There's been quite a run, for instance, on *The Grapes of Wrath*, and if any book gives a cock-eyed view of American life, well, you couldn't find a better example than that; incest, murder, rape," he said, the fox eyes bright. "Nobody can account for three copies of it being on the shelves up here. Maybe you could start asking the students a few questions, just asking around in the library, being casual about it, just keeping your ears open in general for what's being said. I'd appreciate that as a personal favor, and you'd be doing the Information Services and Intelligence a service, too." His voice ceased for a moment, and Jaeger thought: *Sleep. That's what I want, sleep.* Then Overstreet cleared his throat, and the voice began again, saying: "They tell me old Schumacher's a Social-Democrat now. Maybe during the war he was more to the left, and that's why they kept putting him behind bars. Would you have any way of—"

Jaeger sat up, abruptly awake. Honerkamp was in the room with them again. A narrow shaft of sunlight, moiling with dusty, golden motes, fell from the high window, silhouetting the musicians' busts, bisecting the dimness, before halting on the slightly soiled canvas of Honerkamp's tennis shoes.

"That was the director of the *Krankenhaus*," he said. His

eyes sought Jaeger's. Having so recently bled and suffered, and kept silent, and keeping the name unspoken still, he was tired, and this time he asked for help. "We have to get an iron lung somewhere, Jaeger," he said. "Christoph Horn has bulbar polio."

Two medical students at the University had made a contraption out of strips of linen bound fast to a curved steel frame. And Christoph Horn's torso rested in this cradle suspended above the hospital bed, his face throttled black by the fingers that had him by the throat, the cords of his neck knotted like rope in the fury of his fight for air. The strips of cloth served as splints for the muscles and tissue that lay flaccid now, and the cradle they formed rocked the breath into his lungs, and then released it, rocking him out of the reach of suffocation for an instant, and then back into its grip, over and over, hand by hand, hour after hour, throughout the first day, and second night, and into the next day. On the upper floor of the hospital, nurses, interns, University students, waited in turn, but, however many answered the call, there were never enough. Each team went back into the sick man's room tired still, and took up the rocking of the macabre cradle with arms and shoulders ligatured by pain.

Jaeger stood that night and the next day with them, waiting his turn to take his place at the apparatus, to rock the spent lungs full with breath, and to rock the breath out of them again, saying steadily, tirelessly, as the others must have said it in the rotation of their tireless weaving, their tender rocking, to the boy who lay strangling on his bed: *This is the way to breathe, Christoph. This is the way it is done. Just in and out, in and out. There's nothing to it. Just in and out, the way you've done it for twenty-one years. That's all.* At four o'clock of the second afternoon, the call from Honerkamp came through. He'd been trying as far afield as Berlin, as Hamburg; and the Niederstadt hospital, which had refused the day before, had now agreed to lend Fahrbach its iron lung. They must get down to Niederstadt with a truck big enough to haul it, and a minimum of fifteen men.

"I'll get the truck and what volunteers I can," Honerkamp's voice came over the wire. "You start now rounding up the men."

An hour to recruit them, Jaeger estimated it as he walked out of the hospital; *three hours down, an hour to load, three hours back. That's eight hours out of Christoph's life. We've got to work fast,* he admonished his own lagging flesh. He mounted the steep, cobbled lane in the heat, seeing suddenly his own drawn face, his own drugged eyes, without recognition for a moment, in the mirror of a barbershop. He stopped and shook himself awake. There were no customers in the red plush upholstered chairs, only the barber watching the street through the pane in the door. Frail as a spider, and watchful as one, he seemed to Jaeger, able to lift only scissors and comb and razor blade, and nothing more, so Jaeger hurried on again. In front of the old house (medieval, cross-beamed with Tudor, ancient as Gaul, yet pressed now into service since the Americans had come) where the *Fahrbach Presse* occupied two floors, and the rotary presses ran below the level of the street, Jaeger stopped a postman in uniform, with a leather bag slung empty on his back.

"You're through for the day?" Jaeger measured the breadth of his shoulders, laid thick with muscle inside his coat, and his neck heavy as a bull's. "There's a man paralyzed at the hospital. It's got him in the respiratory system. He can't breathe. Will you ride down to Niederstadt tonight and help bring back an iron lung?"

"An iron lung?" the man repeated slowly. In his uncertainty, he seemed ready to grin. A day's growth of beard sprang tough and blond along his jaws, and there were drops of sweat on his upper lip, and pearls of it caught in the yellow stubble that bristled like straw in the cleft of his chin. From under the coat of the winter uniform, his flesh gave off great blasts of heat. "I've got an old wound from the war. I couldn't do any lifting," he said.

"Then forget about Niederstadt," said Jaeger. "But they need volunteers at the hospital now. They need someone quickly to take my place." He fumbled a moment in his inner pocket, and brought out a card. "My name's Jaeger. I'm from the *Presse* here." The postman's fingers were damp with heat as he took the card in his hand. "They need men to keep the apparatus functioning until we get back with the iron lung."

"I'm to go into the room where the sick man is?" said the postman slowly. "But what he's got's catching, isn't it?"

(*Yes, catching, contagious,* dreamed Jaeger. He felt himself submitting now, and he tried to shake his flesh awake. *I must keep to facts,* he rebuked himself. *I will take note of the fact that a German named Jacob Heine described this paralysis as an entity, communicated by the secretions of the nose and throat and bowel. No class or group, no elite, no proletariat, is exempt, oh, postman! It would not help to join a party or wear an emblem on the sleeve. If it hesitates, as it is said, to attack the colored peoples of the earth, this entity, then that is a facet of its prejudice; and when attempts are made to prevent the spread of it by solutions which block the portal of entry to the nose, it holds its sides in its twisted hands and snickers: "No! Oh, no!" It has a marked affinity for nerve tissue, oh, postman, and rather than use the blood stream for communication, it travels— like love—along the nerve pathways and enters the centers*

269

*of the spinal cord and brain. If it gets the chance, it will
seize the muscles of the extremities of the thorax, and hold
them fast. It will hold on to them forever, if it can; forever
and ever, again like love.*) Now he had shaken himself
awake, and he was running quickly up the stairs. In the
Presse office, old Schumacher looked up from the work on
his desk, and listened.

"We'll start in the make-up room," he said, and he got
to his feet. "A board-of-health inspector came in yesterday."
As they went down the winding stairway, Jaeger felt under
his soles the wood of each tread scooped hollow by time.
"He wants the polio cases kept out of the press. They can
go on with the University seminar, and keep the swimming-
pool open, if we don't give the eighteen cases of polio any
publicity."

"Eighteen!" said Jaeger, startled out of the benumbment
of the dream.

"There'll be a front-page piece in tomorrow's edition,"
Schumacher said from below him on the spiral stairs.
"There'll be an editorial urging the closing of the pool, and
the cancellation of the two-week seminar."

In the make-up room, Schumacher rapped on the table
for attention, and Jaeger spoke briefly to the men. When
he was done, they talked for a moment among themselves,
and then five of them rose and took their shabby coats, their
old felt hats, from the row of them hanging by the door.
From the rotary-press room, three more followed him into
the hall.

"Get something to eat," Jaeger said to them. "Meet me
at five in front of the America House."

On his way to the riding-stables, he cut through the University grounds. They were quiet, abandoned, now, but in
the avenue of shade under the big oaks, a man stood water-
ing the grass. It was the physical potentiality of men that

mattered to Jaeger: the width of their shoulders, and their youth, and the soundness of their limbs. He was like a butcher, eyeing them, feeling the structure of their bones, judging the value of flesh still on the hoof. The grass was lightly beaded with water, the sun came gently through the branches, the quiet lawns were enclosed by dignity and peace in a frame made by the far, grey stone steps, the distant Gothic arches, the tall, mullioned windows like candelabra burning in the sun. By rights, he was a student, said the young man with the hose in his hands when Jaeger had spoken to him, hastening to correct any false impressions of his status that the work he was now doing might have conveyed. He was perhaps too soft for the job to be done in the night ahead, thought Jaeger. He was plump as a baby, and downy-cheeked, but there was a stubborn, tough thing in him too. Although the University was officially closed, he was doing some extra work that he needed for credits, he said, and he was repaying the *Rektor* by helping tend the grounds. As he shifted the fan of water from shade to sun across the emerald grass, Jaeger shook his head at the sight of the dimples in the soft flesh of his hands. Research for his thesis was taking all his spare time, so it wouldn't be possible for him to go to Niederstadt that night, he said; nor would it be fair to his parents, who were bearing the expenses of his years away from home. He felt he owed them every instant of these years, just as he owed them every *pfennig* they had spent on him, and that they could not afford to spend, with six other children, younger than he was, making demands on them, and they stinting themselves for the other children too.

At the west gate, Jaeger turned off the gravel path, and walked up the flagstones to the caretaker's door. He thought: *There is a son here, a young man recently come back.* But it was the old man himself who opened the door, and who stood in the sun on the worn piece of carpet at the threshold, leaning on a dark wood cane. "Our Wolfram, I tell you he's a lazy lout," he said, speaking with naked gums once Jaeger had had his say. The small, faded, misted eyes, rimmed raw, were fixed on Jaeger's face. "Since he's back, he sits out there in the kitchen, doing nothing but whittling at a piece of wood. I swear, they changed him over there in Russia. He's not like a good German boy any more. But he'll go, I'll make him go!" His voice quavered high, and the bones of his knuckles showed white on the cane. It might have been this, the conflict he had been waiting for. "A word out of him, and I'll break this cane over his back! That's the kind of language he understands!" But now, in the rheum of his eyes, there were tears like drops of glycerin, too indissoluble to fall. "Sometimes I think he isn't a German any more!" he said in plaintive grief.

Jaeger hurried on toward the *Schloss*, and it seemed to him that there would never again be, or perhaps had never been a direction offered, never a long furtive passage leading to the dark heresy of sleep. He had begun to mistake haste for languor, the past for the present, to confuse sight, and taste, and hearing, with sound. The vapor that hung like a veil between him and time no longer parted before house, and wall, and tree, so that he believed as he moved forward that he was at the same moment slipping backward down the hill. But there, like a colored slide projected on the mist, was the *Graf*, svelte, elegant, erect, the grey *Loden* of his *Steirer Anzug*, trimmed with bottle green, his long, corrugated neck supporting the bird-neat, prim head. On this head was worn a glossy, olive felt, with two immaculate pheasant breast feathers, speckled brown and red, secured in its band, the suit and the hat proclaiming their own season at the same time they defied the dilapidation of his country's estate. There he drifted, upright on the

mist, a monocle glinting in his eye as he surveyed the strawberry beds.

"We need your three grooms. We need them tonight,"
Jaeger said. He raised one hand, seeking to push aside the
vaporous curtain, but the folds of it did not stir. "We need
them to help bring back an iron lung on a truck from Niederstadt."

"For Christoph Horn," the *Herr Graf* said. It was not a
question the nasal voice asked.

"There's not much time left," Jaeger said.

The *Graf* fixed the monocle more firmly in the socket of
his eye and looked down at the strawberries. In this likeness
of a living man which the magic lantern cast on the screen,
his skin had the substance of tissue paper stretched over
the intricate framework of ancient, aristocratic bones.

"Oh, you will save him!" the voice said, the words faded
and far, as if a sound track had gone temporarily awry. "Po-
liomyelitis, if we wish to be technical, may be considered an
American disease. They have a monopoly on it, as on chew-
ing-gum. So now let the Americans take care of Christoph
Horn! Let them put all their modern methods into action,
let them bring their modern equipment forward, and put
the religion of their materialism into practice now! We are
the conquered. We can merely stand by and watch the farce
of pragmatism being played. Our old legends speak of a Dr.
Faust who took the wings of an eagle so as to fly through the
eternities that lie between heaven and earth, those expanses
through which no mortal is entitled to fly. For we know
there are hallowed places that man must bow his head before
and not trespass on, and not desecrate with his manipula-
tions and his ingenuity. Let the Americans take care of
Christoph Horn. Let them bear the onus of the iron lung!"
he said; and he went on saying: "There is no one here
trained to work with the Lipizzaners as he does, that is true.

But out of the vast morass of ignorance and hysteria and misrepresentation by which we are Occupied, let one truth be preserved: that it is the old horses of the Spanish Riding School, the old warriors, who train the young grooms, as well as the old, trained riders who educate the stallions to the rein. For centuries, unaltered by the events of wars, uninterrupted by the course of revolutions, this has been so. Attempts, attempts without number, have been made in other countries to establish classical riding-schools, but throughout history they have failed; they have failed because the decades of work were misunderstood, distorted, when transplanted to foreign soil, and the language between horse and rider, between rider and horse, could not be translated into any other tongue. Let us take care of our traditions, then, while the Americans take care of Christoph Horn." There was a whimsical smile on his faded lips, and his voice was light and dry, like dead leaves blowing across pavingstones. "The American army has trucks and men. Let them do what is to be done," he said.

"This time we can do without the army," said Jaeger, the force of his voice startling them both. The tissue of the *Graf's* face seemed paler, more crumpled, than before. "This one thing we can do without the army, without any army. I have nine civilians, German civilians, ready to go."

"*Herr Gott*, for a little wisdom!" breathed the *Graf*. His likeness flickered out of focus for a moment on the screen. "You are a newspaperman, and I call you that knowing the limitations the title bears. You are a journalist, which means you have no choice but to be unscrupulous, that you respect no man or his privacy, that you have dispensed with all those standards which cannot be altered or dispensed with, by which the cultivated live. We used to say here in Germany that journalism was a trade for Jews. By that, we meant for the man who did not fit into any circle or stratum

274

of our society. But we have had to modify our expressions since a man who was himself an outsider from every stratum of German life carried things too far. You were made a member of a profession without honor by the authority of the Americans," the *Graf* said, "and *Herr* Schumacher was given—also by the Americans—the exalted name of editor. Before you leave these grounds at my request, I must ask you to consider the qualifications of those who selected you, screened you, and gave you your public roles. The German press, licensed by the Americans! What is it but a joke, a tragic joke! Any country which accepts the doctrine that, offered the alternative of a government and no newspapers, or newspapers and no government, should choose the latter, confirms the illiterate and the ignorant in the depths of their ignorance and illiteracy. Give them comic strips instead of diplomatic treaties! That is what that rebus means," he said. "Give them weather-reporters, however unreliable, instead of directors of foreign and domestic policy!" Jaeger heard the far, dry sound of the *Graf's* mirth, bitter, ailing, like an ill man coughing in the mist. "The Americans have made you an authority. Very well—go to them for help!" Without any warning, the sound track functioned normally again, and the *Graf's* voice now blared louder than in reality. "I will tell my grooms there's no need for them to neglect their duties here and go!"

Jaeger did not recall passing under the medieval arch, or crossing the courtyard, not knowing until he stood on the dust-whitened timber of the Lipizzaners' quarters and felt the water trickling from his temples into his neck, that he must have stopped at the fountain where the horses drank, and taken up water in his hands, and wet his face and hair. "Siglavy Marina" said the black letters on the plywood wafer on the stall door, and the fish-eyed stallion stood, deep-chested, on his clean bedding of straw, whinnying words of greeting through the velvet trumpets of his nose. Other than this, there was no sound. Jaeger mounted the narrow stairs to the floor above, and to the right and the left the doors stood open on the bare disorder of men's quarters—of men who required nothing more than an ancient, quilted comforter, and a pair of boots, and a pair of riding-breeches, and a leather-bound crop, as full equipment for their lives. On the unmade cots was the unclean linen, long unwashed, in which young celibates had tossed at night, seeking to still the clamor of their flesh. Under the cots lay discarded socks, unmated shoes, and the smell of sweat, and horse, and saddle, hung heavy on the air. There was still no sound except Jaeger's footsteps on the wood, and the whinny and sneeze of the stallion turning below. But at the end of the hall, one door was closed, and Jaeger walked down the narrow passage to it, and knocked on the panel of reddish wood. When the door opened, he felt no shock at the sight of the girl standing there. She wore tan jodhpurs, and her white shirt was open at the neck, and he knew this was merely the next likeness, in colors not quite as bright as life, to be cast for a moment on the vaporous screen.

"Come in," Milly said. Her small face was grave, and pale as the flower faces he had seen once with Walter in the evening grass. "If you would like to sit down," she said, but he did not sit down. She had closed the door behind him now. He saw that the narrow bed was smoothly made, and, at the head of it, a fresh sheet turned back on the Scotch plaid blanket, and the pillow waiting in its smooth, starched case. Under the bed, three pairs of shoes, the heels of them worn, but the leather polished, stood in an orderly row. "I have fixed things up a little," she said; she made an uncompleted gesture with one hand; "his jumping cups and his racing trophies. I brought some silver polish from the house and worked on them." The loving-cups, with a tracery of words and dates on their gleaming metal flanks, and the medals, the tricolored cockades, the silk rosettes, were arranged on the table in the sun. "They won't let me go to him in the hospital, so I'm straightening things up for him for when he comes back—" She stopped speaking, and he did not want her to stop, fearing that if her voice faded out then she herself might slip from focus before he could say the things he had to say. "Even if he has to walk on canes, it won't make any difference," she began again, and then he believed she said the word "marriage," perhaps that she and Christoph would be married. "We'll make our living raising horses, Lipizzaners. We don't know where yet, but that doesn't matter. I'll have some money of my own when I'm twenty-one. That isn't very far away."

There was no lip-salve on her mouth; it was smooth and pale like a little girl's mouth. Her lashes were as thick as tassels, tangled and black around her suavely tilted eyes. She lifted her face to Jaeger, and her lips parted, and the weight of her hair brushed soundlessly across the pure white collar and shoulders of her shirt, and her breasts pointing in the white linen seemed far too heavy for her delicate bones to bear. So heavy they seemed for the small, belted waist, for the childish hips in the riding-breeches, that for a moment Jaeger thought to cup a hand beneath each breast so that the weight of them might rest, firm as ripening fruit in its satin skin, within his trembling palms. (But he did not move, for now the stampeding of horses' hoofs could be heard below them in the Lipizzaners' stalls, the stamp and thundering on wood of their wild, snorting revolt, and then the splintering of timber as if the partitions had been kicked away, the old walls shattered, and the frenzied clattering of their escape heard in the courtyard as they swerved around the drinking-fountain, their iron shoes striking fire from the stones. Three abreast, they pounded through the arch and out upon the open road, the sun emblazoned on their foreheads, their nostrils spread wide. The mare galloped riderless, fleeing in panic from the ordeal of birth, from the pain of the foal's legs unfolding within her, racing with the stallions toward impunity, toward the flowering fields of male ravishment, of cloverheads, and crested dog's-tail, and a surf of grass. And on the stallions' bare, supple backs rode Christoph Horn and Millicent, the twin streams of silky muscle and sinew and hot, pounding blood flowing between their delicately spread thighs. Jaeger was suddenly filled with savage rejoicing, watching Neapolitano Virgilia and Siglavy Marina bearing them away; knowing that all they fled, escaped from, lay forever behind them: the clamor of outrage, the keening of the bereaved, the fiercely pronounced dicta of their time and place, all scrapped, discarded, flung to the four winds for the sake of the magic power that raced in sweetest anguish through their loins. Whatever might happen to the rest of them so precariously seated in the saddle, feet gripping the stirrups, hands holding for dear life to snaffle and curb, Christoph and Milly rode free of them, without stirrup or rein, the eloquence of the knee crying out: "Go faster, faster, my darling!" or: "Take the hill galloping, my angel, my foal, my colt!" or: "Rise to the obstacle, the fence, the hedge! Stretch to the ditch, the gully, my love, stretch flat to the high, unwinged fascine!" The ground the stallions pounded over was mosaicked with the faces of the living: Lieutenant Stephany's was there, and Honerkamp's, and the faces of other men, and even of women, but Jaeger could find no feature of Catherine Roberts' face. In the singular way that mothers have of accompanying their daughters in passionate silence to the threshold of love, and even beyond it, to their marriage beds, Catherine Roberts may have been either ahead of them, letting the barriers down so that they might race through unimpeded, or else keeping pace beside them in their furious flight. But if, like the others, she followed some image of herself in hope and pain, the story was different for the Colonel. There on the terribly beaten soil lay the remnants of his features, pitilessly ravished beneath the horses' hoofs, stamped on, massacred, nearly effaced, no longer bearing any resemblance to the face of man.)

"I think I am going to have a baby," Milly whispered, standing there in the sun. "I can't tell yet, but I hope I am. I told my mother this last night." She looked down at the dust from the stable that lay like golden powder at their feet. "You don't—you didn't—I mean—my breath, did you?" she said in a low voice, not looking at Jaeger. "Not since Christoph—not for three days now. If he gets better quickly, gets well, if nothing happens to him, I'll never— I mean, you see, Jaeger, don't you, that I won't need to any more if Christoph—" Jaeger began saying now the things he had come to say about Niederstadt, the iron lung, the truck about to go. She listened, her head down, her eyes moving back and forth as if pacing the boards, her breasts so heavy, so beautiful, in the white linen, her hips so narrow in the breeches, that Jaeger, speaking of men and their obligations, wanted to let his hands move down from her shoulders, curving a moment to her breasts, and then slip, trembling, to her hips, spanning her small waist with his open palms. When his voice had ceased, she said: "They're all giving lessons now, the grooms. We can find them in the outdoor ring. I can stay here all week with the Lipizzaners, night and day. I know how to care for them, and no one else really needs me anywhere. That means two grooms could go with you."

She turned, and Jaeger followed her down the hall, down the timber stairs, a sleepwalker following her through sleep out of the precarious moment of infidelity. But only one groom dared defy the *Graf*. He was the oldest, the least fit, bandy-legged, broken-winded, like a carelessly fed and heedlessly ridden horse. He had asked one question: would the Americans pay for the time? But even though Jaeger had shaken his head, still he came. It was just after five o'clock when they reached the America House, and the unwieldy German truck and the nine men were already there. *We are twelve, counting the driver*, Jaeger thought. *Only twelve. That isn't enough.* He walked unsteadily up the steps, past the plaque with the date engraved, and the words: "The America House is a gift from the American people to the people of Germany."

"I have got only twelve," he said as Honerkamp came running through the door.

"There are men in the library, the music room, the science room! Just get on the truck!" Honerkamp called over his shoulder. He was gone again, the air still spinning with his presence. When he returned, six men followed him down the steps. "I've even got you an electrician! You may need him!" he shouted louder than the roar of the motor under the rusted, agitated hood. "We'll allow seven hours! Seven hours!" he shouted through his funneled hands, and the truck began to move. "I'll be at the hospital, replacing you there!"

But it was closer to nine hours when they returned through the steep, narrow streets of the town, the truck climbing slowly because of the weight it carried now. Jaeger knew, in the summer cold of the late-night hours, that he must have slept in brief, broken snatches on the way back. They had had a blowout at midnight on the *Autobahn*, and it was then, as he sat by the side of the road, smoking and watching the men at work in the headlights' glare, that the little electrician from the science room, agile and weightless as a boy, had mentioned the current in Fahrbach.

"The lung runs on a hundred and twenty," he had said, taking a Camel from Jaeger's pack. "The hospital current in Fahrbach could be two-twenty. You know how those old houses are—one floor one current, the next floor something else. If that's the way it's going to be, I'll run for a transformer when we're there."

It seemed to Jaeger that there would never again be any need for sleep, that this state which was neither waking nor sleeping, neither sharpness and sweetness of perception nor annihilation such as people succumbed to behind the drawn shutters of their houses and their lives, that this state of dogged enterprise alone had the power to endure. Even the electrician's words were a part of the enduring power of their enterprise that was not to be diverted in its course, and not to be dammed, that slid over boulders and effaced them, that moved through sleeping and waking, night and day, without digression, bearing the monstrous obstacles of life and death like twigs on its surface, carrying them off as lightly as fallen leaves. It was half past two when they rolled the lung through the double doors of the Fahrbach hospital, and they knew then that the current was wrong. They knew an instant later that the lung would not take the corner of the hospital stairs. *So we carry him down in his cradle, rocking him, rocking him, carefully, while they go for the transformer, and we set up his room here in the entrance hall, blocking the door with the iron lung so that death cannot get in. It is not difficult,* Jaeger told himself in strange elation, staggering with sleeplessness now. *There is nothing difficult about keeping death at bay.* He knew the only difficulty that remained was to persuade all of humanity that there was no line between sleeping and waking, and that the flesh, the nerves, the brain, required no nightly annihilation in order to function accurately. At three in the morning, Christoph was placed in the iron lung, and, at once, as if the hand of God had touched him, the veins in his neck unknotted, the gasping and sobbing of his breathing ceased, and they watched as the dark blue of his face was restored to the pallor of flesh again. His eyes found the tilted mirror fixed over the lung's black, iron throat, and he smiled in weary, ancient sophistication at the sight of the twelve men it framed. And then, scarcely audibly, he began to sing a childhood song of a bird, bearing a message in its beak, that came to rest for a moment on his foot.

When the Colonel's voice roused him, Jaeger did not know the hour of the day, or, if it came to that, what the day itself might be, or through what sequence of events the Colonel should be standing in his room. Although he had perhaps just stepped through the door, still he was clearing his throat and slapping his pockets as if he was eager to be off again, but there was no look of irritation in his eye.

"There are big goings-on out in Ober-Pastau, Jaeger," he said. He stood close to the bed, his ruddy flesh packed solid in the olive-drab of his pants and shirt, the smell of his hair lotion (fresh, pungent, as male as gunshot) mingling with the sweet, stale effluvium of whisky as he spoke. "I've been chasing all over town looking for you," he said, a smile twitching at his mouth. He was oddly, jubilantly triumphant, but what war he had won Jaeger did not yet know. The mottled silk of the paratrooper's scarf was unloosened at his throat in the heat, and he seemed relieved now of some burden he had always borne before. "Your paper said you'd been up all night, or a couple of nights, and so you were sleeping all day. Well, now it's time to wake up. It's five o'clock." Jaeger had raised himself on his elbow, and he looked at the sunlight filtering through the shutters' ribs, thinking that protocol must be hopelessly violated if a civilian of any nationality lay recumbent in pajamas while a high-ranking officer stood upright by his bed. "I'm glad to see you're not worrying over the business of the *Deutschmarks* last Saturday night," the Colonel said. He appeared to wink an eye at Jaeger, in indication that this was just one more of the uproarious jokes they shared. "I was pretty well shot with worry myself over my daughter that night, you understand. I didn't know where she was, and civilians a little too quick on the draw roaming all over the woods." He offered it half-humorously, with none of the avowal of apology. "I'd be interested to know who gathered up those *D-Marks*. Probably that old fox, Knau!" He was laughing outright, standing close to the bed in the heat. He said he was doing his own leg-work today because Lieutenant Stephany was off on a mission of some urgency. "Unofficial. An assignment concerned with the heart," he said, and he tapped his chest, his eye giving the humorous signal again. But for once his shoulders had ceased to toss and jerk, having cast their own unbearable weight away. "Not always the most reliable organ, the heart, Jaeger," he said; and Jaeger, leaning on his elbow still, was suddenly bleakly aware that this was the first time English had been spoken in his room, and not by the voice he had dreamed would one day come to speak it in tenderness here. "Old Knau does pretty well for himself," the Colonel said; "and now the old sly boots himself has seen the giant boar! It charged him somewhere around dawn this morning down by the blacksmith's place. He telephoned Headquarters, and I was in Niederstadt when the message got through. I came right back, hell-bent for leather, but still I'm late. But they're hot on the trail out there, a slew of Germans, a dozen dogs. They say the dogs have drawn some blood. We're to get there fast with the guns."

"There's just this," said Jaeger, trying to get the facts quite clear; "could you tell me what day of the week it is?"

When he touched his jaw, the bristles rasped under his fingertips, and his tongue was dry and rigid in his mouth.

"Day of the week? It's Friday," the Colonel said. He had taken a step or two back now, and he straightened his scarf, preparing to go. "It might very well be the showdown, Jaeger," he said. "It might very well be the last act for that pig. Big as a calf, Knau described it to me once, after his wife had seen it. Well, big as a bull is how Headquarters relayed the message to me now. This is the chance that hunters wait a lifetime for: the weather right, the dogs all primed, and men's tempers hot because of the damned beast's audacity. Shy as wood doves, they say of these wild pigs, but this one charges like a bull. He's ready to gore a man to death." And then, perhaps because Jaeger did not speak, the Colonel's voice altered, became quieter. "I need you with me to straighten out any language difficulties, Jaeger," he said. "I'm picking up a kind of working understanding of the language, but I'm still not good enough. And it might just prove quite an adventure for you. You might even get a story out of it for your newspaper, with photographs. I've got a camera in the car," he said. And *Friday*, thought Jaeger; *so it was this morning, just this morning, that Christoph was put into the lung.* "Look, Jaeger, I'll wait for you downstairs," said the Colonel. He studied the watch on his wrist. "How's twelve minutes? Forget about shaving. I've thrown some extra things in the car—a raincoat, some boots. You may find you'll need them if we have to keep going over rough country for any length of time. And after the trek, you can keep them, Jaeger. I'd like you to. You've done me services every now and then, but I'm not going to make the mistake of offering you German currency again. You can't be bought, is that it, Jaeger?" He stood in the center of the small, hot room, the light in the shutter ribs behind him, smiling at Jaeger, the line of his teeth white as a china cup, no hint of guile sounding in his voice. "One of these men of principle, not met with every day," he said. In the cracked mirror hanging on the wall was the reflection of his heavy shoulders in the olive-drab, and the grey hair smoothly combed on the back of his wide skull, clipped close on the roll of dull red flesh above the paratrooper's scarf. "There's a basket of victuals and a bottle in the car," he said. "You can eat and wet your whistle on the way." And on the way he went on saying that the story of the boar was going like wildfire through Fahrbach and God knew where else, and that it had even been mentioned in a newscast on the Armed Forces radio. The size of the pig, and the length of its tusks, and the fury of its attack on the forester, he said, had been gaining by leaps and bounds throughout the day. So it was more than likely that a flock of unauthorized civilians might turn out; unauthorized, the Colonel repeated, because no more permits were being issued by Headquarters for the area. The limit was four, he said, and he had picked the four of them up so as to restrict the place to his own activities. "We'll keep our eyes open for our contraband friends in the jeep. This might be just their time to strike," he said as they drove. They were far in the country now, but the light had not yet begun to fade; it was merely cooling, thinning, as it poured across the hills. The Colonel pushed the car hard and fast along the flower-and-tree-and-field bound road, and out of his deep contentment, his jubilation over the look of things ahead, he said this time he would give the unauthorized no quarter. This time, if he so much as clapped an eye on them, they would not get away. "Now that you've got a couple of sandwiches and a cup of good strong coffee under your belt, you'll be able to help me lay them low. I'm almost regretting that regulations prohibit my putting a gun in your hands." Having stated this quite jocularly, he was even more pleased with the situation than before, and he went on saying it would give him the keenest kind of pleasure to run the unauthorized to earth, to shoot their tires, to ram them into a convenient ditch. "The keenest kind of pleasure," he repeated lingeringly, and his elbow nudged Jaeger softly in the ribs. "That's what you ask of a woman, isn't it, Jaeger?" he asked, his voice almost a caress. "Isn't that what you're always hoping to get out of a woman, the keenest kind of satisfaction, once you've got her where you want?" They had come to Knau's house in the village street, but the Colonel did not turn into the courtyard, for the forester had been out with the men and the dogs, he knew, pursuing the boar since early day. He drove on past the blacksmith's forge, past the slow parades of ducks and geese, their breasts an opaque white in the gathering lilac of the dusk, their snowy rumps twitching as they spoke their words of insult to the passing car. As the station wagon rocked out the lumber road, the Colonel began to hum deeply, contentedly, off-key. "You know, it occurred to me this afternoon, in the twelve minutes that I waited for you, that peace is the interval allowed us in which to recognize the enemy," he began saying to Jaeger then, selecting his words with care, "and that war is the corrective action that recognition of him must eventually take." Out the long way through the open fields they rocked, and when they had reached the threshold of the woods, the Colonel's hand slackened on the wheel, and the car seemed to draw of its own volition to one side of the road. There it halted, slightly tilted upon the sloping shoulder of the ditch. "Let's have a drink before we start off," the Colonel said. He reached forward and pulled open the glove-compartment door, and there were the carelessly folded maps of this country or another, and an open pack of cigarettes, and a pair of sunglasses with only one lens left in the tortoise-shell frame. His hand, with greying hairs sprinkled on the back of it, and the heavy links of his silver identity bracelet slipped forward from the wrist, pushed these things aside, and under them could be seen the flask in its tan leather jacket, and a revolver, black and sleek and viciously muzzled, with no holster to keep it in its place. The Colonel took out the flask, and then the pack of cigarettes, and snapped the compartment door closed. "Pass me a couple of paper cups from the lunch kit," he said. He said nothing more until they had each drunk a swallow of the whisky down. "Who was it said that a pessimist speaks of a half-empty package of cigarettes while an optimist speaks of it being half full? Well, I'll be the eternal optimist, Jaeger, and tell you that this fine flask here was just half full. And I'll be even more optimistic and add that I've got an untouched fifth back there with the guns, so we needn't go too easy," he said. In the silence, they both drank from the cups again. "I don't think I had much trouble recognizing you, Jaeger, and recognizing Seth," the Colonel said, speaking with insidious dispassion. "I'm referring to recognition of the enemy. With you, it must have been that first day you walked up the hill. It wasn't the cut of your face or figure, or anything you did, as I remember. It was just your God-damned saintly eye." He sat with his body relaxed in gentleness behind the wheel, but from time to time his eyes flashed their blaze of blue at Jaeger as he spoke. "You know, Jaeger, you, you're the kind who could kill a man, and no jury anywhere, in any country, would ever believe it was you. If the corpse stood up in the grave

287

and pointed you out, and said: 'There's the fellow who picked up a knife and stuck it right into my heart, and kept on twisting and turning it until I was dead,' still they wouldn't believe it, they wouldn't take even the victim's word for it. Because of that pure, heroic look that women apparently sicken and pine for, because of that gilded halo that's beginning to be a little tarnished that you like to wear. Here, let's fill them up again." He unscrewed the cap of the flask, and poured the whisky into their paper cups, dividing it more or less evenly, shaking the last drops out. The flask was empty now, and he reached for the glove-compartment door, and laid it in among the maps. This time, he took the revolver out. In his left hand, he held the paper cup of his drink, while the revolver fitted with exquisite ease and comfort into his other hand. "As for me," he said, looking down at the weapon reflectively, "even if I missed, I would be judged, and sentenced, and executed for my intention. That's the difference, chemically, between you and me. Even if I failed, do you understand, Jaeger, I would be condemned, and I would face a firing-squad—no, I would not be granted that honor, I would be hung—and I would rot in the grave, and in one or two women's memories, as a murderer, although I had never brought it off." He began to laugh quietly, looking down in something like affection at the sleek bluish muzzle of the revolver in his hand. The dusk was coming like slow smoke out of the woods, rising, it seemed, out of the earth itself, and drifting on imperceptible currents through the windows of the car. The Colonel lifted his paper cup again and drank deeply, and then he turned his head and looked at Jaeger in the failing light. "Would you mind going around to the rear of the car and getting the bottle? It's lying back there with the guns. I want to fill the flask up again. Well, what's the matter?" he said when Jaeger made no move to go. He went on speaking gently, almost caressingly, to him. "All you have to do is open the door, and get out, and turn your back on me for no longer than half a minute, and get the bottle, and then come back. You're not afraid of me, Jaeger, are you?" he said. He be-began suddenly to laugh. "Now you get the point of my argument, don't you? Now you see what I was try-ing to say. All I have to do is sit here with a service re-volver in my hand, and the thoughts that go through your mind are libelous. I don't understand it. I don't know what gives you the idea I might involve you in a hunting ac-cident. Oh, I've got your measure now, Jaeger!" he said. "Don't ever try to look like a man again, at least not when I'm around!" He sat relaxed behind the wheel, laugh-ing in pure contentment, looking down at the revolver in his hand. "I've got your measure all right, and Seth's meas-ure, too. I don't say the enemy has taken any ground in this particular engagement, but I estimate his menace by the extent of his harassment of my positions. So, for reasons of health—not mine, oh, no, but Mrs. Roberts' and my daugh-ter's—I've asked for reassignment. The polio scare came at the right moment for my strategy. There was even a case of polio up at the riding-stables, up there at the *Schloss*. You may have heard about it. And I find my daughter clean-ing out stalls, and picking out hoofs like crazy, right in the place, thinking no one else could take care of the horses, wanting to sleep there with them at night, so I did the only thing there was to do. I packed my wife and daughter up in two hours, less than that, and drove them down to Nie-derstadt. Lieutenant Stephany's at the airport with them now, putting them on a plane for home." He drew his left forefinger slowly, gently, along the blue muzzle of the re-volver, laughing quietly as he sat behind the wheel. "You didn't expect that, did you, Jaeger? You and Seth Honerkamp had other plans in mind. But now it's over and done with. It's all over except for the shouting, and maybe the shooting, and I'm happy. I don't care what they hang me for now as long as I've straightened things out. So watch how I lift this little fellow, how my finger fits around the trigger. Lieutenant Stephany is probably kissing them now, kissing them good-by, and neither you nor Seth Honerkamp are in the picture. You've been deleted. You're looking straight into this little fellow's mouth; and he wants to speak to you, Jaeger, he has something he wants to say to you very clear and loud."

It was the sound of a car approaching behind them on the lumber road that made him turn. Jaeger could see it in the mirror above the windshield, coming without haste, a jeep rocking over the ruts turned lilac in the dusk, between the fields of emerald grass. And even while it was still far, they knew this was the vehicle that all the nights of early summer had awaited. They knew there would be sacking tied over its license plates, and, under the powdering of dust, its army-issue tan. The Colonel moved quickly now, leaning forward in his seat, slipping the revolver into his back pocket, retrieving the paper cup from where he had placed it in the panel ash tray. He flung the last swallow of whisky into his throat, folded the cup over twice, and crushed it in his hand.

"All right," he said. "If you're looking for trouble, O.K."

He opened the door of the car, and stepped down, pausing a moment to adjust the paratrooper's scarf at his neck, and then he placed his arms akimbo, and took his stand. His feet were planted wide, his legs straddling the blades of grass that grew luminous, tall, unhindered, on the curved hump of the lumber road. But if he had no intention of letting the jeep pass, the jeep itself had no intention of passing. It advanced, blunt-nosed, square-rigged, a few more lengths in the dust, and then it halted. From the driver's side of it stepped a young sergeant, wearing jump boots and fatigues, who snapped his hand to his temple in salute. From the other side—dwarfed by the widely opening fields, by the incalculable arching of the crystal sky, outdone by the densely woven forest that was more ruthless, more furtive, more complex in its conniving than any man—stepped a civilian with long incisor teeth and a pepper-and-salt cap of hair.

"Well, if it isn't Overstreet!" the Colonel called out, with true pleasure and astonishment. His right hand fell to his side again, having returned the young sergeant's salute. "I'm glad to see you and the army out on a joint operation tonight. I like it. I like to see the two teams pulling together, as far as they can. I didn't think it would be you, but I'm pleased, I'm very pleased, Overstreet. You and I have always set a good example to the others, pulling together, and that's why we've been able to accomplish all we have. Isn't that true, eh, Overstreet? Isn't that true?" And now his elation was carrying him beyond himself. He stood rubbing his hands in uncontrollable delight. "Maybe we're just hunters by nature, Overstreet, you and I, hunters and killers, and the others are the hunted, all of them, every God-damned one of them!" He went grinning and dancing and walking on air down the lumber road toward Overstreet, ready to take him in affection in his arms. For an instant, he glanced up at the evening sky, as if in salute to the plane that somewhere bore his wife and daughter out of the reach of fumbling hands, out of the pollution of strangers' dreams, sending them home, their virtue still intact, their flesh still undefiled. "To act quickly, with courage, and to act in time—above all, to act in time," he was saying, and he clapped Overstreet on the shoulder now. "That's the secret, eh, Overstreet? That's the heart of all security action as well as of military strategy. Once you've got hold of that . . ." And then, for the first time, he seemed to catch sight of the potato sacking masking the license plate below the bumper of the jeep, and he angled his chin in its direction. "I see you're keeping your identity disk in order for inspection. But you'd better get your vehicle out of the middle of the road." He spoke to the sergeant's long-lipped, Irish face. "Pull it in behind my car. Then start getting your equipment out." When the sergeant was behind the wheel again, and the jeep's motor coughing, the Colonel looked down at Overstreet and winked one eye. "This is big business tonight. The reports say he's as tough as a bull. Come over to the car and we'll have a snorter before we get going," he said; but the thoughts were moving fast in the other man's small skull.

"The M.P.s don't like it when the license plates get all fouled up," he began to say through the barricade of his long-toothed grin. They walked over the earth and the grass of the lumber road, and Jaeger watched them come. "I got a talking-to from the M.P.s just last week, so we're playing safe. They want to be able to read the numbers five miles away and in the dark or else they hand you a ticket," Overstreet said. "Once we're back on the main road, where there's macadam instead of country mud, we'll take the sacking off again." As they passed, Walter's voice seemed to whisper across the slow beginning of the night: ". . . the second time I saw him, I could see the ferns and violets through his legs. It wasn't quite dark, and he passed so close that I saw the blood of animals underneath his fingernails." "You see what I mean, sir, don't you?" Overstreet said.

"You don't have to apologize to me," the Colonel said pleasantly. They had stopped by the rear door of the station wagon, and the Colonel twisted the metal handle, and reached in across the guns. "Let's get down to business now," he said. "This is the biggest safari I've undertaken over here. There're fourteen Germans out ahead of us, beating the woods, the *Krauts* spread over a broad piece of country, and the adversary worthy of it, from all reports. They've got a dozen dogs already on his tail. It's not just a little matter of picking off a grazing deer, but something big, something with dimension to it. You and I and the sergeant here will close in for the kill."

"That's why I brought the camera and flash-bulbs along," said Overstreet, grinning. "I want a permanent record of it. You, Colonel, with your foot on its neck, leaning on your gun, once you've brought it down."

"Oh, Overstreet, come off it, you joker!" the Colonel said in absolute delight. He stood there shaking with laughter in the dusk. "Leaning on my gun! The usual stance! Oh, that's wonderful! But we'll get him, we'll get him all right, Overstreet, we'll get him!" He held the bottle of bourbon by its slender neck as he turned his head in the growing dark. "Jaeger, hand me a couple of paper cups out of the lunch box, will you? And then you'd better get into those boots and slip on that waterproof coat, and be ready to set off. It's a summer-weight coat. You'll get a lot of wear out of it still. I ought to be hanging on to it myself, but you're entitled to compensation, Jaeger, so here I am giving it away. Jaeger!" he called, raising his voice. "Where the hell has Jaeger got to? Where the hell is he going? Hey, Jaeger!" he shouted out.

But Jaeger was taking the lumber road back to Ober-Pastau, and nothing would stop him now. As he walked toward the far, clustered lights of the peasants' houses, either the aching sense of loss in his heart, or the whisky giving speech to his blood, stirred in him without rancor, saying: *So they are gone, their voices, their scent, their mermaid eyes, and I am left with my countrymen.* Now he walked through the German countryside like a refugee, an expellee, like a German at last, walking the roads in search of the pieces of his life, seeking the ruins of a house he had never owned, the traces of wife and children he had not had, carrying all that was left to him in his empty hands, as the others bore all that they owned in rucksacks on their backs. *The Germans, my countrymen, whispered his blood, they have set out on this kind of hunt since the first beginnings of time, the beast they pursue in righteous vengeance conjured into being so long ago that they cannot conceive of life without it. They believe that it charges them, God-fearing, peace-loving men, as they walk homeward through their fields at night, armed only with hoes, spades, rakes, with the tools of peace and industry. And my part is to tell them that there is no giant boar. I must say to them it is not France, this beast breathing fire and brimstone at their thresholds, not Russia, not England, or America, but that it is all men who have another vision, another faith. It is Schumacher, as it is Fritzludwig, as it is me, myself, and if I accept this, and remain on the sidelines of their Armageddon, then I will be able to see the way ahead lit by the lamps in a few men's windows, marked by the wayside signs of separate men's identities. And that will suffice me. That must suffice.*

Again, he did not stop in Ober-Pastau, but walked past the courtyards, past the dungheaps shrouded by the night, walking through the village that settled in quiet like a bird on its nest in the evening, and beyond it onto the road that wound through orchards, through pastures known in the darkness by the smell of freshly cut hay. When he reached the macadamized road that linked hamlet with village, village with town (running toward Kastel to the north, toward Fahrbach to the south), he took the direction of

294

Fahrbach, walking steadily, untiringly, his head down. Four hours later, as he crossed the open market place, the church clock of Fahrbach struck midnight. He was aware of no weariness in his flesh until he heard the ring of his footsteps on the cobbles, and then it seemed the gait of a lame man that accompanied him, one step bearing the weight more heavily than did the next one on the polished stones. The alleyways and lanes he took, he knew as well as the lines in his own palms, and he descended the familiar flights of stairs that led from level to level of the town. There were lights in the hospital windows as he passed by, and then, without warning, the front door opened, and Jaeger paused tentatively in the shadows beyond, and saw it was Honerkamp who came out, and who waited in unaccustomed hesitation before coming down the steps to the street. *Something has happened, something has failed,* Jaeger decided quietly; but what the look of Honerkamp's shoulders, his muted step, portended, he did not want to know.

"Hi, Mr. Honerkamp," Jaeger said, watching him come.

"Hi, Jaeger," said Honerkamp without surprise. They walked on, side by side, not speaking, along the narrow sidewalk in the dark. It was warm, and at the first street-crossing, Honerkamp took out his handkerchief and wiped his face. "Well, it's over," he said. "It was over about twenty minutes ago." *I won't believe it yet,* thought Jaeger: *not until we've reached that streetlight ahead.* "He was too tired," Honerkamp said.

And *Poor Milly, poor Milly, Milly, Milly,* thought Jaeger, and he saw her on the drunken horse, riding on alone. *Poor Milly, bearing Christoph's flesh and blood within her, and Catherine holding the lost, and the lonely, and even the dead, against her hotly beating heart.* In the train, he had touched it with his fingers. He had felt its pulse in the deep cup of his hand.

'I can't see the reason for his dying," he said stubbornly.

Before they took the last street to the America House, they saw the nimbus of blanched light that was cast up from the open square. And, ahead, in the hushed town, there sounded now the rhythm of hammering, and men's voices calling out.

"I'm getting the thermometer set up," Honerkamp said, as if continuing a conversation they had begun somewhere before. As they took the corner, Jaeger saw there were floodlights beamed from the two top balconies of the America House, and in the illuminated square a truck and derrick waited, and workmen swarmed in the center of the open place. A dozen or more shouldered an obelisk onto a platform that others still constructed from new timber, men dressed in discarded articles of G.I. clothing, matched incongruously with worn but viciously fitted German military boots. The obelisk was shifted on high, decked gaudily in red and silver, numbered in black, until it swayed in grave admonishment above the sleeping, immune houses of the town. Honerkamp and Jaeger watched the men place this giant replica of a clinical thermometer upon the stage that had been set for it, watched them hold it upright in this final dress rehearsal for the performance that would open the next day. It stood perhaps thirty feet tall, and it soared upward as suavely as a rocket, fashioned of building-lathes and Bristol board, and so boldly graded and numbered with poster paint that it had the festive look of a float for Mardi Gras as the kneeling carpenters drove nails into its base. In the simulated glass tube that ran the length of it, the silver paint of the mercury was halted at 37.3°. "And from there, which marks normal, as the contributions come in," Honerkamp was saying now, "we'll push it up to forty-one, forty-two degrees, and even beyond, to the limit that man's capacity for burning heat can go. You can see the D-*Mark* figures just below the temperature gradations. The goal is five thousand D-*Marks*, or forty-two and a half degrees. When we reach it, that's an iron lung for the Fahrbach *Krankenhaus*, and perhaps a respirator, too." It was something like this they did in America, he was telling Jaeger. It was something they did at home in Community Chest drives. Each time a hundred dollars was added to the fund, the silver paint representing the mercury would rise a tenth of a degree. The entire week was to be given to it, he said: the school children of Fahrbach collecting funds from door to door, the newspaper following the campaign, listing the contributions every storekeeper and each individual gave. All this had never before taken place in Hesse, perhaps never before in Germany. "You can see what it would do," Honerkamp said, "each child knowing he is taking part." Because of Schumacher's editorials, the *Oberbürgermeister* had closed the swimming-pool and the movie house, he said, and the seminar would not take place that year.

"There were eighteen cases on Thursday," Jaeger said.

"There are twenty-six of them as of tonight," said Honerkamp, "and two already dead. And tomorrow the children will set out again, ringing doorbells, knocking at doors, asking that an iron lung be given them before it is too late. Too late," he repeated. He looked at Jaeger out of eyes set in the dark caves of his fatigue. "Let's go inside and talk for a while before we go to bed." They turned away from the relentless light, so brilliant that no shadow was cast by halted object or moving man, walked out of the sound of voices and the knotting and unknotting of the men, and walked up the steps of the America House. "When it arrives, the Fahrbach lung, we'll set it up temporarily here in the main hall, with literature to explain its functioning. I want even the peasants to come and look inside its iron heart and know what it can do." He pushed open the great white front door, and Jaeger followed him in, and the door sighed closed on the glare and clamor of the floodlit square. "Right here is where I want it to stand," Honerkamp said. He halted in the gracious arena of the hall and indicated with his squared hands where the lung would best be on display. "Right here, where everyone can walk in from the street and take a look at it, and where those who are reluctant to come inside can see it from the door. There's already been opposition to the idea," he said, and the mask of weariness and worry slipped sideways on his face in the moment that he laughed. "Some of the *Krankenhaus* boys want the showing to be behind closed doors, reserved for the medical elite. What private honor, they asked me, is conferred by a degree if the common man is permitted public access to the secrets of the trade?" One crystal-petaled chandelier was lit in the white bowl of the ceiling over their heads, and a second glittered as if hung with icicles above the open fan of the handsome marble stairs. Honerkamp said: "We will have to work faster than before, Jaeger, and with more intelligence than we've shown this far. There is no time to dream, no time to eat or sleep or shave our faces, none. There is no time to think of the women we might have loved, and who might have loved us in return." He interrupted himself then, his voice saying bleakly: "Yes, I know. I walked up to the house early in the evening. I know they've gone." Then he went on with the rest of it: "We will have to go on looking haggard and bearded, as we look now, because of the other things we've undertaken to do." He laid one hand on Jaeger's arm, the words he spoke so explicit that they seemed to be pointing out a direction for them to take, or that they had already taken without being fully aware. "For some, we can do nothing. It is already too late," he said, and they began to mount the stairs, "but there are others for whom it is still possible to act." *Too late, too late,* whispered their feet on the unblemished marble; *too late, too late,* on the polished inlay of the upper hall. "If it should prove too late for me, then you will go through with it without me, Jaeger. And you will do it just as well without me, perhaps better without me being here." He stopped before his office door, and took the key from his pocket, and opened it. When he flicked on the light, the skeleton could be seen grinning at them from the corner, and as he passed by, Jaeger read again the inscription that ran below the jointed, ivory bones of the dead feet. "Shall the individual bow before the power of the state?" Sophocles' words asked still. "When the lung arrives, it must be given a ceremonious welcome," Honerkamp said, as if speaking aloud the behests of his final testament. "It will come by train from Hamburg, and the *Herr Oberbürgermeister,* and the *Herr Direktor* of the *Krankenhaus,* and all the children of Fahrbach must be at the station to receive it with songs—yes, singing—and flowers in their hands. If that is corny, well, that is all right, as long as they learn from that reception at the station that it is their property, not American, and not an adjunct of the German medicos, but theirs, acquired because they walked from door to door for it, defying everything their history had established for them, just as you too will continue to defy it, Jaeger." Honerkamp stood on the other side of the executive's desk, his face quite humble, weary, yet furiously intent. "I would like to make it clear that it is the opinion I have of you, and the opinion you have of me, and the opinions we both hold of the skeleton over there, that is our posterity. Perhaps we have saved ourselves by the simple formula of being what we are, and so we have won, the three of us have won, and what we have won the others cannot take away. It may be too late for me to speak out for Dardenella in any courtroom—it may be, I mean, that they will not let me testify. So this is one more thing you will have to do for me. All we need to tell them is simply what we know, which is probably what we have been doing in our lives so far. If we do not speak out as loudly as we can for Dardenella, saying he was never in the woods that night, while other men were whose names we know, then we've turned away not only from him but from each other, and from the skeleton that life framed too, ending it for him crouched alone in a cellar, unable, in his country, in his time, to fit an act to his belief, whatever it was. I tell you, Jaeger, however final things seem now, well, still I've won, because what the skeleton failed to do, I was able to do here." He looked down at the confusion of papers on his desk, and he began to set them in some kind of order, placing one or two letters to one side, and one or two to the other, his hands seeking along them for one document that possibly said the entire thing and yet was not of much greater importance than any of the others lying there. But he could not find it, and after a moment of silence he said: "I've been fired, Jaeger, riffed, declared surplus. I've been kicked in the seat of the pants. I have to go. It's apparent I haven't been doing the right kind of job here. I'm to be replaced."

"But this is insane, this is madness," Jaeger said, his voice stricken.

"I can ask them to let me know the specific charges," Honerkamp said, "and they will advise me that I have the right to answer these charges in writing, under oath or affirmation, and to submit my reply, together with such statements, affidavits, or other documents, that I may desire, within thirty calendar days from the date of receipt of the letter which they have not written yet. I will perhaps be allowed an administrative hearing on the charges, and given the right to appear personally, or to be represented by counsel or representative of my choice, and to present evidence in my own behalf through witnesses or by affidavit. I may even be permitted to appeal to the Secretary of the Army in the event an adverse decision is upheld against me. But in the meantime I must get out."

"But all of us, Germans, Americans, we can testify—" Jaeger began, but Honerkamp interrupted him.

"It is too late. It is two o'clock in the morning. Let's go up now and turn the floodlights off, and then we'll go look for something to eat. Wurst, pickles, *Kraut*, nightingales' tongues." He gave a laugh. "Eating always makes things easier," he said.

A NOTE ABOUT THE AUTHOR

Kay Boyle has been well known to readers at home and abroad since the publication of her first short stories in 1930. Her compassionate understanding of people springs from a varied career, or a number of careers, since her birth in St. Paul, Minnesota. She studied the violin at the Conservatory of Music in Cincinnati, and architecture at the Ohio Mechanics Institute; she has been a switchboard operator, a secretary, and a fashion copywriter in New York and Paris; she has ghost-written two novels, done numerous translations, and served as foreign correspondent for *The New Yorker* in Germany from 1946 to 1953. Out of those five years she spent in Germany, while that country was shaping a new future after World War II, comes the background so vividly delineated in *Generation Without Farewell*. Although she now lives with her family in Connecticut, her years of residence abroad—in England, France, and Austria—which began in 1923, give Kay Boyle an identity with Europeans shared by few American writers.

Miss Boyle won a Guggenheim Fellowship in 1934, and the O. Henry Memorial Prize for the Best Short Story of the Year in 1934 and again in 1941. Among more than twenty published volumes are *The White Horses of Vienna*, *His Human Majesty*, *The Smoking Mountain*, *Three Short Novels*, and *The Seagull on the Step*. *Generation Without Farewell* is Kay Boyle's thirteenth novel.

A NOTE ON THE TYPE

This book is set in ELECTRA, *a Linotype face designed by* W. A. Dwiggins (1880–1956), *who was responsible for so much that is good in contemporary book design. Although much of his early work was in advertising and he was the author of the standard volume* Layout in Advertising, *Mr. Dwiggins later devoted his prolific talents to book typography and type design, and worked with great distinction in both fields. In addition to his designs for Electra, he created the Metro, Caledonia, and Eldorado series of type faces, as well as a number of experimental cuttings that have never been issued commercially.*

Electra cannot be classified as either modern or old-style. It is not based on any historical model, nor does it echo a particular period or style. It avoids the extreme contrast between thick and thin elements which marks most modern faces, and attempts to give a feeling of fluidity, power, and speed.

This book was composed, printed, and bound by The Colonial Press Inc., Clinton, Mass. The paper was manufactured by S. D. Warren Co., Boston. The typography and binding designs are by George Salter.